Don't Hex Witches

Jeni Conrad

Author's Note

As a teacher who has dealt with teens for many years, not to mention was once one herself, I wanted to bring up an issue in this series that many people struggle with. But for some, reading about it may be uncomfortable or even triggering. This story contains themes of an eating disorder. I am not trying to promote it or glamorize it in any way but rather trying to highlight the struggle a person might have with it and how damaging it can be. The issue does get resolved, but it takes several books to do so. If you or anyone you know struggles with an eating disorder, there is help. https://www.edreferral.com/

Contents

Chapter 1 - Trina

As I watched Noah carry my sister's (for now) empty body to his order's vehicle disguised as a catering truck, I fingered the place on my collar bone where the golden family heirloom had sat for years. I had taken it off last week to help find Hanna and hadn't put it back on yet. It was stored in a safe place so I could always find it if I needed it, but right now, maybe more so than ever, I needed to use the powers.

"This better work. The last time I checked, we weren't on the best of terms with the necromancers. Not to mention, she's been ignoring Noah's texts and calls for a while. Honestly, I'm surprised he's agreed to this at all," Brandon, my sister's ghost friend wearing 90s skater clothes, said while standing beside me on the porch.

Mom was hovering over Noah, making sure he got Hanna inside and secured properly. She was also drilling him for more details about what we were going to do next and how the whole thing was going to work.

"I'm pretty sure he's got feelings for her. Else, like you said, he probably wouldn't be doing this." I watched the tender way Noah lifted the blanket and brushed a strand of hair out of Hanna's pale face. We were hoping the blanket would keep anyone from asking questions about us putting a body inside of a van.

So far I had done a decent job of not crumbling into a ball of pained sobs. When I saw Hanna slumped onto the carpet, her neck twisted in a way that shouldn't have been possible, I had almost dissolved into a tearful puddle but somehow resisted.

But watching Noah touch her cheek and then shut the back of the van, putting my sister out of sight, was even worse.

"Of course he has feelings for her. Any normal guy with eyeballs who spent any amount of time around her would develop feelings for her." Brandon grunted in annoyance.

Pressing my lips together tightly so they would stop trembling, I nodded. "She is one of a kind. How long do you think it takes for a ghost to materialize after a person...loses their..."

Brandon knew what I was trying to say, bless his heart, and didn't need me to continue. "I don't know. We've never had to figure it out. There was that one time that Stephanie took an herb and died for a moment. As far as I know, it didn't take her ghost very long to be ready for Hanna to summon her, but that whole thing was under super different and odd circumstances."

"Okay... I'm trying hard here not to feel like I've been left out on some interesting adventures you guys have had." I darted my eyes back to him for a second, blinking quickly to push away the tears.

I told myself to stop being stupid. This was only a temporary thing, and we were going to get her body and spirit back together quickly and easily. It didn't matter how the necromancers felt about everything right now. I would make them put her back together no matter what.

"That you did." Brandon bobbed his head, a wistful smile on his face.

"I still can't believe that Caleb is responsible for all of this..." I trailed off, wondering if I should join Noah and Mom's conversation so I could be updated on the next steps but feeling too lethargic to walk over there and face everything.

"Well, yes, but not really him, you know?" Brandon put his hands into his pockets and rocked back and forth on his toes.

"Yeah..." I wondered how much I should be worried about the vampire. The concern for him was muted by what his body had done under Rose's command. While I had more than regular feelings for the tall, dark, and handsome bloodsucker, I had been trying to fight their appeal. This whole thing with my dead sister was helping him become less attractive. Even if it hadn't been strictly his fault.

But it was. If he hadn't been invited into our house, the spell would have kept Rose out. I was still missing the piece of how he'd gotten enthralled in the first place, but I was certain that somehow that whole thing had been his fault too.

Mom gave Noah a quick hug, which kind of surprised me, and he turned to give me a wave. I returned it half-heartedly as Mom walked back through the grass and Noah got into his van and drove off.

"Don't worry, honey. We'll get her back together in no time." Mom pulled me into a hug, but I wasn't sure which one of us needed it more.

"I know. We will," I said into her hair, soaking up her comforting embrace.

"I do have to point out the irony of my haunt now being this house, apparently," Brandon said after giving us a few seconds.

Mom and I parted, and I glanced at Brandon, letting Mom know he'd said something and where he was standing.

"Brandon says his haunt is now our house. Normally, I would have laughed and ignored it as another silly joke, but as Hanna is no longer here to use her powers, I'm inclined to believe him." I blinked back more tears as I focused on the logistics of the situation.

Mom furrowed her eyebrows. "Well, how do we know it isn't just your powers keeping him here instead of sending him back to his haunt?"

"Because I tried going back to my previous haunt before, and nothing happened. I don't feel that usual draw to the skatepark. Plus, Hanna had said there was something about being captured inside the crystals that reset a ghost's haunt," Brandon answered before I could come up with anything.

I relayed the message back to Mom, still feeling weird about having to copy his words so other alivers could hear them.

"Interesting. Maybe it's a theory we can experiment with more later. Right now..."

But before she could finish her sentence, an arcanist was suddenly standing right next to us on the porch.

"Right now, y'all need to go inside, sit down, and prepare yourselves for what I need to tell you. Where's Hanna?" Phoenix omitted the apology I felt was deserved for scaring the bejeezus out of both of us.

They looked more frazzled than I'd ever seen them look before. I mean, sure, I hadn't spent a lot of time with them, but still. The longer side of their bright red hair was mussed and tangled. Sweat beaded on their forehead and upper lip, smudging some of their makeup. It was probably their appearance and sense of wild urgency that stopped us from complaining about their sudden arrival.

Mom recovered quicker than me, looked around the quiet Tuesday-morning neighborhood as if a wild beast was going to spring out from behind the nearest mailbox, and nodded her head toward the house. "We have news for you too. You may also need to sit down."

Frowning, Phoenix followed us inside our spell-protected house where we'd given access to them when they had come over for Thanksgiving. Brandon followed as well, of course, just as curious as we were about what they had to say.

"Would you like something to drink?" Mom went straight to the fridge and pulled out milk and then to the cupboard to grab the hot cocoa mix.

If there was ever a time I needed sweet, warm chocolate, it was now.

"You wouldn't happen to have a mimosa in there somewhere, would you? Or maybe a strong whiskey." Phoenix sank onto one of the kitchen table chairs.

"Sorry, dear. Best I can do is some cocoa." Mom plucked three mugs off the shelf.

Phoenix sighed dramatically. "I suppose that will do."

Mom probably would have smiled at least a little from the exchange, but it was a statement on how she was feeling that she didn't respond cordially. Instead, she got about business.

"What did you come here to tell us?" I also sat down at the kitchen table.

Brandon frowned down at the chair next to me, giving it a meaningful look.

Sighing and shaking my head, I pulled it out for him so he could sit down without half his body poking through the table. It would have been distracting for both of us.

Phoenix quirked an eyebrow at my odd behavior but didn't comment on it. "I have some bad news, I'm afraid."

I scoffed. "Not as bad as *our* news."

Phoenix pressed their lips for a second. "Perhaps you had best go first then."

"Rose somehow possessed Caleb, used his access to our house to climb in Hanna's window and murdered her." I kept my gaze straight onto the wooden grains of the table instead of locking eyes with my mom. I knew if we saw the pain in each other's faces, we'd dissolve into blubbering messes.

"Oh—" Phoenix cursed and put up a hand to cover their mouth. "I came here to warn you about her, but I can see that I'm too late. I'm so sorry!"

We were quiet for a time, the only sound coming from Mom's spoon as she stirred the milk heating on the stove. Even Brandon seemed to understand it was not the time for any smart remarks.

Normally, I probably would have told Phoenix it was okay and that we didn't blame them, but I wasn't sure I could say that honestly. The magic users were supposed to have been watching Rose, keeping her from doing any more harm.

Finally, Mom spoke with a quiet voice, still looking down at the stove. "What happened?"

Phoenix sighed, their shoulders slumping, and gave both of us a sad, compassionate look. "I'm so sorry for your loss. I wish I could have been here earlier to warn you, but things happened all at once and very suddenly."

When neither of us responded, they kept going. "We're a bit fuzzy on the details, and a lot of this is our fault. Maybe the necromancers should have taken control of Rose, after all."

I stared Phoenix down, willing them to get to the point instead of continuously pausing as if waiting for us to tell them everything was okay.

Because nothing was okay.

"Right... So we had Rose locked up in the safehouse where we kept prisoners. These rooms are specifically designed and magicked to keep magic users trapped, unable to cast spells, locked up, and away from hurting anyone. Unfortunately, Rose's reach into our coven was stronger than the matron or I ever guessed. Someone, we're still investigating who, somehow managed to lure your vampire friend into the safehouse. We know that he wouldn't have come had he known what the real reason for his presence was, but somehow, he was convinced he needed to drop by and give us a visit. I'm guessing it had something to do with a desire to protect Hanna or get more information."

"How kind of you to give him the benefit of the doubt." Brandon looked at them flatly as he rested his head on his hand, his elbow on the table.

I might have been trying not to think of the vampire in any kind of fond way, but I couldn't help myself from prickling a bit from Brandon's comment. Caleb would never have gone somewhere where he would knowingly put us at risk. At the very least, he wouldn't have gone in there agreeing to become Rose's puppet.

I was certain of that.

"Okay... So how did Rose get her hands on him? Does she even need to touch a vampire to control one?" I asked, wishing I knew more about how everything worked. It was true I was new to the occult thing, but I had learned some from Hanna and her stories in the last few months. But I still felt like I didn't know nearly enough.

"You would have to ask a necromancer how the details work. All I know is that Caleb was in the same room with her, she was able to possess him, and using his vampire strength and skills, he broke her out. Our prisons are meant to protect against magic users, not vampires. We know we need to rectify this now, but hindsight and all that." Phoenix took a mug of cocoa from my mom and frowned into the swirling brown depths. "Y'all can't imagine how sorry we are. Believe me when I say we want to make this right, and you can consider the matron and me, at least, in your debt, willing to help you however we can...especially after what has happened to Hanna."

We let the quiet settle in between us after Mom sat in the chair on the other side of Phoenix. There was no way I would tell Phoenix that we forgave them or the coven. It might have made them feel better, but if anyone deserved to feel bad right now, it was them.

Nothing was going to make up for their failure, certainly not a simple verbal apology.

"Can magic users bring people back to life like necromancers can?" Mom asked, disturbing the heavy silence.

I was sure Hanna wouldn't have gotten tangled up with the necromancers on Steph's behalf if the magic users could do such a thing, but I waited for Phoenix to respond in case I was overlooking details.

"I'm afraid only the black witches may be able to do that, but I tend to avoid that crowd. They're a bit...deranged. Not to mention, whatever they would bring back wouldn't be Hanna. It would be something different, even if it was wearing her body. No, the best bet would be getting a necromancer and a Seer to put her back together. Like how Hanna helped her little blonde friend a few weeks ago."

Mom picked up her mug and blew over the top. "I suspected that was so. We've already called Noah and had him take her body to the order so they can keep it preserved until we can find her ghost. I was hoping we could cut them out though, since we're not sure how upset they are with her."

"Or what cost they will require for doing such a task," I said with a frown.

"Maybe we should have figured that stuff out before we let the boy take her body already." Brandon crossed his arms on the table.

Phoenix "tsked" and shook their head. "Yeah, it's a shame we need to work with them, but I'm afraid that's our best bet. Whatever they require in return, if I can help, I will."

"Thank you," Mom said. "What kinds of things do they usually ask for? It seems all they wanted for helping Hanna with her friend was simply for Hanna to track down a ghost and get information from it. That doesn't seem so bad."

I stirred my spoon around the cup idly watching the swirls of cocoa and bubbles. "Maybe, if she'd been able to accomplish the task before she died. The way they see it, we might owe them *two* debts, and after the whole debacle with Rose and the magic users, with Hanna clearly on the side of the witches, they're bound to be angry and demanding."

"And I can't even say I blame them," Phoenix said quietly into their mug.

"So what's next? What did Noah say?" I glanced at Mom, suddenly unable to find the appetite to even enjoy a comforting cup of hot chocolate.

"He said they'd get in touch. It was almost like he was as unsure about the whole thing as we are. I'm wondering if he's worried about what the leader will say, too, but he did assure me that Hanna is important, and they would want to help her come back if they could. However, I'm afraid, Trina, that we're going to have to tell them about you. I know keeping your powers a secret was important, but you're going to have to help them get Hanna back together."

Phoenix narrowed their eyes and turned toward me. I felt heat rush to my cheeks under their inspection. "Wait a minute... Are you saying...?"

I sighed and nodded. "Yes, I'm a Seer, too.

They looked at me as if they'd never seen me before. Their meticulous shaped eyebrows furrowed down under forehead wrinkles as their penetrating grey eyes stared down into my soul. "How is this possible?"

"Gran was just as confused when she found out Hanna could also see ghosts." I dropped eye contact and looked back at the mug. "Apparently there is usually only one every other generation. But not us. Yay. We're so lucky."

"If people got points for sarcasm, you'd have just gotten at least ten or so." Brandon quirked an eyebrow at me.

I ignored him, trying to also ignore the pain I felt when I thought about Gran. There were many choices I regretted in life and waiting so long to take off that stupid necklace was rising higher on my list. It ended up off my neck anyway. Why didn't I do it when I could have talked more with my grandma?

It was probably something I was going to regret for the rest of my life.

"Yes, that is my understanding as well." Phoenix nodded. "There can be more than one Seer on the earth at a time, of course, but per family it's usually only one every other generation. From my time when I was friends with Rose, I knew she was aware of your grandmother as a Seer. I suspect she set up a shop here nearby after your grandmother passed so she could keep tabs on your family. She had to have known at least one of the grandchildren would have received the gene."

I shuddered. "Creepy."

"Very." Mom gave me a compassionate look. "Let's try to keep Rose in the dark about your powers as much as we can. We probably shouldn't even let the matron of the coven know. Only the inner circle, if we can help it. We had to tell the necroes, of course, so that they understand how we are going to be able to perform the spell to bring her back, but hopefully they'll keep that secret to themselves.

"Hate to burst your bubble here," Phoenix said with a wince, "but did Caleb know what Trina could do?"

Mom's eyes widened. "Oh no. Can she access his memories and knowledge like that?"

"Perhaps not directly, but she can easily compel him to tell her everything. We should assume that she already knows." Phoenix frowned and took a long drink of the cooling cocoa.

"Great." I sunk into my chair and leaned my head back on the top of it, staring at the ceiling. "That makes things harder. She's free, has a new pet who happens to be someone we care about and can enter our home at any moment. We've got work to do."

"Well, I can at least reset the wards on the house so he can't come in again." Phoenix stood and grabbed their bag.

Mom nodded and stood as well. "Yes, let's do that right now, just in case. We're lucky he hasn't come to murder the rest of us yet."

"Perhaps Rose is planning something else for us," I grumbled, mostly giving voice to my discontent, but the truth of my statement wasn't lost on any of us.

Chapter 2 - Hanna

"So there I was, standing in my own room, and my vampire friend, who was supposed to protect me, came in and snapped my neck. How rude!" I said to the dandelion struggling to grow in the cold winter grass.

Our town didn't get a lot of snow until January-ish, so all the plants that were vibrantly green in the summer looked brown and sad in December without any of the white stuff that helped make wintertime pretty.

At least, that's what time of year I was guessing it was based on the weather and holiday decorations on the houses across the street.

I was laying on my stomach but didn't feel the cold from the moist ground seeping into my clothes. I couldn't feel the chilly wind making the weed's leaves twitch and the grass wave. I couldn't even feel my own arms as they rested upon each other, my chin sitting on the back of my hand.

It was like I was empty but unable to quite understand or feel how empty I was.

Being a ghost was weird.

"When do you think the apocalypse will happen? What will it be like? Probably have something to do with a bunch of countries setting off all the nuclear weapons. We might even blow our whole planet to smithereens just because a few groups of humans couldn't get along. Humans are dumb."

The dandelion's only response was to sway in the wind.

I'd had a lot of time to think, unsure how many days I'd been dead or even how many days I'd been a conscious (sorta) ghost. Time passed oddly. I suspected my ghostly energy ran out sometimes because I would blink during a brilliant sunrise only to open my eyes again to the still quiet of night.

During my free-thinking time, I came up with way more questions than answers. In fact, I wasn't sure I came up with any answers at all. I could tell my memory was fuzzy and getting fuzzier by the day, which didn't help me connect dots.

I wished I'd died with a pen and notebook in my pocket so I could keep track of all my thoughts. Too bad I had only been in jeans and a t-shirt with nothing useful in my pockets at all. It was also what I was stuck wearing for eternity. I didn't even have any shoes, but of course, that didn't matter as my ghostly feet made no real contact with the sharp sticks and rocks.

I had been reasonably surprised when I'd first opened my eyes and realized where my haunt was. Prior to being dead, I would have guessed the school or my house, the places I spent most of my time. It would have been funnily ironic if it was the pancake restaurant I used to adore. Thank goodness I wouldn't have been able to smell. That would have been real torture.

Even popping up next to Frank inside the movie theater would have been not so bad. But no, none of those.

Instead, it was grass, picnic benches, and a sizable area filled with concrete, ramps, half-pikes that curved, and rails where the skaters came to play.

And, because fate liked to tease me, this all happened right after I'd freed Brandon and reset his haunt.

I'd never seen another ghost haunting the skatepark, and, as far as I knew, there still wasn't.

Except now there was me, alone with the weeds and the laughing kids who didn't care about the cold wind or the solitary ghost laying in the grass.

"Yay," I said aloud, mostly to hear my own voice and reassure myself that I hadn't faded away completely.

I watched the sun slowly travel through the sky. I'd never taken the time to do that in life but now I had nothing but time. Time to watch kids come to the park and zip around. New kids showed up, old kids left, and parents walked back and forth making sure everything was okay. Sometimes I felt like I was trapped in one of those time-changing scenes in a movie where things moved quickly and faded in and out of each other.

Other times I felt like I was in a slow-motion scene watching a few seconds pass by in what felt like hours.

It was clear to me now why Brandon had been so excited to realize I could see and hear him. I wondered if his boredom attached him to me more than his actual liking of me. Would we have become friends if we had both been alive? Would he have even spared me a second look as he skated around the park, rolling on the board that he had loved in life so much?

I'd seen ghosts cry before but so far hadn't had the energy to let myself get there yet. Maybe ghosts didn't usually do that on their own but only around the alive me because I had given them extra energy to feel things. Yay me.

At some point, I had no idea how long after I died, or what day of the week it was, I noticed a few kids arrive at the park that tickled something inside my brain. I didn't understand the sensation at first, so I merely stayed where I was, sitting on my favorite picnic bench, elbows on my knees, and my head in my hands, and watched the newcomers.

There were two that particularly stood out to me, although I didn't understand why. One was a carefully put-together girl, my age, with expensively bought blonde highlights, and, what I already knew somehow more than saw, haughty blue eyes. She had her arm looped around the elbow of a guy, again about the same age, with dark hair that kept falling onto his forehead.

There was something about the way he pushed his hair back that stirred the most reaction from inside my chest, but it wasn't until the girl laughed, apparently in response to something the guy had said that my memories flushed back into me like someone had shoved my head into a toilet and given me a swirly.

"Holy cow." I stood from my bench. I knew if there had been a heart inside of me it would have been pounding heavily with the appearance of my friends.

Or people who had been my friends at one time.

Noah had brought a skateboard, and as I walked closer to them near the park entrance, I could hear their conversation.

"I'm not sure about this." He looked down at the concrete and held his board with the arm that wasn't stuck to Andrea's side.

She waved her hand in frustration. "Oh, come on. I'm sure it's just like riding a bike. You'll remember how to do it again before you even realize you're doing it."

"Noah!" I yelled, some dumb part of my brain thinking that if I was loud enough, he'd be able to hear me.

"Maybe we'll start over here where we're out of the way, and it's flat." Noah steered Andrea to the side of the concrete area, less in the way.

Andrea sighed. "I thought you had neat tricks you could show me. Instead, this is like watching someone try skating for the first time. Boring."

"Hey, this was your idea. Remember? If it were up to me, I'd be...doing something else." He put the board down on the flat sidewalk.

The more they talked, and the more I studied their faces, getting close enough to see the light dusting of freckles on Noah's nose, the more memories came back to me. This was the first time I'd seen Andrea since Noah had told me the truth of their relationship and what she was.

Narrowing my eyes, I leaned in to study her, wondering if I'd see the side of her ear start to detach from her head or her skin molt as she decomposed. But there was nothing wrong with her appearance. In fact, I got so close I could see the peach fuzz on her cheeks and upper lip. Not even an eyelash was out of place.

"Boo!" I wiggled my fingers right in front of her eyes.

There was no reaction, of course, as she unhooked her arm from Noah's and took a step back. "This moping is absurd. You've got to get out of the house and do something you love. Football doesn't seem to be helping you, and neither does hanging out with friends, going to see movies, minigolf, and all the other stuff we've tried. I thought skating like you used to enjoy in middle school might help. You'll never know if you don't try."

Moping? Why would Noah be moping?

He sighed and put one foot onto the board and pushed off, going slow and careful. His balance wasn't as graceful as it could have been, but, overall, it wasn't too bad.

In my own mind, I was becoming somewhat of an expert after having spent days—maybe weeks, whatever it was—watching the kids practice and zoom around. I had no idea what the technical terms for everything was, but I could watch someone and appreciate their skill level compared to the others.

Andrea stepped back some more, getting onto the grass so she was out of the way, and put her hands into her jacket pockets. I followed, not because I was worried about getting ran over by someone on a skateboard but more so curious about what she was.

In life, we'd been friends for a little while. If you can call it friends. Mostly, she copied off my math homework and used me to make her seem more popular. There had been a few good things to come out of our relationship, though, like how I had gotten to know Stephanie and Noah.

I'd had a crush on Noah for all of middle school and becoming Andrea's friend had felt like a dream come true.

It was funny how priorities changed as one grew and matured.

When Noah had first told me that Andrea was a zombie he had to essentially resurrect every day so her father wouldn't find out that the necromancer order had botched their daughter's initial resurrection spell, I'd thought it was one of the funniest things I'd ever heard.

Even now, as Andrea was watching Noah try to get his footing again on the skateboard, she was fiddling with her hair and using the camera feature on her phone to check her makeup.

She always looked so put together, and because of how vain and rude she was, it seemed hilarious that she was actually an undead creature that required a necromancer to be around at least once a day to protect her body from falling apart.

But now, it wasn't so funny. Instead, it was kind of sad and that was coming from me—a former friend and now dead person no one could see or hear.

Perhaps I got too close while studying her because something weird happened as I was leaning in over her shoulder.

He was focusing on the skating, still working on balance before going down to try any of the ramps.

Apparently deciding this was going to take a while, she put her phone away and took an unexpected step back, probably heading toward the picnic tables so she could sit down.

Usually when an aliver walks through a ghost, it's not a big deal. They might feel a slight chill or something, but the ghost isn't impacted much. Before I had died, I would have said that the ghost might get slightly uncomfortable based on Brandon's reactions to it. However, I had been walked through several times, and it hadn't really bothered me. Perhaps Brandon had just been making jokes. Or maybe it had bothered him on an intellectual or emotional level. It was something I was planning on asking him if I ever got to see him again.

When I got to see him again.

Despite the usual ghost rules, when Andrea stepped backward into me, something different happened.

Instead of feeling nothing when her body passed through my own, I felt a dark coldness. It was almost like there was an empty space inside her body. Curious, I placed myself more in line with her and found my point of view shift from being a spectral apparition into being...well, Andrea.

In awe, I lifted my arms, which turned into her arms. I moved them up and down like doing some kind of weird zombie dance and then moved her fingers in front of my face and wiggled them.

"Woah." I grinned, getting a giddy idea. As quickly as I could, I put my hands into Andrea's carefully smoothed hair and mussed it all up.

I was cackling to myself as I whipped her long, dyed-blonde hair into a frenzy when Noah walked up to me, a concerned expression on his face.

"Andrea? Are you okay?"

I froze, suddenly remembering that if I could use her body, other people could see it. "Uh..."

"Did you get a bug in your hair or a nasty itch? I can help you look for it." Noah dropped his board onto the grass next to me/us and reached his hands up as if to help me with whatever debacle I had gotten myself in.

"Oh, yeah. A spider. Totally that." I managed to find Andrea's voice and speak. It was surreal to hear her lower tones come out of my mouth instead of my own.

"Good gravy. You could have asked for help instead of creating this mess." He gently tried to smooth down the hair.

I was surprised at the care he took to pull out each strand from the tangles and found myself watching his concentrated face as he stood so close to me, his eyes focused on his task.

After I had quieted, and he realized I was watching him, he glanced down with an amused smile. "You sure made a mess of this. What? What are you looking at?"

I smiled back at him, feeling probably more affection than I would have if I hadn't been a lonely ghost for a while, facing eternity without ever feeling the touch of anyone else again. "Nothing. Sorry. Thanks for helping me. Have you found the spider yet?"

He shook his head and went back to his gentle search. "Not yet. Mostly just trying to fix your hair. I know how you hate having it messed up."

"Right. Well, I'd like to see what *you* would do if you could inhabit the body of your former enemy, or frenemy, as the case may be."

"Wait, what?" He dropped his arms down and looked into my eyes again. "What are you talking about?"

I grinned and winked. "I had some pretty cool powers in life. Not that I would have admitted it when I was alive, because I'm so humble. But it looks like I've gotten some different kind of ghost powers in death, too. I mean, yes, Gran had possessed a vampire before, but that took two other Seers pushing her into the body that was dead already. Maybe it works here because Andrea is a zombie and all that. You really should tell her the truth, by the way. But this didn't take nearly as much work as helping Gran possess the vampire queen. In fact, I didn't even know it was happening until I was suddenly able to move Andrea's hands."

Noah took a step back from me and stared. "What is happening? Hanna? Is that *you*?"

"In the flesh," I looked down at Andrea's body, "so to speak."

"Is this some kind of joke?" He looked around, maybe trying to find out if there was a hidden camera or a group of mischievous kids giggling at him from behind a bush.

"Maybe. I don't know. If it is, I'm not in on it." I shrugged and looked down at my feet. "Man, these shoes are killing me. I don't know how she can stand wearing them."

Furrowing his eyebrows, he got closer again and peered into my eyes. "Is it really you, Hanna? How is this happening?"

"Like I said, I think it's because she's a zombie. I mean, something is inside of her, but not a traditional spirit, I guess. Other kids have walked through me and nothing happened, but I guess they all had souls or whatever it is that makes someone not a zombie. I have no idea." I tried to give him a reassuring smile, but judging from his expression, it was probably more deranged than intended.

"Okay, let's go over here for a minute." Noah grabbed me by the elbow and glanced around in case someone was overhearing our odd exchange. None of the kids that chilly afternoon paid any attention to us after having gotten over my weird hair fiasco.

I grinned thinking about the possibilities of having a body.

Noah steered me to a table, and we sat on the bench.

"Seriously. These shoes are terrible." I wiggled out of the wedge booties Andrea had thought to put on this morning.

"Don't take off your shoes! It's too cold for that. People will think you're crazy, and after the hair situation, they are already questioning it." Noah bent down to put them back on my feet.

I sighed dramatically. "Maybe I want them to think Andrea is crazy. That's the least amount of payback I owe her."

He sat up and frowned. "I suppose I can't begrudge you that. How are you here? Your mom and sister have been looking all over for your spirit."

"They have? Trina is using her powers more? That's awesome!" I smiled and then frowned quickly. "I hope they haven't been too worried. I didn't mean to..."

Noah grabbed my hand that had been sitting on my lap. "I know. It's okay, Hanna. The order has your body, and your family has been trying to find your spirit so we can put you back together again." He shook his head and chuckled. "I have to say it's funny that this is your haunt. No wonder they haven't been able to find you yet. I would have pegged the school or your house. I never would have guessed it would be the skate park."

"Wouldn't you? It was Brandon's haunt..." The sadness sank into me, stronger than when I had been a ghost.

Apparently being dead didn't only mess with your memories but also muted your emotions.

"Oh, right. I guess that makes sense... I just haven't wanted to admit to myself how much you cared for him. It seems silly now considering...everything, but I was jealous of the ghost. And if his old haunt is your haunt, well then, I guess I had something to be jealous of." He tried covering up his discomfort with a flirty grin, but it wobbled too much to be effective.

"Yeah well, not sure any of that matters now. I'm dead. He's dead. Though after he was enslaved in the crystals and I freed him, his haunt reset. How ironic is that? He did mention something about trying to go back to his haunt in the few minutes we had together, but nothing happened. Do you think his new haunt is my bedroom? Have you talked to Trina about it at all? Can I use your phone right now and call her?"

My voice raised in pitch as I spoke, getting more and more excited about having a body again.

"Woah." Noah raised his hands up in a calming motion. "Let's slow down here. First, it could be dangerous for you to be inhabiting Andrea's body. Perhaps it's been too long already. What kind of effects could it have on you? Are you using up ghostly energy which will help you get closer to a poltergeist? What about Andrea? This could be hurting her in some way or she may be able to remember everything that happens when you're possessing her. Don't get me wrong. I've been worried sick about you and am so glad to be able to talk to you, but I also want to make sure we're not making anything worse."

He squeezed my hand, and it was nice to be able to feel the warmth from someone's touch again. "I care about you, Hanna. I don't want anything worse to happen to you or to anyone else we care about. We've got to be careful about this whole thing."

I sighed. "I suppose you're right. Yes, it's too good to be true that possession like this wouldn't have any consequences. I'll give you your girlfriend back. Can you at least promise to tell Trina and Mom where my haunt is?"

Noah smiled sadly and nodded. "Of course I will. Before you go, though, I just have to ask. Was there ever any chance for the two of us? Well, I mean, if we were both single and free to do what we wanted."

I considered my options as I stared at our entwined hands. The last thing I wanted to do was scare him away. At the moment, he was the only chance I had at talking to anyone. "Maybe. But it doesn't do to dwell in hypotheticals. You're Andrea's boyfriend, and I would never cross such a line."

Figuring that would make for a good exit, I somehow gathered the parts of myself that were ghost and stepped out of Andrea, leaving the warmth of her body and the connections to my memories and emotions.

Chapter 3 - Trina

"Where else have we not tried? Oh! Maybe we can go to the movie theater tomorrow. I remember her talking about some other ghost she knows that haunts there. She also liked to go see movies, so that could be a place." I fiddled with a pen as we sat at the kitchen table compiling a list of other places we could check for Hanna.

Mom nodded. "Yes, let's try there. After that, maybe we could check that pancake restaurant she liked so well."

"Right. Sounds good."

"Okay, I know this is going to sound slightly self-centered, but what about the skatepark?" Brandon asked from his chair to my right.

Mom took the notebook from me and slid it across the table to add the two new places to the list, heedless of Brandon's words. It had taken me several days to get kind of used to having the skater kid, almost-boyfriend-of-my-almost-dead-sister, and smart-mouth-extraordinaire haunt our house.

The hardest bit was listening and talking back to him when others were around. Even though I *knew* Mom understood what was happening, I still felt awkward and dumb. I wasn't sure the weirdness would ever go away.

It made me miss and appreciate Hanna even more.

"The skatepark? Why would her haunt be the skatepark?" I scrunched up my nose and looked at the place where Mom only saw an empty chair while I saw a blue-toned, transparent teen from the 90s with spiky hair and pants so big you could fit several legs in them at once.

He shrugged, and, to his credit, there was a sheepish grin on his face. "Maybe because she missed me?"

I scoffed and shook my head, turning to Mom. "Brandon says we should check the skatepark because she'll be missing him."

Mom's eyes darted to the empty chair and back to my face. "I suppose that's not a bad idea. She sure was...upset when he was gone. There are worse ideas, certainly, and we're nearing the end of our list. We might as well add it."

I gave Brandon a pointed look while she scribbled it down. He beamed a dumb smile as if he'd won some kind of sibling-type argument.

"Ugh, I can't wait until we get her back. Then I can put that necklace back on, and *she* can deal with you." I gave Brandon a side-eye. "I have no idea why she likes being with you anyway."

Brandon sat back in the chair and chuckled. "I'm like a wart. I tend to grow on ya."

Rolling my eyes, I shuddered my shoulders. "Ew."

Mom's lips twitched as she listened to my side of the conversation, used to hearing us bicker.

"Well, it's late. Best we get to bed and pick this up in the morning." Mom put down her pen. "How much homework do you have? If you could do some tonight, we can have more time to look tomorrow."

It was Friday night, a week and three days since Caleb's betrayal, a week before Christmas break, and the mid-part of my senior year. Frankly, I'd been a straight "A" student until Hanna's temporary separation from her body. Now, my grades were under severe threat of dropping, which would make me lose the scholarship to Virginia Tech I'd worked so hard to qualify for.

I was struggling with the guilt of having to find my sister's ghost while the long-term consequences were staring me in the face. Mom and I had talked several times about it, and she knew I required the extra push to focus on schoolwork once in a while.

"Yes, I can work on some Trig for a bit. Although, my head is killing me." I rubbed the spot that hurt the worst, wishing I could put enough pressure on it that the pain would ease.

"I'm sorry, sweetie." Mom patted my hand that was laying on the table. "It's probably stress and tension. Thankfully you'll have more time to catch up on your work over Christmas break. Maybe if we're lucky, you'll get some time to rest, as well."

"Don't forget that you need some rest, too. I know you scaled back some on your photography, but you've been working hard and trying to find Hanna with me. I'm sure you're tired."

She nodded, a small wistful smile on her lips. "I'll sleep when I die, perhaps."

"I wish I could tell you you'll get rest when you die, but so far, I've found that to be a lie," Brandon muttered, and I wasn't sure if that was more for himself or for me.

The next morning, I was up by nine, something unusual for me on the weekends but had become much more common recently. As I spent time in the bathroom fixing my hair, I waited expectantly for

Hanna's impatient knock and muffled call for me to hurry up so she could pee.

It didn't come, of course, and the heaviness in my chest threatened to squeeze out emotion. So far, I'd managed not to cry about any of it. Not even when Noah's muscled arms carried Hanna's body out of the house and to the necromancer's van. I didn't leak a tear as we lied to Dad telling him that she went on an unexpected trip with her friends for the holiday, making sure to take all her studying with her so she wouldn't be penalized at school. I certainly didn't cry when Mom and I had taken walks through her favorite stores and the school, trying to find the haunt where we were sure her ghost was waiting patiently for us. I hadn't even teared up when all those places turned up empty—of anyone I wanted to talk to, anyway.

I was very proud of the fact that I hadn't cried when Brandon had told us what had happened, including the bit about Caleb being under Rose's spell. Mostly, I avoided thinking about any of it except to stoke the anger inside so I could use it for more energy.

There was no point in getting sad since it was only a matter of time before we were back together, laughing in the kitchen as we followed Gran's old cookie recipe.

Because there was no point at all in accepting that she would have crossed over and not become a ghost. There were way too many unfinished things for that to happen.

All we had to do was find her.

"Are you ready?" Mom's voice sounded from the other side of the bathroom door.

I opened it with a small smile. "Ready enough. Want to head to the restaurant first?"

She nodded and walked toward the kitchen. "Might as well stop and get some breakfast while we're there, you think? It might take some time for her ghost to show up and find us."

I shrugged even though she wasn't looking at me. "I guess."

Brandon popped out of the wall as I walked past Hanna's bedroom. The first few times he'd done it had scared the crap out of me, but now I was used to it. The poor kid seemed to be somewhat of an extrovert, craving social interaction.

"Can I come with you?"

I sighed and turned to look at him when we reached the front room. "We've been over this, Brandon. A ghost isn't supposed to be able to leave their haunt. I know Hanna had the power to work around that, but there's no reason to assume I can do the same thing."

"Can we at least try it? Pretty please? I've been a good boy patiently waiting by myself during the quiet hours while y'all are at work and school, but I've got to get out of the house. What if you can take me with you, but you won't ever know because you won't try?" Brandon's eyes were wide and pleading, probably used to getting his desired results from the puppy-dog face.

"Might as well let him try. What's the worst that will happen?" Mom picked up her purse from the kitchen table and turned to me. She hadn't been able to hear his side of the conversation, but we'd been through it enough by now that she knew what he was asking.

"The worst? That he'll be able to come with us and drive me crazy with his incessant comments. It's like having a snarky narrator that only I can hear hanging over my shoulder all the time. Isn't it enough that I have to put up with him while we're at home?" I rubbed my forehead in frustration.

"Ouch." There was some pain in his tone as he gave me a pouty lip. "I'm not that bad, am I? What if I promise to be quiet?"

"I'm sorry. I'm new to this whole ghost thing, and it's hard enough ignoring the pleading comments from the random strange ghosts we run into, let alone your smart mouth."

Mom chuckled softly to herself as she waited patiently for me to finish speaking with someone no one else could see.

"You think I'm smart? Oh please." Brandon put a hand over his mouth as if blushing in gratitude.

I rolled my eyes, remembering that Hanna had done it a lot, and now I completely understood why. "Ugh. Whatever. We can try but don't blame me when you find out you're absolutely stuck here."

"Yay!" Brandon clapped his hands with a giddy smile on his face.

"Did Hanna do anything special to make her powers allow a ghost to come with her?" I asked, unsure how any of it worked.

He shrugged. "Not really. The first time she didn't think it was going to work either, but I kept on walking next to her side. We were both surprised when it worked."

"Easy enough." I put my phone into my back pocket and pulled on my jacket that had been sitting on the armchair of the couch. "If it does work, remember you promised to be quiet."

He motioned zipping his mouth closed and throwing away the key.

"Ready?" Mom's eyes twinkled with amusement.

"Yes, the sooner we find Hanna, the better, for lots of reasons."

Brandon gave me a cheesy grin which I tried to ignore.

As we stepped out of the house, I looked around at the neighborhood in the bright morning sunlight. It had gotten a little warmer during the day yesterday so there was misty fog settling around the cool trees. Beams of sunlight filtered in through the leaves and dew, making the world look so innocent you would have never suspected vampires roamed around, just snapping necks willy-nilly whenever their necromancer/witch masters told them to.

Mom gave me a tight smile as she saw me pause on the porch. "The sooner we're in the car, the better."

"Yes, let's get into the car." Brandon strutted past me as if he belonged with us alivers.

Shaking my head, I followed his lead but ignored his protests when I went to sit in the front seat.

The witches had redone the magic spell around our house so presumably Phoenix was the only occult creature that could enter there. But that didn't mean we were safe outside. Rose and Caleb were out somewhere running amok and causing whatever havoc Rose decided she wanted to descend on the world. With his darker skin, Caleb was able to withstand the sun better compared to his pastier brethren, and even in the bright morning sunlight he could run by, murder us, and run away so fast someone watching would have assumed we'd simply fallen to the ground on our own.

Phoenix had given us assurances that the coven would help and keep an eye out for us, but I was sure they weren't around every second. Gryphin and Mr. Tyler had agreed to help watch out for me at school so I wouldn't have to miss out on my studies.

There was a possibility that the vampire queen was hiding somewhere nearby as well. We hadn't heard from her since the night she'd made us agree to let her murder Rose in exchange for information about Brandon and his family she thought we might find useful. I knew she at least valued Seers enough to want to make sure one didn't die...or at least *another* one didn't die. If she valued her chance at Rose, we were her best bet. Even if she used us as bait, as long as she protected us when it came down to it, I was fine with that.

As for the information Kieran had given us, I hadn't had the heart to share it with Brandon yet. It was clear he didn't know we knew about his death or that Rose was actually responsible for his sibling's murders, but it didn't feel right for me to share all of that with him. Mom and I had both agreed that it was something Hanna could tell him when we found her.

As I put my hand onto the handle of the car door, a red SUV drove up and stopped in front of our house.

"Oh, I hope this isn't bad." Brandon stood next to me with hands on his hips.

Mom got out of the car but kept the door open as she moved to stand between me and the newcomers.

I was slightly relieved to see Noah climb out of the passenger side but still unsure how much we could trust him. The driver swung the front door shut and walked around to greet us with a resolutely friendly smile on his face. I vaguely recognized him from the night the necromancers helped us storm a vampire seethe and free Hanna, but I didn't know his name.

"Good morning," the driver said, stopping a few feet from my mom.

Noah trailed in after him and gave us a greeting smile that was more awkward than I'd seen him usually display.

"Good morning," Mom replied, a tight edge in her voice. "Can we help you?"

"Yes, you can, actually," the man said with a quick glance in my direction.

My chest tightened at his look. While we had expected them to come calling, that didn't mean I was ready for whatever they were going to ask.

"Mr. Fellows has a task for you. Well, two, actually, since your family owes the order already. Then add to that the favor you want from us, I'm afraid we require some extra work before we can grant your desire. I'm sure you understand why we expect payment first, considering what happened last time," the man said.

I glanced at Noah for reassurance, but his eyes stayed on the grass sparkling with light frost. Trepidation flitted through my chest as I considered what would make him not want to look at us. Did he know the jobs we were going to have to perform for the order?

"Okay. We understand there are costs to what we need, and we intend to fill our end of the bargain as best as we are able, but we work as a team. If you want access to my daughter's powers, then you'll have to deal with me. I've already lost one daughter, and I'm not about to lose the other while I live and breathe."

The man smiled and nodded. "Of course. We understand. A mother's love is one of the most extraordinary things in this world. We wouldn't dream of causing anyone more fear or pain. There's enough of that in this life already."

"I'm glad you understand. What does he want us to do?" Mom glanced behind at me, probably to make sure I was still standing there.

"If I know these guys, it's not going to be something easy or fun. He better not expect us to find the goat," Brandon said, confusing me more than helping.

"He would like to discuss things with you himself. Do you mind coming with us? I'm afraid the longer we stand in the open air with Rose and her pets on the run, the more dangerous it is," the man said, taking a step back toward the SUV.

At least we agreed on one thing.

Mom glanced back at me again, her eyes questioning. It didn't seem wise to trust them enough to get inside their vehicle and go with them wherever they wanted, but we'd already made our decision by giving them Hanna's body. We would have to follow it through.

I nodded at Mom and stepped up next to her. "Let's go. The sooner we can get this over with, the better."

"Are you sure? We could be going into some kind of trap." Mom leaned in to whisper as if the necromancers wouldn't know what she was saying.

"We've already given them Hanna. Might as well get in bed with them. It's the only way to bring her back," I said.

She gave me a scandalous look.

"Metaphorically, of course." I shook my head.

"Caleb would probably be upset if you got in bed with a necromancer," Brandon commented as he waltzed over to the van.

I didn't bother to dignify his comment with a response, figuring he'd be gone as soon as we pulled away from the house.

Mom walked quickly back to the driver's side of our car and grabbed her purse before shutting the door.

Then we went together toward the SUV the necroes had shown up in.

The driver opened the door for us, and Mom climbed in first. I got in after her. Brandon attempted to follow but frowned as if something was stopping him from leaving the curb.

Heedless of what was happening with the ghost, the driver shut the door, and it swung through Brandon's body as he stood staring forlornly.

"Well, guess I'll see you guys when you get back," he said, barely audible from outside. "Too bad you don't also have Hanna's unique skills, but it makes me wonder what extra abilities you have. One sister can't have talents beyond normal Seers and not the other."

Noah and the driver got into the front seats while Brandon spoke. I gave him a slight wave as the car started, but I didn't really know if he could see me through the tinted windows.

Mom watched me wave, and we locked eyes communicating the knowledge that we were alone in this odd adventure.

An hour and thirty minutes later, we were walking out of the necromancer's headquarters house, or at least that's what I was calling it. It was one of those big houses I would have loved to explore under different circumstances. As it was, I wanted to get out of there as fast as I could.

I'd seen the order's leader a few times but hadn't really talked with him before. He was creepy—like make your skin crawl creepy. I didn't know how Hanna had been able to put up with him so far.

And this was coming from someone basically in love with a vampire. If I thought someone was creepy, then they were definitely creepy.

"So that's just great." Mom sighed and put her hands into her jacket pockets.

It had warmed up some, but there was still a brisk chill in the wind as we waited for our car to come pick us up. The necroes had offered to drive us back home again, but we'd insisted on using an app for a ride. We'd had enough of their company, thank you very much.

Noah hadn't been in the room while Mr. Fellows had explained what they needed from us, and I hadn't seen him on our way out. The task we'd been given seemed innocent enough, although there was probably more going on than we realized. However, I was pretty sure it wasn't the reason Noah was avoiding even basic eye contact with me.

Something else was up.

"Perhaps we can do two things at once. Keep an eye out for Hanna as well as talk to the ghost. Honestly, I'm relieved that he asked us to contact Susan, the same task he gave Hanna before she... Well, anyway, I've at least talked to this ghost before and maybe we can get somewhere with her."

Mom pressed her lips together and nodded appreciatively. "Nice. Probably smart that you didn't tell him you've already had contact with her."

I shrugged. "I figured it would be best to keep whatever information we have until we can come to him with some actual answers."

"Or at least answers we were wanting to give him." Mom glanced back at the house behind us, several paces away as we stood on the curb. "I don't feel good about any of this."

"Me neither." I left it unspoken that we didn't really have a choice and we both knew it. We were willing to do anything to get Hanna back, including making a deal with the devil, or at least a guy who freaked me out as much as the devil probably would.

Maybe even more.

Chapter 4 - Hanna

After Noah and Andrea had left, she having no memory of being taken over momentarily by a ghost, I felt a bit sad. It was like the few minutes I had felt alive again, literally, were making my death more starkly contrasted than ever.

It was nice to have something to look forward to, but without anything to distract myself so that the time passed by quickly, the momentary thrill was merely a form of torture instead of a bright spot in my existence.

It hadn't mattered to me that Noah had concerns about what I had done. Andrea seemed totally fine, if not a little confused about how she had gotten so quickly from the concrete to the bench. I was sure Noah could figure out how to get her to think she'd just had a small minute of forgetfulness.

Certainly, it couldn't be that hard for a necromancer to convince a zombie of stuff, and if it was, I'd assume that person wasn't very good at their job.

There was a small chance that Noah wouldn't come back to chat, but there were many reasons to think that he would. First, he seemed so happy to talk to me. Second, there were a lot of questions we had for each other. Third, he was going to tell my mom and Trina where I was so they could get to work on putting me back into my body.

They would have to come back to talk to me then. If we were really lucky, Trina would be able to escort me to the necromancer's house and they could cast the spell, and everything would be right in the world again.

Thinking about Trina using powers to help me leave my haunt, I realized I hadn't even tried it myself yet. If I had the power of easily possessing a soulless body, so to speak, then perhaps I had other powers as well.

It was dark out and the park was empty, so I judged it to be some-time late. I was sure it was cold but couldn't feel it. I counted that as a good thing since I didn't particularly like shivering all the time. There were some perks about being a ghost.

Another one was I didn't have to worry about getting fat. Frank had seemed eager to want to eat again, but I felt content not having to wage that battle any more. If I did come alive again, I was going to do better at eating healthier, if not more food. Vegetables were always a good bet, and after feeling so weak the last few days before death, I was more inclined to try avoiding being so sickly.

I walked toward the fence that surrounded the skate park, hoping that trying to walk out of one's haunt wasn't painful. The dark, empty trees swayed above my head in what must have been a strong wind. The houses around the park were dark except for the occasional porch light. Even most of the Christmas lights had been turned off. Not a single car drove by in the long minutes I contemplated the darkness. It wasn't like I had anything else to do.

This was the time I hated when the world felt the emptiest, and I felt the most alone.

I paused at the end of the sidewalk, remembering when I'd been there the first time with Brandon. I'd told him he wouldn't be able to pass beyond this point and had told him goodbye while he had grinned and merely continued to walk down the street with me.

What had given him any indication that I could somehow escort him out of his haunt? It could have been that he'd never talked to another Seer before, unaware of our usual limitations, and that he'd only been hopeful that he could continue to hang out with me.

At the time, I'd felt his attachment to me seemed a tad unhealthy seeing I was a stranger, but as I stood on the empty sidewalk staring at the gum-riddled concrete, I understood intimately why he had been determined to hang around.

Setting my lips together in a thin line of determination, I lifted my foot and tried to push it past the line where the fence of the park met the sidewalk.

I couldn't do it.

Thankfully, it wasn't painful. It was as if an invisible wall stood between me and the outside world—unmovable, didn't budge an inch, and firmly ignored any of my ghostly pleas.

Of course, if it had worked, I would have felt really dumb for taking so long to figure it out. So there was that, I guess.

I had been foolish to try.

On heavy feet, I went back to the park, sat on a bench, stared at the empty grass, and watched the wind tousle tree branches.

Sometime later, days, weeks, whatever, Noah and Andrea came back. I hadn't even noticed them come into the park at first, busy as I was talking to my new dandelion friend. It hadn't grown much, but it was hard to gauge time by that since it was winter, and the plant wasn't going to be able to grow a lot anyway.

It wasn't until Noah took a seat on the picnic table bench in the back that I even realized they were there.

"I thought we were here to skate. You acted so excited to come back. I still don't get why *I* had to come, though. As much as it was fun watching you wobble around last time, it would probably be easier for you to have fun without your bored girlfriend waiting for you." Andrea looked at him with crossed arms as she stood, not joining him on the bench.

Noah's eyes bounced around the park, unable to focus on any one thing. "Yes, I'll skate in a minute. Just going to get some stretches in. I didn't realize it was annoying for you to watch me skate. You're the one who suggested I come here the first time, remember?"

She sighed. "Yes, but that was me trying to get you out of your funk. And it worked. So do I really need to come back here? I need to get my nails done. Not to mention that something about this skate park is starting to give me the willies."

I grinned openly, not having to worry about her seeing my expression while Noah glanced around some more, avoiding eye contact with her.

"That's because it's haunted," I said, using a spooky voice.

"Can you blame me for wanting to show off in front of my girlfriend? We'll hang out here for a little while then I'll take you to get your nails done, my treat. How about that?" Noah finally looked at her with a charming smile.

She sighed. "Fine, but you're also buying me a boba."

"Done." Noah nodded resolutely and went back to looking around the park.

I considered their conversation and why Noah was really here. I was pretty sure it wasn't because he actually wanted to skate, but I didn't want to barge into their conversation. Plus, he had been the one worried about the effects of possessing Andrea.

But he was clearly looking around for someone. What would it hurt to check and make sure that someone wasn't me?

Feeling weird but also eager, I stepped inside Andrea's body, hoping it would be that easy again. It was, but I couldn't help wondering what Andrea experienced when I did it. Did her essence or whatever was left in her body just take a nap? Where had her soul gone? What exactly *was* a zombie?

I quickly forgot the existential questions when I had arms and legs and skin again.

"I suppose I'll get used to this if I keep doing it." I examined Andrea's hands.

"Oh, you're here! I wasn't sure how to get your attention or even if you were around." Noah stood and put his skateboard down.

"Where else would I be? It's not like I could go get a manicure." I examined Andrea's current set of acrylic nails. They were so long, I wondered how she even buttoned her pants.

"Yeah... Well, I've got to bribe her somehow. This isn't possible without her help, or, believe me, I wouldn't be trying to drag her along."

"For some reason, I do believe you."

We shared a knowing smile about our mutual friend.

"So what did Mom and Trina say when you told them where my haunt was? I bet they laughed at the irony." I took a seat on the bench and curled deeper into Andrea's jacket which was much more fashionable than functional. It was both uncomfortable and thrilling to feel the icy wind trying to get through the jacket and tapping at my nose.

Noah put a hand through his hair to push it out of his face. It didn't work as it was just the right length to fall back down. If he didn't like it in his face, he really should have gotten a different haircut. I suspected he didn't mind, and it was once an action I enjoyed watching.

"I haven't had a chance to tell them yet. Things have been busy… I promise I'll tell them soon!" He said the last part with sincerity when he saw my face scrunch up in concern.

"They still don't know where I am?" I wasn't sure if I was more upset because I'd been sitting in anticipation, waiting for contact from them, or because I was worried how sad they were. Either way, I was upset.

Noah sat down next to me and grabbed my hand…or Andrea's hand, whatever. "It's okay. I've seen them. They're doing well. They're working with the order to prepare putting your body and spirit back together, but David is refusing to do it until they follow through with their part of the bargain first. I super promise that when it's time, your family will definitely know where you are."

I frowned, my gaze shifting from his eager hazel eyes to where our hands were warmly interlocked. We hadn't ever held hands like this when I was alive. "What kinds of things is David asking them to do? Nothing too dangerous, I hope?"

"Of course, not dangerous. I don't know the details myself, but the last thing David would want is to lose another Seer. He's eager to keep Trina safe and available for the use of the order. In fact, I wouldn't be surprised at all if he had a secret detail of minions keeping track of them all the time."

"I know that's supposed to make me feel better, but it doesn't." I curled my lip thinking about a zombie shambling around the bushes, making sure a vampire didn't pop in and murder my family.

"I know it might be kind of creepy. I also know that you don't fully trust the order, but I can promise on my soul that they want to keep your family safe. It might not be for the same reasons as yours, but at least they'll continue to protect them." Noah smiled tentatively.

"I guess that's helpful... With Caleb on her side, I worry they're sitting ducks for Rose to hurt them as easily as she hurt me."

Noah squeezed my hand and pressed his lips into a regretful frown. "I'm sorry I wasn't there to help. As much as Caleb and I don't like each other, I can't imagine he would ever willingly put himself in a position where he would have hurt you. Rose must be more powerful than we suspected."

"Yeah... When he gets freed from her grasp, he's going to feel pretty bad about it. Do you know how much a vampire can feel while being enslaved by a necromancer?" I asked, resisting the urge to caress Noah's thumb where it interlocked with mine, not necessarily to give him pleasure but more to feel something while I still had skin.

"As far as I know, they're mostly aware of the whole thing. It's not like whatever you can do with Andrea's body where she has no memory or realization of what happened. Neat trick, by the way." He paused to smile.

I gave him a weak smile back. "Thanks."

"The vampires are fully aware of what's happening to their body. They just can't control what they do. If you ask me, it's only what they deserve after enthralling their human prey and draining all the blood out of them until only a dry husk remains."

"But not all vampires are like that. Caleb was different, right? As far as I know."

Noah shrugged. "Probably?"

"Before I forget to ask again, can you fill me in more on what happened at the storage unit? Why were you in the unit when we broke that spell?"

His eyebrows furrowed for a second as I changed topic so quickly. "Oh, I'm a bit fuzzy on the exact details, but one of the witches contacted our order, told us where Rose was hiding out, and was waiting for us when we arrived. I think her name was Peaches? I only remember because it was kinda weird."

I nodded. "Yeah, it's a weird name. The matron was able to contact her through the coven's bonds even through the spell."

"Didn't know witches could do that. Cool. Anyway, she was standing there with a plastic container of water and a small bag of orange powder. After meeting us, she told David about the storage unit and how there was a spell inside we needed to break. She said that doing so would trigger Rose's presence, and we could do with her what we wanted."

"Oh, I'm not sure the matron knew that Peaches told the necroes that," I said with a sideways frown.

Noah nodded. "That makes sense. She didn't want the order to keep Rose."

"And look at how good that turned out," I muttered. "Maybe we should have let you guys take her after all."

"But what about those ghosts you were so worried about? Did you manage to free them?"

I nodded. "Yes, most of them. There are still at least three missing. And they also happen to be Brandon's siblings. It seems kind of important to free them...but I forget about the important things a lot now."

Noah rubbed the back of my hand with his thumb. "That must be hard."

Worried about the amount of time we'd been chatting and if there were indeed consequences from me possessing Andrea's body for long, I prodded him to keep going with the story.

"Oh, so Peaches told us that to break the spell we'd need to find a specific picture and dump it into the orangey water. She gave us precise instructions, and since I'm the apprentice and unable to do much yet, David told me to break the spell while they waited for Rose to show up. Once we found the unit, I went inside and prepared the water. It was so weird, though, because before I could even begin looking for the picture, I saw a small hand come out of nowhere, pick up a magazine, and dump it into the water. Then the hand disappeared. Do you happen to know about *that*?"

Laughing, I filled him in on the ghosts, how I knew about Brandon's siblings in the first place, and that they'd been trying to help free us from the spell.

"Wow, it must be seriously so cool to talk to ghosts like that, and yet I get the feeling that you don't necessarily enjoy it," Noah said.

"It was super scary when I was a kid, so I just learned to ignore them. Plus, my mom freaked out when I mentioned Gran coming back from the dead. It made me a bit wary of the whole thing."

Noah nodded. "Makes sense. I didn't realize it all started when you were a kid. That would be scary."

We sat for a few seconds in silence. There were only a couple of people at the park despite the afternoon being sunny. The chill breeze of the incoming winter had probably scared most of them away.

"Shouldn't we be getting worried about the side effects of me possessing Andrea? You seemed pretty freaked out by them last time." The discomfort of touching him finally overwhelmed the desire for human contact, and I pulled my hand away from his, putting it into Andrea's jacket pocket like the other one was.

"Probably. But nothing has happened yet, right? Do you feel tired or like your energy is draining?" He also buried his hands into his jacket pockets.

"Not really...but that doesn't mean it's not taking energy." I scrunched up my face with slightly disturbed thoughts. "Guess there's really no one to ask about it either. I don't have a huge knowledge of Seer and zombie relationships, but as far as I know, this isn't something that is usually possible."

"I guess it's like the other Seer powers you can do that others can't. Maybe since you had extra powers in life, you now have extra powers as a ghost?" Noah nudged a pebble on the concrete with his shoe as he spoke.

"Seems like it. Other humans have walked through me, and nothing happened. I think it's because Andrea is...what she is. I keep thinking of her as a zombie, and now that we were talking about the fight at the storage unit, it makes me think about all the zombies the ghosts were able to possess using my powers as a Seer. Maybe it's because I could do that kind of thing."

Noah shook his head. "That was seriously impressive. I think you managed to surprise even David and Rose. I mean, if you think about it, it was dumb for Rose to kill you when you were able to do that. That was an amazing display of power, and she should have kidnapped you and made you her own personal Seer."

"Thanks, I guess? But it wasn't that great. It helped the magic users win, which then led to Rose escaping and my death. In a roundabout way, I killed myself."

Noah nudged my shoulder with his. "Don't think of it like that. You're amazing. I mean, just getting to talk with you like this is amazing."

"Perhaps we may get brave enough that I can even keep parading around as Andrea. Do you think anyone would notice if she was suddenly less vain and better at math?"

We shared an amused smile.

"People would notice," he nodded, "for sure."

"I suppose it wouldn't be very ethical." I looked down at her shoes. At least they were slightly more comfortable than the ones she'd had on last time.

"I suppose," Noah copied my phrase, his mouth twitching into another smile.

"You promise you're going to tell Mom and Trina where I am? They might not be ready to get me back into my body, but at least we could talk and maybe I could make them feel better." I looked into

Noah's eyes steadily, hoping the gaze would help him understand how important it was because he hadn't gotten the message the last time.

He nodded. "Yes. I promise. See you around, H."

I left a smile on Andrea's face as I pulled my ghostly spirit out of her body. I stayed long enough to watch as she blinked a few times and looked around. Noah's smile faded as he stood and stretched his back.

"Alright, I think I'm ready now. I'll just get in a few passes, and we can leave. Okay?"

Her eyebrows creased and she kept blinking and looking around the skatepark. "Okay…"

I retreated to my spot in the grass where my dandelion friend was and stared at it listlessly for a few minutes, days, or weeks.

Chapter 5 - Trina

After stopping by the pancake restaurant and staying long enough to eat, hoping we'd given Hanna's ghost plenty of time to show up if she was there, we walked to the car.

"Well, that doesn't mean her spirit isn't here or anywhere else that we've checked. Maybe she doesn't have enough energy to show up in the small moments we've visited. I know I don't understand as much about the ghost world as Hanna does, but I do know that energy is hard to get for ghosts sometimes." I got into the car and put on my seatbelt.

Mom put her hands on the steering wheel but didn't start the car right away. Instead, she stared out the window with exhaustion and sadness on her face. "But we're sure we're going to find her, right? We're sure she hasn't passed on to Heaven?"

I put my hand on her upper arm, trying to convey love and companionship. "Yes, we're sure. We're going to find her even if we have to look for a long time. We won't give up."

Pressing her lips together, Mom turned to look at me. "I'm so glad we can do this together. I don't know what I would do if you weren't able to talk to spirits or ghosts or whatever you want to call them. Can you imagine what this would feel like if we didn't have the hope of putting her back together again?"

I could see the emotion welling up in her eyes as she considered how she might feel if Hanna couldn't come back. Unwilling to let myself feel anything close to that but still tearing up from seeing my mom so near devastation, I smiled resolutely despite my watery eyes. "That's not going to happen. We'll find her. We will. We just need to keep going. The worst thing we could do for her right now is give up."

She nodded, wiped away a few tears, and started the car. "Exactly. We can check out the movie theater later since it might not even be open yet. In the meantime, let's go talk to Susan. Maybe we can get some progress with her."

"It speaks volumes of how much we love Hanna that we're willing to go hang out under the overpass with all that smelly garbage and those scary hobos," I said, trying to make a joke but mostly failing.

Twenty minutes later, we pulled into a grocery store parking lot near the tent city. I was still surprised that town officials hadn't cleared it out yet, but it looked as dirty and creepy as ever. Mom and I had been here together once before when I'd contacted Tracy and worked to help her cross over. This was also when Hanna was missing only a few weeks ago. She'd ran away after Thanksgiving dinner and was busy solving mysteries with the witches, but we hadn't known that for several hours.

At least it was daytime, hopefully safer, and people would get less angry at us wandering around loudly calling out for ghosts.

As I stepped out of the car, I could see several blue forms floating around the alivers and heaps of garbage. An alive lady pushed a cart full of stuff I wouldn't want to sort through as we crossed the street and headed into the dark shade of the highway overpass. Cars constantly drove above us, giving the space a rushing echo sound that I suppose one got used to after a while.

Tracy, the pioneer lady who had been churning butter for decades, perhaps centuries, was gone. I'd helped her pass over after researching what had happened to her family after her neighbor had murdered her. The task had been simple enough, but it had felt good helping someone find peace.

If we could get past all this other drama with witches and necromancers and vampires, maybe it wouldn't have been so bad being a Seer, focusing on helping lost souls get to where they needed to go.

"I wonder how they get through the winter down here," Mom said quietly as we tip-toed our way past tents, cardboard boxes, overflowing dumpsters, and snoring heaps that could have been possible people underneath all the dirty clothes.

"I don't know. One thing I do know is the city really needs to do a better job at helping these people. It's not right."

"Agreed." She trailed behind me as I kept an eye out for Susan, a ghost who would have blended in easily with the alivers here, except for the whole being dead and blue situation.

Once we'd made it nearly halfway in, I was beginning to think we probably should have brought Gryphin with us again. Caleb had been busy getting information about Susan and Brandon's family the first time Hanna and I had come here, so we'd gotten Gryphin's help. We hadn't needed his physical protection, but the knowledge that we did have it—should we need it—had been reassuring.

Speaking of the wolf, I thought about how many things that were mere myths and stories a few months ago. Nearly all of them had turned out to be real, dangerous and lurking in our naively human world, and I thought I had handled these revelations well.

No one gave me credit when Caleb revealed he was a vampire, first to Hanna during an odd fight with Mr. Tyler on the lawn, and then to me later, after Hanna had explained what had happened.

I didn't even freak out when we found him chained up in the basement of the seethe and needed some blood to heal and help us escape. Well, okay, I might have freaked out a little bit, but considering the entire situation, I deserved more credit for handling all the disruptions to my beliefs about what was really out there.

"Susan?" I thought I glimpsed a blue movement heading behind a large concrete pillar.

I picked up my pace, and Mom scrambled behind to stay with me. As I rounded the pillar, I came face-to-face with a ghost, but not the one I wanted.

This one was an elderly man, stooped at the shoulders, wearing a cable knit sweater, slacks, and loafers. He was glaring at me beneath his bushy eyebrows and over his glasses.

"Why are you making such a racket? You're going to wake the dead," he grumbled as I stopped short.

Stifling my laugh at his unintended joke, I tried to smile pleasantly. "Oh, hello. Excuse me. I thought you were someone else. Sorry."

He narrowed his eyes, and he studied me shrewdly before turning his gaze onto the world around us. I could see the moment when he "woke up" as a ghost and realized his surroundings were not what he had seen them to be for however many years he'd been dead.

"Where are we? What's happening?" he muttered.

There were way too many things on my plate to add another ghost needing help to the list. I felt bad leaving him there to wander, especially after I had awoken him and popped his happy, clueless ghost bubble.

"Don't worry about it. Feel free to go about your business as usual." I stepped around him and continued making my way through the nearest path, hoping he wouldn't follow me.

He did.

"Hey! Wait! At least tell me where I am so I can get back home," he hollered.

I walked faster, wanting him to get the message. Mom scurried to keep up with me, probably not really understanding what was happening but trusting me to lead her through it.

The elderly ghost was faster than he probably would have been before death, if his lumbering old man footsteps were any indication. "Wait a minute!"

By this point, I was basically running to the car, feeling ashamed for waking him and frightened at the same time. Some of the alivers had noticed my apparent distress and may have thought I was running away from my mom or had to suddenly rush to the bathroom or something equally silly, but I didn't care. I just wanted to get away from the whole thing.

Talking to ghosts was scary. Not because they were scary like they were going to eat me like a zombie, but more because they made me feel things I didn't have time to work through.

"Ah, I see you've met Barnabas. Once you get him talking, he never shuts up." A ghost appeared next to me and easily kept pace with my hurried steps.

"Susan!" I said, stopping abruptly, causing my mom to almost fall on top of me. "I've been looking for you!"

"What's going on, Trina?" Mom asked, panting and grabbing my arm.

"Stop running away!" the elderly man, Barnabas, I guess, said.

"Susan!" an aliver said from where he was standing about fifteen feet away, adding to the chaos.

"What's going on over there?" Another person shouted from somewhere else.

"Okay, let's just take a breath." I inhaled slowly and then choked on the nearby smell of something rotting.

"Trina, are you okay? What's going on?" Mom bent over to look me in the face and put her hand on my back.

I waved her off, pulling my shirt over my mouth and nose to cover the smell. It helped a little. "Yes, I'm okay. I think. Susan, I've been looking for you."

The middle-aged woman ghost wore a toboggan that squished her hair down and out the sides, but somewhere around the eyes I found familiar features. She put her hands on her hips and looked at me closer. "I remember you. Why are all these Seers coming out of nowhere and bothering me?"

"Have we met before?" Barnabas asked, standing partially through my mom and leaning in to get a better look at Susan.

Susan sighed and shook her head. "Yes, for the last time, Barnabas. We're ghosts haunting the same place. We've talked several times." She turned to me and jabbed a thumb in the elderly ghost's direction. "Poor guy has more memory problems than he probably had in real life. And judging by the looks of him, that was a lot."

Mom stood close to me, unable to hear what the ghosts were saying but offering her silent support and patience as I sorted through the conversation.

"I think I would have remembered talking to someone as rude as you." Barnabas lowered his glasses and glared at Susan.

"Then how do I know your name?" Susan fired back, her head bobbing in a sassy way that reminded me of another ghost I knew.

He sputtered for a few seconds, unable to come up with an answer to that.

I took the chance to steer the conversation back to where I wanted it. "Hi, Susan. My name is Trina. We have met before when I was working with Tracy. Do you remember that?"

Susan stopped shaking her head at the elderly man and turned to me again. "Yes, of course I remember. It's only been a few weeks."

I restrained myself from commenting on how a ghost's memory isn't reliable. I needed to stay on her good side, and she was already sporting an attitude. "Right. Of course. Well, this time I'm here to offer you some help. Is that something you would be interested in?"

Her eyebrows narrowed, and she glanced at Barnabas as if he was going to be able to tell her if I could be trusted or not. He merely glowered as if still trying to figure out how she knew his name.

"What kind of help?" she finally said.

"Whatever help you want. Maybe talking about your life will help you start to figure out what we need to do to cross over?"

Mom gave me an encouraging smile. It was nice to have her support, but I still felt weird knowing she could only hear my side of the conversation. Perhaps I'd get used to it eventually.

Susan scoffed and shook her head. "What is it with Seers and wanting ghosts to cross over? If y'all got rid of us, you'd be out of a job. That's why you're really here, right? Someone sent you I bet. There's no way you came to hang out in this place on your own."

I sighed and rubbed my neck awkwardly. "Can I level with you, Susan? Let's just be straight up instead of playing games or having an attitude. Can we do that?"

Her eyes narrowed. "Are you saying I have an attitude? In my experience, it's the teenagers that have that issue. I would know. I...almost raised four of them."

Pressing my lips together in sympathy, I tried a different tactic. I needed to get her to trust me before she was going to give me any kind of help. "Alright, I'll be fully honest here. Yes, the necromancers sent me to come talk to you, but—"

She bristled, sinking into her shoulders. "I knew it! Those jerks won't leave me alone!"

I held my hands up in a calming, pleading motion. "Wait! Don't disappear yet! I'm trying to be honest. Yes, they sent me, but there is another reason I want to talk to you more than trying to help those turds. I dislike them as much as you. The bigger reason is we're in contact with who we think is your son, Brandon. Do you remember Brandon?"

Susan froze. Only the blinking of her eyes told me she had heard me.

"Who's Brandon?" Barnabas put his hands on his hips as his head swiveled back and forth between Susan and me.

"That's my son," Susan said, her voice in a whisper, her eyes on my face. "How do you know about my son?"

"He haunts our house. Actually, it's quite a funny story as his first haunt was the skatepark, but then he got stuck inside a crystal which reset his haunt that now happens to be my sister's bedroom. She was...is a Seer too, and you actually met her once before, and—"

Susan held up her hand, and I trailed off, realizing I was probably going too fast.

"Brandon is a ghost? He should be in Hell." She frowned.

"Aren't we already in Hell?" Barnabas muttered to himself, or us, I didn't know or care.

It took all I had not to quip back at Susan, telling her that she should also be there based on the deal she'd made with a necromancer, soul-eating witch. Not to mention she let her only surviving son think he was responsible enough for the accident that he killed himself.

Instead, I forced myself to say, "He's not. Well, not yet? I don't know how these things work. What I do know is that he's always got something to say and drives me crazy."

"That does sound like Brandon..." Her eyes were still narrowed and studying me.

"I wish I could help you guys get together and meet." I frowned, realizing it was true.

I sincerely wanted to help them, but whether it was to distract Brandon enough that he'd stop being so annoying or because I genuinely cared about them, I couldn't be sure. "If my sister were alive, she would be able to escort Brandon here. She has a special Seer power that can allow a ghost to travel outside their haunt as long as they're with her. Don't worry. We're going to resurrect her soon, and then maybe she'll be able to help you two get together."

She was shaking her head before I finished my sentence. "And that's why you're here. The necromancers want you to get the information they've been trying to wrangle out of me for years in exchange for bringing your sister back."

I worked past my surprise at her astuteness and focused. "Yes, exactly, but when she comes back, you and Brandon can reunite and chat and catch up as much as you want. You'd like to see him again, wouldn't you?"

"Wait a minute. I may not know a lot about the occult world, learning most of it after I died, but the last guy told me there was only one Seer per family every other generation. How come there are two of you? And if your sister has extra powers, why wouldn't you?"

It was my turn to pause, taking in her questions. "I—I don't know. Wait. What other guy?"

Barnabas decided at that moment that he was bored or perhaps the weird memory situation of ghosts started acting up, because he shook his head for a few seconds and then wandered off, muttering to himself.

I couldn't say I was sad to see him leave.

Susan waved her hand in the air as if to push away the topic. "Just the last Seer the necromancers commissioned to come talk to me a few years ago. He died after we had gotten kind of close, actually..."

She trailed off and sobered as if talking about the Seer was bringing back some deeper feelings she'd pushed away.

Chills ran down my back, and I shivered deeper inside my jacket. "He died? How did he die?"

Mom stepped closer to me, linking her arm through my elbow and offering support and warmth.

Her movement drew Susan's eyes toward her for the first time, but the ghost must have decided her presence wasn't anything to worry about.

"Uhm, it's a bit fuzzy, but I seem to remember giving him the answers he was tasked to get. We parted as friends, I think, but as he walked across the parking lot," she pointed vaguely in the direction where we had parked our car and frowned, "something happened. I seem to have an image of a huge guy walking in my line of sight, making a quick movement, and then walking away, leaving Clayton's body... His name was Clayton."

"Oh, that's terrible." I was suddenly nervous again and realizing we were sitting out here easily in the open where Caleb could come by and snap *our* necks. If I thought a car would stop him, I would have suggested moving it closer so we could all climb inside to continue our conversation. But as it was, I doubted the metal would stand up to a determined (or enslaved) vampire. "Do you know who it was? Why did they do it?"

Susan's eyes kept looking at the parking lot as if lost in the memory of what had happened there. "I don't know."

"Do you think it's dangerous for me to be talking to you?" I asked, my voice small. I didn't want to alarm my mom, but it was an important thing to know.

As expected, my mom's grip clenched, pulling me in tighter. "Trina? What's going on?"

Susan pulled her eyes back to my face with some difficulty. "Perhaps. I told you working with those necromancers is dangerous."

"Do you think it was them that had the Seer killed? That doesn't make sense after he just got the information they're looking for," I muttered the last part more to myself as my thoughts caught up with my mouth.

"Not them directly, but maybe someone who doesn't want them to get the information. There's a reason they don't have it yet, and maybe it's a good one." Susan gave me a pointed look. "You need to leave. Find another way to bring your sister back. Tell Brandon I don't want to put anyone else at risk, not even to talk to him, but I do love him. More than I ever told him while we were alive."

Before I could protest, she popped out of sight as if someone had flipped a switch somewhere.

"Wait!" I said too late, my hand stretched out into the open air.

Mom's eyes were darting around us with worry. "Trina? Maybe we should get out of here. Did Susan leave?"

"Yeah, that's a good idea." I steered Mom back through the chaos and across the street into the sunshine.

I knew Caleb was able to move around in the sun, but the bright light helped me feel a little better.

We got into the car, and Mom clicked the lock button before even turning the vehicle on. As we drove home, I filled her in on what had happened. Understandably, she had been confused with the whole running thing at first, and we both agreed that the interaction with Barnabas had been odd.

Then when I told her everything Susan had said, Mom's grip on the steering wheel gave her white knuckles.

"We can't keep doing this. It's dangerous! Do you think David knew what he was sending us into? Did he know what he had sent Hanna into? He has to know that the previous Seer was killed. Why wouldn't he at least offer us some protection? It seems it would be in his best interest to give us escorts at least, so we don't end up murdered after finally getting the information he wants," she said, her voice rising in pitch the more she spoke.

I put a hand on her arm, trying to calm her while still feeling upset and scared myself. It wouldn't help the situation if we got in an accident because she was worked up. "Okay, breathe. Perhaps he was worried that giving us an escort would garner more attention. I don't know, but we don't need them. We can ask Gryphin to come. I'm sure he would be more than happy to help us out, especially if it's eventually going to help out Hanna."

Mom took a long inhale and held it for a second before releasing it. "The wolf kid, right? Yes, we should ask him. At least we would be able to trust him more than the necromancers. How do we know they aren't going to murder us after they get what they want?"

I frowned and watched our familiar neighborhood pass by as we neared home. We had decided it would be best to retreat there where we knew we were mostly safe and then decide what to do.

"We don't know that they won't. But what other choices do we have? It's not like they'll agree to hand us back Hanna's body and let us go after we've gotten in this deep. The best thing we can do is make sure they see us as too valuable to murder."

Chapter 6 - Hanna

More time passed. I wasn't sure if it would have been good or bad to have a functioning watch with the date and time. It may have made me sad to see the time passing in spurts and jumps, but it might have been nice to have something else to focus on.

At least I was haunting a place that had some small amount of activity, even if the skatepark was pretty empty during the day while the kiddos were in school. If I had been haunting a place with no activity, I was sure I'd turn into one of those lost, mindless ghosts in no time at all.

It also helped that Noah brought Andrea by. The third time they came to visit, it was raining. The park was empty of anyone except him and an umbrella-toting Andrea whose pouty lip told me she wasn't happy.

I couldn't blame her.

"This can't be safe, skating in the rain. I don't get why you're suddenly so obsessed with coming here, and I still don't know why *I* have to come." Andrea's voice whined through the park, talking loud enough to cover the sound of the water pattering on her bright pink umbrella.

"I'll make it up to you. I promise. What about going to Starbucks? We won't be here long. You'll barely notice." Noah headed toward the picnic tables, looking around for me, I presumed.

Why he bothered to look for me, I didn't know. Maybe it was his way of indicating he wanted me to come out and talk with him.

Not like I could stay away when Andrea was just sitting there, soulless, ready for the easy takings so I could feel something, remember things, and experience life again—if only for a few minutes.

I didn't bother waiting for her to sit down or for him to come up with a reason to sit on the wet benches and stepped into her, finding it was becoming easier with each time.

"You know you need to get more creative to explain why you keep dragging her here. She might even begin to remember being possessed. We don't know enough about what is happening," I said by way of greeting.

His smile pulled at something inside of me, but it was hard to define. Probably a mixture of guilt and happiness that someone out there in the world who was alive and knew about me.

"Yeah... I hope she doesn't remember any of this. It would be hard to explain." He ran fingers through the wet strands of his brown hair. "Have you noticed feeling angrier after the possessions? Is it taking energy and going to turn you into a poltergeist?"

I took a second for self-reflection and shook my head. "I don't think so, at least not enough to notice."

"That's good." He came closer to me, dropped his board onto the pavement, and ducked inside Andrea's umbrella.

I watched as a rivulet of water slid down his nose and dripped off the edge downwards. Once upon a time I would have been thrilled to get this close to him, but things had changed. Now I found myself happy to talk to anyone, but I did manage to feel guilty for letting him think it was because I had personal, romantic feelings for him.

If he had liked me only a few months ago, things might have been different. But his affection had come too little too late, and there was another guy who haunted my thoughts, so to speak.

"Please tell me you've told Trina and my mom where I am." I looked him in the eyes, hoping he didn't feel like it was a good time to lean in and kiss me.

It felt bad to use him like this, but it was all I had—unless some other almost-zombie wandered into the park and I got lucky enough to figure out what they were before they left again.

Something looking like regret passed through his hazel eyes and my heart sunk. "Hanna...I—"

"Why haven't you told them? They must be so sad and worried." I tried to fight the tears that welled up in my eyes but not too much.

He put a soft hand on my cheek, or Andrea's, it was a bit hard to remember this wasn't my body sometimes. "Can you blame me for wanting time with you all on my own?"

I frowned, my heart picking up in pace but not from pleasure at hearing his words. More from guilt. Perhaps I had been leading him on stronger than I'd realized.

"Noah, you and I aren't—"

He shook his head sadly and put a soft thumb on my lip. "I know...but I—I couldn't help but pretend for a minute. Can you blame me?"

I furrowed Andrea's eyebrows. "Yes, I can. I'm dead, my family doesn't know where I am but could talk to me if they did, and you're keeping it from them. Not to mention, I'm inhabiting your girlfriend's body. None of this makes sense or seems ethical. We should probably end it all as soon as we are able."

Dropping his hand, he pressed his lips together as he thought. "You're right. Of course you're right. I'm sorry. I'll tell them soon, I promise."

I sighed, breaking eye contact and watching the rain stream off the side of the umbrella for a second. "Can you tell me more about Andrea and how this whole thing works? I get that the order somehow botched the resurrection spell. David did warn me about how dangerous it was and that it doesn't always work out. But do you all know what went wrong?"

Noah ran his fingers through his hair again with a sigh. "The spells aren't like science. There could be many reasons why. Like maybe one of the order members wasn't putting enough strength into their casting. Maybe someone messed up a few words enough that the chanting didn't work clearly. Maybe we didn't kill the goat at just the right moment. We don't know. What we do know is that when her spirit merged with her body, it didn't respond in quite the right way. The body rose like a simple zombie, not like Andrea's spirit was in there. The Seer we were working with—"

"There was another Seer?" I couldn't help asking.

He nodded. "One that worked with the order for a time. Seers are rare, yes, but they are around."

"Oh, right. I guess that makes sense."

"He said that her spirit was in there somewhere, but it wasn't fitting quite right. That's how David knew something had gone wrong. Apparently, that is one of the things that could happen from a botched spell. David then called me over and helped me cast another spell, further interlocking Andrea's spirit with her body. I found out later that he chose to have me do it because he knew I would be the best option for getting close enough to her every day as we are the same age and go to the same school. Then, after all that, we had to recruit a witch to erase her memories of the death and the whole incident in hopes that it would help her live a more normal life."

"Seems cruel to recruit you into that without your permission or telling you what the spell would require. You explained that each spell takes a cost." I turned away from the rain to look him in the eyes again. "What does the spell cost you, Noah?"

It was his turn to look away. "Nothing that isn't worth saving a life."

"But *every day?*"

He sighed. "These are all necromancer secrets I'm telling you right now, things I shouldn't be saying."

I chuckled dryly. "Dead men tell no tales, or in this case, dead girls."

A small smile flitted across his lips. "I see those pirate movies have paid off."

I shrugged. "So why do you do this for her every day? It seems like a lot of work for one girl, a silly high school cheerleader who cares more about herself than she cares about anyone else."

"Like I told you before, the order is family...or maybe more like the mafia, if you want to think of it like that. We do what they ask."

"So David could tell you to jump off a cliff, and you'd do it?"

He looked around the empty park, soggy and grey in the winter wind. "David would not ask me to do anything that wasn't important. I know this because he uses his own powers once a week to restore the cost it takes, so I don't age. It would be bad if I visibly wilted in front of the students and teachers over time. Can you imagine this old guy on the football field?"

He laughed, but it was slightly strained. I didn't join in his mirth.

"But what does David do to offset the spell costs on *his* body?" I creased my eyebrows, considering what Cordelia had said when they'd been discussing who would take custody of Rose. "Wait…Do you think he… Why did he want Rose so much?"

Noah's mouth tightened, and his eyes kept darting around the park, telling me that he either knew more than he wanted to share or had at least suspected what I was getting at.

"Noah? It seems like it would be a very handy thing to know how to suck in a soul like that for an aging necromancer. Would you still follow David if you knew he was devouring innocent souls?"

It was surreal to think and say something so offhandedly like that, but I was working the angle to get him to wake up.

His gaze was quick to come back to mine. "I *know* he's not taking souls like that. I can feel it in my gut. Besides, wouldn't we all notice if he suddenly looked younger?"

"Maybe, unless he knew how to siphon the energy slowly instead of taking a whole soul like Rose does. Didn't you say something about a necromancer doing this a long time ago? Do you know what David thinks of this guy? Has he seemed particularly interested in finding him? What's this guy's name, anyway?"

I wasn't sure why I asked the last bit. Maybe because it would be easier to refer to the incomprehensible bad guy by his name instead of dude-who-consumes-souls.

Noah rubbed at the back of his neck for a second. "It started with a 'T', I think. I'd have to look it up. It's been a while since anyone has even talked about him. I only know about him from my necromancer lessons."

"Thomas? Tim? Terry?" I asked, tilting my head to the side as I suddenly struggled to remember any names with my foggy, ghostly brain.

Noah shrugged it off. "It doesn't matter. There is no way that David is taking in souls or even planning on it. That matron planted weird ideas in your head. We only want Rose so we can give her the justice she deserves for perverting our magic in such a way. That's it. Nothing else."

I pursed my lips to the side, annoyed that he was so close-minded but understanding that it would take more than a few coincidences to make someone question their family and core beliefs.

"You never answered why Andrea gets such treatment. Didn't you say something at some point about her dad?"

"Oh, right. Yes, her dad is a big deal with the order. I've never met him personally, but David seems to be willing to go through a lot just to help him out."

I frowned. "You're Andrea's boyfriend, have to see her at least once a day, stalked her family to vacation places and everything, and have never even seen her dad?"

"She lives with her mom and stepdad. Her real dad isn't around much. Or maybe ever. I get the feeling he's into some big business stuff, probably closely tied to the order in some way."

"And that never made you question the whole situation? Seems as sketchy to me as anything could be."

"Not everything is like the movies." He chuckled. "Sometimes people are just busy doing things. Maybe he and the order work hard earning money for charities that help starving kids. You don't know."

"And neither do you, it looks like."

He rolled his eyes. "You've been hanging out with Caleb too much. Not everything in the world is wicked and has nefarious intentions."

I shook my head. "No, just the ones I usually pick to trust."

"So dramatic. Nothing is ever boring with you. That's actually one of the things I like about you—"

I held my hand up to stop him. "Listen. I've got to level with you here. I feel like I've led you on too much. Yes, I am happy to see you, but it's because you're my friend and I have someone to talk to. It's not because I have any romantic feelings for you. I'm really sorry to have to say this, but I want to make sure it's clear."

He studied my face so long I was worried he was going to try to kiss me again like he'd done at my birthday party. Finally, he sighed for like the third time that day. "Yes, I know. I get it. You don't have to keep saying it. You're in love with someone else."

Memories flooded my brain of the morning of my death. Brandon and I had actually admitted those feelings to each other. I'd been trying to avoid thinking about many things that were going to make me sad in death, and that memory was one of those. Sure, now we were both dead, but we were even more unable to spend time together. It was worse than one of us being alive while the other wasn't. At least back then we'd been able to talk to each other and even steal a few kisses here and there.

"I... I guess you're right. It's taking me a long time to admit it, and it still feels weird to say, but yeah. I think I'm in love with someone else."

Noah smiled sadly and stroked my cheek again. "It's okay. The heart wants what the heart wants."

Chapter 7 - Trina

On Saturday afternoon, after we'd eaten lunch and sat together at the kitchen table while I did homework and Mom worked on some stuff for her photography business, I decided it was time to figure out what to do next.

We'd needed a few hours of normalcy before facing what we had just gone through and what else we were supposed to be doing. I guess it was our way of coping with the whole situation.

Brandon hadn't appeared when we'd come home and didn't make an entrance the whole time we were there. I wondered if he needed some resting time. So far, it didn't seem like I had the other power Hanna did, which was to lend more strength to the ghosts she was around.

It was nice to have some quiet time without him. I had no idea how Hanna put up with that kid so much.

If I were to keep count, that put Hanna's gifts up two to my nothing. Susan's question spun around inside my head, even as I tried to ignore it. She'd said something about Hanna's gifts and how I should have some extra powers of my own, but so far I got nothing. Even though I had hid from my gifts for a while, it was still discouraging to hear all the things Hanna could do but I couldn't.

Maybe that was the whole point.

I had stifled myself so much that I only had the "normal" Seer powers. Well, after this whole thing was over and Hanna was back, maybe I could go back to wearing the necklace and not having to think about things like that.

About three-ish, I put down my pencil and sighed. "Mom, we can't hide in our house under this spell forever. We have too much to do."

She finished what she was doing for a second or so and then looked at me. Her eyes were tight with worry and stress. "I know, but I also can't bear the thought of losing you. Even going outside is a danger. How do we know Rose won't send that vampire after us again? It's just so scary to think about."

"Yeah... I mean, I'm not sure what I would have done to earn her anger, but perhaps being a Seer is enough."

Mom nodded soberly.

"What if we stay in public areas and also take Gryphin with us? Do you think that would be safer?" I asked, fiddling with my penguin-shaped eraser. I had a dedicated eraser just for my math homework since I tended to mess up a lot.

"Safe enough. We've got to find her or else all this nonsense for the necromancers will be for nothing."

"If we can even get what they want." I sighed.

Mom shook her head. "Nope. We got this. We'll get the wolf kid's number from William, er, Mr. Tyler, and beg him to hang around with us."

"Hopefully the wolves won't ask a favor in exchange or else we might end up owing favors everywhere before this is all over."

"Whatever we have to do, it's worth it," Mom said as we shared a resolute smile.

An hour later, Gryphin pulled up in front of our house in his van. It felt weird getting into it with my mom and not Hanna. I'd been inside it once before when we'd gone to the underpass with him as added protection, just as we should have earlier that day.

I was glad we'd gotten some progress with Susan, but it still hadn't been much. We needed to figure out how to convince her to give us the information. She might have figured that was the end of us, but I wasn't about to give up.

In the meantime, we were going to keep looking for Hanna's ghost.

"Hello, Ms. Sanchez, Trina. How are y'all doing?" Gryphin asked as he jogged toward us across the lawn.

We hadn't asked him to escort us from the porch to his van, but it looked like he was taking his guard duties seriously.

I smiled at his broad shoulders and beefy arms but not perhaps for the reason most girls would smile. He looked like he could hold his own in a fight. However, as much as I wanted to see Caleb again and try to figure out a way to help him, I wanted to avoid him even more. Phoenix had assured me they were researching ways they would be able to set him free without hurting him, but they had confirmed my suspicions that a necromancer would be far better equipped to figure out how to do that.

There was Noah, of course, but I didn't know him that well and wasn't sure where he stood. I had no idea how much we could trust him or if he'd be willing to help Caleb. For all I knew, he'd want revenge on Hanna's death and stake the vampire before we could try to set him free.

As much as I liked Caleb, though, nothing mattered if we couldn't get Hanna back into her body. Maybe once she was up and going, she could help me figure out how to help Caleb.

Of course, if we didn't free Caleb before bringing Hanna back, I suppose Rose could simply make him kill her again.

"We're doing well, thank you. And thanks again for coming out here with such short notice. I'm sorry we're feeling a bit needy." Mom climbed into the front seat after Gryphin had opened the door for her.

"Oh, it's no problem. Actually, I've been eager to help. I've been going on my own missions to see if I could sniff her out," Gryphin said before he carefully shut the door as soon as Mom sat down.

I climbed into the middle seat as he was helping her, but before I could slide the door closed he was there with a friendly grin and tugged it shut for me.

Mom and I shared an amused smile while he jogged around the car and got into the front seat.

Once he was settled and started the van, I asked, "What do you mean 'sniff her out'? Is that something a werewolf can do? Find a ghost?"

He sighed. "No, not really. I mean, sometimes we know when a ghost is nearby, and we may be able to sense it, but we can't talk to them or wouldn't even know who the ghost was. It's just..."

Mom smiled as he trailed off and patted his upper arm. "You wanted to help. It's okay. As a person who can't see or talk to ghosts either, I understand."

He chuckled and checked the mirrors before pulling out onto the road. "Exactly. I felt so helpless sitting there and not doing anything."

Mom had told Mr. Tyler about Hanna's death the evening it had happened, mostly to keep the wolves informed and to ask if they'd known anything that might have helped us. He had then told Gryphin, and they'd both volunteered to help keep watch over me during school hours at the least.

"Well, now you can be our macho bodyguard. Isn't that fancy?" I said, trying to bring in some positive vibes.

"Absolutely! So where are we headed to first? The skatepark? She hung out there a lot." Gryphin kept his focus on the road as he spoke.

"The movie theater first. We haven't been able to check that out yet, and we often went there as a family. She also mentioned a ghost she was helping haunting there. It seems like the next best bet." I settled into the seat, wishing it was a little more comfortable.

"Okay." Gryphin shrugged and turned the van into the direction of the theater.

After a few seconds of quiet, my curiosity got the best of me. "So where did you go looking for her ghost? Did you sniff out anything interesting? When did you go? Must have been at night or people would have freaked out seeing you run around as a wolf. Or maybe you can smell just as well in human form."

Gryphin chuckled. "Where to start... Well, I can smell better than the average human in this form, but the wolf can pick up smells even better. So first I would stop by a place in the daytime as a human and check it out. If there was anything resembling a ghost smell, then I'd come back later at dark as a wolf and see if there was anything more I could pick up."

"What does a ghost smell like? What places did you go that smelled like a ghost?" It was kind of freeing to be able to ask an occult creature random questions about what they could and could not do.

Mom glanced at me from the front seat. "You sure are nosy."

I gave her a cheeky smile.

Gryphin waved it away with one hand while keeping the other on the steering wheel. "It's fine. I don't mind talking about it, but I may trade you for some questions about being a Seer. I've always wondered what that is like."

"Anytime. Although I have to admit I don't know as much about it as Hanna does. Guess you can ask her the stuff I don't know when she comes back."

"Of course. So I sniffed out the school first, naturally. Billy, er, Mr. Tyler, as you call him, helped me out there. He was already familiar with the ghost smells of the school, but we figured another nose wouldn't hurt. Oh, and a ghost kind of smells like... Well, part of it is smell, but it's also connected to a feeling or awareness. If that makes sense. I don't know how to explain the smell. Maybe like peppermint but more acrid?"

"We'll take your word for it." I smiled as he glanced at me in the rearview mirror. "We checked the school, too, and didn't see her. Oh! Did you know there is a ghost haunting the cafeteria? She's been super distracting as I've been going to school without my necklace in case Hanna pops up somewhere."

"What kind of ghost?" Mom asked, her eyebrows raised in slight alarm.

"Just some old lady who used to work there, I guess. She kept yelling at the staff to do a better job, fix their portions, and stuff like that.

Thank goodness they couldn't hear her. They would have been so annoyed."

"I bet." Mom nodded appreciatively. "It was probably annoying for you."

"I'm getting better at tuning them out. Mostly."

Gryphin checked his mirrors and blind spot before changing lanes. "Yeah, I sensed a few in the school, but Billy confirmed they were nothing new. In a way, it's kind of a good thing. I mean who wants to haunt the school for the rest of your days?"

"At least you'd have entertaining stuff to watch and not feel too lonely," I said, finding myself thinking more and more about haunts lately. If it were up to me, I'd want to haunt somewhere with a lot of people, so at least I wouldn't feel completely alone.

"That's fair, I suppose," Gryphin said.

Mom turned to look at Gryphin. "Where else did you check?"

"Oh, you know, places around town. Like I said, it's not an exact science for a wolf. I had no idea if I was sniffing out ghosts that had been there for decades or Hanna. I'm sorry I couldn't be of more help."

"Don't say that. You're helping us now more than we can repay." Mom gave him a grateful smile.

"Especially if we run into a certain vampire, and you have to fight him off. Oh. No offense, but do you think you could take a vampire while in your human form?" I asked, feeling like that question was crossing some kind of line but needing to know the answer anyway.

Gryphin frowned. "I hope it doesn't come to that. Mostly because if we are somewhere public, others could get hurt. If Rose is around like she was that night in the meadow, I can firmly say I'd be no match against her and the vampire, especially if she has souls to eat. If it's just the vampire on his own... It would be a lot better if I could shift before he attacked, but since it takes so long, that's usually not an option."

"So what is it? Are we asking you to come help us only to put you into danger, too?" I asked, suddenly worried we'd only dragged another person in to suffer if it came down to a fight.

"No, I wouldn't say that. I'm glad to help, and I've had training since I was young with how to fight the bloodsuckers. It's kind of a tradition in most wolf packs, anyway. At the very least, I could be enough of a distraction so that y'all could escape and get out of harm's way, and I heal fast so as far as going up against a vampire, a wolf, even in human form, is a formidable ally to have."

Mom and I exchanged looks. I judged from her expression that she was having similar concerns about putting him in danger only to help us. Shaking my head slightly, I gave a half-shrug, trying to convey that there wasn't much else we could do.

"Thank you for helping us," Mom said, putting heavy sincerity into her voice. "Let's pray that we don't run into anyone dangerous. I'd feel terrible if you got hurt."

Gryphin shot her a kind smile. "Don't worry about me. Like I said, just happy to help."

We pulled into the theater parking lot, and Gryphin guided the van to an empty spot which wasn't hard considering it was still early in the day. If there had been a new movie to come out that week, it wasn't a popular one.

As we headed inside, I was in between Mom and Gryphin who kept his eyes sweeping over everything. I couldn't help but also let my eyes roam, trying to catch sight of a tall, dark, and handsome creature that I had very confusing feelings for.

The smell of popcorn, fresh and stale, greeted us as we opened the doors and walked into the lobby area of the theater. Loud music and scenes from movies played over the speakers, keeping pace with the several large TV screens. There were a few people playing arcade games and two working the concession stand, but there wasn't much action going on.

Mom gave me an encouraging smile as she let me take the lead in our search for Hanna. I wasn't completely sure what the best technique for finding a ghost without drawing awkward glances from strangers was, so I opted for taking a seat on a bench with a good view of most of the lobby and even some of the hallway beyond.

Mom and Gryphin sat on either side of me. His eyes were alert still, watching all the dark corners. Several of the people in the lobby gave him looks, spanning from obviously checking him out to competitive assessments of his broad shoulders. Despite having hung out with Caleb for several years, another one who drew attention when we were in public, I still wasn't quite used to sitting with someone everyone wanted to visually appreciate.

Telling myself to focus, I got out my phone and pretended to be preoccupied with it while trying to covertly scout out the area for ghosts. Usually, I was insanely grateful that the ghosts couldn't look at me and tell what I was right away, but for the first time ever, I was wishing it was more obvious I was a Seer.

I caught a glimpse of a ghost passing through a wall, crossing the hallway, and passing into another wall, but it wasn't Hanna.

"This is hard." I sighed. "There are so many people here, which I'm grateful for because we're less likely to be attacked by a vampire, but

I'm also annoyed because if I start chatting up a ghost, I'm going to look crazy."

"Why don't you hold your phone up to your ear, so it looks like you're talking to someone?" Gryphin's gaze moved over to a mom struggling to keep her toddler away from the arcade games.

"I guess that is better than nothing," I said. "This whole thing is still new to me. Why am I feeling so nervous?"

Mom wrapped one arm around my shoulders and gave me a light squeeze. "It's okay, sweetie. At least you know that you can leave this place, and the ghost can't follow you out."

"Ugh, yes. Poor Hanna. That's how she acquired Brandon."

Mom and I shared amused smiles, having recently gotten to know the kid pretty well.

"You can pretend to be talking to me if you want. That way I'll be nearby in case something happens. I'll even nod and smile at you to make it look more legit," Gryphin said, his roaming eyes finally landing on mine.

Something happened then to my stupid heart and body—I got lost in those sharp, yet somehow soft grey eyes, and I liked it. His energy was the opposite of Caleb's, sweeping me away into a forest with soft rushing winds playing through the leaves above us and birds chirping happily. I got so lost that it took me a second to come back to earth, and when I did, my heart was beating quickly.

"Trina?" Mom leaned around my shoulder and glanced between me and the wolf. "Did you see a ghost?"

"What? Oh, no. Well, yes, but not the one we need. Sorry." I shook my head and blinked a few times.

Gryphin's mouth twitched up at one corner, but he didn't say anything about my daydream into his eyes.

Annoyed with myself, I stood and looked for the best ghost to strike up a conversation with. Perhaps I could get lucky, find an already awake ghost, and ask them if they'd seen any new ghosts pop up here recently.

The first one I eyed didn't look awake at all. He was wearing 70s disco clothes and performing some kind of dated dance I was grateful I didn't need to know in my time. It was interesting to watch him roll around, though, since he was wearing skates, reminding me of what Hanna had said about this being a roller rink before it was a movie theater.

I bypassed this ghost, with Gryphin walking beside me trying to look like we were just hanging out, and wandered around the lobby until we were standing in front of a cut-out movie poster of a bunch of friendly, cartoony aliens posed together like a family on vacation.

"Well, I guess this movie would be something kids would enjoy." Gryphin put his hands into his pockets and studied the bright image of the cut-out.

As I stood there considering what else to do, a ghost suddenly walked out of the wall and through the cardboard cutout. He had long, wavy dark hair, a Led Zeppelin t-shirt, a leather vest, and fitted, torn up jeans.

"Yup," he paused to stand next to me and assess the room, "must be a Saturday."

Unsure how to strike up a conversation with a ghost while trying to appear casual in public and not freak the ghost into popping out, I figured a calm statement or two would be the best bet. "How can you tell it's a Saturday?"

Gryphin glanced at me for a second, noticed my eyes were to the side, and a knowing smile grew on his face as he figured out what was happening.

As for the ghost, his eyebrows furrowed, and he turned to look at me. "Hey, I know you. You're the sister, ain't ya?"

"Oh, yeah. I guess you probably would have seen me before if you've been hanging out with Hanna. My name is Trina, and as you've probably guessed... I can also see ghosts."

He nodded, his hair sliding into his face a little. "I'm Frank. So where is the little Seer? I haven't seen her around nor been summoned to do her bidding in a few days. I have to say I'm missing our odd missions."

It was weird to feel emotion flood my chest and eyes while the logical side of my brain reassured me several times that Hanna wasn't gone for good and that we'd get her back.

The emotions didn't care.

I took a breath to steady myself before answering, but my eyes still burned at the corners. "She's gone... I'm not sure how much you know about Rose, but—"

"Oh, I know plenty about that freaky deaky lady. What happened? I thought the witches caught her crazy butt and shoved her into a deep, dark dungeon."

I glanced around, hoping Gryphin's presence was enough to deter anyone from thinking I was talking to myself and was happy to find not a soul was looking at me. Maybe chatting with ghosts in public wasn't that big of a deal. Despite how weird I felt about it still.

"Are you aware that she can control vampires?"

"Yes, but they took down her pet at that storage place... Wait... Did she get another one?"

I nodded, and Frank's eyes narrowed as he put the pieces together.

"And...that one guy is a vampire and has access to your house." Frank cursed and shook his head. "We should have seen that coming."

My lip quivered slightly on its own. "Yeah, we should have, but it's okay. We're going to put her back together again."

"Like Humpty Dumpty?" He chewed on his lip for a second. "You know that didn't work out so well for the egg."

Anger pushed out a few tears, and while I was currently facing away from Gryphin, he heard the pain in my voice and put a comforting hand on my shoulder. "What else can we do? We have to get Hanna back. We can't let that witch win!"

Frank kept shaking his head and muttering curse words to himself.

Mom came over then, perhaps unnerved by my emotional outburst. "Sweetie? Are you okay?"

I pressed my lips together and inhaled slowly through my nose. "Yes, I'm fine."

"We can go if you want," Gryphin said from my other side.

Shaking my head, I turned back to Frank. "So you think we should just let her die and move on? Is that really what you think is right?"

Frank grumbled and put his hand into his hair, running it through the waves. "I don't know. Nothing about this seems right."

"Okay, well, while you stew about ethics and how unfair the world is, can you at least confirm she isn't haunting this place? If she was, surely you would have seen her by now," I said, trying and failing not to come off as angry.

Frank turned to study me and frowned. "I'm sorry. You must be hurting. I honestly know what it's like to lose a sister, and I really am sorry. No, she isn't here. Can I ask what you plan to do once you find her ghost?"

"I'm sure you can figure it out. Thank you for your time," I said in a grumble and turned to walk away.

"Wait! I want to help!" He followed me to the doors, heedless of my mom and Gryphin escorting me on either side.

Stepping near the wall so we weren't in the way, I turned and looked at him. "If you really want to help, you can start by not being so judgmental and helping me figure out *what* to do instead of telling me what *not* to do."

Mom and Gryphin exchanged confused glances but moved to stand to the side with me, still nearby so we continued to appear to be talking to each other.

Frank surprised me by chuckling. "You two sisters are so alike in your stubbornness, although I do have to say you seem just a tad more down to earth than she was...is. Anyway, fine. I'm sorry. I'll stop pointing out the flaws of everything. What can I do to help?"

"Honestly, I'm not sure. I appreciate it, though. Right now, we're trying to work on the task given by the necromancers so we can earn their help to put her back together again, and no comments from you about how insane that is, please. We're also trying to locate her haunt. She's been dead over a week, but we still don't know where she's haunting."

"Okay, what kinds of things do the necromancers want from you? Hopefully not digging graves and pulling out bodies to use for zombies."

I frowned and widened my eyes. "Is that a thing they would ask? No. We're not doing that. Just getting information from ghosts, things people like to ask from Seers, I guess."

"And is it too much to assume that you have the same power as Hanna that allows ghosts to travel outside their haunt?" His face was a bit too hopeful for my liking.

"No, sorry to disappoint. I can promise you though that if I had that power, Brandon would be following me around everywhere. So in a way, I'm kind of grateful I get to have moments of peace, even if he is haunting our house now."

Frank laughed and shook his head again. "Oh man, that's some irony right there. Alright. So if Hanna could do those extra things, what extra things can you do? It only stands to reason that if there are two Seers in one family in one generation, and one has special characteristics, then the other would too."

I sighed and adjusted the bag strap on my shoulder, glancing again to see if anyone was giving us extra attention. "I don't know. As far as I can tell, I'm a regular Seer. Nothing special beyond that."

Frank's eyes shined amusingly. "Being a Seer is special enough, but you haven't found anything *yet*. Maybe we can work on that together. You already know that you can't travel outside a haunt with a ghost. That's good progress. Next, let's see if you can command a ghost to do something. Go ahead. Tell me to do a cartwheel."

I scoffed some and glanced at Mom and Gryphin, who of course had no idea what the ghost was saying. Mom gave me an encouraging, slightly confused smile while Gryphin regarded me with kind eyes.

"Right. Okay. Fine. Do a cartwheel," I said, earning an amused eyebrow from Gryphin.

Frank looked down at his body as if waiting for it to launch into motion. "Maybe try saying it a bit stronger. I know Hanna sometimes had trouble getting me to do things compared to other ghosts. I suppose I've got a stronger will than others."

"This is weird, but I do want to figure out if I have extra gifts." I cleared my throat, glanced around again, content to see that most people were busy playing arcade games, talking to each other, or ordering popcorn. "I command you to do a cartwheel!"

We waited for a few heartbeats before Frank shrugged. "Alright. Well, that doesn't seem to be in your wheelhouse. You have homework then. When you leave here, try to summon me like Hanna could do. If it works, then we can chat some more. If it doesn't, then you'll have to come back here and visit me again. I'm sure finding out what you can do is lower on your to-do list, but I'm also here if there's anything else I can help with to get Hanna back. Technically, she owes *me* a few favors, but I can't help but feel a bit of a soft spot for the girl."

I gave him a tight-lipped smile and a nod. "Okay. I'll try it and let you know. Thanks, Frank."

He nodded as we turned and left the theater. While it did kind of feel like I'd just been given another task to perform, it made sense that I should find out what else I could do. Maybe there was something I could do to help ghosts, and, if we were lucky, help Hanna.

Chapter 8 - Hanna

In the hours of alone time, slowly losing memories, I stared up at the clouds and watched them take different shapes and thought about what my unfinished business might be. There were tons of obvious things like telling my parents I loved them, getting to say goodbye to my family, or even kissing Brandon for real.

Then there were the things related to my powers. Perhaps I was meant to solve a certain ghost's issues, but I hadn't been able to do it in life. Or maybe I only needed to get the information for the necromancers, and then I would cross over.

From what I'd seen, or at least what I thought I'd seen in life, when a ghost finished their business, they crossed over whether they wanted to or not. As far as I could tell, the very definition of having your unfinished business finished was that everything was finalized and solved, and you were ready to move on.

But whoever made the rules about the whole thing didn't take into consideration the current moods and feelings of the ghost. It was like the decision of what the ghost needed to do so they could cross over was cemented at death, and even if the ghost changed after being dead, it didn't matter.

Which made being a ghost even more confusing. If we aren't kept on the earth to grow or learn more so we could work toward finishing our business, then what was the point?

It made whatever turned out to be the unfinished business stuff a huge deal. It was important enough that a spirit was trapped in this world, unable to move beyond. Except some of the ghosts I'd helped cross over hadn't needed anything important. Some of the things were almost silly despite trapping their immortal souls forever.

Others had required very important things. One of the young, ghost girl I'd helped, Clara, had needed to assist in the death of a vampire lord, while her sister had only needed to know what had happened to Clara in life.

In fact, as I thought, I realized that several ghosts had only needed to know something important to them before they crossed over, making information as important and subjective as anything, I supposed.

I rolled over and stared at my dandelion friend whose blossom had finally turned into the wispy seed phase. It would be gone soon, free to float on the wind. Half of the seeds had already taken flight, and seeing it change made me sad. It could grow and progress while I was stuck, unable to do anything but talk to a weed.

Chapter 9 - Trina

After the theater, we still had a few hours of daylight left. Not that it really mattered to Caleb if we hid during the dark, but we still felt better doing things when we could see, so we headed to the skatepark.

It just seemed like the next best thing to do.

Gryphin pulled the van over onto the side of the road in front of the park. I was surprised to see there was plenty of activity despite the chilly air and occasional drizzle of misty rain. It probably helped that it was an early evening on a Saturday, so the kids were out of school and maybe had nothing else to do.

A few parents lingered around the edges of the park, hunching down in their jackets and chatting with other parents or staring at their phones. I took a second to appreciate their dedication to allow their kids to come play even in the wind.

As I stepped out of the van, my eyes roamed over the scene, trying to spot a glowing blue figure. Unlike the other places we'd visited, this one was smaller and there wasn't much space for a ghost to hide.

There was nothing to see.

"I don't think she's here," I said as Gryphin and Mom met me on the sidewalk.

Gryphin glanced toward the park, the grey curls of his hair twitching in the wind. His jacket was thin, but that didn't seem to cause him any discomfort in the chilly air.

It was probably way cozier to cuddle up to a wolf than a vampire. The few times I'd been close to Caleb, his skin had felt like the cold marble of a tomb. It probably felt nice on a hot day but wouldn't so much on a cool one.

"I suppose it wouldn't hurt to look around some more and wait. I know you said sometimes it takes a while for a ghost to appear." Mom pulled her jacket hood up over her head to keep in some warmth.

I shrugged, feeling more and more disheartened with each place we visited. I was determined to believe we'd find her and that she hadn't passed on, but it was getting harder and harder to keep up the optimism with each blow to my hopes.

Kids hollered at each other, laughed, and talked animatedly. Wheels rolled smoothly down concrete curves, and the boards clacked when someone crested a deck, paused, and then went back down. The wind shuffled the almost-empty trees above us, and cars drove down the road nearby, the tires crunching loose rocks on the pavement.

We walked quietly to one of the tables further away from anyone else. Mom sat on the bench, resting her back on the tabletop and facing the park with her purse sitting snugly in her lap. Gryphin sat on the table, his heavy boots resting on the bench with his elbows sitting on his knees as he looked around. I sat on the other side of him, also sitting on the top because it felt weird to be lower than him on the bench.

Crossing one leg over the other, I rested my chin on my hand, my elbow digging slightly into my knee, and watched the kids play.

"At least if this were your haunt you could watch the skaters," Mom said, her voice just loud enough to carry over Gryphin.

He nodded. "I'm sure there are worse places to haunt. Didn't that Brandon kid spend a few decades here? Doesn't seem like it would be too bad."

"I don't know. Maybe. There don't seem to be any other ghosts here, so I'm guessing Brandon was alone that whole time. Even if you have something to watch, I'm sure you would get lonely with no one to talk to after a while," I said, my voice heavy with the disappointment that was seeping into my chest.

"But it's not so bad if you have visitors," someone said on my left where a blue form slowly materialized. She was copying my sitting position, but her mouth wore a giddy smile as we locked eyes.

"Hanna!" I yelled so loudly that Gryphin and my mom jumped. Several people looked over at me in concern.

I didn't care.

"It's about time you got here," she said as we both leaned in for a pointless and probably odd-looking hug.

I dropped my arms with a quick disappointed pout while Mom and Gryphin scrambled up from their seats and stood in front of the both of us, trying to at least make my interactions with the empty air less distracting for those alivers in the park.

Gryphin's broad form blocked most of the view while his eyes sparkled with cheery happiness. Mom stood next to him, staring at the table where Hanna was sitting, unable to see her baby girl but still putting a trembling hand over her mouth as tears winked in her eyes.

"I'm sorry it took us so long. I guess we should have listened to Brandon's suggestion earlier. He's going to be so annoying for days when he finds out he was right the whole time," I said, wishing I could at least hold her hand.

Hanna smiled, beaming at each of us. "Sometimes that kid does have some good ideas. I'm guessing he couldn't come with you?"

I frowned again and shook my head. "Honestly, I've been kind of relieved he wasn't following me all over the place, but right this second, I wish he could be here to see you, too."

"But it's okay because y'all are here! Can you tell Mom I wish I could give her a hug?" Hanna asked, her gaze lingering on the darker bags beneath Mom's eyes and the tears that were escaping.

"Okay, but it might make her cry even more."

Mom looked up at my words, and I gave her a soft smile. "She says she wishes she could hug you."

Her chin trembled for a second, and Gryphin wrapped a warm arm over her shoulder. "Oh, sweetie. You'll be able to soon, once we get you back in your body. All we have to do is finish up the task for the necromancers."

Hanna's eyebrows furrowed, and she looked at me. "What kind of deal did you have to make?"

She was already shaking her head while I explained.

"There was no other choice. We can't just let you stay dead!"

"Yeah, but what do they want in return? It costs them an awful lot to cast a resurrection spell. I saw how hard it was for them to fix Stephanie, and that's only if everything goes well. I don't want to end up like Andrea!"

I frowned. "What's wrong with Andrea?"

"Don't you remember? I told you that she is a zombie. *Her* resurrection spell went amiss. Now she has to have Noah recast a spell on her every day or else she'll like rot or something, I don't know, and no one wants to find out."

Goosebumps spread down my arms. "Oh yeah... We laughed like forever about it. It's not so funny to think about that happening to you."

Mom was watching me worriedly. "What's she saying? What could happen?"

"If the spell goes wrong, a necromancer will have to recast it on her every day," I said with a pensive frown.

"What?" Mom and Gryphin exchanged worried looks. It must have been too intimate for him to hold her shoulder while also looking her in the face because he dropped his arm.

"Well, not the same exact spell because the first one requires lots of members and energy, but a lesser one that still requires a cost. Each spell a necromancer performs takes part of their age. It's like they get old right in front of your eyes. Which is why Rose was eating souls, to somehow that restores her youth," Hanna said, the words rushing out of her blue lips.

"Okay... So I get why the necroes would demand high costs for their favors and why Rose might want to eat a soul, though I'm not saying either of those things are right," I hastily added the last part as Hanna's eyes widened in concern for my morality, "but I am saying I understand a bit more about what's going on."

I locked eyes with Mom, and we shared a resolute nod before I turned back to Hanna. "We still think it's worth it to help the necroes and get you back in your body. You can't expect us to just let you die and that be the end of that. Plus, I *cannot* handle Brandon haunting me for the rest of my life. You've got to be there to distract him before we both go crazy."

Her mouth puckered into a laughing smile. "You guys could always move. At least you know he won't be able to come with you."

"Nope. You're coming back. That's the end of that discussion." I folded my arms across my chest and gave her a pointed look.

"I know I'd like to see you again, at least," Gryphin said, a wistful smile on his face. "It's not much fun talking to a table and hearing only one side of the conversation."

Hanna's expression softened in a way that made me grin. Perhaps Brandon wasn't the only guy she had eyes for these days. I couldn't blame her, though. The wolf was pretty to look at, and his heart was as pure as any I'd met.

"Tell him I'm glad he came, not just because it's nice to see him again, but that I'm glad he's there to help you guys out. You never know when Rose might send Caleb back. I've been really worried. I'm guessing Brandon told you everything that happened?" Hanna said, her focus shifting as she spoke.

Before I responded to her questions, I told Gryphin what she'd said.

His smile lit up the park like the clouds had parted for the sun to shine through. "I'm just glad I can help in some small way."

I turned back to Hanna. "Yes, he told us. I still can't believe it." Shaking my head, I snuggled deeper into my jacket. "I hope Caleb doesn't realize what he's done. He'll be tormented for eternity once we set him free."

Hanna shook her head as well. "*If* there's a way to set him free. What if he's stuck like that until a stake finally gets shoved into his chest?"

I pressed my lips together to smash down the pain I felt at the thought. "No. There has to be a way. We just need to find it."

Hanna patted through my knee with her blue hand. "I'm sorry. You're right. If I found a way to free the ghosts from the crystals, I can find a way to free him. Maybe the witches will have some ideas. Or even Noah. Speaking of Noah, I'm guessing he finally told y'all where my haunt was. He's visited me at least three times so far but took forever to tell you where I was. I mean, I *kind of* get why he did it, but still..."

She trailed off as she saw my confused face.

"What? No. Noah didn't tell us anything. We only stopped by because Brandon and Gryphin thought it might be a good place to check. Wait. Are you saying that *Noah* has known where you were this whole time?"

Mom's eyebrows scrunched, giving her forehead wrinkles a chance to shine. "Noah knew she was here? Do you think he knew when we saw him?"

Hanna watched our exchange with a frown. "So Noah didn't tell you where I was?"

I shook my head. "No, but that might explain why he couldn't look us in the eyes. That sneaky—"

"Trina!" Mom scowled. "I taught you to talk better than that, though I have to admit that word aptly describes this supposed 'friend' of Hanna's."

Hanna didn't look as scandalized as I felt she should have been. Instead, she looked sad.

"I was worried he wouldn't tell," she said as she fiddled with her blue fingers. It was weird to talk to ghosts even though I was slowly getting more used to it, but it was even weirder to talk to my own sister. I could literally see through her head, though it didn't help me to understand what she was thinking any better.

"Why wouldn't he tell? That's just rude to keep us from you like that." I exchanged frustrated glances with my mom.

"Do you think the order told him to do that?" Mom said, her eyes darting to the table where she thought Hanna was sitting.

Hanna shrugged. "I don't know. It's possible, but I get the feeling it was more because he wanted to keep me as his secret for a bit. I maybe...might have led him on a little because I wanted his help and just had to have someone to talk to. Oh! Aren't you guys going to ask me how we could talk?"

She practically vibrated with excitement, and I felt dumb for not wondering about that right away.

Before responding to Hanna, I repeated her answers to Mom's questions and then turned back to her. "Oh, yes. That's a good point. How did you manage to talk to him?"

"I can possess zombies now. Like before when I was a Seer, I ordered those ghosts to take control of the zombies so the necroes would allow the witches to take Rose, but in death, I can kind of glide into one without a Seer's help. Isn't that cool?"

I would be lying if I didn't admit that ugly jealous feeling I sometimes had towards Hanna showed up again. I thought I was past that, you know with Hanna being dead and everything. I'd hoped that my grief and sadness at her loss would overshadow any petty and jealous feelings that may be tempted to show up.

Guess not.

Part of the reason I felt so frustrated about my lack of special Seer skills was because Hanna had been able to use hers in amazing ways. It had been much easier to ignore when I was denying myself the powers in general, but once I'd taken off the necklace and faced the facts about who I was, the jealousy had begun to fester and grow.

Why wasn't I able to do anything extra? Not only could Hanna take a ghost out of its haunt, she could give them extra energy, summon them from their haunt, *and* command them to do things, *and* give them the ability to possess a zombie.

While I hadn't yet been able to try all of those things, I certainly couldn't do the first or command them. There was no reason to indicate that I would be able to do any of the others either, and it stung.

Realizing I better explain to Mom and Gryphin, I cleared my throat and turned to them. "She says she's able to possess a zombie without a Seer's help. She can glide into one and take control."

Hopefully I said that factually instead of with a simmering, jealous tone of voice.

Gryphin raised his eyebrows and nodded in appreciation. "That's really cool, actually. If we could get her a zombie body to walk around in, she could do nearly normal human stuff."

Mom and I gave him alarmed looks.

"Except she'd be a zombie!" Mom said, her shoulders shuddering. "No thanks."

"Yeah, probably don't want to be dropping limbs while wandering around the house or something. Others might get concerned about the stench at school," I said, unable to help myself from jumping into the zombie jokes.

"No, but like Andrea is a zombie!" Hanna said at first to all of us and then turned back to me. "Does she smell like one or look like one? Yes, sure, it's not ideal, and if we get the resurrection spell at some point,

I wouldn't want to end up like her, but on the other hand, it's not so bad."

Shaking my head, I turned to Mom. "She's pointing out how good Andrea looks while still being a zombie." I looked back at Hanna. "So Noah and Andrea showed up to the skatepark, and you figured out you could possess her and that's how you and Noah have been talking?"

She nodded, her eyes wide with excitement. "Isn't it cool? I mean, we joked about letting me have her body for a while and just going to school and being normal and stuff, but we're not sure what the side effects of it could be. It wouldn't be good if I turned into a poltergeist after all of that."

"Or if something bad happened to Andrea," I pointed out with raised eyebrows.

"Oh, right. Or that. So far, we've only chatted for a few minutes each time. Nothing seems to be happening yet, though."

"Not sure that means that it won't." I turned back to the alivers and filled them in on what she'd said.

"Yeah, it sounds sketchy. Perhaps it would be best to avoid doing any of that unless it's really needed. Now that you know where her haunt is, she doesn't need another body to talk to people," Gryphin said, sounding more like an adult than the teen he was supposed to be. He didn't look like one either, though.

Maybe werewolves grew up faster than us normals or maybe he was older than I thought he was.

"Of course, but it's cool to know we have it if we need it, right?" Hanna said, still beaming.

I gave her a half-hearted smile. "Yes. It's good to know. What about other powers you might have as a ghost? Do you think you have any more? We may need all the help we can get before we can fix everything."

This included finding out if I could do anything extra, but I left that part unsaid as it was more of my burden.

She shrugged. "That's it, as far as I know. My memories don't work as well as they did, although being in Andrea's body has helped bring them back some, and I sure don't have unlimited energy. Sometimes I fade out, and when I come back it's a different time of the day or maybe even a whole different day. Time is weird here. What's the date, anyway?"

I told her and she sighed. "Yeah, it feels like it should be a lot later than that, and also that time has passed too fast. I know it doesn't make sense."

My smile was more genuine then as I was capable of feeling sympathy while still trying to stuff away the jealousy. "I'm sorry you're a ghost. We've all really missed you. You probably already knew that, but I just wanted to say it in case you didn't."

She patted through my leg again. "Thank you. It is nice to hear it. So tell me what the necroes want in exchange for bringing me back to life? Is my body being preserved? If I have to go back to it, I want it to at least be free of rot."

I chuckled and shook my head. "Of course. That was the first thing we did—called Noah over to bring your body to the order where they can take care of it like it should be. As for what they asked of us, so far, it's been to finish up the task you were supposed to do."

She winced. "I'm sorry. I didn't mean to die."

"Of course you didn't. No one blames you."

"And we don't blame Caleb, either. We'll find a way to bring him back. I'm sure you've been worried about him."

"You know... I've been so busy worrying about you and figuring out how to find you while still going to school and not being murdered by a vampire in broad daylight to think much about him," I said softly, realizing it was mostly true.

I had been trying to get rid of my feelings for Caleb. Being in love with a vampire was worse than being in love with a ghost, in my book. Honestly, though, I wasn't sure if that was because it was creepier that he drank blood or more that he was basically three hundred years older than me.

It was super frustrating my heart and body liked someone my brain told me was not good to like. I had been hoping this whole murder thing would help me like him less, but, instead, I found myself feeling sorrier for him and wondering what kind of mental torture he was under while Rose was in control of his body.

"It's funny how even in death you know me better than I know myself," I said after sorting through some thoughts and giving her a side-smile.

I noticed Mom's eyes softened as she listened to my side of the conversation but decided to ignore whatever sappy Mom moment she was having.

"Of course I do. I'm your sister. What I am having trouble remembering is what the necros had wanted from me..." she trailed off as she narrowed her eyes and studied Gryphin's boots standing in front of her on the pavement.

"It's okay. You get a pass since you're like a ghost and all."

We shared a smile.

"They asked us to find out whatever we can from Susan about some dude named Theodore McCutcheon. Does that sound familiar?" I said.

"Uh, oh yeah! And Susan is Brandon's mom!" Her head whipped over to look at me as if the conversation had reminded her of that whole situation. "Wait, he doesn't know yet, does he? Did you tell him? That's literally what I was going to let him know when... Man, the more I think about it, the worse the timing is! If she had killed me earlier, then Brandon and I could have had the same haunt and be hanging out together for the rest of eternity."

I blinked a few times. "Yeah, that sounds really awesome. Y'all could take turns scaring people who had no idea you were there."

She narrowed her eyebrows into an annoyed look at me. I returned it with a cheerful smile.

"No, I haven't told him about that. I figured that was something you could do. I *did* tell his mom, though. We went there just this morning, although it feels like forever ago already, to try and get some progress on the task. I was hoping that telling her about Brandon would get her to cooperate more with us, but no such luck," I said the last part with a shake of my head.

Hanna sighed, taking in air or plasma or whatever ghosts took in with their ethereal lungs. "I don't know why the necroes are so obsessed with hearing whatever she knows. The times I tried to talk to her, she was super frustrating."

"Well, it's comforting to know that at least one thing hasn't changed while you've been on your vacation," I said dryly.

Mom lifted her index finger as she spoke. "Don't forget to tell her about the other Seer. I don't know how it relates to all of us, but it seems like something she may want to know."

Nodding, I turned back to Hanna. "She's talking about something we did manage to get from Susan, which partly explains her reluctance to help us. There was another Seer that chatted Susan up. I guess they got kind of close because Susan seemed actually sad about what happened to him."

Hanna glanced at Mom with worried eyes and then back to me. "What happened?"

"He was murdered on his way to the necroes with the information, right in the middle of the parking lot and in front of Susan. That's the main reason she doesn't want to help us. Whatever information she has for the necroes, someone else doesn't want them to know it."

Gryphin's green eyes fell to me as he spoke. "How do you think they knew that Seer had finally gotten the information he needed from the ghost? From what we know of Susan, he probably had to visit her several times, but it wasn't until she told him what he wanted to know before he was killed. Coincidence or not?"

"He has a super good point. Not to mention, how high are the odds that we already know the person who hurt this Seer or that this is completely unrelated to whatever we are working on here?" Hanna leaned back on the table and tapped her fingers as she thought.

"I don't know how we're supposed to know any of those things," I said with a shrug. "It's clear we need more answers, but, to me, none of it really matters so long as we get the necroes to help us get you back into your body."

"Yeah, unless I get killed again right away or they go after you."
Hanna frowned. "We've got to be careful about all of this or it'll be
pointless. I wish we had a vampire we could rely on."

I sighed and turned my gaze to the skaters in the park. As evening
came on and the air got more and more chilly, there were less and less
people. I didn't blame them. My butt was cold from sitting on the
cool tabletop, and my toes were starting to feel slightly numb. "Unless
you want to hit up the vampire queen, we've got nothing on vampires.
We do have some help from the wolves, thankfully," I shot a smile in
Gryphin's direction, "but perhaps we ought to ask the magic users for
more help. It's their fault that Rose has escaped anyway."

Hanna popped her shoulders back with energetic agreement. "Yes!
Even if the matron won't get involved, which she should like you said,
at least Phoenix would be willing to help us. Let's get them in on it,
gather what information we have, and figure out what to do next after
that."

Mom nodded after I repeated Hanna's words. "Sounds like the best
thing to do. We'll keep talking and sleep on it and see what else we can
come up with. Hanna, I wish we could take you home with us."

Her words hadn't been meant as a dig toward me not having Hanna's super awesome extra Seer powers, but they felt like it anyway. If I
was as good as Hanna, we could have her around us all the time and
not have to leave her in the park.

But I was just me. Yay for us.

"I know. It's okay, Mom. At least you know no one can hurt me
anymore." Hanna's voice was chipper like she meant it as a joke, but I
didn't repeat it well enough to convey her attempt at lightening things
up.

Mom's smile grew sad. Gryphin and I moved to comfort her on either side. As we said goodbye to Hanna, I felt a mixture of sadness, pain, and struggling hope.

Yes, my sister was dead, but we had found her. We had a way to talk to her, and we kind of had a plan of what to do next. At least Brandon would be happy to hear she hadn't passed on, and that he'd been right about her haunt all along.

Chapter 10 - Hanna

As I watched my sister and Gryphin support my mom on the way out of the skatepark, I could feel the strength from their presence ebb away. It was like seeing their faces and talking with them had helped bring back more of myself than I'd felt as a ghost thus far.

It was almost as nice as being inside a body again.

I was also sad to see them go when I felt like I should have been going with them. My place was with my family, in my house, not at the skatepark in the cold where no one could see or talk to me.

For some reason, I was sadder after their visit than before. Sure, I was happy they were doing well, working on a plan to get me back with them, while trying to avoid a vampire on the loose. Still, the tears in my mom's eyes hurt the most.

It was one thing to imagine her pain, while it was quite another to see it.

Not long after they left, the skatepark emptied out and dusk settled in. Still sitting on the table where my family had been, I stared up at the sky watching the clouds float by and the colors change.

After thinking about my family, my thoughts drifted to Brandon. I couldn't help the smile perking onto my face at the thought of him bothering Trina incessantly. He had probably nagged them until they'd figured out where my haunt was. He had also probably tried going places with her, but that had not worked out, obviously. He'd probably been chatty and dropping sarcastic comments and inappropriate jokes while she was trying to do homework or talking to someone else.

It was funny how the things he did that annoyed me when I was trying to operate as a normal human were also the things that I enjoyed about him. I'm sure it helped that imagining him doing them to Trina was quite entertaining. In some ways, she deserved it as she'd had that necklace all along, while I had to grow up seeing and hearing the ghosts.

I mean, yeah, it wasn't really her fault since she didn't know I could see them too, but I had to admit it felt kind of good to know she was feeling some discomfort.

Sometime after dark as I was watching the stars peek through drifting holes in the clouds, a car door slammed somewhere nearby, and two sets of footsteps headed in the park's direction.

Curious and finally bored of watching the sky, I got up from the table. It was odd not to feel stiff after sitting there for so long or cold in the nighttime air, but I could take the advantages of being a ghost where I could get them.

Before I reached the fence of the park, Noah and someone else that wasn't Andrea walked in. I backed up needlessly in surprise as they passed by on the sidewalk.

Noah was in jeans, a t-shirt, and a jean jacket with various band patches on it. His hair was slightly mussed, but the wind kept it from slouching over his forehead.

The old man with him was clearly out of place. He was wearing one of our school's shirts, several sizes too big for him, with a set of sweatpants, also too big. Flip-flops provided cover for the bottom of his feet if not the tops in the cold air. His hair had at one point been slicked into a comb-over but was currently flapping in the wind. Whether or not he still needed them, a pair of scratched glasses sat on his nose. Compared to Noah's height and football muscles, the man looked small, frail, and hunched. He could have been built better in his youth, but time had stolen his strength, if it was ever there at all.

Adding to his odd appearance, the way he followed Noah in through the gate, kept a few paces behind him, and didn't utter a word had my eyebrows furrowing.

"Hanna? Are you here? Can you hear me?" Noah asked, his eyes roaming over the park. "I thought we could perform an experiment or two. Can you try possessing this body for me?"

I frowned and assessed the old man again. Part of me was tempted to ignore Noah and let him leave the park without having made any interesting scientific discoveries. I had practically begged him to tell my family where I was, and he'd lied about it.

Maybe he'd had no intention of telling them where I was the whole time.

Deciding he at least needed to know why I was upset with him, I took a ghostly breath and walked into the old guy.

"Hanna? Hello?"

"Yes, yes. I'm here, although I seriously considered not getting into this bag of bones. Is this the best you could do? What happened to Andrea? She was way more pleasant to possess even if I pretty much hated her guts already. Plus, you don't deserve to talk to me after what you pulled," I said with the old man's gravelly voice.

Startled, Noah's eyes widened as I worked through my tirade. "Woah. Okay, first off, do you know how hard it is to get a body these days? It's not like earlier times when you could stumble upon a vagabond in a ditch somewhere that no one would miss. There are rules and cameras, and you know, it's just a trying time to be in the zombie business. Not only is it super hard to find a body to use, but it's also even harder to find one in this good a shape. To be honest, I was feeling pretty proud of myself for this discovery."

I glared and folded my arms across my chest. "The least you could have done was give him a jacket. It's freezing out here."

"Well, in my defense, zombies don't usually complain of the chilly air. I'll have to remember that next time, ghost princess," he said the last bit sarcastically and made me want to slap him.

"How about answering my other questions? Couldn't come up with a lie good enough to get Andrea over here this late at night? Why not command her as your zombie slave?"

He tipped his head to the sky and sighed. "This is not how I was hoping this would go.

"Oh, it's not?" I bobbed my old man's head in a sassy way. "Were you hoping that your new ghostly girlfriend would lovingly enter into an elderly corpse and jump into your arms with grateful kisses?"

He barked a laugh that broke some of the tension in his shoulders. "Okay, fair enough. No. That's not what I was going for."

"And I hadn't meant to make you laugh. You're supposed to be getting angry and become as upset as I am. If you can't tell, I'm mad at you," I grumbled, hoping my bushy eyebrows and deep forehead wrinkles were menacing when furrowed.

A smile danced on his lips, but he had the decency not to laugh again. "Okay, I see. And why are you mad at me? It's got to be more than this body. If anything, I thought you'd be happy to have something to walk around in for a minute. I was thinking we might even see if you could leave the skatepark while inside a body."

Hope and excitement flared through the anger, but I wasn't quite ready to let go of it yet. "Nope. You don't get to sweet talk me. I'm upset because you never told my family where I was! They found me today...or yesterday, depending on the time, all on their own. We had a lovely talk which included the fact that they had seen you, but you hadn't even looked them in the eye or given them any clue that you knew where I was."

"Oh."

"Yeah, oh." I frowned and crossed my arms. It was weird to do that without having breasts in the way, but I hoped the effect wasn't lost.

"Right," he said, looking away and rubbing his neck.

"And I'm sick of your excuses about how you want me to yourself or whatever. I'm beginning to think that the order told you to do that to keep my family from progressing so that y'all never have to put me back together. After all, you have Trina to do your Seer work. What do you guys need me for anymore?"

I hadn't realized I'd felt like that until the words came out of my mouth. I had been so used to feeling special and being the only Seer (or at least the only one who anyone knew about) that it was hard for me to adjust to having Trina around who could do almost everything I could do.

I understood why my family would want me back alive, but why would anyone else care? Trina was probably much easier to work with since she was nicer and smarter than I was. She probably wouldn't have talked back to the vampire queen like I had or maybe not even done the stupid things to help Rose.

Maybe Trina would be the better Seer, and I should stay dead.

Noah must have seen some of the pain and confusion cross my face because he focused back on me and frowned. "First off, the order doesn't know where you are. I haven't told a single soul about finding your ghost. Like I said, I wanted you all to myself for a little while. It was nice having my own secret for a time. I'm sorry because I understand it was selfish, but I'm not sorry for the time and conversations we've been able to have. We've never been left alone like that just to talk, and I wanted to take the time to do that. I hope you don't hold that against me."

I stared at him with my old-man arms still crossed. "I do."

He sighed. "Fine. The other thing I need to point out is that you are more than your powers. So what if Trina is a Seer too? Do you know how rare it is for two to be born in one family in one generation? Even with that, add all the extra stuff you can do. You're nothing short of a miracle, Hanna." Taking a step closer, he grabbed my shoulders and looked into my eyes as if to convey how sincere his words were. "And even if you couldn't do a darn thing except help a cheerleader with her math homework and weren't able to see a single ghost, you would still be a miracle. You're funny and fun and enjoyable to be around and kind underneath all that sass. You think I've been busy with Andrea and being a football player, and all of it, but I've been busy watching you through the whole thing."

Knots formed in my stomach that I didn't know how to interpret. There was some gratitude at his words, warmth from feeling that at least someone appreciated me for me, but it was all coated in a shell of guilt. I enjoyed his comments as a person and a friend, but there was no way I could return the depth of his feelings.

Not after all we'd been through, and it had nothing to do with the business of dealing with corpses.

"Noah, I appreciate your kind words, I really do. It kinda feels important to reiterate that I'm not interested in you in a romantic way..."

He held his hand up and shook his head. "No. You don't have to tell me again. I get it. I do, but that doesn't mean I'm going to stop telling you how I feel. Maybe it'll change as time goes on, but for now, I care more about you than most people in my life."

If I'd had my own body, I know my cheeks would have been blossoming into redness, but hopefully that was not the case in this saggy bag of bones.

Unsure of what else to say for the moment, I let his words drift off into the nighttime air as we studied each other.

Finally, Noah broke out into another chuckle. "I'm sorry. This is hard while looking at you like this."

I allowed a small smile to peek out of the body's face, wondering how many teeth I was missing. "It's hard being like this. Why couldn't you have just brought Andrea out again? She wasn't my favorite person, but it's much easier to be her."

He was shaking his head before I finished speaking. "I'm afraid of the effects of what we are doing. As hard as it was to find a body this well preserved, it's worth not running the risk of harming Andrea in some way. We don't know what happens to her when you take over, and I'm not sure we want to find out. This body was legit dead," he saw my eyes widen and he put his hands up to stop me from completely freaking out, "but not very long! It's fine. I got the freshest one I could, okay?"

"This is insane. I can't believe this is happening to me. Did you dress him in one of your shirts?" I held up the over-sized Willow High School t-shirt. "The least you could have done was gotten him something that fit a little better."

"Is that really what you're worried about when this is the first time you've had a body with...manhood bits? I mean, sure they might be a bit saggy and less attentive than another body's man parts, but—"

"Ew! Can you please stop?" I nearly gagged, trying desperately to keep my mental awareness of the body from traveling downwards so far.

He was laughing way more than was decent, but eventually it grew on me, and I started joining in.

Slowly, his mirth dissolved into a pleased kindness as he smiled down at me. "Ready to do some ghost science? Think about the possibilities if this works to let you leave the haunt."

"Yes, I could take a lovely trip to the pharmacy where I could refill my prescription meds, and then go to the local watering hole where I could complain about today's youth with all the other old men. Very exciting."

That earned me another chuckle. "If that's what you really want to do, then let's do it, by all means, but I was thinking you could go visit your family. I know you said they dropped by today, but did they happen to bring along a certain other dead person?"

I couldn't feel an actual heartbeat but if there had been one, I know it would have picked up pace at the mention of Brandon. Then I remembered what I looked like and frowned.

"I'm not sure I want to see him like this... I mean, I really miss him, but this whole image may ruin any feelings he has or has ever had for me." I narrowed my eyes. "Wait a minute... Was that your plan all along? I'm on to you, mister!"

"What? No! This was seriously the best option I had, okay? Sheesh. You're getting so hung up on this that I'm starting to wonder if you're as vain as Andrea."

That shut me up. I gave him a pouty lip that was probably silly looking on this old man.

"Oh, don't look at me like that. I was just kidding. We don't have to go visit anyone or do anything you don't want to do, but let's just see what is possible. Shall we?"

I nodded and took a step before another thought came to me. "It strikes me as we were so worried about what effects this possession thing might have on Andrea's body, but what about my spirit? Is this just another power I have because I had some ghostly ones in life or am I using up precious energy that will eventually turn me into a poltergeist? I don't even have a cool old church to haunt."

He smiled at the reference to Clara, the girl who had turned into a poltergeist while haunting the church-turned-homeless shelter. "That's definitely a concern, but again, I don't know how we'll figure it out unless we test it."

"And how do we test that, exactly? Decide if I feel tired? I'm the one that is supposed to be an expert on ghosts, but I have no idea how any of this works," I grumbled with a frown.

"Perhaps we can start with a series of questions. Do you feel tired now?"

I shrugged. "Hard to say. Not more than usual?"

"Okay… So ghosts don't stick around when they have low energy, right? Like they disappear for hours or days at a time?"

"That's my understanding. Usually when ghosts spent more time around me, they got more solid and present. Brandon spent so much time with me that I'm not sure he ever needed to faze out."

"And what about you now? How often do you faze out? Can you tell?" Noah's eyes were so intense that I was a bit startled by his focus. Apparently, he had a passion for ghost science.

Was ghost science even a thing?

I looked up at the tops of the stark trees as I tried to think about it. "I'm not sure. It's hard to tell. The only way I can judge it is by the hops in the time of day, but my memory is also terrible and trying to remember how often I see the hops or blips is impossible."

"Can you try to guess? Maybe we can make a vague judgment on if it's getting worse or not."

"But even if it is getting worse, how do we know it's because I've been possessing zombies and not just the natural waning of ghost energy over time?"

That slowed our pace for a moment as we both thought about it.

"I suppose all we can do is our best," Noah finally said and ran a hand through his hair.

"Even at the risk of turning me into a poltergeist?"

"That's up to you. I'm not going to make you do anything you don't want to. All I'm trying to do is help, but I get the feeling that you'd rather risk it, at least a little, so that you have something you can do to pass the time and maybe even help your family."

I gave him a pouty look. "You seem to know me pretty well. It's true. I'd rather experiment than sit here and watch the grass not grow in the winter weather."

He smiled softly. "That's what I thought. So. Ready to take your new ride for a spin?"

Chapter 11 - Trina

It was late on Saturday night, and I couldn't sleep. The day had been so full, my head was spinning from everything that had happened. The biggest two moments, of course, were when we'd further upset Susan's ghost and when we'd finally found Hanna.

Her ghostly blue face had looked the same as she always had, except it felt totally different. It had been surreal to see her like that and even more surreal to have to tell Mom and Gryphin what she was saying even though she was sitting right in front of them.

There was some happiness and relief at seeing her, of course. We knew where she was, and as soon as we could finish the tasks from the necromancers, we could unite her with her body, and everything would be good again.

Hopefully.

Mom, Gryph, and I had decided we'd figure out what to do with Susan tomorrow, which was Sunday, so I had one more free day before I had to go back to school. Thankfully, there was only one more week and then Christmas break which should give me extra time to figure out stuff and hopefully catch up on the homework I'd been struggling to complete.

Finally knowing where Hanna was should have freed me up to focus more on other things... Unfortunately, that also included focusing on Caleb.

I couldn't help but think about him as I snuggled deeper into my pillow, wondering if he was scared or angry or feeling anything at all while under Rose's spell. What was he out there doing? Had he tried to come back into the house and found that we'd respelled it so he couldn't enter anymore? It was possible we were worrying about him popping up out of nowhere for no reason, because Rose could have moved on completely and focused on whatever else she wanted to do.

There were too many questions and not enough answers.

Brandon still hadn't been back when we'd gotten home. I suppose he was still saving up energy since Hanna wasn't around to feed the ghostly need or whatever it was she did to make the ghosts stronger. It had been nice to have a break, but again, the space allowed the difficult thoughts to come in.

Caleb and I had been getting kind of close lately. We'd even gone on a date, or at least hung out with just the two of us instead of with all our other friends. It hadn't been awkward at all. Honestly, it'd been fun and enjoyable.

Which I'd been annoyed with at the time since I was still trying to push away my feelings for him. I'd partially agreed to go on the date in hopes that my heart would get over whatever crush it was fostering.

Too bad it had done the opposite.

I had hoped that after hearing what Caleb had done to Hanna, all my feelings would have been washed away, covered by the pain and horror of what had happened. Instead, my stupid heart decided to feel sadness and worry for what he was going through rather than anger at what he had done.

Frustrated and wanting something else to think about, I decided to try out Frank's suggestion and summon a ghost. Uncaring if it was weird to summon a random ghost to one's bed in the middle of the night, I closed my eyes and tried to remember what Frank looked like in as much detail as I could.

He had long, wavy hair, a band t-shirt I couldn't remember the name of, a vest, and torn jeans. His eyebrows were thick, his nose only a little crooked, and his mouth was always tilted into a sarcastic sneer or angry pout.

Feeling nothing, I sighed and rolled over to stare at the ceiling.

The feelings of jealousy and inadequacy sunk back into my chest as I soaked in the darkness of the night. It didn't seem right that Hanna would get all these extra powers while I got just the basics.

There had to be something else I could do.

The next morning, I woke up with scratchy eyes and a heavy head. Somehow, I'd managed to sleep in a tiny bit more than I had been lately, even on the weekends. Perhaps finding Hanna had helped ease some of my anxiety even if I'd struggled for a while to fall asleep.

Mom was sitting at the kitchen island nursing her coffee and doing something on the laptop when I stumbled in after using the bathroom and washing my face.

"Hey, sweetie. How did you sleep?"

I didn't bother to answer except with a grunt as I opened the fridge and got bread, butter, and jam out to make toast.

Brandon sauntered in from down the hall, his hands in his pockets, and a happy smile on his face. "Y'all ready to get started on the day?"

I groaned as I pushed down the toaster button and turned to face them.

Mom's eyebrows were pulled high up her forehead as she regarded me. "Something wrong? I was expecting you to feel much better about things today."

"Brandon's back. I suppose we ought to tell him the good news," I said, my voice groggy and tired.

"We could." She shrugged. "Or we could just let him suffer for a little longer."

That made me smile a bit and even more so when he started twitching his head back and forth between us. "What good news? Did you find her? Did you?!"

My smile was all the answer he needed, and he started jumping around the room like he was at some kind of punk rock concert, his giant pants flaring with each bounce.

"Well? Is he happy?" Mom asked, watching my face.

"I think you could say that."

My toast popped up, and I turned back around to the toaster.

"Where is she? Did you find her at the movie theater?" Brandon asked, moving through the kitchen counter until I was forced to see his face instead of my toast.

"Hey! Don't get your ghost juices on my food!" I swatted him away until he backed up to stand next to me.

"Well? Tell me!"

"It pains me to say that you were right the whole time. She's at the skatepark." I licked my finger after putting the jam on my toast.

"I knew it!" He jumped around again in a circle a few times. "The universe has too good a sense of humor not to do that to me."

"Yeah, well, I can only guess that it's your fault. If you hadn't been making her hang out with you so much, she probably would have haunted the house or the school. So it's your own fault, in a way, that you guys aren't able to spend time together as ghosts," I said, taking my stuff to the stool next to Mom.

She took a sip of her coffee. "I suppose that's one way of looking at it. Though we can't blame him for everything. It's not his fault she died."

I shrugged while Brandon leaned over the counter, put his chin on his hands, and got a bit too close for comfort. "So? How is she? Did y'all talk about me?"

Rolling my eyes, I crunched a bite of my toast. "Not as much as you'd have preferred, probably. We had a few other things to talk about besides you."

"Of course." He nodded sagely. "You also had to talk about how handsome and good looking I am."

"Sure. Whatever makes you feel better. It's your world. We're just living in it," I said dryly.

Mom shot me a slightly amused look that also told me to behave.

"Well? How is she? Does she miss me or us or you or anyone?" Brandon's eyes filled with eager concern that nearly made me feel something for him.

"Yes, she misses us. As far as we can tell, she's fine. Getting used to the whole ghost thing, not having a body, being unable to leave the haunt, and having only a select few people to talk to, but would you believe that Noah's been chatting her up for at least a few days and hadn't told us?"

Brandon's forehead wrinkled and his eyebrows narrowed. "Wait. How can he talk to her? Necromancers aren't able to speak with the ghosts, can they?"

I was already shaking my head. "No, it's just another one of Hanna's many tricks. She had special skills in life and has them in death now, too. Andrea is basically a zombie, and Hanna was able to possess her. You weren't there, but when she was alive and we were battling the necromancers at the storage locker—long story short—but she was able to force all the ghosts into the zombie bodies and stop them from listening to the necromancers. So then, of course, now that she's a ghost herself, she is able to possess a zombie body."

I tried to keep the bitter tones out of my voice, but I wasn't sure I succeeded very well.

Brandon's eyes widened as my story progressed. "Woah."

Mom studied me for long enough that I felt awkward and shifted in my seat. I had a feeling she was going to bring up her suspicions at some point, but perhaps I could keep her distracted enough that she wouldn't remember to ask silly things like how I was feeling.

"Yeah, it was a whole thing. I'm sure she'll tell you all about it once y'all can talk. There are some more things that you should know as well, but I can't tell you. It's best if you hear them from Hanna," I said, referring to the heart-breaking details we'd learned from the vampire queen.

Brandon frowned. "Why do I feel like I've missed a lot of important stuff?"

"Because you have. You were gone for a while, but that's not important right now. What is important is that we're mad at Noah and definitely suspicious of his behavior. It's possible the necromancer order told him to hide her from us."

"Did Hanna get a chance to ask him?" Brandon kept frowning. "I don't like the idea of him chatting her up like that and not telling anyone. It's creepy."

"More than creepy, it's rude. She said he seemed to just want to spend time with her. Perhaps he likes her more than any of us guessed."

"I guessed." He huffed and stood, folding his arms across his chest. "I knew he was no good all along."

"I mean... Yeah, it's suspicious, but I'm not sure we can label him as a villain quite yet," I said, taking the last bite of my toast and washing it down with some orange juice.

"Well, maybe you can't, but I can."

"Okay. Have at it. The only problem is that we need him and the order to put Hanna back together. It almost doesn't matter if they're evil or not. Hanna is too important."

Mom grunted, maybe disapproving, but I didn't stop to let her try and change my mind. "We've got to get her spirit and body back together. They've already got her body. All we have to do is talk to your mom and get some information for the necromancers. That's not evil. It should be easy if she'd only cooperate."

Brandon's head darted in my direction, and he froze as if the lack of movement would help him hear me better. "Did you say...*my* mom?"

"Oh," I felt my cheeks color, "have we not told you yet? Oops."

Mom's mouth pressed into an amused smile-frown, nodding encouragement for me to fill him in.

"What are you going on about? You've got to tell me now!" Brandon's hair seemed to be sticking out even more than normal.

I filled him in on the necromancer task that was originally given to Hanna and then passed to us. I told him as much as I knew about the interactions between Hanna and Susan and then updated it with our conversation from the day before. The whole time I talked, he only interrupted me five times while otherwise staring like a fish gasping in air.

"Why. are. you. only. telling. me. this. now?" he asked after I'd finished.

"There have been other things on our minds." I gave him a pointed look. "The worst part is this isn't everything, but I think Hanna needs to tell you the rest. It'll be better coming from her."

He frowned and glared. "Just tell me."

"Nope. Not going to do that no matter how much you ask. Now, can you give me any insight into what we can do to get your mom to spill the beans?"

He continued to glare at me, so I merely glared back.

Finally, he sighed and threw his hands up in surrender. "It's funny how y'all think I'm the annoying one. Ugh. Fine. When it comes to my mom, I have to admit I'm like the worst person to figure things out with her. I was always messing up around her. Nothing I ever did was to her liking. Even when I fixed the twins' hair in the mornings because she was gone somewhere, she'd complain about my efforts after they'd gotten home in the evening.

"If I tried to clean something, she'd grumble and go behind me and 'fix' it. I'm not surprised at all that she wouldn't be motivated to helping you by being able to talk to me. She's probably upset that I even turned into a ghost or something. Hell, for all I know, I'm doing the entire ghost thing wrong and have messed up terribly."

"Well, you *have* managed to change your haunt into a teenage girl's room," I said with a teasing smile to cover up the sympathy I'd felt for his pain.

"Yeah, exactly."

"It must have been hard growing up like that," I said, thinking about the other stuff we hadn't told him.

His mom must have been a real peach to go looking for a witch after her husband left her for another family, and then, even worse when she agreed to whatever price the witch was going to take, even at the risk of her own children. Not to mention, she went to a witch to get revenge on the most likely innocent bystanders of her husband's new family. All things I was waiting to let Hanna tell Brandon.

The last thing he needed right now was to feel more animosity toward his mom. He could be as mad at her as he wanted *after* we'd gotten what the necroes needed.

Then there was the other thing we hadn't clued him in about, which was Hanna had found his siblings, kind of. They were also ghosts trapped inside a crystal and on our list of impossible situations we needed to solve.

But again, not for me to tell him about.

"There were worse parents out there. I was just glad to have my siblings around to help cushion her annoyance of me...until..."

I wasn't supposed to know more about that situation than he knew, so I tried to pretend I didn't. "Until what?"

He waved his hand at me in dismissal. "It doesn't matter. What matters is that no use of me will help motivate her to talk to y'all."

Mom was watching me through our exchange, so I updated her on the things Brandon had said. She frowned as I told her about his mom's apparent dislike of her own child and was shaking her head by the time I finished.

She took a breath. "Sometimes moms just want to help their children learn but don't necessarily know how to go about it. It's hard being a parent, you know. Each child is different, and a technique that would help one kid will only discourage another. It's impossible to do everything right all the time. I'm sure his mom's heart was in the right place."

Brandon scoffed.

I gave him a tentative smile. "Let's just give her the benefit of the doubt for now. What do you think will motivate her to talk to us?"

"Perhaps we need to ask why the necromancers want to know the information first. Maybe there's a reason she doesn't want them to know it. Didn't you say that right after she finally told that other Seer, he was killed?" Brandon said, one of his eyebrows pressed down in thought further than the other.

I shrugged. "Yes, but how do we know it's related? If it is related, who killed the guy, and why wouldn't they want the necroes to know the info?"

"I'm pretty sure we can assume it's related with it happening so fast," Brandon said.

"We talked about all this yesterday with Mom and Gryphin and came to the conclusion that we really don't have enough information." I sighed and placed my head on the kitchen island, my cheek pressing onto the cool countertop.

Brandon tapped his lip and walked back and forth through the dining room table. "More information. Well, Noah kinda owes us now. Maybe we can get him to talk more about why the necromancers need the info. What's the guy's name again?"

"Theodore McCutcheon."

"Right, that guy. If he's so important the order has to know about him, maybe Noah has heard of him."

"Even if he has, he probably won't tell us." I pushed myself up and took my dirty dishes to the sink.

"Who?" Mom asked, following my lead and cleaning up her empty mug.

"Noah. We're going to see if he'll help us get more information. Then...I guess the next best thing is to hit up Susan again, as much as I don't want to."

"It's so sad to see that homeless camp," Mom said with a downward tilt of her mouth.

"Plus dangerous. We'll have to see if Gryph is up for another adventure today."

Brandon dug his hands deep into his giant pockets as his shoulders slumped. "I really wish I could come with you guys. As fun as it is to hang out in an empty house all day, I worry about you when you're gone."

Feeling that familiar anger of inadequacy, I gave him a sarcastic frown. "Guess you'll learn to be better company. Maybe you won't bore everyone so much."

"How rude." He pouted at me while his arms were folded.

I shrugged and walked away from him to go get ready. "I'll text Gryph, find out when he's free, and then see if Noah is willing to try and get back on our good side," I said for Mom's benefit as I walked into the hallway and toward the bathroom.

About two hours later, Gryphin and I settled into a booth bench across from Noah and Mom. She looked small sitting next to the broad football player, but I probably looked even smaller sitting next to the large shoulders of the young werewolf.

"You look...tired," I said to Noah, interrupting the awkward silence as we stared at the menus.

He glanced up at me with eyes that were red and underlined with dark circles. His normally fun and relaxed hair seemed a bit more frayed than usual, and his movements were slow as he picked up his glass of water to take a sip. "Thank you."

Mom gave me a scolding look, but I shrugged it off with one shoulder.

"I didn't sleep well last night...and the one before that and the one before that," Noah said, his voice rasping low in his throat.

"Good."

Mom gave me another look while Gryphin grinned in my peripheral vision behind his menu.

We'd chosen to meet at a restaurant even though I wasn't sure any of us were particularly hungry at ten-thirty in the morning. It seemed public enough that we'd be relatively safe, but Gryph had agreed to come with us just in case. I was kind of surprised that Noah had come, but perhaps he did feel some guilt from not telling us about Hanna.

I hope he did.

Noah put down the menu, placed both palms over it, and looked right at me. "Listen. I know you're mad. You have every right to be. I should have told you guys where Hanna's haunt was. If it helps you feel any better, she already lectured me about it, but, you know, if y'all need to weigh in too, then I understand."

His words took some of the fight and anger out of me. Mom and I locked eyes, and she gave me a soft smile. Sighing, I looked back at Noah. "So long as you feel bad about it, understand it was wrong, won't do anything like it again, and are willing to help us out now, I suppose I can forgive you."

Gryphin's grin grew, but he was smart enough to keep it hidden.

Noah sighed and shook his head, picking his menu back up. "Yeah, yeah. All of that. Fine. I'm sorry for keeping it from you, if it helps you to hear that."

"It does, dear," Mom said with a kind smile.

"Whatever helps you sleep at night, which you seem to need some desperate help with." I put my menu up to block my smile.

Sure, I was mad at him but not that mad. He had left it too easy to torment him, and it wasn't like he didn't deserve it.

He groaned and put his menu back down. "If y'all are just going to sit here and insult me, I think I'll go home and get to bed. I haven't slept yet since yesterday, and I'll have you know it's because I was working on something with Hanna."

That made us pause, and all three of us put down the menus and stared at him. Of course that was when the server decided to come over and get our orders. Distractedly, we placed our food requests and handed the menus over before we could bombard Noah with questions after the server left.

"What did you say?" Mom asked.

"What kind of things were you working on?" Gryphin said at the same time, his raised eyebrow telling us exactly what things he was worried about.

"Well, you obviously have to tell us now." I gave him a steady glare.

"Relax. I was planning on it. Did Hanna tell you about Andrea and what she's been able to do with the zombie body? Which, by the way, is a super big secret the order would punish me for you guys knowing about, so you *have* to promise to keep quiet about that." Noah's eyes were pinched at the edges.

I waved it off. "Of course we won't tell your secrets. We wouldn't want to let the order know anything other than what they have to know."

Gryphin and Mom grunted their agreement.

"Okay." Noah looked at each of our faces one by one, so we knew how important it was to him. "Well, I wanted to know what else could happen when she was in the zombie body, so through some difficulties on my end, I procured a body for us to experiment with, in a way."

"Why didn't you just use Andrea again?" I fiddled with my straw wrapper.

"We didn't want to mess up what the order has worked hard to preserve with her, so I decided it would be better to try things out with someone less important. You know, just in case things went wrong."

"You guys sure have gone to great lengths to keep Andrea's secret." Mom pushed her lips into a pensive frown.

"Yes, she's important to the order. You don't have to tell *me* what we've gone through." Noah shook his head. "Not trying to be rude. Just saying I've taken the brunt of the work, and it's been difficult."

"So what did you guys try with the new zombie body?" Gryphin asked, steering us back on track.

A small smile spread over Noah's lips. "Perhaps I should let Hanna tell you the details. Let's just say it was a productive night. Now, can we get to why y'all wanted to meet with me today? Something about the order, I assume."

Chapter 12 - Hanna

"Remind me never to get old." I was trying to get used to the zombie body of the old man and figure out how to navigate around without falling over. His legs were wobbly, his back was stiff, and while I couldn't feel much pain like I'm sure he felt in life, it was still a struggle to get the old muscles and bones working.

"You're telling me." Noah scoffed and shook his head.

"Oh, right. That's probably not a good joke to use around necromancers." I gave him an awkward smile. Or attempted to. I had no idea what kind of expressions were coming out of my zombie face.

"Yeah, not generally. It's okay, though. We're used to it." He stuck his arm out for me to grab as I walked on the sidewalk toward the skatepark's exit.

I didn't take his offering, determined to stand on my own feet. Plus, even if I fell down, what was the worst that could happen? The guy was already dead.

"Or you could just steal souls to gain eternal youth." I gave him a side-eye.

He sighed loudly. "No. We don't do that. I've told you before, that's one of the biggest sins a necro can commit."

"Are you sure David knows that?"

He groaned and shook his head again. "Yes, I'm sure. He wouldn't do that."

"Perhaps you should remind him, just in case."

Giving me a flat look, he paused as we neared the exit. "The moment of truth."

"Actually, I can usually stand on the sidewalk outside the fence. It'll be stepping off the curb that will really be the test. Not sure that this body will be able to handle even that. We're not going to run any zombie marathons or anything, right?"

"It's more of a matter of will with these bodies. Sometimes they try and push back, but the strength of the necromancer comes from his will. If he's strong enough, even the oldest and most decrepit zombies can do what you need."

"I'm not a necromancer, remember? I'm a ghost trying to walk around in some old man's legs."

"I'm sure you'll figure it out," he said with a smile as we crossed the sidewalk and approached the road. The neighborhood was quiet at this time of night, and it was rare for a car to pass by.

I took a deep breath in my old rattly lungs and stepped off the curb. It felt no different, but there I was, not standing inside the haunt.

Noah and I shared a triumphant look.

"Guess we answered that question. How do you feel, though? Any more tired than before?" He peered down as if visually inspecting me.

I looked down at myself as well, at my too-big t-shirt, baggy sweatpants, and age-spotted hands. "Again, it's hard to tell. Right now, all I can say for sure is that I do feel old and cold. Heh. That rhymed."

"Well... I guess we'll just keep tabs on what you're feeling. If you start to get drained or whatever, we can stop. It wouldn't do to find out what you can do if we simply turn you into a poltergeist."

"I can agree with that. So what else do you want to 'experiment' with? I will not try eating brains. Despite being a zombie right now, I have no desire to try one."

Noah chuckled and waved it off. "That's not a necromancer zombie thing. That's only the ones that get sentient on their own."

I froze as I had started to turn back to the sidewalk in case a car did come by. "Wait. What? Zombies on their own is a real thing?"

"It's rare. I wouldn't worry about it. Anyway, feel like trying to help your mom and Trina out?"

"Oh, and I suppose help the order while I'm at it?" I stepped back onto the sidewalk.

He shrugged. "Right now, it's all the same thing. We want all the same things. I just thought maybe you'd like to try and see if we can make some progress. They were only given the assignment this morning, or yesterday, but it wouldn't hurt to see if we can help."

"Did the order put you up to this or is it cheating to help someone with the favor they owe the order?" I rubbed the stubble on my chin. It was weird to have stiff hairs on my face, but no weirder than the other new body parts I had.

"I don't know. Maybe." He shrugged his broad shoulders again. "I do know that it feels like the right thing to do, and we can see how much you can walk around inside a zombie. I mean, it's better than being a lonely ghost in a skatepark, right?"

"Yes, yes. We've been over this. Alright, let's go see Susan. That's what they're supposed to be working on, right? Learning about some dude from Susan for some reason."

"Yeah, I don't know the specifics as David didn't feel like pulling me into the loop, but that's not too strange as I'm simply an apprentice and don't get involved with all the order's stuff. Do you happen to remember where the ghost is that they need to talk to? And the name of the guy we need to ask this ghost about? Susan? Is that her name?"

"Yes and yes. I see your car. Let's get inside, and I'll tell you where to go. Will you still make me wear a seatbelt even though I'm already dead?" I said, finding that the more I joked about it, the more I could handle the absurdities of the situation.

"It might be best to take care of this body as long as we can... You know, just in case."

"Ugh, I guess."

We climbed into his vehicle, and I obediently buckled my seatbelt like a good little zombie.

"So where are we going?" Noah asked as he started the car and checked the mirrors.

"The underpass area where that homeless camp is. Do you know where I'm talking about? It's probably dangerous to go there during the day and worse during the night, but you look like you know how to handle yourself, and I'm dead, so what should I care? The hard part will be getting Susan to cooperate."

He nodded and pulled onto the road. "Yeah, we should be fine. So why is she being uncooperative? Did your family tell you more about that?"

"Yeah, so there was another Seer sent by your order, and the moment she told him what he wanted to know, he was murdered on his way to see you guys. We have no way of knowing why or how or what happened exactly, but it all seems too coincidental not to connect. You wouldn't happen to know anything about it, would you?"

Noah shook his head. "No idea, but I agree that it sounds odd. And so this ghost is worried about telling you the information the order is asking for in case something happens to the people she tells?"

"I guess? Honestly, just going off what appears to be her personality, I'd say she was being stubborn just to be stubborn."

"Maybe she would be more willing to give the info she knows if the person she tells is already dead and can't get hurt by whoever doesn't want the order to know it. Although, I'm struggling to figure out who wouldn't want the order to know the information."

"Seriously, you see the order, your family or, whatever you want to call them, through rose-colored glasses, as my Gran would say. They just can't do anything wrong, can they? Why is it so hard to imagine the order doesn't have enemies? The magic users and they are already at each other's necks. I'm surprised there hasn't been a battle yet, honestly."

Noah ran anxious fingers through his hair, making sure to keep the other hand on the wheel. "I'm not blind. I know we don't always do everything perfectly. I'm just pointing out that I'm not sure who would be trying to keep the info from us. As far as I know, things aren't that bad right now."

"Yes, because you know everything that's happening in the order," I said, my voice dripping with sarcasm, and I added an eye roll for good measure.

His shoulders slumped, but he kept focus on the road instead of getting mad like I'd expected. For some reason, the sight of his growing defeat finally made me feel a little bit bad for him. I was sure it was hard to find out that one's family, the people one trusts most, might not be the upstanding citizens they appeared to be.

"Look, I'm sorry. I'm not trying to be mean, though I know I'm not doing a good job at being nice, either, but I don't know how else to get you to understand the order may not be the group of people you think it is," I said, trying to put kindness into my soft voice.

"Yeah, it's fine." He waved it off, but we both knew it wasn't. "Let's focus on the task right now. We're going to look for the ghost named Susan, which I assume you'll still be able to see even while in a zombie body, right?"

I furrowed my eyebrows. "Actually, I'm not sure. I—" I cut myself off as I glanced out the window and saw a ghost shuffling down the sidewalk. "Nope. Scratch that. I can still see the ghosts."

"Okay, one more thing we've learned with our experiments. Sweet. So we find this ghost and ask her about someone? What was the name the necromancers gave you?"

"Uh... Oh, Theodore McCutcheon."

His whole body froze, and I got worried for a second that he'd forget to stop for the red light we were approaching.

"Uhm... Noah?"

Thankfully, some auto-pilot response kicked in as he slowed the car and took the chance to turn slowly and stare at me. "What did you say?"

"Theodore McCutcheon?" I was worried I'd gotten the name wrong or something, but I was pretty sure that was it.

Gritting his teeth, he turned back to look at the road. Both of his hands were on the steering wheel, squeezing onto it with white knuckles.

"What? Do you know him or something? If you know about this guy, then maybe we can skip talking to Susan altogether. I mean, it would be pretty ironic if the necroes have been looking for info on this dude for a while, but you just happen to know what they need to know, and they never bothered asking you about it because you're only an apprentice. Wouldn't that be funny?" I asked, finding myself rambling in hopes it would thaw whatever panicked ice he was turning into.

The light turned green, and he pushed the car onwards but didn't look back at me. The muscles in his jaw flexed tightly for a few seconds before he spoke. "That's not it. No. The order knows as much about this guy as I do, probably more, now that I think about it. Did they say why Susan would have info on him? Why this specific ghost?"

"I'm not one hundred percent sure on why her, but something else that's kinda funny is she's actually Brandon's mom. You know, my ghostly friend I hung out with a lot? That guy. This ghost is his mom. Isn't that so crazy that it's such a small world? I haven't gotten the chance to tell him or introduce them yet before Rose took me out, ugh, so frustrating, really. But seriously, isn't that wild?"

Noah didn't answer right away, the thoughts in his head a mystery but clearly working quite hard. "Yeah, you told me about that before. It is odd. Something like that seems like more than a coincidence."

"I guess. But no one could have known that Brandon and I would have ended up friends while his family is messed up in all this Rose crap. That part has got to be a coincidence."

"Could be. Do you know how Susan and McCutcheon are connected?"

"No idea. Sounds like you know who he is. So who is he? Maybe that will help us figure out how she knows him."

Noah sighed and ran his hands through his hair again, messing more than fixing. "Do you remember that guy I told you about who used his necromancer powers like Rose does? Eating souls to give him more power and youth?"

I frowned, feeling like my heartbeat should be picking up in alarm. "Yes?"

"That's him. Well, one of his aliases, at least. The last I'd heard was that he hadn't been around in years and was possibly dead. He's bad news, Hanna. Super bad."

"Well... I know that Susan was involved with a witch because she was angry at her ex, but I don't know how that would connect to the most evil terrible necromancer in history."

"She went to a witch, you say?"

I nodded and then when I realized he wasn't looking at me, I said, "Yes. Kieran, the vampire queen, told us that she had been keeping tabs on Rose for a long time. Mostly because Rose has a nasty habit of killing Seers, and Kieran wasn't too happy about it. So Kieran said Susan was one of Rose's patrons at one point, went to her for revenge on her ex, and Rose told her there was going to be this hefty price. But Susan didn't care. The worst part is that, according to Kieran and her super vampire spies, Rose didn't actually need to take anything to make the spell, but she had Susan's three children killed as an excuse for it and captured their souls."

Noah slowly looked at me long enough for a blink or two before turning back to the road. "That's a little intense. And I thought being the necromancer who had to date a zombie was bad."

"Yeah, well, I still haven't been able to tell Brandon about all of this. The worst part is that he was driving the car when Rose caused the accident and took his three younger siblings. He blamed himself for the whole thing and ended up killing himself."

"Wow... that's terrible."

I nodded and looked sadly out the window.

We were both sorrowfully quiet for several moments, long enough to arrive at the parking lot across from the homeless camp under the overpass. The clock on the car said it was nearly one in the morning, and under normal circumstances, I would have been terrified to approach a bunch of unpredictable homeless people whom I was probably going to anger by waking them.

I shivered in my old man body as I stepped out of the car. It didn't help that I was basically skin and bones without a jacket and that the winter wind was cutting through the air. It hadn't bothered me much at the skatepark, but after being inside the warm car, I guess my body had started feeling more.

Noah came around to the passenger side of the car and draped his rather large letterman's jacket over my shoulders. It would have been a sweet gesture if I weren't a hundred-year-old zombie.

I still smiled up at him. "Thank you."

"Just don't get your zombie cooties on it."

"As long as no one attacks me, I should be able to handle that."

Gravel and glass crunched under our shoes as we crossed the parking lot and then the road. The area was always busy during the day, and there were still cars passing by periodically even in the middle of the night.

There were a few fires glowing amongst the tent city, snapping at whatever wood inside giant metal barrels. A few people stood around them, warming their hands clad in holey gloves while staring listlessly into the flames or talking to each other in low tones. Outside the small circles of firelight, the rest of the place was in shadow with lumps of darkness where I assumed tents or piles of belongings lay.

Noah hunched deeper into his jean jacket and shuddered. "This place makes me sad."

"Me too."

"Do you see any ghosts?" he asked as we stood on the sidewalk, pausing before we entered the area.

"A few. Not the one I need though," I said, my eyes straining to see much into the darkness and past the smudged glasses. "Oh, there she is."

Noah looked in the direction where I was pointing but of course couldn't see anything. "Well, I've got your back. Let me know what you need help with."

"Probably best to look alert and make sure no one tries to rob me of my tacky t-shirt." I began walking toward Susan.

She was standing off to the side, staring at the concrete wall someone had decided to graffiti and label the area as their territory like tagging was a human way of peeing on stuff. But there was probably pee there, too.

I was glad she was off to the side with less chances of me disturbing someone who would want to beat me up.

"Susan?" I said quietly, trying not to spook the ghost. The number of times I'd been worried about scaring off a ghost was truly ironic.

Noah followed closely behind, keeping his eyes open and scanning the area. I didn't feel quite as secure as I would have had Gryphin been with me, but it was better than being alone. Even though I was dead, I still didn't want anything to happen to the old man's body, mostly because I wasn't sure where we'd get another one and Noah didn't seem to consider Andrea's body a usable possibility.

Susan didn't respond to my call, so I tried again. "Susan Matthews? It's me, that Seer from a few weeks ago? A while ago? I don't know. Time moves weirdly when you're a ghost, as you know, of course."

She slowly turned around to look at me, her eyebrows pinched in confusion. "What?"

"I know I look different than before, but this is just a body I'm borrowing for a minute. Rose had me murdered by enslaving my vampire friend, so my necromancer friend got me a body to possess because even though I'm technically a ghost, I've somehow gotten the powers to possess zombie bodies. I'd step out and show you so you could remember who I am, but I'm afraid if I do that, I'll get zapped back to my haunt."

Susan's eyes narrowed as I spoke, probably giving her way more information than her ghostly mind could keep up with. She glanced at Noah who stood closely behind my left shoulder and then back to me.

"You must be the girl they're trying to resurrect. Looks like you've got a body after all, and you don't need my help anymore. Plus, I don't associate with necromancers."

"Wait! No. *Please* help us!" I brought my wrinkled hands together in a pleading motion. "I'm already dead so whatever fear you have for someone dying for knowing the secret doesn't apply here. You can tell me. No one can hurt me anymore."

That gave her enough pause to keep from disappearing at least. "Why do you think I'd be afraid of you dying?"

"Oh, my mom and my sister came up here today and told me that's what they suspect is stopping you from telling us what you know. Is that right?" I asked, trying to seem non-threatening by hunching over and giving her a polite, tentative expression. "Someone you got close to was murdered after you told him the info the necroes are looking for, right?"

She frowned and glared at me some more. "Are you the girl that has powers to bring ghosts out of their haunts and who knows my son?"

I chewed on my lip and nodded. "Yes, we've become pretty good friends. Mostly at first it was because he was so excited just to have someone to talk to and that he could travel around with me as I went to school and stuff."

Her lip perked up on the side as if she might smile. "That kid was always very social." Then she sobered and her shoulders deflated into a slump. "He killed himself, you know."

I nodded. "I know. I'm sorry. That must have been difficult to deal with."

While it was true that I pretty much blamed her for the whole thing, I did feel bad and was still trying to earn her trust. It probably wasn't right to say any mother deserved to go through that kind of pain, and if any mom did deserve it, it was her, but still. However, that wasn't something any decent person would wish on another.

She looked down at our feet, not really seeing them I suspected. "I didn't deserve them. My kids. They were good kids, but I took them for granted."

"Do you want revenge?" I asked, a small plan blooming in my chest like a tiny rose.

"Revenge?" She tilted her head to the side like it wasn't something she had considered possible.

"If I get my body back, I can take down Rose. We actually already have a vampire queen who wants to do it for us. I can bring Brandon here to talk to you, and you can hash out whatever feelings you want to discuss, and even more than that, I can free your other three kids. I know where they are as well." Speaking those words gave me a feeling of power I hadn't felt in a long time, if ever.

I knew I was right. When I got my body back, I would fix it all, and that felt powerful and freeing. Hopefully, Susan could feel that too.

"You could do all that?"

"Sure. I mean, I was going to do all that anyway. I care about Brandon. I want him and his family to be happy. Plus, as a Seer, it's pretty much my job to help dead people. All you have to do is tell me what the necromancers want to know about Theodore McCutchen, and we'll be golden. After all this clears, I can even help you with your unfinished business if that's what you'd like."

She thought about it, looking around the underpass where she'd lived for several years, probably even before she died, pausing to stare at Noah who was cluelessly standing with his hands in his pockets and looking around, and then back to me. I gave her an encouraging smile in hopes that would help her make the decision I needed her to make.

"Okay. But only because you're already dead, and yeah, revenge sounds pretty nice too."

Chapter 13 - Trina

"We were hoping you could tell us more about the necroes and why they needed this specific information. If we have that, maybe we can convince Susan to help us." I took a sip of my drink.

Noah's mouth twisted into a teasing, sort of assessing half-pucker. "When I said that Hanna and I had a productive night, what I meant was we got the information the necroes, and you guys by extension, are looking for."

All three of us paused what we were doing and turned to stare at him.

"What?" Mom asked.

"Why didn't you start with that?" I asked, feeling a little like pulling out my hair.

"What did she say?" Gryphin's forest green eyes were wide with excitement, seemingly as invested in this project as we were.

Chuckling enough to make me want to slap him upside the head, Noah said, "We were able to convince Susan to help us by using an already dead person to get the information. Plus, we... Well, Hanna, offered her revenge for what happened to her family. It won't be any extra work since she was already planning on helping Brandon and his siblings and taking care of Rose. It all kind of worked out nicely."

"Except for the whole we haven't done it yet part. It may be way harder to do than for us to talk about, but we can worry about that later, I guess." I continued to fiddle with my straw wrapper. "So? What's this secret info the necroes are so desperate to get?"

"I'm afraid you'll have to ask Hanna about that. She wouldn't tell me. I could only hear Hanna's side of the conversation, as you may be familiar with." Noah nodded toward Mom and Gryphin.

They returned his nod with amused smiles and glances at me.

I stared flatly at all of them. "Well, you're no help at all. You should have just texted me to go talk to Hanna, and we could have skipped this whole event."

Of course, the server came by right then and dropped off our food. We acted like the happy group of friends we appeared to be, or whatever, and munched on our meals for a minute. I wasn't feeling too hungry, but the club sandwich I'd ordered was delicious with the perfect amount of tomato to meat to cheese to bread ratio.

Noah dabbed his face with a napkin before speaking again. "I would take this time to say that you guys called me to this meeting."

I sighed in exasperation and sat back into the booth. "We only did that so we could make more progress on this task."

"How was I supposed to know that? I thought maybe you were going to ask me out to the winter formal." Noah's grin made me want to slap him upside the head.

Mom held up her palms with a soft smile. "Let's take a breath. This is good news, isn't it? We need to get the info from Hanna and go to the order and let David know what she found out. Then we can start preparations on getting Hanna back into her body and put all of this behind us."

"I hate to be a downer here, but if Hanna wanted the necroes to know, wouldn't she have just told ol' boy here?" Gryphin shot a thumb in Noah's direction.

I had turned to him as he spoke and found that sitting so close to him in the booth while looking him in the eyes was kind of overwhelming. I looked away quickly. "He's got a point. Maybe this is something the necroes shouldn't know..."

I frowned as I trailed off, feeling deflated.

Noah glared at Gryphin. "Don't call me 'ol' boy'. I'm certainly younger than you."

"Yes, and that's something to be proud of." Gryphin's smile wasn't the usual kind one he used on me and Hanna.

"Woah, now." Mom again put her hands out across the table in a calming motion. "We're all on the same side. We all want the same things."

"We need to go talk to Hanna. We're wasting time here. Once we know what the info is, then we can decide what to do with it." I grabbed one last drink of my soda and prepared to stand up once Gryphin had slid out of the booth.

"Agreed, but we should at least pay for our meal." Mom looked at me with raised eyebrows before pulling out her purse.

I groaned and gave her a look.

"Listen, I know you guys are worried about the order's intentions. I know it looks...odd for the other Seer to have died after just learning this information, but I'd like to point out two things." Noah pushed his plate away enough for him to rest his elbows on the table and his chin onto the backs of his hands. "First, you can't bring Hanna back without us."

"We know that," I snipped, folding my arms across my chest.

"Second, the order isn't nearly as bad as you guys are thinking it is. I've been associated with them my whole life through my uncle and family. I've been around the meetings and activities. We're good people only wanting to help protect others from the bad things out there as well as create a safe place where we can practice our craft. Whatever this info is, no matter who it is about, David, the leader, would only use it for good things." He took a breath as if trying to also convince himself. "It isn't worth keeping it a secret at Hanna's expense."

"Yeah, yeah. Let's pay the check and get out of here." I knew we had no choice but to use their help, but that didn't mean I wanted to admit it to Noah. Something about him made me itchy.

Later, after Noah had parted with a cheerful wave, a comment to keep him updated, and an offer to let him know if we needed more of his help, Mom, Gryphin, and I talked in the van as we headed back to the skatepark.

"Can we at least give him credit for helping us when we were so stuck with Susan?" Mom glanced at me from where she sat in the front passenger seat.

I sighed and rolled my eyes. "Sure. He can get credit for that, though it seems like Hanna did most of the work."

"He had to get the body from somewhere." Gryphin shrugged as his eyes met mine in the rearview mirror for a second.

"Yeah, woohoo. Let's get him a cake."

It began to rain as we parked on the side of the road. "Awesome. You wouldn't happen to have a few umbrellas in here, would you, Gryph?"

"Not that I know of," he said with a sympathetic side smile.

"Oh well. Hopefully you don't smell like a wet dog."

He chuckled, thankfully taking the joke as how I'd meant it and not something mean. Maybe not having Hanna around to make those kinds of quips had made me try to step in and fill in the role. Or maybe I was feeling angry, frustrated, and backed into a corner.

As I stepped out of the van and felt the first sprinkles of rain on my hair, I took a calming breath. Me being grumpy wasn't going to help us with any of it.

I could do this.

Mom looped her arm in with mine as if knowing that I needed some extra support. She patted my hand as we walked into the park. "It'll be okay, honey. We'll figure it out."

"Then why do I feel like we've made a deal with the devil? There's nothing concrete I can put my finger on. It's the vibes."

Gryphin walked behind us as we headed towards the tables at the back of the park. There wasn't a soul there so far, alive or dead, and we had the place to ourselves.

"I know. Right now, let's focus on what we can do and get it down to one task at a time, okay?" Mom gave me another pat on my hand.

"Okay, *Dad*." I gave her a teasing smile, so she knew I wasn't trying to be mean.

She shook her head and smiled. "Your father isn't perfect, as no man is, but there's still plenty of good things about him."

"I'm sure his next girlfriend will worship the ground he walks on," I mumbled as I pulled away from her to sit on the bench with my back to the table and my eyes scanning the park.

Mom tsked at me with her tongue and shook her head again. "Behave, Trina."

"So? Can you see her yet?" Gryphin sat next to me.

We were at least two inches apart, but I could still feel the warmth radiating from his arms.

"No." I frowned and kept looking around. "I really hope she's not resting after having such a crazy night. That would be just our luck. Hanna finally gets the answers we need but is in ghost limbo so she can't tell us."

"I was hoping y'all would come back here," a deep voice said from behind us.

My heart did three twirls and a roundoff before I could spin around to confirm it was who I knew it was.

"Caleb?" I asked, eyes wide.

He stood on the other side of the table wearing a dark suit Rose had probably forced him to put on. Usually, he preferred to dress more casually. Or maybe that was only the version of him I knew, the one who was trying to fit in with the high school kids. He'd been around for three hundred years. There would never be enough time for me to know everything about him even if we spent the rest of my life together.

"What are you doing here?" Gryphin stood and stared at the vampire who seemed to be completely immune to the rain.

Mom gasped and grabbed my arm as if she was going to be able to protect me for some reason.

Caleb didn't even glance at Gryphin as he stood with one hand on his hip while the other rested at his side. "Imagine my surprise when after I got rid of one troublesome Seer, I quickly learned her sister is one, too. It's bad luck for you guys that this is the vampire I've chosen for my new pet. He knew all about you and your family. Speaking of, what are the odds of two Seers in one family in one generation? It's unheard of, and I should know. I've studied Seers for a long, long time."

I was sure the vampire could hear the erratic beating of my heart. It was honestly so loud that my mom probably could hear it, but I wasn't sure if it was pounding throughout my body because I was terrified or thrilled to see him. It was as if the very sight of him made my stomach clench and my heart ache, which was stupid, of course, but my body wouldn't listen to my brain.

Then again, not every part of my brain agreed. It was stupid how much I had liked him, still liked him, despite what he had done. Or at least what his body had done while under the control of Rose.

"What do you want, Rose?" I asked, also standing and glaring. "We've been expecting you to send your goon again. Honestly, I'm surprised you've stopped to chat before murdering us all. That's not usually your style."

Caleb rolled his dark eyes and groaned. "Great. I can see you're just as pleasant to talk to as your sister. Listen, if I wanted you dead, you'd all be dead. Werewolf or no."

Gryphin's hands balled into fists as his stance shifted. "I dare you to try it."

Mom slowly stood and placed herself between me and the table, thus Caleb as well. "There's no reason to get violent. We can talk as calm, relaxed adults. We recognize your strength. Please tell us why you're here so we can all go on our way."

Caleb smiled unlike any smile I'd ever seen of his. When he was himself, he frequently used a predatory grin that showed off his teeth, not quite as pointed as when he needed to feed, but this smile was missing the teasing gleam in his eyes. It was all lethal monster.

"I appreciate the credit. I don't kill *every* Seer I run into. Only the ones who deserve it or have proven that they're not going to be cooperative." Caleb shrugged one big shoulder and flipped his hand over his neck like he was pushing back invisible, luscious curls. "Can I be honest for a moment, though? It's usually because I lose my temper, but I've had time to calm down. You have nothing to fear from me as long as you stop trying to help the necroes. They're trying to get the secrets to my magic, you know. Neither of us want that."

I narrowed my eyes, trying to understand. "Why not?"

"Oh, I'm surprised you have to ask. Do you think eating souls is a good thing to do?" Caleb's eyebrows pinched upwards as his lips perked into a feminine-looking pout.

I was both disturbed and amused by watching my heavily-muscled friend display such girly mannerisms. It also hurt my heart to see him right in front of me but seem so far away. He wasn't the guy I'd grown such strong feelings for. He was lost somewhere inside himself and hopefully there would be a way to get him out.

"Of course we don't, but I'm surprised that you care. Wait... How is us helping the necroes with information from this ghost helping them to start eating souls? Why do I feel like you know more about what we're doing than we do?"

"We can't trust her," Mom said quietly.

"I know, but we can at least hear her out. It seems like she's telling us more than the necroes did about what we're really doing for them."

I wished I could talk to my mom telepathically so we didn't have to say this stuff right in front of Rose.

As for Rose/Caleb, he merely smiled condescendingly as we spoke. "She's right." Rose looked at my mom and then back to me. "I've come here to tell you not to give the necromancers the information they want. I know what you need, and I'm willing to help. I can put Hanna back into her body just as well as they can. Stop working for them, and I'll help you with your little problem."

"Yeah, a problem *you* caused!" I pulled my eyebrows together in anger and shook my head. "I can't believe I'm even hearing this. Can you believe it?"

I turned to my mom who was staring wide-eyed at Caleb.

"The trickery in this one is thick," Gryphin said as if quoting some kind of wolf saying he'd heard growing up.

Caleb laughed, but it sounded more high-pitched than usual. "Believe me, working with me and my coven is much better than dealing with those necroes. Think about the concerns you already have working with them. How do you know they can be trusted? How do you know what you are doing for them is the right thing to do?"

I gritted my teeth and spoke tightly. "You're the one who killed my sister. You snapped her neck with those very hands. You've taken control of one of my best friends, and I know you've manipulated Hanna into doing things for you she never would have done otherwise. Plus, you eat those poor ghost souls. None of these things I can stand for."

As I spoke, I took slow steps around the table until I was at the end of the side, closer to Caleb than I should have ever gotten, but with his super-fast vampire speed, I doubted a table between us would offer much protection. Like he said, if he wanted to kill us, he would have already.

Caleb waved his hand into the air nonchalantly. "Fine. Suit yourself. There are other things I can do to stop you and them. Oh, and Gryphin, sweetie, I can't help but admitting some triumph here. You might want to run home soon. I have a feeling your daddy is going to need your help."

"What? What are you—" I started to say, but he was already gone.

Gryphin's face was pale as rainwater dripped off the end of his forehead curl. "What did she say?"

Mom held her hands up to calm him. "Remember we can't trust her. It could be a trick into distressing you."

He glanced at my mom and then whipped out his phone. I knew from experience with trying to track Hanna's phone that there wasn't much service out at the werewolf territory, but there must have been a landline or a certain provider that worked out there because Gryph tried to call someone.

After a few tense moments, he looked back at me and put his phone down. "No one is answering. I should go check it out."

"We're coming with you." I stepped back around the table.

"We are?" Mom asked with wide eyes.

"Well, you don't have to come. In fact, it would be safer for us to drop you off at home, but I'm coming. They may need my help as a Seer since I know all of this started with the alpha's mate's death. Right, Gryphin? Hanna was working with you guys on that?"

Fear and indecision battled across Gryphin's face as he looked at me. "Yes, she was helping, but then... We found out that Rose's previous goon was the one that killed Sarah and then she showed up again and trapped her spirit. Hanna was able to free her, and while things with the pack haven't been completely settled, I had hoped…"

I pressed my lips together angrily and shook my head. "She did this. She did this whole thing but why? What's the point in all of this work and set-up?"

Gryphin shrugged his shoulders helplessly. "I don't know, but I do need to check it out. Come with me if you want but understand you could get hurt. If there's a werewolf battle or something going on, I'm not sure I can guarantee your protection. Normally, I wouldn't even consider letting you come along, but you're right. It might be solved by helping my dad get out of whatever ghost reality he's living in by finally solving Sarah's issues."

He turned to my mom and grabbed her hand. "Please stay home. I know that leaving your daughter to do this alone must feel difficult, but I can assure you that it would be much easier for me to protect her if I wasn't worried about you as well."

Her hand was shaking as she frowned and looked at me. "Go fix this. Help the wolves and stop whatever insane plan Rose is trying to pull together. We can't let her win anymore."

Chapter 14 - Hanna

So it turns out that possessing a zombie and walking around in its body for a few hours takes a harsh toll. I couldn't feel the energy drain at the time, but when we finally got back to the haunt, and I released the body, I slept for a long while.

Or whatever it was called that ghosts did to gather back their energy.

It felt like sleeping but deeper. As if I was simply not...there. Maybe that was what crossing over would be like.

Chapter 15 - Trina

After dropping Mom off at home and giving her a tearful good-bye where I reassured her over and over that everything was going to be fine, Gryphin drove the van out of town, going much faster than I was comfortable with. I understood his rush, but that didn't mean I had to enjoy it.

"What do you think we'll be getting into? What's been going on back at home? I feel bad for not asking you more about it during all this time we've spent together. I'm not usually this selfish and self-centered as a friend, I promise."

Gryphin kept his eyes focused on the road as he pushed the van as fast as he dared while still being able to take the turns. "Honestly, I've been trying to keep out of it. It was stupid of me to put my head in the mud and take a blind eye to everything, but I guess I figured it would sort itself out in time."

I awkwardly patted his leg, trying to appear sympathetic and not scared for my life as he careened down the gravel road. "We all have our coping mechanisms."

"Maybe if I had been there more for him, he wouldn't have lost so much of his hold on the pack. I'm worried that the third-in-line will call a challenge to my dad's power. If that happens, someone will die, and I'm afraid my dad isn't as strong as he used to be."

I frowned, considering his words and wondering how I could use my skills to help. Talking to the ghostly mate didn't seem like it would be super helpful, but I was certainly in no position to do any fighting, and I was pretty sure I didn't have the proper negotiating skills to deescalate such a situation.

Maybe the ghost would have an idea of how to help.

Gravel and dust flew behind us as we bounced up the road to the werewolf commune. I'd never been there before myself but had heard plenty about it from Hanna. Usually, I was fascinated by her stories and wondered how daily life worked in such a place, but, as we pulled up to the area, I only felt dread and anxiety.

"It occurs to me that this is a place where vampires aren't welcome. I wonder if it would have been safer for me and my mom to hide out here...but then we wouldn't have been able to find Hanna or do the tasks the necromancers want done," I said the last part in answer to the first part of my half-formed question.

"Not only that, but it's definitely not a safe place to be, especially now." He gave me a glance before he pulled into the lot where other cars were parked. "I shouldn't have brought you here. Please don't get hurt."

"I'll try my best." I forced a small smile and pretended I was braver than I felt.

"I wouldn't have brought you here if I didn't think you'd be helpful. I'll try my best to watch out for you, but as I have no idea what we are going into, I'm worried about being able to keep my promise."

"It's okay. I promise if I die, I won't haunt you."

"Funny." He gave me a side-eye and shut off the van.

We hopped out into the cool evening air, and I was happy to see that the rain had stopped, even if my clothes were still damp and starting to chafe in places I was going to have to air out later.

Glancing around, I could appreciate the freedom of the place. Trees surrounded the small village and, while they were spindly and naked in preparation for snow, I could imagine how beautiful they'd be at other times of the year.

The beauty was only slightly marred by the yelling coming from somewhere nearby. I couldn't make out the words, but it was clear several people were angry.

Gryphin and I exchanged looks of concern.

"What do you want to do? I'm sure you could get there faster without having to worry about me, but I don't want to get lost and to help if I can." I felt my heart pick up pace in anticipation of whatever we were going to run into.

More shouting sounded, drawing Gryphin's eyes toward the village area where the buildings were set up. "Okay, stay behind me. If I tell you to run, run. Don't look. Don't hesitate. Just run. Head to the van. I'll keep it unlocked in case you need to use it for shelter. It won't stop a wolf, but maybe it'll slow them down enough until I can get there to help you."

I nodded, considering that maybe I shouldn't have come and let them fight this thing out for themselves.

Too late now.

Gryphin grabbed my hand and pulled me into a quick jog. I knew he wasn't going at his full speed, trying to stay back for me, but I was grateful for it since I wasn't in the best of running shape.

We didn't worry about being quiet as the clamor of voices and shouting was so loud, it covered any of our footsteps or heavy breathing. As we weaved closer toward the middle of the village, I saw glimpses of a huge bonfire roaring and several shadows around it. The shouting got more distinct, but I still had no idea what was going on.

When we finally arrived inside the clearing, Gryphin grabbed my shoulders and steered me toward a tree. "Hide here until you feel like you can see a ghost that will help us out. How are you at climbing trees?"

"Uhm, passable, I guess?"

"Okay. Do that if you feel threatened and can't make it to the van, alright?"

I nodded, my eyes wide and staring at the ring of werewolves gathered around a roaring fire.

Gryphin gave me a solid nod in return with a quick squeeze of my shoulders before he whirled around and jogged toward the group.

The sun was sinking behind the already dark clouds in the sky, making everything dimmer quicker. Light from the fire was helpful in revealing what was around it, but it was also blinding in a way that made more shadows. From partially hiding behind the tree, I could see several people yelling at each other. Most of them were in human form, but there was at least one wolf in the middle.

Hanna had been right—werewolves were giant. Even on four feet, the wolf in the middle was taller than the upright humans.

"Yes! This has lasted long enough!" a woman shouted from the crowd as the wolf prowled back and forth inside the circle, sometimes blocking the burning firelight from my face for a second.

"It's time someone else stepped in!" another person shouted.

There was a pause, and I got the distinct feeling I was missing parts of the conversation. Hanna had told me something about wolves being able to communicate with each other while in wolf form, and I began to suspect that's what was happening. The large wolf in the middle was holding some kind of rally, working up the members of the pack to support them into action.

And my stomach sank with fear as I had an idea about the action they were going to take.

"Hold on!" a man spoke up, pulling away from the main group of people. He had dark hair, a rounded face, and narrow eyes.

He must have had a higher rank in the pack, because most of the others turned to look at him as he entered the circle. Or at least that's the best I could guess from my limited knowledge of werewolves and how they worked.

"Sarah is gone. We've all felt the pain of her absence, most of all Bertram," the man said, speaking loudly and looking forcefully into each person's eyes.

Some in the crowd snarled and grumbled at the mention of the alpha's name.

"But," the man said loudly and paused until everyone was quiet again.

The wolf inside the circle continued to prowl around, and the man was brave or stupid enough to put his back to the animal.

"But that is no reason to disrupt the order of the pack!" He yelled the last few words in emphasis.

Several spoke up at once, but I could only pick out a few statements.

"You only say this because you're afraid you'll be next!"

"Bertram isn't strong enough to protect us from other packs any-more!"

"We need someone we can depend on!"

"Gordon should lead us!"

The wolf's eyes reflected the firelight and sent frightened shivers down my shoulders and back.

"Wait! Let's all calm down." Gryphin emerged from the crowd and stood beside the first man.

More jeering and grumbles met his words.

"Ah, the whelp!"

"About time you decided to show up. Afraid we'll take you down with your inept father?"

"Of course you don't want change. You like being the alpha's son!"

Pain and fear made my heart pound wildly as I watched behind the tree. Gryphin was such a sweet kid who seemed so chill and polite that everyone should like him. Considering he was willing to risk his life to help me and my mom when he barely knew us told me a lot about his character and kind heart. Why would they be so mean to him?

The wolf tipped his head back and howled into the dark, grey sky. Several of the humans howled with him, making the hairs on my arms stand up.

Then, much to my horror, several people started chucking off shirts and shoes, hunched over or dropped to their knees, and began what I could only assume was the change from a human to a werewolf.

"No! Wait!" Gryphin stretched his arms out to either side as if he could prevent the others from going wolf.

The first man looked worried and placed a hand on Gryphin's shoulder. I couldn't hear what he said to him over the sounds of bones crunching, human howls of pain evolving into animal snarls mid-way through, and continued shouts from others.

Gryphin sent a worried look in my direction. I didn't know if he could see me in the darkness from so far away, but I gave him a shaky thumbs-up to know I was safe just in case.

The large wolf near the fire howled again. More howls answered him, coming from those half-changed, but also from somewhere else.

If I thought I'd been scared before, it was nothing compared to the chills I got from the sounds coming from the woods. The answering howls were eerie, echoey, and while they were loud, they sounded like they were very far away.

From another dimension, even.

Several in the circle paused and looked alertly toward the woods, almost if they were scared of what was coming, and if *they* were scared, I certainly should be.

Then another howl rang out across the clearing that was deeper, less ethereal, and seemed to make the very trees around us groan.

Chaos, well, slightly more than was already going on, erupted around the fire. The man and Gryphin disappeared into the crowd. The wolves who were changing seemed to speed up their transformation, and the large wolf in the center took a few steps past the fire and away from the woods. His ears were flat against his skull, giving me a feeling about who was approaching.

The ghosts arrived first, spilling into the clearing on giant, silent paws. It appeared that I wasn't the only person that could hear their creepy howls, or at the very least, sense their presence. Several of those in the crowd growled or danced nervously on their feet, feeling something had changed.

Then the alpha, I assumed, broke through the trees behind the lodge and loped into the clearing. I was surprised to see the wolf was slightly smaller than the one already by the fire, although both were bigger than a family-sized van. Apparently, size wasn't all that mattered for a wolf to become an alpha.

But I had a feeling we were about to see how much size would matter.

The ghost wolves prowled around the circle, some snarling slightly. Most of the humans had made the change into wolf form, and there were so many big shadows roaming around, that I rarely saw the fire anymore. None of them were as tall as the alpha or the challenger wolf, I assumed his name was Gordon judging from one of the shouts someone had made.

The alpha—I didn't know what Gryphin's dad's name was, but again inferring from the comments of the others, I guessed it was Bertram, stepped toward Gordon, a deep growl coming from his chest.

Then a ghostly wolf separated themselves from the pack and started walking toward me. As they walked, the blue-hued wolf turned into a slim woman, her hair cut short to her chin, and a small smile on her heart-shaped face.

"Can you see me?" she asked, her voice barely audible.

I nodded, glancing around to make sure no one else was giving me any attention. Everyone seemed to be focused on the two wolves staring at each other, having what was probably another conversation I couldn't hear.

"I thought I could feel your powers from behind that tree. They feel similar to another girl I know, but you aren't her, are you?" The woman talked as she approached. She was stark naked after changing out of her wolf form but didn't seem concerned about it in the least, so I tried not to worry about it either.

"No, that would be my sister. I'm Trina. She's told me some stories, so I'm going to guess that you are Sarah?"

She nodded with that soft smile and stopped a few feet away from me. "Yes. It seems that whatever potion they gave me has allowed me to change now from wolf to human. It took me a little while to figure out how to do it since it's completely different from doing it in physical form, but I eventually got it."

"That's pretty cool. Are any of the other ghost wolves able to do that?"

She shook her head. "Just the ones who have been fed a potion that was in a girl's pocket when she died and became a ghost."

I chuckled awkwardly and glanced back at the crowd of wolves, most of them all animals now. I didn't know which one was Gryphin, or if he was even mixed in with them, but I knew enough about him that there was no way he would abandon me. "What's happening?"

Sarah turned slightly to watch the pack situation while still talking to me. "The third is challenging the alpha for leadership. I'm afraid this has been a long time coming. No matter what happens, this isn't going to end well, and it's pretty much all my fault. If I hadn't gone to that witch—"

"Wait, I'm going to stop you right there. Hanna told me what happened, and since then, there have been even more developments. Rose came to visit me herself—oh, after killing my sister, Hanna, I should let you know."

"What? Hanna's dead? How terrible!" Sarah placed a hand over her heart with sad eyes.

"Well, she's a ghost, and we're going to put her back together, so it'll be okay. But Rose warned Gryphin about what was happening here tonight. She's behind this whole thing. She killed you on purpose so that this would happen. I'm willing to bet that this third guy challenging the alpha is working for Rose or is at least on her team. Whatever happens, the pack does not want him as a leader." I tried to speak quickly as I put the puzzle pieces together so we could figure out what to do before the fight broke out.

The wolves had started growling louder, and most of them were taking on aggressive stances. The two in the middle stood out starkly next to the roaring fire as the others backed up, widening the circle. Whatever conversation or argument or discussion the pack was having, the tensions were rising.

"Pack rules dictate that if a challenge is issued, no one can interfere. The alpha and the challenger fight until one of them is dead. If it's the alpha, well, then, we have a new one until he can be challenged," Sarah said, her eyes on the wolves.

"We can't let that happen! Please, help me figure out how to stop this!" I tried not to shout but fear and panic made my words louder than I wanted.

Sarah glanced between me and the huge wolves, her eyes wide and sad. "I'm not sure there is anything we *can* do."

"Dang it." I gasped for breath as I watched the two wolves charge, dodge, snap, snarl, and attempt to rip each other's throats out. "I guess we'll have to figure out how to make sure the right one wins. If he could see you here, maybe that would give him more motivation to win. Maybe he'd be able to pull back on the strength he used to have."

Sarah moved to stand next to me, her arms folded across her chest as if holding herself together. "I don't know if that would help, but it's something to try, at least. Do you happen to have those glasses Hanna let Gryphin use to talk to me in the meadow?"

I frowned, vaguely remembering Hanna had said something about glasses at one point. "Wait, the glasses. What did they do?"

The bigger wolf, Gordon, slashed out at Bertram too fast for him to dodge and drew first blood. Several of the pack members howled their approval while a few flattened their ears and whined.

"They allowed him to see and talk to me just like a Seer would. Do you know what happened to them?"

"I think Hanna said Rose stole them away...but maybe we could use something else," I said, the wheels turning inside my head. Hanna had been able to do so many extra things as a Seer, and I couldn't do what she could, but maybe we'd get lucky, and I could do something else.

I looked around in the darkness, waiting for an idea to strike me. Meanwhile, Bertram feigned to the left and then jumped to the right where he got a good hold on Gordon's neck. Gordon shook his body but didn't dislodge the other's hold. He turned into a roll, using his longer reach to snap at Bertram's belly, causing the other wolf to let go and spring back.

There was the tree bark, crumbling leaves, a cabin about ten feet behind me, the shoes I had on my feet, my pants, my jacket, and then my eyes landed on a gold bracelet Dad had given me last year for my birthday. I didn't wear it a lot because I didn't want to risk losing it or tarnishing it, but for some reason when I'd gotten up that morning, I'd wanted to put it on, hoping for a bit of luck.

I slipped off the bracelet and brought it closer to my face in the dark. There were small crystals inset into the metal that were probably not real diamonds, but it was still precious to me. As much as I didn't want to give it away, I was desperate to see if I could do something special. Oh, and help the werewolves if I could. Guess that would be good, too.

As I pondered how one would go about making an item imbued with ghostly powers, Gordon seemed to gain the upper hand, giving me less time to figure out how I was supposed to help. Bertram jumped on Gordon, but the bigger wolf used his hind feet to slash and push the alpha away. Blood sprayed into the air and gleamed on his claws in the firelight.

Sarah gasped and put a hand over her mouth.

If I was going to do anything, it needed to be now or never.

Closing my eyes, I focused on the bracelet. I thought about the curves and how it sparkled in the sunlight. I imagined someone putting on the bracelet, and their ghostly body turning into a full human one. I pushed on the metal, mentally shoving energy and power into it from the deepest part of my spirit.

Snarling roars rang out through the clearing as I opened my eyes and handed the bracelet to Sarah. "Put this on and go save your man."

Her eyebrows furrowed as she looked at my bracelet and back to me. "What are you doing?"

"Just trying something. Please go along with my insanity with confidence and maybe we'll get lucky."

She shrugged, put her fingers out and somehow made contact with the bracelet. Both of our eyes widened as her fingers started to fade into a peachy hue.

"It's working," she said, looking up at me.

"Of course it is. Now go help him!" I gestured to the alpha who was currently struggling underneath the larger wolf.

Nodding, Sarah slipped the bracelet onto her wrist and ran toward the firelight. With each step she took, her body grew more solid and material. My heart lifted higher in my chest.

Maybe I was worth something after all.

"Stop!" Sarah screamed as she pushed her way through the wolves. Each one she passed froze at the sight of her until nearly the whole clearing was quiet except for Gordon's growls as he prepared to rip out the alpha's throat.

The ghost wolves also gave her all their attention, stilling their pacing and anxious movements.

"Let him go, Gordon!" Sarah's voice rang out and bounced off the towering lodge nearby.

Slowly, the bigger wolf turned to look at her. She seemed so small compared to his hulking form and even smaller when Gordon regarded her with his bloody mouth hanging slightly open.

As for Bertram, he lay panting in the dirt, his massive rib cage moving in and out as he stared up into the dark sky. But his ears were tilted toward Sarah as if considering if he'd really heard what he'd heard.

"Shame on you for taking advantage of Bertram right now! He's grieving and not quite himself. In fact, the whole pack is grieving." Sarah gestured to the wolves around them.

Bertram snarled and snapped up at Gordon while he was distracted, causing the bigger wolf to hop off and away from him. The alpha struggled to stand up, clearly wounded as blood pooled onto the dirt beneath his heaving stomach.

However the wolves communicated with each other in animal form must have also worked for her in human form or ghost-human form. I had created her, but that didn't mean I knew what she was.

Or how long it would last.

"Yes, I understand he's been distracted, and the pack needs a strong leader. I get that. I've been here the whole time, remember? Oh, right now I'm using the powers of a Seer Gryphin brought to help us. You all owe them a thank you."

Several wolves turned to look at another rather large animal with grey fur that must have been Gryphin. He stood tall and proud and nodded gratefully in the direction I was still unsuccessfully hiding in.

"Ancient tradition? I'd say coming back here after I'm dead and wearing a physical form so I can talk with you all is also breaking ancient tradition. Gordon, I'm calling you out in front of everyone. Even if you nearly beat Bertram, you are not fit to be the alpha. Tell them all who you are working with. Tell them how you've managed to become bespelled into a stronger and more powerful wolf. I can feel her sticky, dark magic on you."

The pack turned to look at Gordon, some with confused tilts to their heads while others lowered their stances and growled deeply in their throats.

Gordon snarled at Sarah and lunged at her with snapping jaws, but where he had been expecting a weak and fragile human body, he met an auburn wolf who had been able to instantaneously change forms.

She met his charge with a swift slap of her paw. While she wasn't as big as the alpha or Gordon, she was faster and fresher to fight, without having any injuries.

Gordon's head whipped to the side with her slap. Too bad the encounter only seemed to make him angrier instead of hurt. Drool and blood dripped out of his mouth as he turned his focus back on the female.

I didn't know all the rules of the pack, but I suspected he'd broken one or at least come close to breaking one because the pack reacted differently than they had before. Instead of backing up and letting the two fight, they grew angry, growling more, hunching down into their legs, and prowled closer toward Gordon.

My ignorant guess was that he'd struck someone he wasn't supposed to. It could have been because she was a female or maybe because she was already dead. The whole thing was absurd, but my guess was it was because they'd already been in a duel between two that wasn't finished. By attacking another person, he'd probably broke some kind of alpha battle rule and messed up the ritual.

Maybe. All I could do was guess.

What was clear is that the pack had turned on Gordon. Even the wolves who had been supporting him a moment before closed in on him. Bertram was at the lead, limping but still menacing, while Sarah moved to stand loyally by his side.

Gordon's eyes darted around him, taking in the odds, assessing what was about to happen, and then focused again clearly on Sarah. He probably said something mean and disrespectful because nearly the whole pack snarled as one and attacked.

I turned away, hiding my face behind the tree. I may have shielded my eyes from the glimpses of violence, but the sounds painted a picture clear enough. Snarls, howls, bones snapping, ripping of other parts I didn't want to know about, and other disgusting noises had me slinking down to my knees and curling up into a ball with my back to the tree and the brutal scene behind it.

Chapter 16 - Hanna

I don't know what time it was when I finally awoke, and I certainly didn't know what day it was. For some reason in ghost science, I appeared in the middle of the skatepark, standing on the concrete in the heart of where all the skaters zigged and zagged, swooped and slid. Thankfully there was no one there at the moment. Not that it would have hurt me had several people skated around and through me.

Bright sunlight peeked through the gaps in the clouds in the east, telling me it was morning at least. The clouds were heavy but breaking up as they turned pink and orange with the sunrise. Rainwater dripped off the tops of the trees, the sides of the tables, and had changed the concrete into a darker grey than usual.

A fresh breeze blew through the park, and I tried inhaling it as it came by. Of course, I couldn't feel the cleansing air in my lungs or even feel it dance on my skin, but the trees and grass seemed to enjoy it so I pretended I could, too.

Aimlessly, I walked up the ramp and left the concrete part of the park and headed toward my usual table. As I waved at my lone dandelion friend in the grass, a few memories flitted through my empty ghostly skull.

Noah. The old man zombie. Talking with Susan. The information I'd needed before death that I was finally able to get out of her but had no one alive to tell it to.

I furrowed my eyebrows, trying to focus more on the memories, recalling details and feelings I had during the encounter. The funny thing about being a ghost was that feelings were distorted.

Sometimes a ghost could only focus on one or two feelings they had while alive and that basically became their whole personality, especially if they'd become a poltergeist. Other times, the feelings kind of faded away, making the soul feel as empty as the blue-hued spirit body.

It was more of the latter for me, which I suppose was a good sign I wasn't turning into a 'geist any time soon. But it became quite a shock when I entered a zombie body, and the feelings and memories came back with the possession of a physical form.

Don't ask me how the whole thing worked. Again...ghost science was weird.

Some time later after watching the dark clouds break up and shift away to some other place, I heard a sound and looked back down to the ground. Two people were walking toward me, and I was disappointed to note it took me several seconds to recognize them.

"Trina! Gryphin!" I hopped off the bench as they made their way to the tables.

Trina looked up with a relieved smile, but there were dark bags under her eyes and her usually nicely done hair was a bit frazzled. "Oh thank goodness." She turned to Gryphin who had a wild glint in his eyes and whose hair was more frazzled than hers. "She's here."

"Good." He nodded and shared in the relieved smile.

"You guys are acting weird. How long have I been gone?"

"Only a day or two." Trina's smile morphed into a tighter one. "It's been an eventful few days. Noah told us that you guys got the information from Susan but that you wouldn't tell him what it was, so we had to hear it from you. Then we came to the park yesterday, and you weren't here, but then someone else was."

Trina and Gryphin shared another look, this one was wide-eyed and scandalized.

"What? Who else was here?" I asked, looking back and forth between them.

"Caleb! Well, Rose as Caleb. But yeah."

It was my turn to have wide eyes. "What! Did he hurt you guys or try? You look still alive right now, but did he?"

"No. I'm sure he could have if she had wanted him to. Gryphin was with us, so we had some kind of security, but it was dark and raining, so there wasn't anyone else here. If she wanted us dead, she would have killed us. Instead, she almost seemed sorry for what she had done to you. It was weird. Anyway, then she said something about a situation with the werewolves. We rushed over there, and there was a huge werewolf fight for the right to rule the pack."

She was talking so fast, I had a hard time keeping up with all the new information she was spouting.

"So this guy was named Gordon, right?"

Trina looked to Gryphin for confirmation to which he nodded, a small smile playing on his lips probably related to how eagerly she was pouring out the story.

"Right. Gordon challenged Gryphin's dad for the role of alpha and then the whole pack turned into giant wolves! When you told me that the werewolves were huge, I had no idea how big you meant! I mean, truly gigantic."

I grinned at her. "Yes, wait until you get to ride one around in the forest. That's pretty fun."

"Wow! I bet it would be! You'll have to give me a ride sometime, Gryphin," she said as an aside and then kept rattling on the rest of the story. "So then the two *huge* wolves started fighting, but then Sarah, the ghost wolf who you were trying to help a few weeks ago, remember her?"

I nodded, finding that as she spoke of her, I could remember.

"Well, she came over, and I just knew we had to do something to stop the fight, mostly because Rose had insinuated that Gordon was working for her in some way and that she was trying to get control of the pack. Can you believe she killed Sarah and started that whole thing to get the pack in her pocket? She's insane!"

I frowned, my mind starting to reel with everything. "Wait. How do you know that?"

"She told us that she had done something to the pack and wanted to show off her triumph, and we already know that she was the one who ordered Onyx to kill Sarah. That must have been the start of her evil plan with the wolves!"

Gryphin's eyes weren't focused on me directly as he could only base my location from where Trina was looking, but he nodded. "She seemed pretty proud of herself. I have a feeling she's one of those bad guys who likes to explain how devious and clever they are so it can be appreciated."

"Ugh, those are the worst," I said with a smile even though he couldn't hear me.

"I know, right?" Trina said, shaking her head. "So Sarah and I knew we had to stop them from fighting, and she mentioned those glasses, remember the glasses?"

I thought for a second and found that I did, but again only after she had talked about them.

"So I got to thinking about them, and it's been weighing on me a lot about not being able to do anything special as a Seer like you can. I mean, you have so many cool and extra powers, I was feeling a bit jealous and dejected that I didn't seem to be able to do anything extra. I didn't want to talk about it, because I was ashamed of the feelings, but there it is."

"I'm sorry. I didn't mean to make you feel that way." I wished I could pull her into a hug.

"You shouldn't feel jealous. It's amazing to be a Seer in of itself. Most of them didn't have extra powers like Hanna, as far as I know." Gryphin pulled his eyebrows together as he looked at Trina.

She waved off our comments. "I know. I know. I didn't mean to have those feelings, and I know logically I shouldn't have had them, but I did. I even talked to Frank about them, and he was trying to give me ideas of what I could do to figure out what my gifts were."

"Frank?" I said, trying to recall someone she obviously thought I should know.

"Yeah, he's that kid from the 70s that acts like a grumpy old man. He helped you with your quest to find Rose and free Brandon. Do you not remember him?"

She watched my face eagerly as if concerned that I was falling apart. Well, my body and spirit had already detached from each other. It was no surprise that my memory was struggling to keep up.

"I kinda do, I guess."

"Well, we can get back to him later. The point is, the extra abilities were on my mind, and when Sarah brought up the glasses, I wondered how they got made and wanted to see if I could maybe do the same thing. And Hanna, guess what? It worked!"

She bounced on her toes a few times holding up a golden bracelet.

Her energy, despite the dark circles underneath her eyes, was a bit overwhelming in my previously-alone ghostly state. I eyed the bracelet she held in her hands and looked back at her face.

"You created an item that can interact with ghosts?" I said slowly as I tried to get the whole picture.

"Yes! I'm not super sure how I did it, and I'm hoping I can figure out how to do it again, but Sarah put this on, and everyone could see and hear her. She had a complete, full physical body!"

Gryphin's smile and sparkling eyes confirmed her story, and I took a closer look at the bracelet. I vaguely recognized it as the one Dad had given Trina last year, and it still looked the same as far as I could tell.

As I reached out to touch it and see if there was a different feel to it, Trina pulled it back out of my grasp.

"Hold on. There seems to be a side effect once you wear it. After Sarah put it on, chided Gordon for his behavior and turned the pack against him—which was super disgusting, by the way. I never want to hear anything like that ever again..."

Gryphin winced and looked at her apologetically.

"Anyway, after that whole nasty business was taken care of, Sarah was unable to take the bracelet off. It scared us for a moment but everything was so chaotic, we quickly forgot about it. Oh! But it was pretty awesome how quickly she was able to change back and forth from a human to a wolf, I guess thanks to that ghostly potion you and Phoenix gave her, by the way."

Gryphin nodded. "I wish I could change that fast."

"And from the sound of it, a lot less painful. Anyway, this gave the alpha and her plenty of time to talk. Things settled down, several pack members went to bury the body, Gryphin changed back into a human, found his clothes again, thank goodness, and took me into the lodge to warm me up and give me some cocoa. Then the most amazing thing happened!"

"You sure are excited for just being in such a terrifying situation," I said, trying to imagine all the things she was describing.

"I'm feeling mostly relief, to be honest. It was scary, for sure, but I'm too relieved to remember how scared I was. So, then Sarah and Bertram were on the other side of the lodge near the kitchen, talking, but it wasn't long before Sarah crossed over! One second she was sitting next to the alpha on the couch, both of them sharing a warm blanket, the next second she was sparkling into the air like dust motes in the sunshine. Bertram gave me the bracelet back with a tear-filled expression of thanks, and we rushed right back here to tell you everything!"

Trina took a few gulps of air, trying to recover from the quick spouting of her tale.

"Wow." I turned to Gryphin for confirmation of her story, but he kept smiling and vaguely staring at the table. "That's...really intense."

"Right? So I was thinking I'd give the bracelet to Brandon," she said, a small quirk to one side of her mouth. "Of course we'd tell him that once he put it on, he couldn't take it off, so we'll let him have the choice of it. There are lots of things I don't know about how it works. Like will he still need to eat and sleep? Will he be able to die?

Will his body age? I don't know *any* of that. I don't even know if it will last longer than a few hours. It could fade with time, but at least you guys could talk for a bit? I do know that even though the ghost has a physical body, they can still see and interact with the other ghosts. The whole thing is quite confusing but so *so* exciting! Wouldn't you love to see Brandon again? We can give it to him first and see what the side effects might be before making you one, too."

I slumped down onto the bench behind me and put my head between my knees, trying to pull in fresh oxygen that never responded to my gasps.

"Oh, I think I broke her," Trina said to Gryphin and then sat down next to me. "I'm sorry. Was that too much information at once? It's just life has given us nothing but sadness for weeks, and we've finally gotten some good stuff to happen for once, and I really wanted you to know about it."

Keeping my head down still, I nodded. "It's okay. I just need a minute."

"Understandable." She gingerly put the bracelet back into her pocket. "We haven't slept all night. Pretty sure I'm running on pure adrenaline at this point."

Gryphin nodded and sat down on the other side of her. "Yeah, all-nighters are not my favorite thing. Oddly enough, being a werewolf puts them as a frequent occurrence, though."

Their mundane chatting helped give my brain time to catch up with everything. I tuned them out and thought about each important thing Trina had told me in a list so I could sort through what I was feeling and what I needed to do next.

First, the pack seemed to be stable again with the main instigator having been…dispatched.

Second, Rose had been behind the whole disruption which made me angrier with her and also concerned. What kind of bigger picture thing was she putting together? What were her motivations and goals?

Third, Sarah had crossed over. That should help with the pack's stability and eased some of the guilt I felt about how that whole situation had played out.

Fourth, Noah had told them I'd gotten the info we needed from Susan, which I still needed to give them so we could get closer to getting my body back. But I needed to decide if the cost was worth it.

Fifth…the bracelet. Trina had found she that could make ghostly items. Perhaps she could remake the glasses. What else could she make? What were the possibilities with that?

Sixth, Brandon.

"What do you mean the ghost can't take the bracelet off once you put it on them? Is there a way to fix that?" I asked, interrupting whatever they were talking about and not caring.

Trina turned to me and pressed her eyebrows together in thought. "I don't know. I could try creating another item that doesn't do that. I'm betting it needs to be gold though, just because the glasses and the bracelet were both gold. I will try it on other materials, of course, but that's just my suspicion so far. So yeah, I could try making another one that does the same thing but isn't stuck on the wearer. I'm not sure if I messed it up when I made the bracelet or if it's another one of those weird ghost physics rules."

"I'm worried about where the bracelet is getting the energy. If it siphons off the ghost, Brandon could turn into a poltergeist within a day, and we wouldn't be able to stop it from happening."

Trina frowned and her shoulders slumped. "Oh, that would be terrible. I suppose the energy does have to come from somewhere and that could be dangerous for the ghost. I'm sorry. I was so excited to be able to help."

"Oh, this does help!" I put a cold hand on her knee that she couldn't feel. "It's actually really amazing! We only need to be careful in case there's a different loophole, that's all."

"What about the glasses?" Gryphin asked, having been able to follow the conversation slightly by listening to Trina's comments. "Do we know where the glasses got the energy? They may work the same way."

"Or I messed it all up." Trina stared down at her shoes. "It's not like I knew what I was doing."

I rolled my eyes to myself where she couldn't see. I did feel bad that she wanted so much to help and be able to do something special, but at the same time, pouting like this was annoying and pulling on the dramatic. "The glasses worked with alive people to help see ghosts. They could have taken energy from the alive person or been imbued with power from the Seer, and that's all the energy they required. Either way, they weren't much of a danger to the ghost."

Trina muttered my answer to Gryphin sullenly.

"Oh, that makes sense. I guess that's no help then." Gryphin sighed.

"And I know if you tell Brandon about that bracelet, he's going to put it on no matter what the dangers might be and find out the hard way. He likes a plan, but he'll like having a body better," I said, giving Trina a pointed look I'm not sure she fully saw.

Gryphin put a hand that I knew from experience was warm and comforting on Trina's shoulder. "Hey, you did help a lot. Sarah was able to cross over, and my dad is alive because of you. You should be proud of what you've done. The pack is very grateful."

I chewed on my lip as I watched her lean toward him into a side-hug. It wasn't like Gryphin and I had ever been together or anything, but he was my friend first. I was glad that she had someone there to offer protection and comfort. I didn't *want* to be jealous that it was the same person whose fuzzy head had helped calm several of my own panic attacks. But even as an aliver, I hadn't been super in control of my emotions.

Trying not to sigh too loudly, I said, "So what do we do next? You guys were able to stop Rose from taking over the pack for now, but if I know her well enough from all this chaos, I would suspect she'll just make another plan to get what she wants. And fun fact, she'll out-live us all. Present company included." I gestured to myself with a flat expression.

Trina sat up, and Gryphin's arm dropped from off her shoulders onto the table behind her. "That's true. Kieran is right. She's got to die."

"Who's got to die?" Gryphin asked, his eyebrows raising in surprise.

"Rose. We may have stopped her this time, but that doesn't mean we'll stop her next time. In fact, I'm kind of surprised she didn't send Caleb here right now to take care of us while we're out in the open." Trina looked around in alarm. "I hate having to be scared to ever leave my house. It's infuriating."

"I know you were so excited to update me with all of this, but you probably should go home, not only to be safer inside the spelled house, but to get some sleep," I said, not wanting them to go but also worried Caleb would pop up with Rose's rage at her plan being foiled.

"We will as soon as you tell us what you learned from Susan so we can get closer to fixing you." Trina turned her blue eyes onto me.

"Oh, right." I fiddled with my fingers in my lap. "Susan was worried that whoever she told the information to would get hurt. She didn't know who killed that other Seer, but she was willing to tell me about it because I was already dead. Should I be worried about telling you guys the same thing? Not only will you have to watch out for Caleb, but you'll have to watch out for someone else trying to murder you before telling the necroes what you know. Maybe it'll be better if I tell them myself."

Trina frowned. "Are you saying you won't tell me what it is either? It'd be so much simpler if you told me, so Mom and I can drive over there tonight. Otherwise, we'll have to get a body for you to use again. Noah already stated how hard that had been the other day."

"I'm sure he's got that old man still. It hasn't been that long. I wouldn't worry about that. Yeah, that's what we'll do. Go home. Rest. Update Mom. Text Noah and get it going. Maybe we can do it tonight and get all this over with. I'd rather tell them myself so whatever happened to that other Seer after finding out the truth, doesn't happen to you."

Chapter 17 - Trina

I stared at the wall of my bedroom, my head on my pillow with my hand tucked underneath it. Late evening sunlight filtered in past the blinds, and I watched as the dust floated around in the streaks of orange. It was Monday, and I had missed a day of school. Not something that I usually wanted to do, especially during my senior year.

I was going to have to stop staying up all night to break up werewolf fights.

Eventually, my eyes drifted to the bracelet sitting on my nightstand.

I had wanted to help so much and then had gotten super excited that something I could do *had* helped. The possibilities were dazzling to think of all the items I could come up with to help ghosts and people communicate. Like, I could have piles of glasses laying around, and when someone had trouble with a ghost, they could use a pair and solve the whole thing. Of course, there were the dangers that came along with that. Hanna had all but confirmed with Rose that she'd killed our Gran trying to get access to the glasses.

Caleb had later filled me in on more of what happened that night, telling me that Gran and Rose had fought in the front room while little Hanna was only a few feet away in the kitchen. Caleb had been too worried about defending the child, like he knew Gran would want him to, that he was unable to stop Rose from firing the bullet that took Gran's life. Caleb had lived with that pain and guilt for many years, and even though he'd been able to get some closure with Gran's ghost and helping her grandchildren, the memory still haunted him.

Oh, Caleb. Poor guy. He'd shown me a side of himself that others rarely got to see. Yes, he was a broad-shouldered, hunky, and sometimes a brooding, blood-sucking vampire, but he was also fiercely loyal to those he loved and had a strong sense of morality.

I really hoped we would be able to figure out how to set him free. The only solution may have been Rose's death, and I was slowly becoming more and more okay with that.

I'd taken a several-hours-long nap and awoken to feelings of disappointment and inadequacy. I was getting sick of feeling this way. I knew Hanna hadn't meant to make me feel bad or take the wind out of my sails. She was simply trying to make sure we didn't accidentally hurt someone else. It was, admittedly, slightly alarming to learn that once the ghost put on the bracelet, they couldn't take it off. But that didn't mean we shouldn't use it.

I was willing to bet my sneakers on the fact that, given the choice, most ghosts would prefer to have a physical body again. It was tempting to try the bracelet out on someone less "important" than Brandon to make sure it didn't turn them into a poltergeist, but that had its own pile of ethical issues I wasn't about to play with.

I guess I was good for nothing...again.

Groaning from sore muscles, I pulled myself out of bed and opened my bedroom door. The house seemed quiet, but that didn't mean Mom wasn't home.

I'd filled her in quickly before getting to bed this morning, updating her on all the things that had happened, including the bracelet and what Hanna had told me. I'd made sure to talk quietly about the bracelet and ghostly stuff in case Brandon was around. I hadn't seen him, but that didn't mean he wasn't lurking like the creeper he was.

After taking my time in the bathroom, showering long enough to get a good scrub and soak in the hot water—doing my hair and makeup in the best way I knew how, hoping to make myself feel better about everything—I headed back to my room to get dressed and check my phone. Usually, I brought it in with me for music and stuff while I got ready, but today I wanted the quiet of introspection.

As I walked around the doorframe and saw who was sitting on my bed, I froze.

"Nice towel. Do you think I need a shower after having not had one for twenty years?" Brandon said, sitting as human and alive-looking as ever on the edge of my bed. The golden bracelet twinkled on his wrist, and while it was definitely a snug fit on his larger bone structure, the look suited him well.

Clutching my towel tighter at the top to make sure it wouldn't fall off, I frowned. "You dirty—!"

Brandon laughed and put up his arms in surrender. "Woah! Don't let your mom hear you talk like that!"

I ground my teeth together as I tried to reign in my fury. "You were listening when I told Mom about that this morning, weren't you?"

A grin on one side of his mouth grew as his eyes twinkled. "Maybe."

"You did hear me say that the first ghost who used it couldn't take it off, right?" My heart pounded in my chest as I felt a mixture of emotions. Hanna was going to kill me if he turned into something that required a priest and an exorcism.

Oh well, then we'd all be a happy ghost family together.

He shrugged. "Yeah, so? As far as I can tell, I'm still dead, so I don't have to worry about getting murdered. It's just like...I'm a ghost but people can see me, and I look normal. Sounded like a good deal."

"Did you also hear me say that we weren't sure where the energy comes from? You could be pulling it from yourself only to turn into a poltergeist and haunt this poor house forever. I doubt Hanna would want to hang out with you when all that's left is a ball of raging screams."

He shrugged. "At this point? Even that sounds better than wandering around this house aimlessly while y'all go out and have adventures without me."

I shook my head, still trying to believe this was happening. "Okay, fine. But now you're definitely not allowed in my room. Get out. Let me get dressed. Maybe go see if you've gotten hungry after twenty years of not eating."

My bed squeaked as he stood, and he gave me the most triumphant smile. "I can touch things now."

"Good for you. Get out."

He chuckled as he left my room, and I shut the door firmly behind him.

About a half hour later, Mom, Brandon, and I were standing in the kitchen looking awkwardly at each other. "Okay, so he put it on all by himself? Did you put it on by yourself? I'm sorry. I'm not used to talking directly to you."

Brandon was leaning back against the counter with his arms folded across his chest. "It's okay. I get it. Yes, I heard y'all talking about it this morning and decided I wanted to try it out for you. You can have it back when I'm done with it. Or just make another one. Whatever works. Isn't it such a neat power that Trina has?"

I couldn't help the thrill of excitement and appreciation that rose up inside my chest, but I wasn't about to start gloating. Maybe I'd save that for when we actually knew what the bracelet was doing.

"Yes, she's amazing with or without the powers." Mom gave me a kind smile before turning back to Brandon. "But I still think what you've done is foolish. We don't know enough about this bracelet."

"It's fine. I feel fine. I'm going to walk to the skatepark and show Hanna my new body, alright? I have a feeling she'll be more excited about it than you two seem to be."

"Well maybe it's time you go get a job and find your own place to haunt...or live. Whatever this is," I said, half-kidding as I waved my arm up and down toward him.

His lips pulled into a frowning pout. "You wouldn't kick me out now, would you? I thought we were becoming great friends."

Mom shook her head. "Of course not. We'll make a place for you on the couch for now. Oh, do you even need to sleep?"

Brandon and I exchanged looks and then both shrugged.

"Maybe?" he said.

"I don't know," I said at the same time.

Mom laughed and shook her head. "Of course, this would happen. Good gravy. Okay, go say hi to Hanna. Have a night out on the town. Just make sure you're home by eleven. We've got a curfew around here."

"Cool." He stood and his eyes were twinkling. "I've got a curfew."

I looked at him oddly. "Congratulations."

"So I guess I'll see you in a few. Noah is coming to give Hanna a body, and we're all meeting with the necroes tonight, right?" Brandon asked before he walked out the front door.

Mom looked at me for confirmation. I'd been in contact with Noah before and after my midday nap, and he'd mostly arranged everything.

I nodded. "We'll be there in a bit. Noah said he'd meet us later."

Brandon nodded. "Okay, toodles."

After eating a quick dinner and waiting for my mom to do a few things for work, we headed out to the skatepark. Gryphin had gone home before I'd fallen asleep, probably to also get some sleep and check in with the pack, see how things were shaking out. He'd seemed optimistic about it all so that helped ease more of my anxiety.

I did still feel a little anxious as we stepped out of the car where my mom had parked it along the street. We were outside without protection, and if Rose wanted to get revenge for messing up her werewolf plans, it would have been a good time. It was probably dumb of us to come out like this, but we had to get stuff done. We'd go crazy staying at home and not making progress with the necroes. So to us, the risk was worth it.

Chapter 18 - Hanna

It was surreal seeing Brandon walk into the park with flesh and bone. I'd been with him in the physical form several times when he'd taken energy from me while I'd been alive but seeing him being able to do it on his own was still trippy.

I was content at first to simply watch him walk past the fence and take a look around, presumably looking for me. It was early evening, the cool November sun peeked through the clouds and lit up his spiky blond hair that I knew to be soft to the touch. His green eyes looked fondly upon the skating kids even though there were only three that evening. A small smile peeked upon my face as I reviewed his emo band t-shirt, giant pants, and wallet chain. Some of the style had come back recently, but not quite like it had been in the 90s. He still looked out of place. Perhaps we'd be able to take him shopping for more modern looks later.

His eyes finally found mine from across the park and that stupid, charming grin lit up his face in a way that made my heart lurch, or it would have if I'd had a heart.

"Hanna!" he called and waved to me before jogging over to what appeared to be an empty table.

There was one parent who was sitting at another table nearby. She looked up from her phone long enough to give Brandon an odd look, but then her attention went back to the phone.

"Well, well, well, how the tables have turned." He met me at our table in the back, put his hands on his hips, and looked down at me in triumph.

I rolled his eyes at his ironic pun. "Trina promised me she wouldn't tell you about that bracelet."

He lifted his arm up to study the feminine piece adorning his wrist. "She kept her promise. I just eavesdropped and stole."

"How Brandon of you."

"Did I just become a verb?" he asked, putting his hand over his chest.

"I hope you're not about to become a poltergeist. I've had enough of dealing with those, thank you very much."

"You guys worry so much. So far, so good." He hopped up onto the tabletop next to me, rested on his hands behind him, and relaxed his legs.

"So how alive do you feel? Like, are you hungry? Can you feel the cold? Most importantly, do you feel tired?" I asked, looking down at his peachy fingers splayed out, wishing I could touch them.

"I never thought I'd say this, but I kind of missed this view." His eyes bounced around from the skating kids to the nearby naked trees and back to my face. "I have to admit, it doesn't quite feel like I'm alive. It's like when I used your energy to become physical. I can feel things with my skin, but I'm not quite sure my organs are working. Can you hear my heart?"

I considered his words and shrugged, figuring it wouldn't hurt to check. Leaning in closer to his chest, I got my ear as close to his shirt as I could without my ghostly body going through him. "Nothing. No sounds."

I sat up and frowned. "I know my emotions are weird in ghost form, and so are my memories, but I would have imagined that this moment would have been exciting and fun. You know, reuniting with you? Instead, I simply feel sad."

"Oh, Hanna." He looked at me, his eyes full of care and longing. "Please don't be sad. Your sister and mom are on their way over here shortly to meet with Noah, give you a body, and get that much closer to putting you back together again. Then we can touch, hold hands, maybe even share a hug or two. I promise not to let go of our hug until you do."

His words didn't make me feel better. Rather they had the opposite effect, and I felt some kind of ghostly tears fill up in my eyes. "I've missed you. It's lonely sitting here every day."

"I've missed you, too. If there is anyone who understands what it feels like to have this place as their haunt, it's me. Can you blame me now for deciding to follow you around even if you were doing something as mundane as going to the store?"

"I can't remember," I said, feeling a few tears escape.

Brandon's eyebrows pulled together tightly as he regarded me sadly. "It's okay. I'll remember for the both of us."

"I feel like there are some important things I need to tell you." My eyes drifted away from his face to his skater shoes. I could see more of them than usual since he was sitting and the big pants were pulled up higher. His laces were a bright, neon green and that surprised me for some reason.

"Trina warned me that you had some things to tell me. None of that's important now. We need to focus on getting you back in your body, then we can spend hours staring up at the stars and talking, our fingers interlocked," he put his hand over mine on the table, neither of us able to feel the contact, "our foreheads almost touching as we giggle together, and give each other all our secrets."

"That sounds cold." A small smile pulled at my lips.

"Don't worry. I'll keep you warm, too hot, in fact. When I'm finished with you, you'll relish the feel of the cold air on your heated skin."

We burst into giggles, unable to take such sultry comments seriously, even if they felt good.

"Hanna? Are you here?" a voice called out from near the fence, pulling our attention away from each other.

The mom on her phone looked up at yet another person calling for my name, blinked a few times, and glanced back at Brandon with confusion. He gave her a cheeky smile and a teasing wave, causing her to frown and turn back to her phone.

We giggled again as Noah walked further into the park.

"I guess he probably doesn't know what I look like." Brandon hopped off the table and watched Noah come closer. His broad shoulders and football-throwing arms were barely disguised beneath the letterman's jacket.

The old man zombie trailed behind Noah. His slumped shoulders and shuffling movements made my knees twinge in memory. Oddly,

I didn't feel dread at being him again. At least I would be able to feel something.

Brandon put on a cheerful smile and waved at Noah when he was within reasonable distance for conversation without having to yell. "Hey, man. Good to see you in the flesh."

Noah paused, the old zombie bumping into him. "Wait, do I know you?"

"Does anyone really *know* anyone else? I mean, do we even know ourselves?" Brandon looked thoughtfully up to the sky.

I chuckled and rolled my eyes. "Glad to see you haven't changed much in the few weeks we've been apart. It's only been a few weeks, right?" I found myself asking since I honestly had no idea.

Noah quirked an eyebrow. "It's too much of a Monday to be able to answer those questions. Guessing from your clothes and how you know me, I'm going to assume you're Brandon, but how did you get out here? How do you have a body? What's going on? Is Hanna here?"

Deciding to put the kid out of his misery, and despite how awkward it would be to hang out with Brandon while I was a wrinkled, old man, I stepped into the zombie.

"Ah, Hank. He's becoming sort of a second home to me," I said, shaking out his sore shoulders.

"His name is Hank?" Brandon asked, his eyes wide at what I'd just done. Perhaps I should have warned him.

As I had that thought, all the memories and things I needed to tell Brandon rushed into my brain. It was weird how any body could help restore my memories even though the physical brain was way different than my own.

Again, weird ghost science.

"Actually, his name was Shane, but sure, you can call him Hank." Noah pushed his lips together and shrugged. "Kind of suits him, actually."

"Brandon! I remember! I need to tell you some very important things," I said, hobbling closer to him and grabbing his hand.

He wore an amused expression as he looked at my wizened, crinkled face and back to our intertwined hands. "Trina warned me you guys had some things to tell me, but she said *you* would have to do it."

Noah sighed. "Great. You guys just got reunited, didn't you? Can we spare all the squishy love stuff for later? We've got a meeting with David. Your mom and Trina are on the way. But first off, I'm really dying to know how he's standing there with a body, and does he expect to go with us? Going to be hard to explain that to the leader."

My shoulders slumped even more than they already were. I let go of Brandon's hand, mostly because I didn't want him to feel more awkward than the situation already called for. It had been nice to feel his skin for a moment, even if I did look like a creepy uncle. "He's right. You probably shouldn't go with us. It could be dangerous."

Brandon put both of his hands into his big pockets and shrugged. "What's the worst that can happen? I'm already dead."

I gave him a flat look and turned to Noah. "It turns out that Trina can make objects that help alivers interact with ghosts or vice-versa. She made a bracelet that Brandon foolishly put on without knowing the side-effects, but it gives him a weird type of physical body. It's kind of in a limbo state, but we...or alivers at least, can see and interact with him."

"Wow. That's super impressive, actually."

I stuck a crooked finger in Noah's face. "Don't you go telling anyone, though. Trina won't become a necro puppet just like all the zombies y'all enslave."

Noah laughed and put his hands up in surrender. "I would never."

Brandon and I shared a look.

"We don't believe you," I said, puckering my lips together and giving him a pointed expression.

"I promise. All this is so complicated anyway. The last thing we need is more." Noah glanced toward the park entrance. "Right on time. Ready to go give your report to David? Do you still remember the stuff Susan told you?"

I followed his gaze to see Trina and Mom coming toward us. They both looked wary of their surroundings, and I'm sure I wasn't the only one wishing they had brought Gryphin with them.

Hopefully they'd be relatively safe from Rose while we dealt with the necroes.

Realizing what we were about to do and having a body to help me remember the situation, I frowned. I'd stalled long enough, especially by insisting that I be the one to personally convey the information, but I still wasn't absolutely certain that the necroes should know what Susan, and now I, knew.

"Hello, everyone." Mom gave us a small smile that widened when she saw my body. "You've aged well, sweetie. Do we need to return you to the old folks' home after we're done today?"

"Yeah, she's probably already out past her bedtime," Trina said, a laugh playing at her lips.

I waved off their comments. "Funny. At least I finally have a body to match my level of wisdom."

Noah coughed into a laugh as Brandon grinned. Mom and Trina shared a giggle.

"What? It's true," I said, putting my hands on my hips, probably both of them having had surgery at some point. "Can we get past this and down to business? Whose car are we taking? Do we need to take two separate cars?"

Trina's eyes landed back on Brandon. "What about him? Is he coming with us?"

I didn't wait for Noah to deny him again. "Yes. He is."

And with that, I set off for the exit of the park with my stiff, wobbly legs.

Noah tried to protest behind me, but I ignored him and found the van we'd used the last time we visited the necro order's house. Brandon caught up and gave me a grateful smile.

"I was afraid I'd have to hang out by myself some more. I'm getting sick of being alone," he said as we walked around the fence and down the sidewalk.

"I know that feeling all too well these days. Plus, what would we do without having your snarky comments to annoy everyone?"

"I know that's right."

Noah grumbled to himself the whole drive, but we ignored him. Mom sat in the front passenger seat while Brandon, Trina, and I were in the back.

"We really should let the oldest in the car have the front seat," I said pointedly, crossing my arms over my chest and feeling the sagging skin on my elbows. "At least I've got more age-appropriate clothes this time. Can you believe Noah first dressed Hank in a Willow High t-shirt and sweats? Talk about uncool."

Brandon glanced down at my plaid button-up shirt and slacks. "That would be uncool. I think out of everyone here, we're definitely the best dressed."

We grinned at each other amid the various scoffs he'd earned from the others.

It wasn't too long before we were walking into the order's house behind an annoyed Noah. I enjoyed hanging out with Brandon again, of course, but the second-best part of having him with me was bothering Noah. I wasn't too worried about him getting into trouble for bringing an extra stranger into the order's headquarters, and even if he did get in trouble, he probably deserved it for something else he'd done.

We met David again in the study, this time crowding into it and making his eyebrows raise. Knowing it was a super weird thing to think, I had a moment of pride to see that the leader's wrinkles were even deeper than my own.

"Okay... Well, I didn't expect such a group. Perhaps y'all should head to the kitchen where there's space for everyone to sit while Hanna and I discuss." David leaned back from his desk and regarded us with shrewd eyes.

Mom stepped up as Noah moved to step out of the room obediently. He paused when he heard her speak.

"Listen, we've worked hard for the order trying to get the info that you requested. Even though Hanna is the only one who knows the results, this was a group effort. We will stay together and see this out. Plus, we're not ignorant enough to assume this is all you will want from us. The next task will likely be related to the info Hanna is about to divulge so we'll hear it anyway."

David's bushy eyebrows cinched as he studied my mom for a few moments. "Very well, but anything we discuss here remains private. We'll know if you reveal our secrets. But I must insist that only you and Hanna remain. The other three aren't essential. In fact, I'm not sure why you've brought them to our house in the first place. Especially this stranger. Who are you, young man?"

Brandon was looking around the room as if he'd forgotten he was visible for a moment. He stood up straighter and blinked a few times. "Who me? Oh, I'm nobody."

David frowned and shifted his gaze to Noah. "Why is he here? A magic user spying on us, perhaps?"

Noah's eyes widened in concern, but Brandon laughed. "Oh no. I wish I could use magic. That would be sweet, but no. I'm nothing special. I can respect you want privacy for your secret order meetings. Trina and I will step outside. They'll just tell us everything you said later, anyway."

I pressed a smile down, hoping the corners of my mouth didn't perk up too much.

Trina gave David her most charming smile and nodded. "Yes. We don't mind waiting outside."

Noah held the door open for Brandon and Trina to leave as Mom and I settled into the two chairs across from David's desk. The door shut softly behind us, and I spared a thought of hope that Brandon didn't annoy Noah and Trina...too much.

"Seriously, you have nothing to worry about. You know Trina, and that's only Brandon. He's my friend and doesn't even know anyone else to tell secrets to. He's fine, I swear." I adjusted my stiff legs in the chair and tried to find a position that was at least semi-comfortable.

"I'm sure what you say is correct, but the order's secrets must remain secret. It is how we've survived. In fact, you know firsthand how bad it can be if someone outside learns necromancer secrets." David's steely eyes bore down on me.

He was right, I realized, as flashes of Rose wielding that purple lightning passed in my memory.

"Of course. We understand," Mom said before I could recover.

David nodded. "Excellent. So please, tell me what Susan had for you. I've waited a very long time for this information."

"Oh, we know," I said, Mom and I sharing a side-glance, "Susan told us about the other Seer you sent. She also told us about how he died crossing the parking lot minutes after she told him what you want to know. Do you happen to know anything about that?"

David sighed, took out a handkerchief from somewhere, and started cleaning his glasses. "Yes, that was an unfortunate accident."

"The timing was too good for it to be an accident, despite how dangerous that part of town may be," I said, watching him behind my own pair of scratched glasses.

"It took time for us to investigate, but there was another in the order who didn't want me to get the info we so desperately needed. That person has since been dispatched, and you have nothing to fear."

I frowned, trying to pick up my different thoughts and put them into a coherent picture. "The Seer was killed by someone in your own order after being on a mission for the order?"

"The order isn't perfect."

I scoffed inside my head, at least wise enough to not do it out loud.

David continued, "We're made of people like any organization who have differences in opinions and sometimes get into conflicts because of this. I can assure you that all is safe now. Please tell us what Susan had to say about Theodore."

I sighed and looked at Mom. She gave me an encouraging nod, and I really hoped I was doing the right thing.

"She said his current name is Mitchell Michaelson." The moment the words left my mouth something clicked inside my old, addled brain. Wasn't Andrea's last name Michaelson? What are the odds of that being a coincidence?

My mom blinked a few times waiting for me to continue. "That's it?"

David chewed on his bottom lip and sat back into his wheelchair; his elbows propped on the armrests as his fingers fiddled with a pen. "That's quite enough, actually. And very helpful. It is also very ironic."

"Why?" I watched him closely, dying to ask if the guy had a daughter who we all happened to know.

His gaze shifted to mine as he slid a smile across his lips, not impacting the rest of his face. "Nothing for you to concern yourself with. Order business. Thank you for delivering on your task. Now your mother and sister need to fulfill one other favor, and we can put you back into your much better-looking body."

I looked down at the age spots on the back of my hands. "Hank has been good to me, but I would enjoy being able to bend my knees again."

"What is our task?" Mom asked. "Nothing bad or dangerous, I hope."

David waved away her concerns. "Of course not. The order requires service and payment, but we understand limits. If something were to happen to you, then we wouldn't get what we need, now would we? I'm afraid you are going to need help to accomplish this, though. Luckily, you've already got a ghost who will come in handy."

Chapter 19 - Trina

I t wasn't completely awkward as we waited in the living room, more for display than actual use. Noah muttered about having something important to do and left us alone.

I took the time to check in with my friends, check socials, and text Phoenix. It'd been a few days since I had touched bases with the magic user and figured they would enjoy an update.

It took me a while to fill them all in on everything that had happened, leaving out my newfound power and only mentioning that Brandon was able to get a body through an interesting situation.

While I tapped away on my phone, Brandon read through some of the magazines that had been stacked on the coffee table. I mostly ignored his random comments about how the world is somehow totally different and insanely the same as it was in his day and other random thoughts he had on current fashion trends.

Phoenix seemed most interested in how Hanna was able to possess the zombie bodies, which suited me fine because at least it distracted them from asking more about Brandon's physicality.

Then we moved to other topics.

Our coven members tell us that Rose is still hanging around the area. I suppose you already suspected this since you saw

Caleb a few days ago. I have to say I'm not surprised to hear she was trying to get her claws into the local wolf pack, pun intended.

I smiled at their lame joke and texted back.

What do you think she's planning? What does she want? And more importantly, how do we trap her again and save Caleb?

I watched Brandon lick his finger before turning another magazine page like the old man he was while I waited for Phoenix's response.

We're working on some ideas, but we honestly don't know what she wants. If it was only to live and enjoy her long life, I'm certain she would have left the state, probably the country, already. There is something nearby that's demanding her attention. We have to figure out why.

A tickle of an idea started to brew in my mind.

What if I try and get in contact with Caleb and see if she'll share her plans with us? She does seem to like to hear herself talk. Maybe I can also see how much of Caleb is still left inside? Maybe he's got some room for free will in there but is biding his time to use it until the right moment.

Phoenix: I understand why you'd hope that from him, but don't you think he would have used that freewill to stop himself from killing Hanna? It doesn't seem like he has much ability to choose. I'm sure he's still in there, only enthralled in a similar way that vampires use on their victims, ironically enough.

I sighed, not wanting to read what they'd said but understanding it sounded mostly true.

Phoenix: I don't think it's safe for you to meet up with Caleb. You could be playing right into Rose's hands. She could simply

be waiting around here to kidnap you. Promise me you won't do anything stupid and let us work our magic.

I frowned as I stared at their words and tried to decide what to do.

Brandon's gaze traveled up from his reading material and looked at me from the armchair across the couch where I had chosen to sit. "What's up? Are you as surprised that the Backstreet Boys made a comeback as much as I am?"

"Huh? No. I'm frustrated and angry. Rose is still out there doing who-knows-what, and we're sitting in a house full of zombie-raising humans doing nothing."

"Don't forget she's out there with you-know-who," Brandon said with a wink.

Shaking my head, I tossed my phone to the side, still unsure what to say to Phoenix. "We can't let him continue to suffer like this. We've got to be able to do something."

Brandon sat up and tossed the magazine onto the table. "I get that. I've spent most of my undead life sitting around and doing nothing. It's maddening, for sure. Hanna is always telling me to slow things down and take it one thing at a time."

I stared up at the ceiling. "That's something my dad says all the time. Speaking of my dad, it's weird that he hasn't questioned us about Hanna's supposed trip with her friends. Guess he's busy with work and getting his lawyers to finalize the divorce."

"I'm sorry that your family is going through that and all of this now. It's kind of a mess. It seems like you've been able to handle it pretty well so far though."

"Only because I'm in a constant state of busy denial," I said, surprising myself with the candor.

He smiled kindly, and it was weird to feel something for him other than annoyance. It was almost like a resigned camaraderie maybe.

"You're stronger than you give yourself credit for, I think. Let's talk things through. Maybe it'll help you feel better. What's our first priority?

"To get Hanna back in her body, I guess."

"And to do that we have to appease the necroes, which is what we're doing right now. Maybe Hanna will get reunited with her body tonight!"

I gave him a flat look. "That feels too easy."

"Well, Hanna got the info they needed, right?"

"I'm sure they'll have more for us to do first."

He shrugged. "Then we'll do it."

"What if they ask us to do something wrong or evil?"

He shrugged again. "It's all for the purpose of something good so that makes it good, right?"

"I'm not sure that's how things work."

"In this case, it does. I'm sure it'll be fine."

"So then what? Hanna gets put back together, and then Rose comes by to kill her again? I doubt the necroes would resurrect her twice."

Brandon pursed his lips and nodded. "Unlikely. So we better make sure it sticks the first time. Maybe that's how we get Rose. We set her up. She comes in thinking she'll get to solve the Hanna issue once and for all, and then we pounce. Incapacitate the vampire without hurting him somehow, because I know you'd be crushed if something happened to him, and then bam! Rose is gone, we've solved our issues, and we can live happily ever after."

"You know, for an emo 90s kid, you're kind of optimistic," I said, trying to figure out how in the world we'd be able to do all that and win with no injuries or deaths.

He frowned and furrowed his eyebrows. "Yeah... I guess being around Hanna so much has changed me. Weird. I didn't used to be so chipper."

"Maybe you only needed to find the right people to be around," I said, remembering that Brandon's life hadn't been so great.

"Maybe."

The door opened from down the hallway and footsteps sounded as I made sure to grab my phone before standing up. Brandon and I turned to greet Mom, old-man Hanna, and the order's leader wheeling in after them.

Hanna looked as grumpy as ever, which wasn't saying much considering her wrinkled face. Mom looked worried, though. Her eyes were pinched on the sides, and the white knuckles she was using to clasp the strap from her bag alarmed me.

I gave Mom a concerned look, but she shook her head slightly, telling me to wait to ask.

"I expect to hear from you all again soon. Good work, Hanna, even if it did take you longer than expected," David said as they came into the large living area.

Hanna rolled her eyes where David couldn't see before turning back to him and flashing a toothy smile. "I'm sure we'll be quicker about it this time."

"I'm sure." David nodded at the rest of us before turning his chair around and going back down the hallway.

As if he'd been waiting for his cue, Noah's quick feet carried him down the staircase. I wondered how close by he'd been and how much of mine and Brandon's conversation he'd heard.

"I'll take y'all back home now, if you'd like. It is a school night, after all," Noah said as he rounded the corner of the staircase and put his hand through his hair.

"I don't miss those," Brandon grinned and then paused, "although it might have been nice to graduate. Huh. Maybe that's my unfinished business. Oh well! Not going back there."

Hanna turned her balding head and looked at her friend. "I guess I'm too old to go back, too. Poor Trina, has to go to school like the young whipper-snapper she is."

I sighed, feeling the familiar pressure of somehow keeping up with all the responsible, normal human things I was supposed to be doing while talking to a zombie possessed by my sister. "I really shouldn't miss any more classes. I want to keep my scholarship."

Mom smiled, though it was still tight at the corners. "You will, dear. It'll be fine. We'll drop you off first so you can catch up on homework and then get some good rest for the next day. You've worked hard and deserve a break."

"And what are you guys going to get into?" I asked as we headed out the front door.

The sun was setting, making the sky turn a soft, autumn purple as shadows stretched out until they connected with others.

"We've got to see a guy about a book," Hanna grumbled in the raspy voice of her current body.

Chapter 20 - Hanna

After Noah dropped Trina off so she could go be a good student, we headed back to the skatepark. We all remained inside the van after he shut off the engine. Noah turned to the side in his chair so he could talk to my mom in the front seat and Brandon and I in the middle seats.

"So do I get to keep this body for a while, or do I need to apply for a zombie-body library card?" I poked myself/Hank in the chest.

Noah looked at me and thought for a moment. "First tell me how you feel. Are you any more tired than usual? How did you recover from possessing him for a few hours last time?"

Mom spoke before I could answer. "She was missing from her haunt for at least a whole day. We tried to go back and talk to her, but she wasn't there." She turned from Noah to look at me. "I'm sorry, sweetie, but I think it drains you more than you want to admit. Perhaps we should work on our plan to get the book for David and let you rest for a few days before we try anything else."

"Alright. As much as I want to get all this over with, I agree. We need to form a better plan. See, Brandon? You can teach an old dog new tricks." I referred to his previous teasing of my plans.

"Aw, look at my friend, all grown up and learning." Brandon patted the top of my balding head with a grin.

Sometime later, some number of hours and days, I couldn't tell, I woke up back in the skatepark. I'd reluctantly given Noah his zombie body back and retreated to the park while the rest of them went off to work on the plan. It hadn't been but a moment or two after I got back to being a ghost that I blinked out, presumably out of energy.

When I awoke, I was sitting in the grass near my dandelion friend. It was during the day, judging from the sun's high position in the sky. Grey clouds muted the bright light as wind played through the stark trees. It was probably chilly out and perhaps even during school hours because the park was empty.

Except for one lone figure sitting on a table a few paces away. He was wearing something new, which distracted me for a moment—modern fitting jeans with a few holes in them, a solid black t-shirt, and a jean jacket. His spiky blonde hair was the same, and I wondered if he had even tried styling it differently or if he'd given up long ago.

"Welcome back to the living." He jumped up from off the table and walked toward me.

"Funny," I said, rubbing my forehead. "I don't feel very much alive."

"You don't really look it either. Was I always so blue as a ghost?" He sat down next to me in the grass, and I wondered how well he could feel the chill of the ground.

I gave him a flat look. "What day is it? How long have I been out? And how long have you been sitting here? Were you here the whole time?"

He looked upward and counted on his fingers as he answered my questions. "It's Thursday. You've been out for three days. About three days. Pretty much. Turns out, I don't need to eat. I tried eating a slice of toast your mom made me but that...didn't go well. I do kind of sleep, though. It's not like out of a need to sleep, I don't think, but more of 'I'm so bored, I'm going to snooze here for a moment' kind of sleep."

"So like the old man you are." I smiled slightly.

"But let's not forget I'm still the younger of the two of us, and *my* hair hasn't turned grey yet."

"Are you sure?" I sat up slightly to look closer at his head. "There could be a few in there since the last time you checked."

He shrugged. "Even if there are, it's less than what you have."

"It only means I'm wiser than you. So tell me about the plan. What's going on? Are you updated on everything or clueless because you've been sitting in a park for three days watching kids like some kind of creeper?"

"I've been careful not to look too weird, thank you very much. Your mom was kind enough to buy me a cheap phone so we can communicate."

"You mean so you can call her to tell her when I appear again." I gave him a look.

"To-may-to, to-mah-to."

"You should probably let her know I'm here. What happens after that?"

"I will in a minute," he said with a soft smile as he looked at me.

"I'm sorry you had to wait so long for me to come back. You probably got really bored." I allowed myself a small moment of joy before getting back to the work of Rose's demise.

"Sometimes. I read a few books and watched a few YouTube videos. Did you know there is a nearby Wifi spot you don't have to use a password to sign into?"

"Well look at you, Mr. Up-to-date." I raised my eyebrows in appreciation.

"Yeah, I'm learning. Mostly I kept thinking about how nice it would be to see you again, body or no, and about how weird it is that I'm the aliver and you're the ghostly blue apparition."

"Except this time, I can't steal energy from you to make my lips kissable," I said sadly, mostly as a joke.

He dropped the smile and looked down at my lips for a second. "That's okay. I have faith we'll get to share a real kiss soon."

If I had blood, I probably would have blushed. "That would be nice. Listen... I've got a lot to tell you from what I've learned while you were trapped in that crystal. There are some things you should know about your sisters and brother. I met them, you know."

"You what?" His eyebrows pinched together.

So I told him about how we got trapped inside the picture spell and how Frank and Brandon's siblings worked to free us. The hardest part was admitting I hadn't seen them since and that they weren't in any of the crystals I'd emptied as of yet. It made sense they were inside a crystal that wasn't tied with my hair since they'd been captured long before I'd ever met Rose.

"Wow... All this time I didn't even consider looking for them because I assumed they were so young and innocent, they would have passed over immediately." Brandon fiddled with a small blade of grass.

"The more I learn about ghosts, the more I'm starting to think being young means there's more unfinished business than not." I put a hand on his knee, but it passed through effortlessly.

"What do you think it'll take to free them? Once we're back to normal, we've got to work on helping them cross over." His voice was quiet, and, judging by the way his forehead was scrunching, he was feeling a reasonable amount of pain.

"I'm not sure, but I do know Phoenix will help us figure it out. They've been so helpful with things like that. So helpful I can almost forgive them for letting Rose escape."

"I'm sure it wasn't only their fault. The whole coven should have been more prepared."

I nodded. "True. So there's more you need to know. I remember once you told me about your siblings and their death, but I had to find out the hard way that it was you who was driving the car when they were killed."

His eyes dropped from mine to the blade of grass he was curling into a tight ball. "And now you know my darkest secret and most horrible guilt."

"Brandon," I said, waiting for him to look up at me before continuing, "it wasn't your fault."

"Of course it was. I—"

"Had nothing to do with it. You were simply a means to an end. I know how crazy this sounds because of how the whole thing connects, but Rose killed your siblings."

"Rose? No, she wasn't there. How could she have—"

"Trust me. We had to make a bargain with Kieran, you remember the vampire queen?"

His sadness morphed into slight horror. "Of course, I remember her. You *talked* to her?"

"Yes. Believe me, it was weird. Caleb set the whole thing up and made sure we were safe. She wanted assurance that we'd let her kill Rose herself in exchange for some information. Brandon, this next part might be hard to hear and is probably why Trina wanted me to tell you instead of having to do it herself, but your mom went to Rose for help. For a spell. She wanted revenge on your father and his new family."

His eyes narrowed at first and then widened as I spoke.

"Rose lied to her and told her there would be a heavy cost for the spell. We've since learned that she didn't really need to take three lives in order to put a spell on three others, but she used it as an excuse to kill your siblings and capture more ghosts."

"I'm not sure what you're saying here."

"I'm saying, Brandon, is that you didn't kill your sisters and brother. Rose did. In a way, your mom did because she agreed to continue with the spell no matter the cost Rose would take. I feel like it's really important you understand this. It. wasn't. your. fault."

Tears pooled up in the bottom of his eyes, making them look shiny and full to the point of spilling out the pain.

"That's right. I also know how you died. You felt so bad about the accident that you..."

He held his hand up to stop me as his lip trembled. "If you keep going, we might accidentally stumble into my unfinished business. I can't cross over now; you need me too much."

I smiled in relief and celebration that he was still the snarky kid I knew despite the pain I'd surely brought to the surface. "Okay, but are you even sure that works now that you've stolen a gaudy bracelet and gained a body? I've been wanting to ask what happened to the clothes you were wearing when you took them off. Did they go back to being ghostly or did we somehow figure out how to clone clothes that are buried in a grave somewhere? Oh, and I also think it would be cool to visit your grave."

He wiped at his eyes with his thumb while using the rest of his fingers to try and block me from seeing his tears. "My grave isn't anything fancy. Looks like all the rest of them. I guess you wouldn't know since your body is currently in a freezer somewhere."

"Pretty sure we want to keep it that way."

"We do." He smiled and went back to fiddling with the grass. "The clothes are still real-looking. I was thinking of selling them as real vintage attire on the internets. I hear you can sell anything on there these days."

"You can, but I hate to break it to you that your clothes might not get much money. Now if you'd died like a hundred years ago, maybe..."

"Dang. A fellow has got to make money. I should probably stop mooching from your family at some point."

"Let's just get through this first, and then we'll worry about getting you a creepy apartment to haunt and a job that will turn you into a real adult."

"Fair enough."

I smiled as we quieted for a moment. The silence wasn't awkward, but rather full of thoughts as he probably worked through processing all I'd said to him.

"What if revenge on Rose is my UB?" he asked after several seconds.

"UB?"

"Unfinished business. I just made that up. Cool, huh?"

"Sure. And that would be bad, because we've got to get rid of her before she causes us any more stress or worse, consumes any more souls."

"Yeah…"

"You sure seem very worried about your UB right now. Maybe crossing over would be a good thing? The spirits always look so happy and peaceful when they leave."

His kind, green eyes moved up my face until they made contact with me. They tightened around the edges. "Nothing would be better than staying here with you."

Emotion welled inside even my ghostly chest. It was so overpowering that I turned immediately to humor to ease the intensity. "Even if Heaven has baskets overflowing with puppies and as many doughnuts as you can eat?"

"Even then."

Warm fuzzies assaulted me, and I'm sure I was grinning like a girl in love. Which I was, I guess. Or at least…a dead girl in love.

"Your UB could be freeing your siblings. What about them?" I asked because I suppose I had an issue with feeling happy.

His smile faded and he sighed, then laid back into the grass and stared at the clouds. "Let's just hope that helping anyone else isn't it.

We'll avoid helping me at all costs and pray that nothing else triggers me crossing over. How does that sound?"

I followed his lead and laid down. The sky was too gloomy to pick out individual shapes of clouds, but the wispy movements held some entertainment. "So you're telling me that you only want to help others and ignore your needs. Is that right?"

I felt him shrug next to me. "Yeah, I guess. It doesn't seem right to deny someone the help they need on an off chance that it will be my UB."

"I agree. So tell me how mad you are at your mom after what I told you. I'll be honest, it made me pretty mad at her, and I wasn't even involved with any of that nor is she *my* mom."

He shrugged again. "Honestly, I'm not surprised. Yeah, it was a terrible thing to do, but my mom wasn't a hero before all of that happened anyway. Mostly I feel bad for Savannah, Shannon, and Justin. It wasn't fair that they should suffer. Do you know what happened to my dad's family after the spell was cast?"

I thought for a second, surprised I had been able to remember as much as I had while being ghostly. Perhaps my long rest had helped preserve my memories for a moment.

"I'm sorry. If Kieran did tell me, I've forgotten. We could try an internet search if you can remember their names and where they lived."

"Yeah, we should do that. If I have any anger, it's toward Rose. There are *so* many ghosts around. Why did she need to create more to enslave them?"

"I don't know." I watched the bare tree branches appear to scratch the sky as the wind pushed them around. "She has a lot of powers but being able to see and talk to ghosts isn't one. Or at least it wasn't until

I was dumb enough to let the glasses fall into her hands. So maybe she killed people because she knew they'd turn into ghosts and knew how to trap them right after death? That's the only thing I can think of. As much as I want nothing more to do with her, aside from her demise, it would be nice to sit down and fire a bunch of questions at her. Too bad she'd never go for that."

"Sometimes we don't get answers for things that happen. It's part of life, if you think about it. Annoying but it happens. Maybe it's best we don't know the reasons for everything."

"Or maybe we'll learn them in the afterlife. Are you sure you don't want to cross over so we can find out all the secrets?" I tipped my head to the side to look at his profile and give him a teasing smile.

He glanced in my direction, and I felt pleasure at being able to bring a smile to his lips. "I'm not going until you do."

I sighed wistfully. "It would be nice if we could control stuff like that. Fill me in on the last few days. Did you guys get the book for David yet?"

"No, but we have got a tentative plan." He rolled over and propped his head on his hand with his elbow resting in the grass. "The first bit is you waking up, so good job! You've done step one already."

"Yay me."

He chuckled. "Let's take the wins when we can, even the small ones."

"Fair enough." I rolled over so we were facing each other. "What's the next bit?"

"This may come as a surprise, but with all the coincidences flying around, it also happens to be that the very man the necroes wanted information about is also Andrea's dad. The necroes knew him, of course, since they've been keeping Andrea alive after messing up her spell. They better not mess up your spell, by the way. The last thing I want is Noah following us around for the rest of our lives so he can cast a spell on you every day."

"Uhm, okay. That's a lot to unpack. Wait…" Something important pinged in my memory about Theodore and some information Noah had told me once, but it felt barely out of reach.

Brandon watched me furrow my eyebrows and try to remember with a small smile on his face. "When we told Noah what we'd found out, he had a fit. I'm certain his convictions toward the order have been shaken to their very foundations."

"Why? I feel like I know, but I can't remember. I don't know how you did it being a ghost and forgetting stuff all the time. It's stupid."

"To be fair, I mostly wanted to forget about the past and only wanted to live in the moment with you."

"You know you can be really cheesy sometimes."

"It's a good thing you like it then."

I gave him a flat look with my eyes, but the corners of my mouth were fighting off a smile, waiting for him to answer my question.

"Fun fact, this Theodore, Mitchell guy is some creepy old necromancer from legends long ago who basically does what Rose does. Your mom's working theory is that Rose has learned the necro secrets from him somehow. They may have even been working together for whatever nefarious plans they have."

"And that's why David was always careful to keep Noah in the dark about what he wanted us to find. Too bad we also happen to be Noah's friends. I kind of remember Noah talking about this old necro guy.

He seemed to think that he was truly evil, like even more evil than we might think necromancers in general are. He's like an extra-evil necro."

"Well yeah, if he's eating souls and then teaching others to do it. I'd say he's evil."

"And I'm definitely not surprised that Andrea is his kid. Though I am wondering about the logistics of how old her mom is compared to her dad. I guess when you're immortal from eating souls, you can still have kids in your...hundreds or thousands. I don't know."

Brandon chuckled again. "Yeah, it makes sense, and now his daughter is a zombie that the necroes are hoping to keep a secret. He's bound to notice at some point that his daughter isn't aging. And if the order's plan was just to wait for him to die, I'm afraid they're going to be very disappointed."

"But wait a minute. Why would David want a book from this bad dude? He told me while Mom and I were in the office that Theodore had the book, but I wanted to get out of there too fast to question it too much." I paused and we locked eyes as we thought things through. It was momentarily distracting to imagine leaning in closer so we could kiss. I had a feeling if we were ever together while both of us had fully functioning human bodies, there would be lots of kissing.

I had a sudden thought and smacked the grass next to me, causing no effect whatsoever. "Oh, I was so right about that guy! He wants to eat souls, too!"

"And thus why Noah freaked out even more when he realized what is happening."

"As much as he annoys me, I do feel bad for him. Finding out that the family you based your life's choices on isn't as good as you thought must have been a difficult realization."

"Honestly, I'm not sure if he's madder about finding out the truth or madder about the fact that they've purposely left him out of it. They were right not to trust him with the information yet. Perhaps they were waiting until he became a more full-fledged member before letting him in on all the details."

"Or maybe David isn't telling anyone in the order, and they're just as in the dark as Noah is. David did say that one of his own order members was responsible for killing that first Seer sent to Susan. I'm betting they knew about David's nefarious plans and wanted to stop them. David found out, probably had them brutally murdered, and then made sure to be more careful about who he was telling his dark ambitions to."

I frowned and started talking again. "So what? He's going to get the book from Mitchell and then consume ghost souls in private? Won't they notice when he suddenly looks a lot younger? It might even heal him from his wheelchair situation, depending on his issues."

"I'm sure he's capable of coming up with another lie to cover that."

"And now I'm wondering why he's involving all of us in this. I get why he only wanted to talk to me at first, keeping the secret to as few people as possible. He had to know I'd tell Noah, though. Especially since I'll probably need his and Andrea's help to sneak into her dad's house and see if the book is there."

Brandon pressed his lips and shook his head slightly. "I have no idea. Maybe this is a kind of test for Noah. I doubt David is very concerned about losing the kid from the order. I don't know. At any rate, he must be desperate to ask you to help him. He knows we'll do anything to get you back into your body, even help him get an evil book that will help him consume souls."

And there it was. The choice we were going to have to make. We couldn't put me back into my body without the order. Noah wasn't capable of performing the spell on his own. David knew exactly what was on the line when he asked me to get the book from Mitchell.

"Trina could make me a bracelet, too," I said, after thinking for a second. "We could both live together like this, solve ghost mysteries, not have to worry about a grocery bill."

His bright eyes softened, and he began shaking his head before I finished. "That is no life, Hanna. Not when you have the choice to live a full one once again. Obviously, the choice is long gone for me. We could dig up my body, but I'm sure I'd look and smell pretty terrible. Not even I would want you to kiss me then."

I widened my eyes in amused alarm. "Yes. I'm going to pass on that. But living in this half-form is better than letting him eat any souls. I'm not putting myself before others like that."

"We figured you'd say that. So we've decided we're going to try and trick him. Even if we fail, it's not like he can kill you more. Then we'll revisit another bracelet idea."

"Or he could hurt you guys. Well not you because you're dead too. But maybe my mom or Trina. He could punish all of us easily. We're already running scared from one necromancer, let's not make it two."

"Okay, how about you look at it like this. Even if we don't help David, he'll find a way anyway. If we can intervene and stop him for good from getting the powers to eat the dead, wouldn't that be worth it?"

I frowned and dropped the arm I was leaning on, so my head and shoulders flopped back into the grass. "Ugh. Why is being the good guy so exhausting?"

"I don't know. Some of the evil plans bad guys come up with seem to be pretty extensive and exhausting."

I sighed. "What do you suppose the odds are that this book is the super evil one with the bad spells we're thinking it is? What if it's only a simple textbook about zombie body parts or something that David loaned Mitchell long ago and hasn't gotten back yet?"

"Let's find the book and see what it is first. Then make the choice of what to do." Brandon sat up and dug a cell phone out of his pocket. "I'll gather the troops. I know your mom has been super anxious waiting for you to return."

"You sure took your time calling her if you were that worried about her feelings." I gave him a small teasing smile.

"Well, you know, I am a teenage boy. I should have some vices. No one could blame me for wanting to spend a few minutes alone with you. Like I said, we've got to take our small pleasures when we can."

I put my hand out to touch his before he could text or call anyone. He couldn't feel it, but he paused as was my intention. "Wait. While we have a second, I was wondering if you wanted to talk about it."

"Talk about what?"

"Well, you know… You've avoided the topic any time I tried to bring it up, but maybe now that you know I know what happened…"

His eyes dropped to the grass, and he chewed on his lip for a second. "I kind of don't want to talk about it for a couple of reasons. One is my UB and accidentally solving that by working through the whole thing. The other is that I'm frankly not ready to talk about it."

"Twenty years isn't enough time?"

He flashed me a small smile. "Guess not."

"Okay, then I guess I want to at least tell you that I understand why you did what you did. I don't want to make you feel bad for hurting yourself, because I get you were in a lot of pain and felt a lot of guilt. But I also want you to know that it wasn't your fault your siblings died. I just really need you to understand that. You didn't do anything wrong. You aren't a bad person."

We sat in silence for a few moments. I hoped it was enough to give him time to let my words sink in.

Finally, he sat back, resting his weight on his hands and looked up at the sky. "Maybe. Maybe not. It'll be nice to talk to them again."

"Don't worry. We've got this."

Chapter 21 - Trina

I finally got notice that Hanna had awoken Thursday afternoon as I headed to my car after school. Brandon's text came through as I dug my car keys out of my backpack. My heart leapt with excitement and relief as I read she'd come back that afternoon and was ready to start figuring out what we were going to do next.

It had been nice to go back to school for a minute without impending issues looming right over my head. I'd been able to catch up on my homework and at least get my grades to a steady place. I had several term papers due after Christmas break, but I was saving those heavy things for when I had the time to work on them.

I probably would have made more progress if it hadn't been for the headache. It started out as a small presence in the back of my mind, but as each day passed, it grew a little heavier. At first, I thought it was a caffeine headache, but no amount of soda helped it pass. Then I thought maybe a tension ache would go away after I'd gotten some rest, but so far, that hadn't seemed to be the case.

Maybe it would go away after Hanna was back and safe in her body, and I could slightly relax. It could have also been from craning my neck over my shoulder all the time looking for Caleb to pop up and murder me at any moment.

I was still struggling to get used to not having Caleb at school. I guess Rose had decided he wasn't wasting anymore time parading around as a high school student and hadn't taken his body back to classes. I probably would have done the same thing if I were her.

Our friends kept asking me if I knew anything about where he'd gone or what had happened, but I'd kept denying it while my heart sunk lower into my chest. Being in our familiar places and with our familiar people was a lot more painful than I wanted it to be.

At any rate, I was relying on getting all this put behind us.

"Something good?" Gryphin asked, that pesky grey curl falling onto his forehead. Sometimes I wanted to get a bobby pin and secure it out of the way. He'd waited for me outside of the school to walk me to my car as protection, kindly requested by my mom.

It was probably a smart thing to do as an extra deterrent from Rose attacking, but I still felt bad for the kid. Surely he'd rather be doing something other than waiting for me outside of the school so he could walk me to my car and then back from the car into my house.

"Yes, Hanna's awake. As weird as it is getting texts from someone who is still essentially a ghost, I have to admit it's been handy having him around so I could focus on school while he waited for her to wake up."

"He might be kind of annoying but seems like a good pup, as my dad would say." Gryphin hopped in front of me a couple of steps so he could open the car door for me.

I smiled gratefully and slid into the front seat. "Thanks. Let's head to the park. I'm assuming you'll want to tag along?"

"Of course. I'm invested now," he said with a grin and shut the door firmly.

I may have sped a tiny bit on our way but not enough to attract too much attention. Besides, it wasn't like it was a far drive.

Mom was already there by the time we arrived, and we all settled onto the usual picnic table in the back of the park. The sky was grey with clouds, and a cold breeze pushed through occasionally, but if I snuggled into my jacket and stole some warmth from the nearby werewolf, it wasn't too uncomfortable.

"How's your headache, sweetie?" Mom asked as I sat down next to her, and Gryphin sat down on my other side.

Brandon and Hanna were across the table from us. It was weird seeing him in clothes from this decade, but it had probably been weirder for Hanna to wake up to his change.

"Still there pounding in the back of the skull. Doesn't seem to be too much worse than yesterday though," I said while rubbing my forehead. "Sure wish meds would work. It's hard to focus on much."

"You've got a headache?" Hanna's eyes narrowed as she studied me.

"Yeah, not a big deal. Everyone gets headaches once in a while." I shrugged it off. "So what's the plan? What are we getting into next?"

Brandon and Hanna exchanged a curious glance with each other while Mom patted my hand in sympathy.

"As far as I've been updated, the necroes want y'all to get a book from this Mitchell guy who also happens to be the father of someone you know from school?" Gryphin asked, his eyes bouncing around to the three people he could see.

Gryphin had been helping out the last couple of days, so he'd met Brandon already. It had been amusing to watch his reaction to meeting the ghost we'd been talking about for weeks. Of course, Brandon wasn't a huge fan of the muscled werewolf that had been spending time with Hanna while he was missing, but I made sure not to mention that he'd also spent some time in Hanna's bed as a wolf, using his hefty weight and soft fur to comfort her.

"Yes, one of my friends from school who also happens to be a zombie," Hanna said, drawing my and Brandon's attention.

Gryphin noticed our glances. "What? What did she say? Hi, Hanna!" He waved in the completely wrong direction.

I hid a smile while Brandon gave him a flat look.

"She said Mitchell's daughter also happens to be a zombie," I said, not wanting Gryphin or Mom to feel out of the loop.

"Okay..." Gryphin's eyebrows raised in curiosity.

"So she has a body I'm able to possess. Does Gryphin know about that?" Hanna said, looking at me.

"Yes, we've had time to catch him up on stuff." I turned to Gryphin. "Hanna is reminding us that she can possess Mitchell's daughter. I'm guessing because she has got some kind of plan."

"Well, not a fully fleshed out one," Hanna said while she and Branon grinned at each other.

It was nice that they were reunited, but it was also kind of sickening and annoying. All I could think of when they made those stupid private looks between each other or giggled at some inside joke was how Caleb was trapped.

"What's her idea?" Mom asked. "I'm not sure I feel comfortable stealing anything from anyone, especially a dark book from an evil necromancer, and then giving it to another, perhaps also evil, necromancer."

"I'm with you on that." I turned to Hanna. "What do you plan to do?"

And Hanna filled us in on her thoughts, which were simple enough but didn't address the ethics of it all.

Mom frowned after I repeated Hanna's plan for her and Gryphin. "I can appreciate the low risk, but I still can't get around the ethics."

"How do we even know this is an evil book unless we see it first? Maybe it's just something about gardening for zombies?" Hanna said with a hopeful smile and a shrug.

"Remind me again of how David described the book for you to find?" I said, not forgetting it at all but wanting her to review and remember.

"He said only there was a book in Mitchell's possession that we'd recognize as it would stand out from the rest." Hanna waved her hand in the air as if it weren't as big of a deal as I was making it out to be.

"And do you really think a gardening book would do that?" I asked pointedly.

She sighed and rolled her eyes.

"If I may," Brandon held up an index finger, "let's not forget that this is all to get Hanna back into her body. We don't really have a choice but to help the necroes. I get not wanting to perpetuate evil. I understand not wanting to allow anyone to suck up souls like this evil necro and Rose can do. If anyone understands that, it's me. However, we have to get her body. Even if we try to appeal to another necro order someplace else, we'd still have to bargain with this current one to release her body. I have a feeling they wouldn't give it up easily. Not to mention, even if we didn't help David, he'd get someone else to do it. Let's just grab the book and go from there, okay?"

Quiet descended on our group as we looked at each other, considering his words.

"I'd say that's fair." Gryphin looked at me with a shrug.

"I don't know... I've seen movies with evil books. They don't usually end well unless you have a chainsaw arm," I said, already knowing I was going to lose the argument.

"As a mother, how is it my right to doom other parents' children's souls because I want to be with my daughter? Where is the line between wanting to save your child and becoming too selfish?" Mom's eyes looked down at the table as she clutched her purse on her lap.

"Tell her to stop worrying and let us do this. We'll figure it out. One step at a time, remember?" Hanna turned her forceful gaze on me.

I sighed, knowing the headache drained me of my fighting spirit. "I have a feeling they're going to do this with or without us, Mom. We might as well give in so we can help instead of getting more worry wrinkles."

An hour later, we met up with Noah and Andrea. They had to come to Hanna because she wasn't able to leave the park, and we really needed the cheerleader's specific body instead of the ol' reliable Hank, as Hanna had taken to calling him.

Whatever lie Noah had told Andrea to get her to the park, it didn't hold up when she saw the odd collection of people waiting for them. Mom had gone home, and her job was to come get us if we were gone too long or something went wrong. From Andrea's perspective, she probably saw two strange guys, one with hugely broad shoulders and the other with an odd vibe standing with a girl she may have vaguely recognized as Hanna's sister.

"What's going on?" Andrea asked as Noah greeted us at our usual table. She stood slightly behind him with her arms wrapped around herself while wearing a thick, but stylish, jacket.

Hanna had explained that Andrea didn't remember the times when Hanna was possessing her, but the before and after the incident was different. If we wanted to keep her in the dark, we had to figure out how to make all of this seem normal and not stick out in her mind as something odd to tell others about later.

Especially if her father ended up asking her about the missing book.

Thankfully, we didn't have to take time and stake out Mitchell's house or figure out where he lived. While Mitchell hadn't been around enough for Noah to meet him, Andrea had spent one weekend a month staying at Mitchell's place, so Noah was at least familiar with the location and the layout.

"We're here to meet Trina about our AP history project, remember?" Noah gave Andrea an admirably confident smile.

"It's weird that they let a sophomore in that class in the first place." I tried to give him an appreciating look.

"Is that the best lie you could come up with?" Hanna said as she stood next to Andrea, licked her finger, and stuck it in the other girl's ear.

"Aren't you Hanna's sister?" Andrea's eyes narrowed as she looked down at my outfit and boots.

I knew they were stylish enough, so I didn't bother worrying about it. Andrea was probably only trying to establish some kind of dominance. "Yeah. Hanna introduced us when she heard Noah was having so much trouble in class."

Noah gave me a flat look out of Andrea's view.

"Okay, fine. But who are they?" Andrea pointed to Brandon and Gryphin who had also gotten up from the bench and were standing behind me.

"I'm Gryphin, a friend of Trina's." The taller boy stuck out his hand for her to shake. "Pleased to meet you."

Andrea took it slowly and limply shook his hand. I had a feeling she probably wouldn't have bothered to return his friendliness if he weren't so darn good-looking. "Hi."

"And this is Brandon." I shoved a thumb over my shoulder in his direction. "Let's get down to it, shall we?"

"Nice to—" Brandon started but stopped when Hanna stepped into the cheerleader's body, not waiting for more meaningless pleasantries. "How rude."

"What? You've never liked her." Hanna put Andrea's hands on her hips and gave him a sassy head bob.

Brandon shrugged. "Still. Doesn't mean I can't be polite and the better man."

"Right. Well, we've got more important things to work on. You can shake her hand later," Hanna said, turning to Noah. "Ready to go?"

He nodded. "Yes. I'm still not sure how I feel about letting David have this book. I've been thinking about it for days, hardly slept."

"That explains why you look like you're the zombie." Hanna wore a sympathetic side-smile.

"As I keep reminding everyone, David is going to get his hands on this book whether we help him or not. At least this way we can grab it and then decide what to do," Brandon said, earning half-hearted nods from most of us.

"Okay, we should get going, before her dad comes home for dinner." Noah turned and led our group out of the skatepark.

"I don't feel great about this." Gryphin leaned in to say to me as we trailed behind the others. "I wish there was another way to help Hanna."

"Me too, pal. Me too." I rubbed the back of my head where the headache was pounding, apparently settling in for the long haul.

Chapter 22 - Hanna

It was so much nicer to be back inside of Andrea's body. Sure, Hank was a good guy, and I imagined he was always kind to his grandchildren around Christmas time, but Andrea's joints didn't creak and resist when I tried to walk. It was also nice not having to avoid thinking about having different body parts than what I was used to.

As I stood on the sidewalk looking up at Andrea's dad's house, I frowned and turned to Noah. "How were we ever friends for so long, yet I've never been here before?"

He gave me a kind smile but didn't need to answer the question. We both knew why.

The Michaelson's house was even larger than the one the necromancer order used, situated in an even richer neighborhood. Considering how old this Mitchell/Theodore guy was, he had plenty of time to save up some money. I spared a few seconds to wonder about his family and how many he had before and how many children he'd fathered over the years.

It was kind of gross to think about.

"Remember, if we run into her stepmom or the maid, you're supposed to act like Andrea, not like yourself." Noah nodded encouragingly.

"The maid wears a uniform or something, right? Just want to make sure I can tell the difference."

Noah laughed. "Oh, you'll be able to tell. Keep the convo short. If all else fails, pull that sassy attitude and retreat to her bedroom. That's what her stepmom is used to anyway."

"I can handle that." I turned back to the car window and peeked my head inside. "We'll be back in a few minutes. If we're longer than thirty, call Phoenix for backup."

"I still want to go with you." Brandon frowned from the middle seat in between Trina and Gryphin.

"Too bad you stole the bracelet and can't be an invisible ghost anymore." Trina's eyes stared angrily at the seat in front of her and her tone was sharp.

That headache must have been bothering her more than she wanted to admit. If I hadn't had so many other things to think about, I would have given her pain more concern. We had time to figure it out later.

Brandon pulled out a pouty lip and crossed his arms over his chest. "Guess you shouldn't have made it in the first place."

I peeked over at Gryphin and raised my eyebrows in silent question.

He glanced over at Trina and Brandon with an amused smile and nodded his head. "We'll be fine. Call if you need help."

Noah grabbed my hand as we walked away from the driveway and toward the house. "Hopefully no one will notice I've left three random people in my car today. We've come here a time or two on Saturdays, but my car is usually empty."

"You're the one who said having extra people in the house would make her stepmom...Er, *my* stepmom suspicious. Maybe we should have left them at the park," I said, trying to get into the mindset of Andrea. She enjoyed showing off Noah and was proud that they were together. She'd want to hold his hand and enjoy the warmth from his skin instead of wishing he were another person like I was currently doing.

"They're there in case we need them though. It's nice to have that reassurance, right?"

"Couldn't you simply summon some zombies to protect us?" I talked quietly as we walked into the house, not wanting anyone to overhear who might have been inside.

"You know that's not how it works. I didn't bring any corpses with me, and I doubt there are any under the floorboards I can pull up."

"I wouldn't be so sure. Have you ever tried?"

It was fun to fall back into friendly banter. We hadn't been able to spend much time alone with each other since Andrea had kept such a short leash on him, but the small moments we'd had at parties or at lunch where we could exchange a few teasing jokes had been pleasant enough.

Enough that it had cemented my crush on him even more, back in the day.

Despite the ease of which we chatted, I didn't feel the return of my previous over-fondness for him. Sure, he was cute and decently nice, but there was someone else I wanted to spend more time with, and it was as simple as that.

Plus, a small part of me was still angry with him for not telling my mom and Trina where my haunt was. He was redeeming himself by helping us and allowing suspicions of David's actions to take root, but it still wasn't quite enough.

"Seems quiet," Noah said as we walked down the foyer.

I tried not to stare too much at the elegant decorations and the high vaulted ceilings but seeing where Andrea lived on the weekends explained a lot more about her.

"It's weird that you've been here a million times, and David has not once asked you to pick up the book. Are we even sure that it will be here?" I kept my voice quiet as we entered the kitchen that seemed as big as my entire house.

"We've got to at least check." He went to the fridge like he lived there and pulled out two sparkling waters.

I grabbed the one he handed to me and took a tentative sip. It was the first thing I'd tasted since dying, and it was as horrible as I remember sparkling water to be. "Am I supposed to pretend I like this stuff?"

Noah grinned and chugged a couple of swallows. "It's probably best if we split up. I'll check the study while you check the bedroom. It might be less weird if you're caught up there than if I am."

I put the drink down onto the counter and nodded. "And I'm just supposed to know it when I see it? I doubt he'd keep something like that out in the open. Could David have been vaguer about this whole thing?"

Something dark flashed through his eyes as he turned his gaze toward the large windows overlooking the backyard with a swimming pool and patio. "It has to be a trick, you know. I've only agreed to help you because I want you to become whole as much as anyone else, but also because I'm worried about you. If something goes wrong, I want to be there to help you out if I can. But honestly, I'm worried that either we'll fail, and our friends will suffer, including you, or we succeed and give a most dangerous book to a most dangerous man."

"I know..." I sighed and leaned back against the counter. "But I don't know what else to do. We can't let things stay the way they are. We've got to take down Rose somehow, free Caleb..."

"Get your body back."

I waved off his comment. "Yeah, that too, I guess. We'll have to figure out another way to keep your order's leader from doing anything crazy. Maybe he only wants to get the book to prevent this other evil necro from doing more evil things?"

The look he gave me was skeptical with one eyebrow raised.

I sighed again. "I thought you were supposed to be the optimistic one, especially when it comes to the order."

He shrugged. "I guess I'm learning better."

"Well, we're not doing much standing around. Meet you back here in twenty?"

He nodded and we parted ways. It wasn't until he'd disappeared down the hall that I realized I had no idea where my own bedroom was, let alone Mitchell's. Shrugging to myself, I decided to explore. Maybe the book would be in a place no one would expect, and it would call out to me, begging to be rescued.

Or to corrupt more people, depending on what the book actually did.

Figuring that the bedrooms were probably up the stairs, I found the elegantly railed staircase and ascended the carpeted steps, trying to keep quiet but also look like I belonged there in case someone else saw me.

The upstairs hallway was wide, and several doors were laid out before me, some open, some closed. I peeked into the open ones first, figuring those were the easiest to assess. It didn't take but two doors to find what I assumed was Andrea's room. She never mentioned siblings, so I figured she was the only kid in the house, though to be fair, I'd never asked about her siblings before either.

The room was not as pink as I would have pictured. White curtains framed both of the large windows. The bed was a dark wood with four tall posts and a white canopy top. The dresser, vanity, and side-tables all matched the same kind of wood as the bed posts, and I took a second to appreciate the symmetry of the furniture as the stuff in my bedroom was random pieces handed down from cousins or things we found at yard sales.

Her walk-in closet was huge, naturally, with rows and rows of clothes I was sure she probably hadn't worn more than once, but there wasn't a book in sight.

Continuing on my adventure, I eventually found an entire room full of books. I couldn't be sure if it was the office and library combined, but guessing from the rest of the house, they had the room to keep the two separate. There were shelves all around the room stocked full of books from floor to ceiling. There was even one of those rolling ladders that allowed a person to reach the highest shelves or fly along the rows like Belle in the bookstore. I was tempted to try that out but restrained myself, trying to keep focused on the task at hand.

If the book was here, then Mitchell was either super smart or super dumb. It would be the first place someone would look when trying to find a book so it wouldn't be a good place to hide it. On the other hand, someone might think that would be too easy and skip this room entirely. As for me, I didn't have any other leads and was kind of following my gut and waiting for sudden inspiration to strike.

Starting with the shelf closest to the door, I looked at one row at a time, enjoying the books as some of them were quite old. Again, Mitchell would have had several years to create this collection. There were probably books in there that were priceless.

Shuffles of feet and humming warned me of someone coming down the hallway. I panicked for a second, trying to figure out where the best place to hide would be, but then I remembered my current body lived here. It would be odd for me to be hidden. Reasonably sure that Andrea probably didn't come to look for books a lot, I searched my brain for excuses as to what I might be doing there.

"Oh, hello, dear," a lady said as she paused outside the room. "I didn't hear you come in."

I smiled but nothing too happy in case Andrea didn't usually go around smiling. If she was anything like she was at school, the smiles were all probably fake anyway.

"Yes, got home not too long ago. Noah and I have a homework project we're working on so I thought I might see if there are any books on the subject in here. He's in the bathroom and will be back shortly to join me. I sure hope we can get a better grade on this report working together than doing it on our own," I said probably way too quickly. Being sneaky and pretending to be someone else was still new to me. Clearly, I needed practice.

The woman walked through the doorway and furrowed her well-maintained eyebrows slightly, clueing me in that I wasn't quite getting Andrea's demeanor right.

Judging from her dress and the way she was looking at me, I guessed this was Andrea's stepmom. I doubted the maid was going around cleaning in a dress I would usually label "club-chic". It was a dark blue, strapless, tight at the waist and cut mid-thigh. She was pretty enough with long, flowing blonde hair, probably as real as Andrea's was, but it was clear she'd had some work done on her face. It wasn't anything I could pinpoint consciously because I wasn't skilled like that, but something about her mouth was "off", perhaps a bit too stiff, a bit too tight. Either way, it made me wonder what kind of woman would marry a super old evil necromancer.

"Don't you usually have Henry go online and get you what you need for projects?" She looked around the room in concern as if this was the last place any person in their right mind would want to be.

I had no idea who Henry was, perhaps someone who worked for them, but of course that's what Andrea would do when she had homework. She'd copied off my math answers for several semesters, why would another class be any different?

Remembering Noah's advice about how to act, I shrugged one shoulder and rolled my eyes where she could see them before turning back to the shelf. "Sometimes I like to do things for myself. Plus, I'm bored, and Noah convinced me that we should do the project together. Once he gets back, I'm sure he'll want to take the lead and do most of the work himself."

"Oh, I see." The woman's tone told me she wore a small smile and that my behavior may be heading in the right direction. "You two sure have been getting close lately. Is there anything you want to tell me?"

I glanced at her, trying to look annoyed. "No."

"Okay, well you know I'm here if you want to talk. I know we haven't always been really close, but you've only got a few years left before you leave for the rest of your life. We should probably spend some time together."

I was half-tempted to sit her down on the nearest sofa, grab her hands, and reveal Andrea's zombie secret, but restrained myself. Once again, I had a job to do, and as fun as it would be to ruin Andrea's life like she'd tried to ruin mine with that stupid video, I was going to take the higher road.

"Yeah, for sure. We'll hang out a lot later when I don't have so much stuff to do." I continued to look at the books, hoping she would go away.

"Right. Of course, dear. Dinner's at seven," she said as she left the room, hopefully thinking that Andrea was totally normal and not possessed by a dead girl from school.

I quickened my pace and searched the whole library room as quickly as I could while still making sure to check all the books. Some of them were frayed and definitely suspicious but none of them stood out to me in the way David had described this book would.

The library had probably been a dumb place to look for a book someone was trying to hide. There could have easily been a secret entrance to a sinister lair somewhere, but I had no idea where to even begin to search for one of those or how to open it.

I found a few more rooms that appeared to be untouched, probably guest rooms, and the master bedroom at the end of the hall. The door was shut, and, guessing from the loud TV sounds coming from it, I assumed that's where Andrea's stepmom had gone after our weird conversation. Not wanting to disturb her again, I returned to the kitchen a few minutes earlier than Noah's designated meeting time.

I sighed and leaned against the counter, looking at the fancy appliances on the other side of the room and wondering what kind of fridge would need a computer screen on it.

"I was quite impressed when David told me you'd found a way to get around. Possessing the zombie body of Theodore's daughter was quite genius though, even I have to admit," a lovely voice said as Rose rounded the corner from the dining room into the kitchen.

As a person who was dead, inhabiting a human body who was also dead, I still felt like I had a mini stroke at the sight of the poised witch. Her light hair was pulled up into a clean twist on the back of her head while she wore a soft-floral blouse with lace trim and navy slacks.

Immediately my mouth dried up, and I had trouble speaking. "Wha? How? No, you've got it all wrong. I live here, but I do need to go."

I turned to run out of the kitchen toward the front door, hopes low that I would even make it as far as the outside when she popped in my way with a blink. I'd seen Rose do some amazing things, including control a vampire and feed it necromancer energy to keep it going strong against any and all enemies, but for some reason, I'd never thought about her using the basic magic user gifts like teleportation. Of course, she could do all that too. Sometimes I wasn't that smart.

"Tut tut. I think it's time for you and me to have a little chat."

Before I could so much as gasp in horror, she grabbed my wrist, and the world spun wickedly around me.

Chapter 23 - Trina

After what seemed like way longer than the twenty-five minutes on the clock, Noah came back out of the house alone. At first, he paused and looked around the neighborhood as if trying to spot something and then jogged toward us as we were still crammed inside the car.

My heart sank at the expression on his face, and I knew something had gone wrong.

Gryphin popped open the door and was outside before Noah had even made it across the lawn. "What's wrong?"

I struggled to follow his lead and climbed out, glad to be out of the suffocating car. It had been nice to be out of the wind, but it hadn't taken long before the wait with two other impatient persons had become unbearable. It had gotten even worse when Brandon started telling us jokes.

Brandon shut the door behind him as he got out of the car. "Where's Hanna?"

Noah's eyes were wide as he shook his head and joined us on the driveway. "She's gone. Not inside the house anywhere. One minute I could sense the zombie presence of my creation, the next, nothing."

"Wait. What? Where could she have gone?" I asked, feeling panic fluttering inside. "Maybe she accidentally stepped out of Andrea's body and got zapped back to her haunt?"

But Noah was shaking his head before I could finish my question. "No. I would still feel Andrea's body inside. She isn't there. I can only feel she's still functioning, but I don't know where."

With wide eyes, I looked at each of my companions, all sharing similar expressions of a horrible worry. Brandon's mouth was pressed into a resolution to hold in the emotions, while Gryphin looked laser focused and ready to prowl out on the hunt.

"Maybe we should at least check the skatepark, just in case?" I said, feeling the pressure from all of their gazes as if it was *my* job to somehow find her even though I certainly wasn't the one who lost her.

We sat in tense silence as we drove. My mind whirled with any kind of situation that could have happened.

"Oh!" I said when we were nearly there. "What if Phoenix popped in and agreed to take her somewhere? They could have gotten a lead on Rose and needed Hanna's help. Of course, Hanna would agree to do that."

"But without telling us? Wouldn't Phoenix have popped up in the driveway to tell us where they were going if that was the case?" Brandon asked, his words tight and tense.

"Yeah, Hanna would have." I picked up my phone for the thousandth time. The only notification was another stupid email of a store ad. Hanna didn't have her phone on her, of course, but she did have Andrea's. She could have found me through a social app and messaged me even if she didn't have my direct phone number. There was nothing there, and nervous energy made me jiggle my knee up and down.

We had already tried calling Andrea's phone several times but hadn't gotten any answer.

I practically ran out of the car and into the park once we arrived. Several kids hanging out turned to look at our group and our panicked rush, but I didn't care.

"Hanna? Are you here?" I jogged toward the tables. There was nothing there, but I wasn't ready to believe I'd lost my sister. Again. "Hanna? Where are you?"

People were trying to politely ignore our weird searching since, to their eyes, there was obviously no one there, but more than one was giving me odd looks.

Noah grabbed my elbow and steered me to take a seat. "Trina, we'll figure this out. Take a breath."

Gryphin sat down on the other side of me while Brandon stood off to the side, his arms folded across his chest and an angry glare for anyone who happened to look his way.

"Where could she have gone?" I blinked at the tears in my eyes and looked up at Noah's hazel gaze.

"I don't know." He shook his head, his hand holding mine comfortingly. "We'll find her. We will."

A dark shadow appeared over us, and I looked up, expecting to see Brandon hovering above with an angry look. Instead, I found Caleb. His eyes were wide and panicked, but his jaw was clenched tightly as if he was straining against something.

"Caleb?" I stood immediately. "You're here for real, aren't you? Did she set you free?"

"No. She doesn't know I'm here. She's busy setting something up real quick. Setting up a spell. She's got Hanna, Trina. You have to save her. Don't come alone. Bring as much help as you can."

"What?" I grabbed onto his jacket, wishing for nothing else except for him to wrap me into his thick arms and tell me everything was going to be okay.

Instead, he grabbed my shoulders and pushed me back so he could properly look into my eyes. "Save her. At the warehouse."

And he was gone as quickly as he'd come, even before Gryphin could reach my side in a protective motion.

I gasped, falling into the space where he'd been standing.

Noah caught me and waited until I was steady again before letting go. "Trina, we can do this. I know some necroes who are loyal to the cause of justice. They'll help us."

"We'll be there, too, of course." Gryphin stood on my other side and patted my shoulder warmly. "I'll text Billy and the pack right now."

"Yes, great, rally the troops. Just one problem."

We all looked at Brandon who had turned from his usual optimistic self to a grumpy downer.

"What?" I asked because he seemed to need the prompt.

"What warehouse is he talking about?"

That stalled our momentum for a second, and I let out a sad sigh. Then something someone had said earlier pricked into my mind. "I'll bet Frank knows."

"Who the heck is Frank?" Noah asked, frowning. "Wait... I think that name sounds familiar. He's a ghost, isn't he?'"

I nodded and ran back to the car. "We need to go to the movie theater."

Chapter 24 - Hanna

As the world righted itself again, and I realized I'd been teleported like Phoenix had done with me a time or two, I had to bend down and grab my knees before I fell over.

At least this time I didn't need to puke.

"Where are we?" I asked in between gasping breaths and looked around while still bending over and giving my brain time to find its way back to Andrea's body.

"Oh, just my little workshop," Rose said in a sing-song voice. "I appreciate you finding a body to inhabit so I could nab you much easier. I seem to be all out of Seer hair to seal you into a crystal with, and we both know it would have been difficult to get you into the trapping circle anyway. Yes, this way is much easier."

Finally able to stand, I got a better view of our surroundings. It was a dim, gigantic space. There were a few overhead fluorescent lights buzzing above, but towering shelves and large patches of darkness made them nearly useless. As far as I could tell, we were in a big warehouse. Our voices echoed and bounced around.

"Now, here's a place just for you, dear." Rose's fingers were like cold, iron vices as she pushed me into a hard metal chair. "I'm sure you'll want to rest after that teleportation. It's always quite potent for people who aren't used to it."

I was too distracted from the disorientation and taking in the rest of the scene to stop her as she used zip ties on my wrists, adhering me to the chair.

In front of me, there was a large table inside a circle. A pentagram was spray-painted onto the concrete around it, and beyond that, several shelves were full of weird things, including the jar I'd seen the necromancers use to write runes on Stephanie's body. This was clearly a resurrection place. On the table, there was a lumpy form buried underneath a tarp. I was instantly running the odds of it being mine through my head.

"Hey!" I finally processed that I was trapped in the chair. "You should be more careful with me. My dad is a very important man."

Rose stood from where she'd tied my ankles to the legs of the chair. "Oh, is it time to play this game? I know you're not Andrea, dear. Couldn't you tell from my comments about how you've found a body to possess? Honestly, I thought you were smarter than that."

"Still. If you hurt Andrea in any way, I'm sure the evil necromancer will come after you. He can do things beyond the other necroes. You know that, right? He can do things like..."

I trailed off, realizing who I was finally talking to. After all this time, I was getting to talk to Rose, and I'd been dumb enough to let her restrain me.

Or at least my body. Maybe I could use that to my benefit somehow... Except the moment I stepped out of it, I would be transported back to my haunt at the skatepark. Wouldn't I?

Or wait. Why would Rose go to the trouble of capturing me if I could simply step out and go back home? There had to be another trick here that I needed to figure out. At any rate, I was too eager to learn the answers to so many puzzles to run away now.

But it helped me to realize I could escape at any moment. I took a deep calming breath and tried to stop panicking.

"Things like I can?" Rose wore a side-smile, using her fingers with brightly red painted nails to gesture to herself. "Where do you think I learned all those neat tricks?"

Footsteps clomped through the warehouse toward us, and they echoed so much, I couldn't tell where they were coming from until a figure entered into our area of sparse light.

"Speak of the devil." Rose shot me a pleased smile and turned toward the man.

He wore a suit, probably very expensive, but I didn't have any knowledge about how to judge that, with a vest and a long, thick coat like I'd seen businessmen on TV wear. His hair was not as grey as I had expected it to be but rather dark as night and combed back and to the side in a stylish way. He wore glasses, but it was too dark to see what color his eyes were. However, I could definitely see the evil smile sitting on his face. It took time to look that evil, I decided. Maybe even centuries.

"Even if I didn't know you were inside my daughter's body, I could tell it wasn't her. You simply don't have the same mannerisms. But please, do be careful. We need Andrea to be alive and well after all this."

I smirked, unable to help using what leverage I could even though it may get Noah in trouble later. "Alive?"

His smile spread even wider, an action I hadn't thought possible. "Yes, well, you know what I mean. She may be dead, but she's more alive than you are right now."

My chest deflated some. "Oh, I was under the impression the order had hid that from you."

He shrugged one shoulder slowly. "I'm a necromancer. Of course, I would be able to tell my daughter is a zombie. But it's okay. At least she'll be able to have some kind of life. The cancer was stronger than all of us. Even the witches I employed to cure her had no luck."

"Then why keep your knowledge a secret from the order? Noah has been bending himself backward trying to help Andrea without you realizing it."

He laughed, the sound deep and guttural inside his chest but not nearly as raspy as it should have been considering his age. "It's good to keep people on their toes. A healthy respect benefits everyone."

I didn't respond to that because I didn't know what to say. It was surreal to talk to the big bad guy while the other big bad guy I'd been chasing for months now was standing nearby with a snarky tilt to her mouth.

What was happening?

"You know all I have to do is step out of the body, and I'll be teleported back to my haunt? This really isn't much of a capture. I'm afraid all you've managed to do is tie up your own daughter," I said, trying to sound confident and haughty.

"Why do you think we put you in that spot immediately?" Rose gestured almost lazily at the floor beneath my feet.

Telling myself I was brave, I looked down and saw another pentagram spray painted onto the floor around my chair. How I hadn't noticed it before was beyond me, but to be fair, there was a lot going on all at once.

"I think you'll find your spirit isn't able to go anywhere. You need to stay because we've got other plans." Rose looked around the dim warehouse. "Where is Caleb? We really do need to get this started."

And then he was standing near the table as if he'd been there the whole time. He hadn't, I was almost sure, but it felt like it.

"Ah, yes, prepare the spell. David should be here any minute with the order. We'll get this first part done and move on to the next." Rose turned around as if completely forgetting about me for a second.

"What spell? David is coming? What's going on?" I pulled at the restraints keeping me in the chair. Rose had been kind enough to at least not make them too tight, but my pulling against them was sure to leave some marks on Andrea's wrists. I wondered how they were going to explain that to her later.

Theodore also turned away from me and went to the shelving area, gathering supplies. Caleb didn't even spare me a second glance before following Rose's directions of checking the pentagram and the sharpness of a ceremonial knife quite similar to the one David had used in Stephanie's ritual.

"You know my family and friends will come for me, right? I have more powerful friends than you certainly realize," I said, trying to get more answers from them, trying to give myself more hope. Maybe if I said the words out loud, I'd begin to believe them.

It wasn't that I didn't know if they would come for me. It was that I had no idea where I was, and they couldn't know either. But even if they did find me in time, without Caleb's help or a whole host of vampires and zombies, my family and friends could, and most certainly would, be hurt.

Maybe it would be best if they didn't come at all.

Rose turned a shoulder toward me and regarded my poor soul under long, black eyelashes. "That's exactly what we're hoping for. That will give us enough time to put you back into your body, and they should arrive at the same time that we're ready to perform the next spell. This includes your lovely sister, though, right?"

Chills paraded down my back. "Uhm, I'm not sure." I really wanted to backpedal on my brave statements. "Why would you need my sister?"

Rose smiled faintly and turned away. "You'll see. No use in ruining the surprise."

For the next several minutes I was completely ignored as the three of them prepared for whatever nonsense was going to happen. Well, Rose and Caleb mostly worked while Theodore found a chair somewhere, kicked back his feet, and picked at his nails.

A screeching sound came from somewhere else in the building followed by footsteps, clomping hooves, random bleats of protest, and murmuring conversation. Then David wheeled around the corner of the shelves with several of the order members coming in behind him, the last one tugging in a huffing goat who did not want to be inside the dark warehouse. None of them looked me in the eyes, avoiding their gaze, except David.

"Hello, everyone. Sorry we're late. Sometimes the goats don't cooperate," David said with his focus all on me. "Hello again, Hanna. So glad to see you were trying your best to follow the task. I wasn't sure you had it in you."

I glared at him as my brain frantically tried to catch up. "This whole thing was a trap, wasn't it?"

David clapped his hands a couple of times sarcastically. "Good for you. Too bad you figured it out too late. I do need to thank you, though, I suppose, because without being able to use you as bait and set up such a trap, I doubt I'd be invited to this party at all. Certain people were hesitant to work with me. So thank you for giving me the leverage I needed. Now, let's get this show on the road. Are we ready?"

"Simply waiting for you, my dear," Rose said with another condescending smile.

Theodore stood, the chair creaking with the release of weight. "This better be worth it. I've studied this spell for centuries. Ann, if you're wrong, you'll be feeling the consequences."

Rose looked at him with more respect than she'd appeared to have before. I remembered Ann had been her first name when she'd been born during a time that had been difficult for witches, but whatever sympathy I would have had for her had been long ago erased.

"Yes, sir." Rose turned to bark orders at the other necromancers who had come with David.

More puzzle pieces connected inside my mind. Rose had learned her tricks from this guy. He'd been pushed out of the necromancer order a long time ago for his crimes, and then at some point had met up with Rose and decided, for some reason, to make her his student.

I still wasn't sure how David fit into the whole thing. I was guessing he wanted to also become a student and erase the unkind costs of magic from his face and maybe even heal his legs so he could walk again. I wasn't sure how strong the souls were when you swallowed one and if they could heal a malady such as that.

And I didn't particularly want to find out.

A clinking sound came from a bag Caleb pulled out from a shelf, and sat onto a table, not the one with the tarped body. I watched in fear as he pulled out several crystals sealed with wax and hair.

Rose stood next to him, put on my family's glasses she'd had in a pocket somewhere, and picked up a crystal.

"Hey! Those belonged to my grandmother! You can give them back any time now. I'm right here," I said, pulling again on the rigid zip ties that were so much stronger than the small rings of plastic appeared to be.

She ignored me, held the crystal with both hands for a moment, and then placed it onto the table. As she continued throughout the pile, three or four ghosts appeared inside the room with each crystal she touched. There were four crystals holding fourteen ghosts in total, making the room quite crowded and loud to my eyes and ears.

Rose looked over her collection of ghosts with a small smile. Most of them shied away from her, but a few yelled expletives in her face to which she easily ignored.

Part of me was impressed by her ability to shut them out. I'd struggled my whole life with that battle, and she had only gotten the glasses recently. Maybe it was simply that she had gotten good at ignoring anyone who opposed her over the years.

Theodore looked around the room, not looking at any ghost directly, and inhaled with a sinister smile. "I do appreciate the combination of magic user spells with necromancer powers. It sure makes soul-swallowing more convenient."

Rose nodded with an adoring, and slightly deranged, wide-eyed smile in his direction. "Yes, sir. I only hope I've been able to bring enough. My supplies have dwindled recently."

She shot me an annoyed look, but I simply gave her a proud smile, hoping I appeared less terrified than I felt.

As for the ghosts, there were only three that I recognized, my heart sinking as they came into view. Somehow Rose had gotten her not-emptied crystals from the magic users when she escaped. The matron, Cordelia, had mentioned something about traitors in her group. They must have helped Rose break free and get her crystals.

"Hey, you can see us, can't you?" one of the ghost girls said as she caught me looking at them with intended attention.

My eyes darted around the room at the alivers, afraid to talk much with the ghosts. It was obviously not a secret what I was, but I certainly didn't want to give up any other information if I could help it.

The first girl nudged the other girl standing next to her. They were identical twins with long, straightened light hair, layered tank-tops, low-rise jeans, and platform flip-flops. "Is she looking at us?"

The second girl turned to study me with a frown. "Seems like it."

I had no way of knowing which of the twins was Shannon and which was Savannah, but I knew the boy's name was Justin. He wore the same dinosaur shirt, loose jeans, and worn skater shoes as he had the last time I'd seen the siblings.

I kept glancing between them and the necromancers and the other ghosts in the room. It wasn't long before several other spirits noticed my panicked eyes and nonverbal exchanges with the first three ghosts.

They started to converge on me with cries for help and disbelief.

"Can you see us? Please set us free! We don't want to be eaten!"

"Please help us!"

"You have to get me back to my family!"

I squeezed my eyes shut, and a few tears leaked through them. "I'm sorry. I'm so sorry."

"Get away from her!" Rose yelled, instantly grabbing the ghosts' attention.

Apparently, she had learned from the last time I'd been in close contact with her ghosts.

As if pulled on by puppet strings, all of the spirits took several steps away from me. Rose passed through them until she was standing in front of me.

"I suppose this could be quite overwhelming for a Seer. Well, no worries, dear. It won't be long before you'll be free of that curse. I'm sure Theodore will enjoy being able to do what you can do."

My breaths came in rapid spurts as I tried to get control of myself again. "What did you say?"

"Yes, that's right. You've hated these powers your whole life. We're going to set you free. Too bad you have to be in your actual body first. That's the annoying bit, but we've promised to restore the cost back to the necroes who have to resurrect your body and spirit. Then we can get down to the real business at hand."

Chapter 25 - Trina

"Frank!" I yelled as soon as I swung open the heavy glass door of the cinema.

Several people turned to look at me with surprise, but I ignored them. Being weird in public was low on my list of concerns at the moment.

Gryphin and Brandon came into the crowded, Thursday-evening lobby and followed closely behind me, offering their support and protection.

Noah had gone to gather any necroes he could find that were more loyal to ethics than the order's leader. He was waiting to hear from me about where we were to meet up.

Brandon, bless him, also started hollering out for Frank even though I wasn't sure they'd ever met before.

"Okay! Relax!" a grumpy voice shouted out over the crowd before Frank fazed through a wall near a fake plant. His hands were up and outward in a calming motion. "I'm right here. No need to wake the dead."

Brandon and I changed our direction immediately and weaved our way through the lines of people waiting to get tickets or concessions until we gathered into a corner, Gryphin's big shoulders keeping us out of sight from most of the people.

"Frank! Hanna said something sometime about you helping Rose in a warehouse one time. Is that right?" The words flowed out of me in a panicked rush.

He frowned, glanced at Gryphin and Brandon but must have sensed the urgency in my voice and didn't ask for introductions to the newcomer. He'd been around Gryphin before, but Brandon was probably new.

"Yes, that's right. Has something happened?"

"Rose has nabbed Hanna. We don't know how or why, but Caleb came by and told us she's in some kind of warehouse. I know the odds are low that it's the very same warehouse that Rose used you to grab other ghosts in, but it's the only lead we've got." It felt like my eyes were on fire and about to pour out burning tears.

"Yeah, that's right. I suppose that could be why she was inside the warehouse capturing the ghosts there because she owned it or was renting it out or something, but still. Those odds are so low," Frank said, holding true to his old-man nature and thinking more about the logistics of things rather than the emotions.

Which was kind of exactly what I needed right now. Even if I was annoyed that he was dismissing my panic slightly.

"Okay, maybe. But we've got to at least check it out, right?" I tried to use Frank's logic to latch onto as an anchor before I completely freaked out and was useless to everyone.

"Do you know where the warehouse was or is?" Brandon was probably as panicked as I was but kept a solid, calm voice as if sensing how close I was to losing it.

Frank took a second to focus on Brandon. He looked the now-solid ghost up and down with a creased wrinkle in his forehead. "What's going on? Are you another Seer? Are they coming out all over the place now?"

"This is Brandon." I talked quickly and waved my arm up and down in front of him. "You helped Hanna rescue him, and thanks to some other insane things, he's got a half-body right now."

I felt bad keeping the bracelet a secret from Frank since he would have also been able to benefit from a similar object I could probably easily make, but there would be time for that later. If he wanted one at all, that is. We still didn't know how it all worked.

"A half-body? So he's still dead and a ghost, but humans can see and touch him? That doesn't seem fair. How in the world did that happen?" Frank asked with a pensive frown.

"We can get into all of that later. Do you know where the warehouse is or not?" I took a breath to try and reign myself in.

The headache was pounding like a series of body-vibrating drumbeats, not making any of this easier.

"I have no idea where that warehouse is." Frank shrugged. "But you're in luck. I spent way longer than I wanted to hanging out in Rose's storage shed while we tried to figure out how to break Hanna and the magic users out of that picture spell. I snooped a bit and happened upon some paperwork with an address on it that could easily be the very warehouse you need."

Gryphin put a steadying hand on the small of my back as if sensing I needed something warm and physical to ground myself with even though he couldn't hear what Frank was saying.

"Okay, so where's that?" I urged him on with my hands, trying to motion him to hurry up.

"Delaney street. 41, I think. That's the best I've got for you." Frank raised his hands and shoulders in a helpless motion.

"Thank you!" I turned to Gryphin. "41 Delaney street. It's our best lead yet."

He nodded. "Let's go check it out."

"Frank, if this leads us to Hanna, I'll make sure we remember to return the favor. Be thinking about what your unfinished business is, and Hanna and I will come back together first thing and help you out!"

"I'll get right on that. Good luck." He gave Brandon another confused study before we sprinted out of the theater and back to the car.

Gryphin parked the van near a long brick building. There didn't appear to be much going on outside of it, including a lack of other cars parked nearby, but I took that as a good sign. Rose wouldn't be trying to use a warehouse full of people doing things, right? She'd want an empty one where she could conduct her nefarious affairs in peace.

I had sent several quick texts to Noah during our drive about where we were headed and why. He'd assured me they would come back us up, just in case.

"So what's our move?" I stood between Gryphin and Brandon, talking quietly in case there were people inside.

"Just a second." Gryphin closed his eyes and took a few deep breaths.

Brandon and I exchanged glances, but if Gryph needed a moment to steady himself, I was going to try my best to stay quiet and let him have it.

"I can smell her," he said as I was about to break the silence and get things moving again.

"Ew," Brandon said. "That's a bit personal, don't you think?"

Gryphin shot him a half-amused, half-annoyed smile. "I'm afraid keeping smells to yourself around a werewolf doesn't work very well."

"Her who? Rose?" I asked, trying to focus on the important things.

"Yes, and the scent is strong, indicating she's spent a lot of time here, coming and going. We need to be careful. I'm betting this is her lair, and if she's as smart as I know she is, this place is going to be loaded with spells and wards. A few magic users would come in handy right about now."

"On it." I pulled out my phone and called Phoenix, figuring I didn't have time to wait for a whole text conversation to come through.

"This is the first time since I've died that I wish I had a ghostly body to return to." Brandon fiddled with the gold bracelet on his wrist as I waited for Phoenix to pick up. "Then I could walk right in through the walls and see what we're getting into. As it is, I'm kind of useless like this... How weird."

Gryphin gave him a kinder smile over the top of my head as Phoenix finally picked up the phone.

"Hey, girl."

"Phoenix! Grab your fellow magic users, grab your spell bag, grab your best wand, whatever. We've got a job to do, and we need your help."

As we waited for them to arrive, Brandon and I climbed back into the van and Gryphin decided to check around the outside of the building. He thought about changing into his wolf form, but since it was still daylight outside, we figured it would be best if he kept in human form for now.

"I know I seem confident and cool all the time," Brandon said into the quiet as we waited for Gryphin to come back.

I gave him a look which only made him smile cheerfully at me before it dropped away quickly.

"But I'm scared. I'm scared for Hanna, and honestly? I'm scared for myself or any other ghosts. Crossing over is scary, but I think what Rose does is even scarier. We've got to stop her. We've got to get Hanna out safely and put everything right again." His eyes were wide and earnest as he looked through the window at the older brick building.

I leaned my head back onto the headrest and closed my eyes for a moment, massaging my temple where the headache was playing wild music inside my brain. "I'm scared, too. You know, putting everything back together as it was includes figuring out how to get that bracelet off you. Maybe I can make some kind of tool that can break the magic around it and pop it off."

"I don't know how that makes sense. What about making one that cancels out the magic from the bracelet? If I wore both items at once, then I could go back to my neutral state?"

I peeked an eye open. "That doesn't make sense about as much as my idea made sense."

He shrugged. "We can work on it later. Do you smell that?"

"Ugh, boys are so gross." I immediately put my shirt over my nose and held my breath for second.

"Oh, no. It's not me. Wait. Can I even fart? Huh." He took a second to think about the great mysteries of the universe.

Despite my nose being inside my shirt mostly smelling the scent of my soap and deodorant, another smell began to leak through the soft fabric. It was a putrid, rotting, stale, and gag-inducing smell that could really only be coming from one thing.

"Zombies," Brandon and I said at the same time as our eyes met in horror.

Then something smacked into the back of the van with a loud crunching sound and the smashing of glass.

I almost forgot my headache in the panic of ducking down behind the seat and folding onto the floormat in terror. Brandon had scrambled into a similar position in between the driver's seat and the middle row where we had been sitting a few seconds before.

Enraged snarls and crunching bone sounds came from the other side of the seats as the van rocked and swayed. The smell was worse as it wafted in through the broken windows, and my heart nearly froze inside my chest as tongue-less snarls and moans grew louder.

"Gryphin?" I pushed my trembling muscles to pull my head up over the back of the seat just enough to see what was happening.

Brandon climbed up next to me and peeked over as well. For someone who was already dead, he sure was acting like a scaredy-cat.

It was indeed Gryphin that had been thrown into the back of the van. He was mid-change, which accounted for the angry snarls and bones snapping as they realigned themselves. Ordinarily, the change had to have been terrible, but Gryphin was probably rushing this one as fast as he could, making the pain as intense as he could handle it.

Beyond him and the smashed van, there was a small horde of zombies descending upon us, thus accounting for the smell and Gryphin's angry change.

At first, I was shocked. The zombies varied all over the place in terms of decomposition and states of dress. Skin, clothes, and even a few bones and organs hung off the zombies in sickening ways. One zombie had no eyes at all, while another had three, an extra one hanging out of its mouth for some reason.

My stomach twisted, but I wasn't sure if it was seeing them or smelling them that was worse. I gagged a few times before I could even speak.

"Holy mackerel! What do we do?" I gasped, wishing I could somehow help Gryphin's change happen even faster.

Brandon's face was pale white, and he swallowed thickly as he glanced over at me. "Do they know we're here? Maybe we keep hiding."

"I don't even know what you're afraid of. You're already dead!" I hissed at him, swallowing another gag as my eyes watered fiercely.

"That doesn't mean they can't cause me pain. What if they rip my arm off? Will it grow back, or will I be an armless wonder for the rest of this undead life? Can you imagine the pain?"

Shaking my head, I peeked back over at Gryphin. He was nearly full wolf, all covered in grey fur. As his spine straightened out and cracked, he pulled himself up between us and the zombies. The horde was only about five feet away from the van then, going slowly as if our demise was inevitable.

"We should help him. He can probably take out a bunch, but we can't just sit here," I whispered to Brandon, looking around for something I could use to smack a zombie with.

"Are you serious? This isn't like a movie where you'll suddenly be able to fight skillfully and save the day. Do you even know how to fight a zombie?" Brandon asked with wide eyes.

"Thanks for the confidence. It doesn't matter. If we don't help him, and he fails, then it'll only be us against the horde. It would be much better to have him by our side than not, right?"

"What about the magic users? Shouldn't we wait for them?"

"Stop being so scared and find something to smash brains with!" I picked up an old umbrella and ripped off the fabric part of it.

"I'm not scared for *me*. Well, maybe a little bit, but mostly for you. Hanna will kill me if something happens to you." Brandon grabbed my upper arm as if touching me would convey more of his point.

I shrugged off his fingers. "Well, like I keep saying, it's a good thing you're already dead."

"Ugh."

I stopped worrying about what he was going to do, looked back at the horde which had finally reached the snarling werewolf, thankfully nearly as big as this van was, and gulped, wishing I had some kind of mask that would keep me from smelling the rotting corpses. "Here goes nothing."

Gryphin snapped out with a great growl that made even the hairs on my arms stand as I eased open the sliding side door and gingerly stepped out of the car, hoping not to attract direct attention from the zombies.

A loud voice rang out over the parking lot that made me momentarily freeze in my crouch next to the van.

"Surrender now, and you'll be spared a lot of pain," a woman said from somewhere behind the zombies. "We've got you surrounded, and while a werewolf might be considerable in battle, I'm afraid one will be no match for the lot of us."

I frowned, trying to recognize the voice. It wasn't David's, I knew that much. I also knew that it had to have been a necromancer, though. No one else could control zombies like this, as far as I knew.

Thankfully it wasn't Noah's either. Him turning against us right now would have crushed my already shaky spirits. It wasn't that I was certain he was on our side, but there was still at least hope that he'd make the correct choices.

The easy assumption was that it was Rose's voice and that she had discovered our trespassing. I should have been scared to suspect it was her, but I was beyond terrified already.

Gryphin's response was to swipe at the nearest zombies, taking down three with his large paw, causing squelching juices to fly into the air and add more potency to the smell. The three crashed into a few others with the stomach-churning sounds of flesh and bone smashing into each other.

I gagged again, my hand against the side of the van to steady me as my eyes watered and vomit came out, splattering the pavement.

"Oh, excellent. They'll be glad to see we've found the sister already. Grab her!" the voice said, presumably gesturing in my direction. I still couldn't see her past the horde of goons, but she had been able to somehow spot me.

The zombies' attention drew from the angry werewolf toward me where I pulled myself up into a standing pose with shaky knees.

I gripped the handle of the umbrella tightly, careful not to stab myself in the eye with the metal spikes. "Come get me you rotting bags of flesh!"

The woman's laughter was drowned out by the grunts and moans of the zombies as they shuffled toward me, hands outstretched and ready to take me to their master.

Chapter 26 - Hanna

"Everything seems to be in place." Marcus, one of David's henchmen I vaguely recognized, stood, holding the ash urn he'd been using to paint runes onto my cold corpse.

It had been surreal when they'd lifted the tarp and my broken body had been revealed. It/I was wearing a similar plain gown to the one they'd put Stephanie's body in with the arms and legs free so they could write the appropriate signs onto my skin.

Part of me was grateful that I'd already seen this whole scenario before, so it was less terrifying. Another part of me was simply scared no matter what they did. If Rose and Theodore had gotten out a ball and were happily tossing it to each other while sucking on lollipops, I still would have been trembling in my seat.

Logically, I should have been happy that they were going to put me back into my body. Wasn't that what Trina and my mom had been working toward this whole time? We hadn't even had to fulfill another favor for the order before they were helping me. It should have been a good thing, right?

Except it wasn't about them putting me back into my body. It was what they were going to do after that.

David pulled out his phone, paused for a moment, frowned, and looked back up at Theodore who was standing next to the table and eyeing my corpse more than I thought prudent.

"There is a group of unknowns outside. Mariah is taking care of it, but she wanted us to know. There's a werewolf and two humans, one of them matching the description of the girl you're looking for." David's eyes bounced to me once before going back to Theodore.

"A werewolf?" Theodore said, voicing one of the many questions I had.

"It's probably the one we've seen hanging out with the family. No worries. One of them can't break through our forces. We need to make sure nothing happens to the girl, though." Rose turned to Caleb. "Best to bring her in here out of the fighting and put her in a safe place."

Caleb didn't respond except to simply disappear, presumably to go get the girl I had a sneaking suspicion was my sister. It made sense, though, from Rose's point of view. Why have only one Seer when you could have two?

I wondered who the other human was, hopefully not Mom. As bad as this whole thing was going to be, I would be even more upset if Mom got hurt or were in danger. At least with Trina, I knew she had some tricks up her sleeve and could maybe help me get out of this whole thing. With my mom, however, she was simply human through and through. The risk for her among this mess was even higher and more dangerous, no matter how scrappy she had proven herself to be.

Unable to do anything but pray, I closed my eyes and sent frenzied good vibes out into the universe, hoping some benevolent being would prevent anything bad from happening.

"Let's get going with the spell so we can work on the next step." Theodore nodded his head toward David.

The order's leader nodded at his followers in turn, and they all took places around the pentagram. I was surprised to see even Theodore step inside as he clearly seemed to be in charge, but perhaps he wanted to be a part of it to ensure the spell didn't go wrong.

Maybe. I was simply guessing as best as I could.

Personally, I had mixed feelings about it. Sure, I wanted to get back into my body, and we were going to use this order's services anyway. But I also didn't want Rose to get anything she wanted, even if it aligned with my priorities.

It didn't matter what I felt though, because things were going to work out how they would while I was tied to a chair and unable to do much more than grunt or damage Andrea's wrists and ankles more.

I didn't bother trying to command any of the ghosts under Rose's control to do anything. I'd tried that before, and it had only been a waste of energy. Not to mention, I was still a ghost with a whole different set of skills than I had with my body.

The spell went pretty much the same as the one I'd witnessed for Stephanie's resurrection. Necromancers chanted, purple lightning lit up the pentagram and crackled around the casters. Wind blew through and around those on the pentagram but touched nothing outside of it. As the feeling of power grew inside the echoey warehouse, David turned and grabbed the poor goat.

I squeezed my eyes shut and turned away as I knew what happened next. Thankfully, the wind, the chanting, and the lightning covered up the sound of the goat's blood rushing out, following along the lines of the pentagram.

Rose had stayed out of the circle, still wearing Gran's glasses, to serve as the Seer as I had done for Stephanie. However, these were quite different circumstances.

I couldn't help growing nervous for the transfer of my spirit back into my body since, if something went wrong, I could simply anti-climatically end up back at my haunt, or worse, end up as a forever-zombie like Andrea.

"Alright, here's how this is going to go. I'm going to bring this body toward yours, once there is skin contact, you move from this body to your old one. Got it?" Rose leaned into my face so there was no mistaking how serious she was.

I blinked a few times, trying to decide how cooperative I wanted to be. There wasn't much I could do in Andrea's body or as a ghost. The chances of breaking free from this insanity were much higher inside my own body with the Seer gifts than they were inside Andrea's.

As much as I didn't want to help Rose, I had sense enough to nod my head stiffly and play along until I could figure something else out.

"Great. I'm sure you'll want to be back inside your real body as soon as possible, even if this current one is a bit cuter." Rose wore an icy smile as she cut the zip ties and pulled me toward the crackling circle.

I suppose I could have tried to overpower her then and run away, but she was right. I did want to go back into my body.

As Rose helped me step through the lightning, into the wind, and over the bloody pentagram, I was worried we'd mess up the spell somehow. Indeed, even if our physical presence going across the circle didn't, we could distract one of the necromancers and they could falter, thus messing up the spell another way. I knew from experience that this was a delicate procedure, and only one small mistake could ruin it for everyone, but mostly for me.

Andrea's hair whipped into my face and eyes while lightning lashed around, crackling and sparking. I worked hard not to keep wincing with every strike but wasn't very successful. It was nearly impossible to see much except my pale body laying out on the table waiting for me to inhabit it once again.

Rose pushed me toward the body, not as gently as I would have preferred, and I stumbled into it and the table. Thankful that the table appeared to be reasonably sturdy, I grabbed onto my body's arm with Andrea's fingers. It was even weirder seeing myself up so close and personal, dead, eyes closed, and looking exactly the same and somehow completely different than I always had.

Unsure if I was doing it right, I pushed my ghostly self down through Andrea's hand and into my arm. It felt weirder than simply stepping in and out of a zombie body, but I found it possible to move to another without accidentally popping myself back at the haunt.

I knew I'd been successful when my perspective changed from standing to laying and staring up at the ceiling. Andrea's body slumped to the floor like the empty vessel it was, and I wondered how long it would take for her to wake up and wonder where she was and what in the world was happening.

As the necromancers stopped their chanting, the wind died down, and the lightning disappeared. I kept my gaze upward at the dark ceiling, more concerned about what was going on inside my body than outside it, for the moment.

It was weird being dead and then not again. It was weird being a ghost for a while and then being put back into a cold body that had been stashed inside a freezer for several days.

Mostly, I felt weak and heavy, unable to care as much about what was going on around me. Somewhere inside, something was telling me I should be concerned and try to escape. That bad things were going to happen if I didn't figure out a way to get free and save the people I loved.

The concerns felt so very far away, and I was so very heavy.

Then the eerie screams of the dead stirred my chilled blood, and I found that I could sit up.

Chapter 27 - Trina

One second, I was brandishing my spikey umbrella, which turned out not to be a terrible weapon as long as I didn't hit myself or my allies, at a zombie head, and the next second I was being snatched up into solid arms and whisked away across the parking lot into a dark building. If I had blinked, I would have missed the whole thing.

"Sit here. Don't move." Caleb's voice was as stiff as his muscled shoulders as he sat me down in a damp and cold corner.

The first thing I did was try to get up and move. He put a strong, cool hand on my shoulder and pushed me back down onto the ground. It wasn't rough but still powerful enough that I couldn't resist.

"I said 'sit'." Caleb glared down at me with his dark eyes.

I exhaled, feeling pain and despair leak into the spaces where the air had been. "Caleb. Are you in there?"

He continued to stare down at me in a dull way, like the empty puppet he was.

My eyes took him in for a few more seconds before moving to look around us. We were inside the warehouse, assumedly, because the ceiling was high above our heads, lit with intermittent, buzzing lights.

They cast a sickly pallor on everything below them, which turned out to be rows of shelving, stacks of boxes, and various random furniture pieces.

Echoes bounced around the walls that were slightly concerning but were distorted enough that I couldn't be sure of what or where the commotion was coming from. Purple streaks flashed out into the ceiling sometimes, cluing me in that necromancer magic was being used somewhere inside. I hadn't seen anything like that myself, but Hanna had explained it enough to me I felt confident in recognizing it.

I deflated some more, pulled my knees up to my chin, and hugged my legs. "I suppose I should be thanking you for rescuing me from the zombies, but I'm more worried about Gryphin and Brandon handling them on their own. Not to mention, what was important enough that Rose had me pulled inside?"

He kept standing there, still as a statue, probably on guard duty until Rose needed him to do something else. It may have been pointless to talk to him, but I kept going anyway on the small hope that he was able to hear me from inside there somewhere.

"Thank you for telling us where Hanna was or is. As I'm sitting here, I'm thinking that whole thing may have been a setup to get me here, but then I wonder why in the world you didn't just grab me then and cut out all the middle parts? Was there a part of you inside that wanted me to be able to call for help? Or did Rose simply want me to bring my allies knowing that she needed to get rid of them anyway to tie up loose ends and having them all in one place like this would be an easy way to take them out?"

I couldn't see his face in the shadows, but I searched the darkness for any sign of reaction from him. As far as I could see, there was none.

"I suppose I fell right into Rose's plans, didn't I? I feel bad about it, but part of me is trying to tell myself to be forgiving. I'm really new to this whole Seer thing, newer even than Hanna. Before a few weeks ago, vampires, werewolves, witches, and necromancers all didn't exist. Even ghosts were only a suspicion. There are too many variables, too many things that could go wrong for me to know exactly what to do exactly all the time. It's honestly not very fair at all."

Quiet broke out over the warehouse and the purple flashing stopped altogether. Caleb looked back toward the heart of the building as his shoulders relaxed only enough for someone studying him to notice.

"Well, Hanna's either in her body now, or they've messed something up." His voice was gruff and quiet, just loud enough for me to catch his words.

"What? Caleb? Are you back?" I gathered my legs beneath me and began to stand up again, but he simply pushed my shoulder back down.

However, instead of looking away again, he settled onto his knees and put a marble-cold hand on my blazing cheek. "I'm so sorry, Trina. I should have seen this coming. I should have prepared for something like this to happen. You're not the only one who has fallen for her tricks."

"Caleb!" I let out a half-sob and grabbed at his hand that was cupping my cheek. "Tell me how to help you and set you free! I've been so worried about you. Are you aware of the things you're doing while under her control?"

He was close enough now that the small amount of overhead light-ing revealed most of his features. His eyes saddened, and he glance down for a second. "Yes. I know what she's had me do. I'm so sorry about Hanna. I would have never…"

"I know." I used my other hand to grab the back of his head and press his forehead to mine. I closed my eyes for a second and breathed in his frost-mint smell, pretending for an instant that he was mine and everything was okay.

"Trina…" he said, his voice soft.

I opened my eyes to look into his, the black pools seeming to stretch into infinity. "We'll set you free. Just tell me how."

"I don't know how. I've been fighting her every second through all of this, but her powers are too strong. Necromancers are truly our biggest weakness."

"There's got to be something, though. I refuse to give up hope. I'm not going to let you go." I swallowed thickly, hoping the lump in my throat would go away.

"Just don't be afraid to kill me if you need to. You already know without me saying it, but I'm going to say it anyway—a million times over, I'd choose your life over mine. Take me down if it comes to it. Beheading. A wooden stake to the chest. Get the wolf to do it. I'm sure he knows how."

"I… I don't want to think about that right now. We're going to find a way to set you free, and that's the end of it."

The tiniest of smiles crossed his lips, but then screams, shuffles, and shouts came from somewhere else inside the warehouse. He stiffened and pulled away from me.

My empty hands dropped back into my lap as I tried to swallow a sob.

All business again, Caleb produced a set of handcuffs from a pocket and snapped one around my left wrist and the other to a heavy table nearby. He didn't even say goodbye as he left, basically disappearing into the gloomy darkness.

I sat in the dim corner listening to the shouts and scuffling sounds echoing around the building and tried to focus on what may have been happening instead of wallowing in sadness and despair.

Chapter 28 - Hanna

Theodore pulled in the last of the ghost and let out a pleased exhale. His skin smoothed and his hair darkened from the greys that had begun to work their way through his scalp.

"Stop!" I screeched, way too late.

The other ghosts screamed with me and backed away from the old necromancer, as far away as they could get. As terrible as it was that he'd eaten one soul, I was selfishly relieved that he hadn't eaten anyone I knew.

David's necromancers didn't seem disturbed at all by Theodore's actions. In fact, several of them watched with a greedy light in their eyes. This led me to thinking David had grabbed only those from the order who approved of the sucking in of souls, which explained why the whole order wasn't there, missing at least two that I knew of.

Rose, still wearing the glasses, simply laughed and shook her head. "Fear is delicious, especially when it's from larger groups of beings. I have to hand it to you, Hanna, these glasses are a game changer. You can have them back when we're done, just in case you feel like talking to your ghost friend again sometime. Well...if he's still around, that is."

With a snarl, I tried to jump off the table and smack that smug smile off her face, but I found my body had been restrained some time earlier with two pairs of hand cuffs. There was room enough for me to sit up, but that was about it. "Hey! Let me go!"

"All in due time, m'dear." Rose went to a different table and picked up a giant book that looked older than she actually was.

Theodore had walked over to Andrea's slumped form near the table. I couldn't help recoiling away from him as much as I could, but he ignored me as he bent over and something silver flashed in his hand.

"There you go, honey. You've played your part well. Now it's time to rest." He inserted a syringe into Andrea's neck.

"What are you doing?" I whispered hoarsely.

"Simply making sure she is asleep. Wouldn't want to expose her innocent mind to any of this." He pocketed the syringe again and bent to pick up her relaxed form.

"Oh yes, wouldn't want to corrupt her at all." I was unable to help myself from rolling my eyes.

Caleb appeared again, his arms outstretched and ready to receive my once-friend's body.

"Take her somewhere safe." Theodore gently placed her into the vampire's arms.

With a blink, Caleb was gone again. I hadn't even had time to ask him about Trina and where he'd stashed her.

Not that he would have answered anyway.

Theodore turned to regard me with shrewd eyes. "Before we begin the next spell, care to explain how your powers work and what exactly you can do? Rose has told me you've got some extra skills that will come in quite handy."

I furrowed my eyebrows. "Uhm, no thanks."

He tilted his head to the side. "Pity. Guess I'll have to figure out how they work on my own."

"What do you mean?" I said, remembering something Rose had said before they'd gotten me back into my body. "Oh."

Theodore simply gave me a condescending smile that sent shudders up my arms.

"Are we ready for the next step?" Theodore turned to Rose.

She studied the book while David rolled himself over to her side.

"Perhaps it would be good to let me consume a soul before this next spell. The resurrection spell takes a lot out of me, and I was weak already. It would be best if I was restored to the most possible energy before doing another, don't you think?" David surprised me with his entreating tone of voice.

I narrowed my eyes and looked at the ghosts who had filtered in among the shelves nearby in an effort to hide. We all knew they weren't able to move very far away from their haunts, which happened to be the crystals now that they were captured, but I gave them points for trying.

Shannon, Savannah, and Justin crouched together behind an old storage container. I only knew this because I saw one of them pop their head up from time to time and update the others on what was happening.

My heart went out to them for the fear they must have felt while trapped with Rose, and the pain that awaited them. They still didn't know that Brandon had died, how and why he'd died, and the entire reason they were dead in the first place. Not to mention, they were still currently trapped under Rose's control, and the odds of them escaping weren't looking good.

While the group was distracted with the book and whatever insane thing they were planning on doing next, I waited for a sibling to look over the container again. Once Justin's head peeked over, I waved frantically at him, hoping he'd get the courage to come closer.

"Justin! Come here! Let me help you!" I whispered, hoping that no one would notice what I was trying to do.

Justin glanced over at the others, and I followed his lead. Rose, David, and Theodore were discussing the merits of when David would get to eat his first soul while most of the other necromancers were talking together in small groups. One of them glanced my way, but I darted my gaze around the room, hoping I looked like an innocent girl just waiting for her powers to be sucked out.

Justin disappeared again, and I frowned, wondering how I could get him closer to set him free without anyone realizing what I was doing.

Then his head popped up again, he looked around, and darted toward my table in a crouch. I had to smile with how he reminded me of a kid playing like they were a super-spy sneaking around the enemy's camp. Which in a way, I guess he was.

"How do you know my name?" he asked as he ducked down behind my table, peeking up at me with wide eyes I assumed had been green in life.

"I know your brother." I kept my voice low. "I can reunite you once we get out of this mess. All you have to do is let my hand go through your chest, and I can free you."

Justin's eyes widened, and he glanced back toward the container. "And my sisters, too?"

"Yes, I just need to—"

"Alright, alright, break it up." Rose appeared at the end of the table, near my feet. "You, get away and stay away."

Justin stood with stiff legs and panicked eyes as he had to obey her orders and walk several feet in the other direction.

"No setting anyone free this time, dear." Rose's smile oozed contempt. "Time for our next trick. Are you ready?"

"I think the better question, Ann, dear, is if *you* are ready," an aged voice said as Cordelia stepped around a shelf, her eyes sparkling with youth that her wrinkled face did not match.

In the next instant, the workplace was flooded with magic users, most of them I didn't recognize. Phoenix was there, throwing out small vials of a potion that exploded into pink smoke, making the nearby people pass out or maybe even die. I couldn't tell exactly, just that they fell to the floor and didn't get back up.

Leah was also there, her small stature darting in and around the shelves, also throwing the pink potion bombs. Three other magic users were following her lead, using the shelves to protect them from the purple lightning the necromancers tried to throw at them.

Cordelia stood in one place and moved her arms around, presumably responsible for the flying objects that were suddenly zipping around in the air, taking hits of lightning or smacking into the heads of the necromancers.

There weren't very many of the magic users, six in total, as far as I could see, but I had to hand it to them. It was very brave to charge in like that, knowing that it would be easy to overwhelm their numbers.

Rose snarled, clutched the book to her chest with one arm and waved the other one around. "Stop them!"

The ghosts filtered out of their hiding places and started to fade into the peach/tan/black colors of their living skin, merging into the corporeal world. A few of the magic users cried out as the ghosts grabbed onto them. Most of it happened behind the shelves where I couldn't see.

Phoenix yelled something out and tried throwing one of those pink potions at the ghost heading toward them. The ghost, who looked like a middle-aged woman in a bathrobe, was completely unfazed by the smokey haze, walked right through it, and grabbed onto Phoenix's arm.

They cursed and tried to shake her off, but their other arm was snagged by a different ghost, one of Brandon's sisters. Then Justin dove in, grabbing for their legs.

I winced, worried that they would kick out and put a boot right into Brandon's brother's face, but the weight of all three ghosts must have been enough to topple Phoenix, and they fell to the dirty concrete with a groan and a growl.

Cordelia winked out before any of the ghosts could get their hands on her, but it wasn't long before the other five magic users were brought, struggling and cursing, into the light.

Rose towered above them with Theodore on one side and David sitting on the other. "Did you really think that would work? And who here is surprised that the matron ran away like the weak girl she is?"

The magic users all gave her angry glares while still trying to pull away from the ghosts. I wondered where all the energy came from for the ghosts to be able to use their physical forms. Knowing Rose, she probably made them use their own energy instead of lending any to them, but that gave the added risk of the ghosts turning into poltergeists over time, which I'm sure would have been bad for Rose. Maybe she had some other trick she was using.

"You might have stopped us, but we took down several necroes, so it was worth it to keep your group from being able to perform anymore dark spells." Phoenix's eyebrows were narrowed angrily.

Theodore chuckled, the dark sound sending chills down my arms. "We have already done the resurrection spell. We don't need so many anymore, anyway."

David's group had been reduced to three necroes who were attending to those that had fallen. They confirmed that the others had been merely knocked out, not killed. While I appreciated that the magic users weren't simply murdering everyone, I did wonder how long the potion would last and when they'd wake up. Hopefully not in enough time to help Rose.

Phoenix refused to give the three staring down at them any pleasure at seeing them upset or defeated. Instead, they glared angrily while continuing to pull against the ghosts.

"Right." Theodore gave the magic users one last annoyed glance. "Let's get going before anyone else crashes our party."

"How long will you be able to hold them?" David asked, leaning in closer to Rose as if not wanting anyone else to hear his question.

"It might not hurt to pull in the zombies," Rose said thoughtfully as she opened the large book again.

"But remember what she did last time with the zombies? She had the ghosts possess them, and they were completely under her control. We couldn't do anything against that." David glanced at me with a distasteful look. I responded with a charming and happy grin.

"That was only with ghosts who weren't under my control. That probably wouldn't be an issue now." Rose shrugged.

David was shaking his head. "Do you really want to take the risk?"

"We can avoid all that once I have her powers," Theodore said, coming to stand next to the table but out of reach enough that I couldn't punch him in the face like I wanted to.

As Rose hefted the book in her arms so she could look at it closer, a screeching sound I was beginning to think was the main door somewhere sounded throughout the warehouse. This time, Rose and her mates didn't seem to be expecting visitors.

"Go find out who that is and stop them," Rose snapped at David's followers.

Caleb hadn't come back yet from taking Andrea to whatever place her dad thought would be safe, but I assumed he was probably out also investigating and following through with the mental commands Rose could give him without needing to see him in person.

It must have been quite handy indeed to have such a pet.

David watched his people go with a worried expression, and I could see the doubt creeping into his face. This wasn't going as well as they'd expected it to, but I didn't know how they hadn't expected some kind of resistance.

"Y'all should just give up now, set me free, and disappear before things get uglier." I flashed my most charming grin in effort to appear brave and confident.

"Wouldn't you love that," Rose said sarcastically and then turned to Theodore. "Okay, you've got to drink this tea we've made. It might not taste the best, but I'm sure it'll be worth it."

Shouts and snarls grew from elsewhere in the warehouse. They weren't coherent enough to make out the words, but something was going on where several people, or creatures, maybe, were *not* happy.

"Looks like y'all are going to have to cut your tea party short," I said, hoping I sounded stronger than I felt.

Ignoring me, Rose turned to the other table, put the book down, and grabbed a thermos. "Drink this but make sure to leave some for me," she said as she handed it to Theodore.

The old man spared a quick glance to where all the cacophony was coming from before popping off the top and taking a few quick chugs. "This is terrible."

Rose picked up the book again. "Magic doesn't always taste good. Touch her arm and hold on until I'm done."

I gave Theodore a nasty look and tried to pull away from his clammy hands but couldn't go very far while being cuffed to the side of the table.

"Well you better talk quickly." Theodore finally got a good grasp on my wrist next to the metal of the handcuffs.

"We better hurry." David's worried glances toward the inside of the warehouse were probably less about the safety of his crew and more about the possible interruption should they fail.

As for the magic users, the ghosts had found various items to stuff inside their mouths so none of them could talk, thus reducing the risk that they'd be able to cast a spell or make plans with each other for escape.

Shannon, Savannah, and Justin were all being good little ghost servants, but judging from the angry glances they gave Rose, it wasn't because they wanted to be. Justin kept looking more at me than Rose, probably wondering what I knew about his brother and how we were going to work through this.

Rose began her chant, and the hair on my arms buzzed to life as if being zapped by static electricity.

"You know being able to see and hear ghosts isn't as great as you might think it would be," I said, trying another tactic. "They're very annoying, always wanting stuff, and it's never anything fun. It's always talk to my aunt this and find my murderer that, and honestly, it's mostly a lot of work and people thinking you're crazy. It's probably best to stick to the glasses and only put them on when you want to."

Rose kept chanting, her voice steady as she was able to impressively completely ignore my chatting and maintain a strong focus. The purple lightning wasn't present, so I assumed this was something more along the magic users' line of abilities, which also explained why Theodore needed Rose's help to perform it.

"Well then, you'll be glad when it's gone and you won't have to worry about it anymore," Theodore said with a nasty smile and adjusted his grip on my arm, so it was squeezing tightly.

Then things started to change which were scary enough that I couldn't keep up the fragile shell of bravery I'd been trying to hide behind. Something inside my body was draining away, something important, something that made up a core part of me.

My head started pounding, and the world shifted until I found myself laying down on the table and looking back up at those terrible buzzing lights. The edges of my vision were blurry, and warm, wet tears welled up in my eyes and spilled over the sides.

"Keep going. I think it's working!" Theodore said, the pain from his strong grip far enough away that it barely bothered me.

Then something loud and eerie echoed throughout the warehouse, making everyone freeze and look at each other with wide eyes. Even I sat up halfway, my neck pulling my heavy head off the table so I could look around.

I knew that sound and the answering howls after it. The wolves had arrived, and not just the alive ones.

Chapter 29 - Trina

I was shivering from fear and the bone-seeping chill by the time Brandon found me. There were terrible sounds bouncing around the warehouse from a direction I could only guess. I had buried my head into my knees, my arm still detained to a nearby table. It also helped with the terrible smell to keep my nose buried inside my clothes.

It was going to take a lot to get used to the smell of zombies. I had no idea how the necromancers put up with it all the time.

I had ventured a few attempts at wiggling and somehow getting the cuffs freed from the metal braces of the table, but even if I had somehow managed to overturn it, Caleb had been smart enough to restrain me to the metal that ran along the inside of the table instead of the legs.

Despite the cold, it had actually been nice to sit in the dark quiet for a time as the headache pounding inside my skull was as strong as ever. I worried that if it got any stronger, I wasn't going to be much use to anyone except as a large paperweight or a couch potato.

"Hiding out here away from the trouble, I see." Brandon's tone was teasing, but he was unable to hide the relief in his eyes.

"Taking your sweet time to find me, I see," I said, my voice hoarse as I mocked him.

"Well, a few things got in the way. First, you know, that whole horde of zombies. I don't think a million billion showers are ever going to free me from the smell."

"Or it could be the fact that you're dead to begin with. Stop trying to be funny and figure out how to get me free." I lifted my arm so he could see where I was stuck.

"Right. I can't help being funny. It's part of my charm and coping mechanisms. Do you happen to know where the key is?" Brandon knelt and studied the handcuffs. "They don't look like the cheap kind you can pop open with a button."

I groaned and rubbed my forehead with my free hand. "Sometimes I feel like just being near you gives me a bigger headache. Of course, I don't have the key. Would I be sitting here if I did?"

Something about the acidic tones in my voice gave Brandon pause, and he turned slowly to look at me. "Wait... You have been even grumpier than usual these last few days... Am I giving you a headache?"

Too tired to think about nearly anything, I groaned. "I don't know. You've always been a pain, but this seems to be quite a bit something else. Maybe I have a tumor, and it's finally killing me."

"Or maybe this bracelet is drawing too much from you and causing issues." Brandon's attention dropped to his wrist as he looked at the bracelet which gleamed an innocent golden hue.

"Guess I am going to die then. There's no way to take it off."

There was a quiet moment between us where the chaos of fighting sounded closer than it had before.

"Or I could cross over." His voice was so quiet that I almost didn't hear it over the snarls and grunts.

I put my arm down from my head and looked at him, blinking slowly a few times. "Did we just figure out that I'm going to be in pain until I'm a vegetable unless you cross over?" I felt satisfied that at least the physicality of his body allowed me to swat his arm. "I told you not to put that bracelet on! That was the whole point of keeping it a secret from you. Now look at what you've done!"

His shoulders dropped as he turned his gaze away from my face and back to the handcuffs keeping me at the table. "Yeah, I messed up. I'm sorry."

Feeling like drawing attention to the pain had only made it more powerful, I leaned my head back onto the cold concrete wall behind me. "Hanna is going to be so mad at me."

"Well, I suppose that's a future problem. Right now, we need to get you free and help her." He kept fiddling with the handcuffs even though it was useless.

"How did you guys get past the zombies?"

"Gryphin and then Noah and some other necromancers showed up. Apparently, not everyone in the order supports that crazy David."

"Huh. Guess Noah had to pick a side finally. I'm glad he's on ours. I bet a werewolf or vampire could pop that metal open easily."

"Yeah, it's a shame you're stuck with the wimpy ghost." Brandon sat back on his heels and sighed.

As he wallowed in self-pity, and I tried to simply stay alive while I battled the headache, an eerie call echoed out through the building that made the hairs on my arms stand up.

Brandon stood, looked around the dark building, and then turned back to me with a triumphant smile on his face. "The wolves are here. They owe Hanna, and they're going to help set her free!"

"Go help them!" I used my free hand to shoo him away.

He glanced once more at my restrained wrist. "We won't forget about you. I'll come back and set you free. I promise!"

"Of course you will." I tried to give him a smile that didn't look pained.

He left, heading toward where all the commotion was coming from. I tried to feel sad that I was all alone again, but my head was hurting too much to think about anything else.

I also tried to listen carefully so I could figure out what was happening, but that was too difficult considering how many clatters, shouts, snarls, growls, yells, and thunks there were. It was impossible to figure out who was making what noise.

The rotting smell of zombies permeated the whole building, and I pulled my shirt up over my nose to try to keep myself from gagging some more. I hated the feeling of my insides trying to become my outsides.

Then a shuffling sound came from somewhere closer to me, and I froze, afraid of what it could be. Sure enough, a zombie rounded the corner of a tall shelf, but it was at least one I recognized. The old man's stooped shoulders barely held up his balding head, and his eyes behind the glasses were vacant and vague compared to the last time I'd seen this body.

"Hank?" I sure hoped he was being controlled by Noah and not somebody else.

The zombie didn't greet me back, but that didn't necessarily surprise me. Instead, he hobbled closer with soft grunts.

I pulled my legs up closer to my chest, unsure what it was going to do. There was no way a zombie would be strong enough to break the metal of the hand cuffs since it only had access to whatever muscles the corpse had, and I doubted poor Hank had been very strong in life. Not to mention, I'd wager that most normal humans wouldn't have been able to break them, even if they'd been a bodybuilder.

Something shiny flashed, reflecting light in the zombie's fingers as he neared me. It was too small to be a dagger or anything too dangerous, but I was still nervous. Thankfully, he wasn't as smelly as some of his other friends...yet. That was probably a big reason Noah had used this corpse for Hanna. He may have been super old, but at least he wasn't too much into the rotting.

He tossed the metal shiny thing at me without warning, and I fumbled to catch it. When I found it tucked into a wrinkle of my t-shirt, I pulled it out and saw it was exactly what I needed.

"Thank you, Hank!" I said to his shuffling retreating form, I supposed he went to go join the epic battle again where he could be helpful by...what? Getting in the way?

Pushing the thoughts about what Hank might do in the fight away, I struggled with my cold fingers to grip the key in the right place. It took a few tries, but I managed to fit it into the keyhole and pop open the handcuffs.

I sighed in relief as my wrist was free, and I rubbed at the skin that had started to chafe. Figuring it wouldn't hurt to have a set of handcuffs and a key with me, even if I simply used them to punch zombies in the face, I unlocked the other side that had been fastened to the table and shoved everything into my jeans pocket.

Then I made my way in the direction Hank had gone, hoping I could somehow help the situation instead of making anything worse. My head continued to pound with pain, but I tried to ignore it with the help of adrenaline in preparation for the oncoming fight.

Chapter 30 - Hanna

Something interrupted Rose's chanting, and it took me a second to figure out what it was. A giant furry creature had pounced onto her from out of the darkness, knocking the book out of her hands which went sprawling onto the concrete and slid under a shelf.

It took me a half-second to recognize the amber fur of the alpha wolf, but the size should have easily given it away. It was clear that my brain wasn't working at full capacity, which was kind of bad considering the amount of quick action and chaos that was happening around me.

The alpha easily outweighed Rose and could have caused some epic damage had she been alone...or not a witch.

Theodore growled and raised his arms, purple lightning started to come out of them before another furry critter ran into him. Tan fur told me it was probably Mr. Tyler, although it was difficult to get a good look at the wolf, and I had no idea how many other wolves in the pack had tan fur.

I pulled myself into a sitting position again, still not feeling quite myself. It was difficult to say what damage the spell had done to me right away, but I took heart and hope in that they hadn't been able to complete it.

The building spun around me as I rose, but I was determined to do whatever I could to help my friends.

Thanks to the chaos, Rose appeared to lose control of her ghosts and they let go of the magic users and then disappeared. I frowned as I watched the colors of Savanah, Shannon, and Justin fade from this dimension into...nothing. I either couldn't see their blue forms at all, or they went back to the crystal.

Panic rose in my chest that I didn't have time to study. They could have easily been exhausted and simply returned to their crystals to rest. That was a simple explanation instead of me being unable to see the ghosts anymore.

Yes, that had to be it.

Caleb appeared out of nowhere, grabbed the alpha wolf off Rose, and flung him into the nearest set of shelves, which also happened to be the same place that the book had gone.

With a yelp, the wolf as big as a small bus went flying and smashed everything in his way as he collided with the shelf.

Without hesitation, Caleb jumped in after the wolf, knowing he wasn't down or out. They commenced a snarling, vicious fight that continued to knock out several shelves and blast through piles of boxes.

Honestly, I didn't know which one I wanted to win as either way, someone I cared about was going to get hurt.

David had wheeled off somewhere in the attack, probably trying to escape without getting injured, the coward.

Theodore wasn't without help either as several zombies came out from the darkness and descended on the wolf attacking him. They weren't strong enough to pull the animal off Theodore, but they were enough to distract him as he began snapping his powerful jaws at the zombies, sometimes catching one and crushing it in half.

My stomach rolled at the sight, and I tore my eyes away to find Phoenix next to me, pulling at my restraints.

"These bloody things aren't coming off." They gave the metal another strong tug.

"Don't you have a spell that could unlock them?" I blinked water out of my eyes and tried to breathe through my mouth. It would be easy to get overwhelmed with the fighting, the snarling, the crunching of bones, and squishing of flesh, but I was determined not to pass out, even though this was probably the weakest my body had ever felt.

I guess getting resurrected after not having been super healthy to begin with, plus being used in a weird spell that had almost finished, took a giant toll on one's strength.

My muscles trembled in almost all parts of my body, and the room kept flipping over as if gravity itself was broken.

Phoenix shook their head. "Not without a concoction of herbs to sprinkle into the lock. I usually carry the blend with me, but I dropped my bag somewhere back there."

They gestured to where Bertram, the alpha wolf, was snapping at Caleb while standing unsteadily on top of the pile of rubble they had created. The vampire was quick, dancing out of the snarling and terrifying jaws of the giant wolf.

"Of course." My voice sounded small and hollow.

Rose appeared next to Phoenix and pushed them away from me. "Stop! We need her to finish the spell. You should run while you still can."

Phoenix fell back onto their hands, giving Rose an icy glare. "Do you think you can win right now? You're clearly outnumbered. I'm sure you're smart enough to realize there are necromancers inside battling the ones you think are on your side. Once they finish their battle, they and all their zombies will flood into this place, taking control over everything."

Rose pursed her lips in frustration and glanced out toward the warehouse that was filled with the sounds of battle.

I hadn't thought about the other necromancers and zombies. David and his people must have run into something else, otherwise, they would have come back to support Rose. Not to mention, Gryphin was out there somewhere, hopefully, uninjured and tearing through zombies.

Forcing my worries for my friend's and sister's well-being out of my head, I tried to focus on what I could do in the here and now.

After a second, Rose looked back down at Phoenix. "You might be right, and for a normal witch, that would probably be a bad thing. But for me and Theodore, it is something else entirely."

Phoenix opened their mouth to respond, but Rose had already gone. Then the tan wolf nearby growled in rage as he was suddenly only attacking zombies as the older necromancer disappeared, perhaps with Rose's assistance.

Caleb got in one more good punch to Bertram's head before Leah popped in out of nowhere, threw another pink potion at the vampire, and popped back out.

Her aim was off by a few feet since Caleb was able to move vampiric speed, but there had been enough smoke nearby that it slowed him down.

I watched in horror as the alpha's giant teeth were about to snap Caleb's torso clean off his body.

"No!" I screamed, trying to reach my hand out, but the restraints prevented me from going very far.

Something else blurred past Caleb, grabbing him just in time as Bertram's snapping mouth clamped down on empty air. There was no way for me to make out who or what had appeared to save my friend, but I was grateful for them all the same. I knew it wasn't Rose because even her teleportation skills wouldn't have been able to grab his body in time. Instead, it had to be something else that could move faster than a werewolf.

And there weren't many things that could do that.

The tan wolf dispatched the rest of the zombies Theodore had summoned easily, if not super disgustingly. As the wolf stopped finally and stood still, I was able to confirm it was Mr. Tyler's intelligent eyes staring out at me.

The immediate area around us stilled as all the bad guys had seemingly retreated. I didn't trust that for an instant but knew enough to take advantage of the small respite we had.

"Can you get these off?" Phoenix asked Mr. Tyler and pointed to the restraints around my wrists.

The tan wolf came for a closer look as Bertram shook off the fight and disorientation of having lost his prey.

I was sure if Bertram was able to talk, he would have been cursing more than my mother would have approved of.

"Let me try." Trina snuck out behind a shelf that hadn't been dislodged yet.

"Trina?" I squinted in hopes that I was seeing what I thought I was seeing.

"Long story short, I've got a handcuff key. Let's see if they're the same." She came toward me and put a small silver doodad into the tiny hole of my handcuffs. "Congratulations on getting back into your body, by the way."

The metal popped open, and she tossed the key to Phoenix to unlock my other arm on their side of the table.

"Thank you and thank you." I rubbed at my wrist where the metal had cut into me.

Before I could say anything else, Brandon ran into the open space around my table. His breathing was rapid, and his hair was smashed down on one side with some kind of dark goop I hoped came from a zombie and not from his body. He was holding the skeleton of what appeared to have formerly been an umbrella, the metal arms bent and also covered in unmentionable fluids.

"Where have you been?" Trina asked with a furrowed eyebrow.

"Are you okay?" I said at the same time, rubbing the other wrist Phoenix had freed.

"You look like you had a run-in with a zombie, and the zombie won," Phoenix said as well.

"There are *a lot* of zombies in here. Gryphin has probably tore fifty of them in half, and they keep coming," Brandon said between gulps of air.

Bertram sniffed around, flattened his ears, and ran back off into the darkness. I hoped he was keeping tabs on us somehow in case Theodore and Rose came back, and he could come save us again.

Mr. Tyler bumped his nose into my arm before running off to follow his alpha.

"They'll probably take care of the rest of them," Brandon said, watching the wolves go.

"The other magic users are also fighting them off. It won't do us much good if we keep only targeting the zombies, though. We need to get at the source—the necromancers summoning said zombies." Phoenix stood and put their hands on their hips as if considering how best to handle the issue.

"Noah and a few of the other order members are fighting against David and his crew, as well." Brandon tossed the abused umbrella into a nearby heap of debris.

"We should really focus on getting the girls out of here before we worry about cleaning out the rest of the zombies." Phoenix turned to help me get off the table. "I have a feeling that Rose and Theodore aren't quite done."

"They won't be until they're dead," I said with a grumble, and looked down at my body. "I don't even have shoes."

"The nightie is super cute though." Brandon took a few steps toward me as if he was going to give me a hug or something while covered in zombie juices.

"Don't come any closer until you get a shower." I put my arm up and used the sleeve of the nightgown to cover the stench.

"Hey, don't blame the player. Blame the game," he said as he looked down at his t-shirt with a frown.

"I'll take you straight home, dear. You don't need to worry about shoes." Phoenix grabbed a hold of my elbow.

"Oh yeah, that's perfect." I smiled gratefully.

Trina paused and looked back into the darkness where werewolf snarls and zombie grunts still echoed around the building. "Should we try to help Noah and the wolves first? They did come to save us and everything. Doesn't seem right to leave them to clean up the mess." Then she turned to an empty place in the room, and said, "What do you mean she's ignoring you?"

"I'll come back and help once you two are safe and sound. You're the top priority here." Phoenix adjusted their hold on my elbow. "Ready?"

"Wait, Trina. Who are you talking to?" I asked, afraid I already knew her answer and even more afraid of what that would mean.

Trina's eyebrows furrowed, and she kept glancing between me and the area next to a shelf that seemed completely empty and free of any ghosts. "He says you talked to him a few minutes ago, but now you're ignoring them. Hanna, can you hear them?"

Blood drained out of my face as the answer was written clearly in my expression.

Brandon narrowed his eyes and took a few steps in the direction Trina kept looking. "Wait a minute... Why do those ghosts look so familiar?"

Phoenix tugged gently on my arm. "We can figure out what's going on with the ghosts in a minute. Let's get you out of here first. That's the most important thing."

But before they could whisk me away to safety, the lights shut off completely, and a whiff of perfume announced another presence on my other side.

"Hello, dear," Rose said into my ear as she grabbed my free arm.

Something happened to Phoenix and suddenly their grip was no longer a steadying presence but a sharp absence.

Without hesitation, Rose teleported us out of the dark warehouse and into a basement somewhere. I could only tell or assume it was a basement because there weren't any windows. Otherwise, it was nicely furnished, large, and quite homey.

It didn't match the nefarious being who shoved me onto a plush sofa as evil glinted inside her eyes.

I was still adjusting to the disorientation of the sudden teleportation, but I must have been getting more used to the quick method of travel because I didn't feel like barfing, and the room didn't spin too fast.

"What do you—"

My question was cut off by Rose disappearing again for a millisecond before popping back up with Theodore. He had Trina and Brandon by the elbows, both looking surprised and scandalized at the same time.

"What are you doi—Ugh, I don't feel so good." Brandon turned to the side and put his hands on his knees. He was breathing quickly as he adjusted.

"Let me *go!*" Trina wrenched her arm free of Theodore's clutching grip and then sunk to the floor with a groan. She held her head in her hands.

I felt some concern for my sister and best friend, but I quickly figured they were simply adjusting to the teleportation. There hadn't even been enough time for them to get injured.

Rose gave the newcomers a smug look before turning to Theodore. "What's with the boy?"

Theodore adjusted the sleeves of his button-up shirt and rolled his shoulders a few times as if ridding himself of the contact of something distasteful.

I didn't know what the zombie-raising, soul-eating creature would find distasteful, but apparently a couple of teenagers did the trick.

"Do you not sense his oddness? He's neither alive nor dead. It intrigued me, and I figured it would be easier to find out more about him now than try to hunt him down later." Theodore went to the kitchen portion of the large room and opened the fridge.

"Yes, I sense his oddness, but *I* figured it wasn't super important considering all the tasks at hand." Rose followed Theodore for a few steps but kept her eyes on us.

Theodore stepped back from the fridge with a beer that I was surprised he'd drink from a can. "He may be more important than you realize."

Brandon stumbled over to the couch and sank into it next to me. "Are you okay?"

I nodded. "I guess?" Then I glanced down at his spoiled clothes. "Be better if you didn't stink so much."

"Couldn't agree with you more." He sat up and whipped off his shirt.

"Afraid that doesn't help the hair situation much," I said, finding myself surprised at how lean and muscled his chest was. It was amazing that I could spare a thought for how sexy someone else was, even Brandon, during such a situation, but there I was, ogling him.

His lip perked up on one side as if he knew exactly what was going through my head, but I looked away, forcing myself to focus.

Trina groaned and put her head between her knees, still sitting on the carpet.

I started to move my own trembling limbs to help her out, but Rose snapped at me. "Stay there! I'm way past being patient. Sit tight. Don't move."

I frowned, but Trina held up a hand to tell me she was alright, just taking a moment to steady herself.

Rose was still wearing the golden glasses, and I had to admit I was impressed she'd kept a hold of them after all that had happened, including being tackled by an alpha werewolf. As Theodore chugged his drink, Rose slowly pulled the glasses off and set them gently onto the nearby dining table.

"I lost the book. We're not going to be able to complete the spell without it." She sighed. This was the first time I'd heard anything but confidence from her, and I had to admit it helped me feel better that even the infallible Rose could get frustrated.

And that we had a hand in causing that frustration.

Theodore sighed and took another drink of his beer. "Why do you think I need this nasty stuff?"

"We need to go back and get the book."

"If it's intact. That shelf fell on it, thanks to your vampire pet," Theodore growled, his dark eyes narrowing.

"Oh yes, I'm fine. Thank you for asking. An alpha werewolf just decided I was lunch, and my vampire pet saved my life."

Theodore shook his head and took another drink. "You better take any phones they have on them before they get a chance to call for help."

Rose frowned and walked over to Trina. It didn't take much effort on the witch's part to shuffle through Trina's pockets and pull out her phone. My sister was much too consumed with her headache to fight back.

Then she stood in front of Brandon and held out her hand. "Give me your phone. Don't pretend you don't have one, because I saw the shape of it in your pocket."

He glared at her for a second before shifting to pull it out and hand it to her.

Something else snagged Rose's attention and her eyes narrowed. "What are you wearing?"

"Huh?" He looked down at his bare chest and zombiefied jeans. Then his eyes fell onto the golden bracelet around his wrist, and he shoved it between his back and the couch cushions. "Nothing."

"That's not nothing. And you're not alive." The elegant witch, hair still somehow mostly intact in the tight bun, studied Brandon for several seconds, more than long enough to make him uncomfortable and squirm on the couch next to me.

"I made it," Trina said from where she was hunched over on the carpet. Her head was still in between her knees, making it so I could only see her disheveled chestnut hair and nothing of her face.

"What?" Rose said.

"Why would you say that?" I asked, exchanging worried glances with Brandon.

The last thing we needed was Rose finding out what Trina could do.

Chapter 31- Trina

I gave Hanna a look, hoping somehow that our sister bond would be able to convey my intentions, but of course we weren't telepathic so all she responded with was confusion.

"You can have it if you can manage to get it off the ghost." I rested my head on my knees where I could still see what was going on but didn't have to hold it up. It was hurting so badly that I didn't even care to get up off the floor. Plus, it's not like being on the couch was going to help us take down Rose any better.

As for the witch, she narrowed her eyes and looked over at Brandon who was still hiding his arm behind his back and giving her a dumb smile.

"Let me see it." Rose stuck out her hand toward Brandon.

At first, I thought he was going to put up a fight, but he glanced over at me and my glazed eyes and must have decided we might as well use Rose in case she could help.

"It makes the ghost physical, but the catch is that they can't take it off. They have to cross over before anyone else can use the bracelet." Brandon raised his arm out for Rose to examine.

Theodore put his drink down and came over to stand between me and Rose. He looked down at my hunched form and studied me a second. "And you made this? How did you do it? Can you make more things?"

I gave a small shrug. "I haven't tried again. Been kind of busy. I'm not sure if it being stuck on the ghost until they cross over was a design flaw I accidentally did or if that's just the way the 'ghost science', as Hanna calls it, works."

With a frown, Hanna watched me cooperate all too willingly. Of course, she couldn't feel the intense headache that seemed to grow stronger every minute Brandon was wearing the darn thing.

"Why are you telling them this stuff? You realize they'll probably kill us after they figure out how to take our powers, right? These are the *bad guys*." Hanna's eyes were wide with fright and concern.

Rose frowned as she gave the bracelet a few harsh tugs, making Brandon wince a few times.

Theodore laughed. "She's right, of course. And now that we know you can do this, we don't even need the spell book."

Rose dropped Brandon's arm and turned to Theodore. "What? Why not?"

"She'll make us something that can do the spell for us. I knew bringing the kid would be important. Are you wishing you hadn't doubted me now?"

Rose looked down at me, still frowning. It hurt to look back up because of the bright lights above her head. It wasn't that the room was brighter than any normal living area, but rather everything with even a bit of light felt bright to me.

"She'll never help you!" Hanna sat up further on the couch.

Rose's smile bloomed across her face in a slow evil way that made me shudder despite the demanding pain in my head. "Oh, I think I know exactly how to get her to cooperate."

"You don't need to do anything but figure out how to get that bracelet off of him, and I'll help you," I said, finding there was still room to feel a bit sad despite the distracting pain. I couldn't decide if it would be worse to help Brandon cross over or to help Rose to stop the pain somehow. Either way, it sucked.

But the headache.

The pain was too much for me to be able to care a whole lot about anything else. After we figured out how to get rid of the pain, I could think about the rest.

"Why would you do that?" Hanna edged upwards on the couch so much she was in danger of falling off.

Brandon grabbed her arm and pulled her gently back before Rose could yell at her again. "Hanna."

The solemn weight of his voice pulled her attention to him.

He didn't say anything, but some kind of message must have passed between them because she frowned without protesting anymore.

Rose watched the exchange with shrewd eyes.

Theodore turned back to look at me. "Alright. I've met a few Seers over the years who can make these kinds of items. In fact, I knew the guy who made the glasses your family seems to think are theirs. It was a shame I had to kill him, though. He wasn't as smart as you in realizing it would just be better for everyone if you worked with me instead of against me."

I furrowed my eyebrows. "Just get the bracelet off without hurting him, and I'll do whatever you want."

"Trina," Hanna said, her voice a pained whisper.

Theodore looked at Rose. "Any spells you can think of that will get rid of the bracelet?"

"Sure. I could dissolve the metal, leaving only slight scarring."

"That doesn't sound good." Brandon eyed the witch warily.

"Don't worry. You're already dead. You can't feel too much pain." Rose wore a fake smile.

"Okay, what supplies do you need?" Theodore asked.

"Are you sure it would be wise to help her first? Maybe we should have her make our item before we get rid of the bracelet." Rose gave me a distasteful look.

"Listen, if you want anything from me right now, I'm nearly sure I won't be able to do it. I don't even think I can stand, at this point." The words came out slowly as they had to work through the fog in my head before exiting my mouth.

Rose glanced back at Brandon before studying me again. "It's taking its cost from you. That's how he's able to stay in this form. It pulls energy from the person who made the item. It makes sense, all things considered. The energy has to come from somewhere."

She turned back to Theodore. "Very well. Let's fix this first, then she can make us what we want, and then I can make us any other items we desire, while you can control any ghosts we need. These two are going to make us virtually unstoppable."

His smile probably would have unnerved me if I'd had the awareness to care.

"I'll send the pet to get what I need for the dissolving spell while I grab some gold items we can use to make what we need," Rose said and then vanished without waiting for his response.

Theodore turned to regard the three of us. "Be good little minions or else I'll have to bring in the undead ones who smell nearly as bad as you do."

Brandon gave him a mocking salute.

Theodore went back to the kitchen and got another beer before sitting down at the table and pulling out his phone.

Hanna and Brandon began whispering harshly with each other, but I couldn't find a reason to care about what they were saying and turned my face back between my knees and closed my eyes.

Not long after, Rose appeared back in the room carrying a bag. Caleb was next to her holding a box of supplies.

Hanna jumped and held her chest at their sudden appearance while Brandon's eyes widened for a moment. I probably should have been surprised to see them come in so suddenly, but there were more important things on my mind.

"Put that over there. I'll make a potion real quick, and we'll get on with this," Rose said as Theodore stood and moved over so they could have more space at the table.

While Rose was working, Hanna and Brandon continued with their quiet argument, and I dug up some energy to try to figure out what they were talking about. Something to do with how to get out of here. Hanna was most upset with being unable to see ghosts. She tried summoning Frank as a test and maybe an effort to use his help to escape, but that was a bust.

Brandon kept reassuring her that everything would be okay and that we'd figure out how to stop these two once they helped us out, but Hanna didn't seem to believe it.

I couldn't say I blamed her.

As Rose worked, Caleb stood by the witch and kept his steely eyes on us as if we were going to try to attack or do something stupid. With his vampire hearing, he was sure to be able to pick up anything Hanna and Brandon were saying, but they didn't seem too worried about that.

I turned my head slightly, still resting it on my knees, and locked eyes with him. At first, they remained empty and focused, but after I kept a steady gaze on him, something shifted and softened in his expression.

We didn't exchange words, but I felt like I'd made contact with the real Caleb for a moment. His eyebrows pulled in slightly as his eyes tightened around the edges.

I sent him a wobbly smile to let him know I was happy to see him, but the exchange seemed to only distress him more instead of comfort.

Finally, Rose finished cooking up whatever she needed and walked toward Brandon. "Give me your arm."

Brandon glanced at Hanna who then glanced at me, her frown deepening, and then nodded at him.

Taking a deep breath, Brandon stretched out his arm. The golden bracelet winked innocently in the light. Rose placed a towel beneath his wrist and prepared to pour something out of a bowl.

"This may hurt, but probably not nearly as bad as you're making the Seer hurt," Rose said, her smile thickly sweet.

Brandon winced and squinted his eyes. "I know I was foolish to put it on. I'm sorry, Trina. I only wanted to—Ow!"

Rose had begun pouring the liquid onto the bracelet while chanting witchy words. I didn't blame her for not waiting for Brandon to shut up. He rarely did that on his own.

Hanna grabbed his other hand and tried to lend him comforting support. I wasn't sure how much it was helping based on the pained contortions of Brandon's face.

Sizzling sounds came from the bracelet, and I managed to feel a sense of loss as the jewelry melted even as relief softened the edges of my headache.

As the metal completely separated and fell onto the towel, Brandon's body began to fade from the real-world back into that blue hue.

Hanna watched in panic as it probably appeared to her that he was disappearing away from her completely. "Brandon! I—I don't know what to say. Don't leave me, okay?"

He smiled as the peach drained out of his face and with soft, blue lips said, "I'll never leave you."

Rose stood, wrapping the towel around the remains of the bracelet. "I don't know why you're getting so upset. He's simply returning to the same form you initially liked."

Then she narrowed her eyes as she took in Hanna's tears and inability for her to focus in on Brandon's ghostly face. "Wait... You can't see him anymore, can you?"

Theodore froze where he was standing a few feet away watching the exchange. "What did you say?"

Rose furrowed her eyebrows and studied Hanna. The thoughts were whizzing around inside her mind in such a way it was almost visible, and I wondered if smoke were going to come out of her ears.

My headache was easing, making my brain feel lighter and my neck stronger. I rolled my shoulders as I sat up straight and put my legs into a crossed sitting position. The relief was amazing, and in it, of course, came the guilt of separating Hanna from her friend. Well, at least we didn't need to make him cross over. That would have been even worse.

"We didn't complete the spell. I know that much." Rose turned to Theodore. "Can you see the ghost sitting there?" Then she looked at me. "He's still there, right?"

I nodded. "Yup, making goofy faces behind your back."

Brandon gave me a glare to which I returned a snarky smile. It was nice to feel some of my personality again.

Theodore was shaking his head. "I don't see anything."

Hanna huffed through a sob. "But if you don't have my powers, where did they go?"

A loud crash sounded from somewhere above our heads, and we all looked up toward the ceiling as if we'd somehow gained the power of seeing through walls and would be able to know what had made the noise.

"What was that?" Theodore asked with a frown.

Rose sighed in exasperation. "This night just keeps getting worse. Pet, go check it out."

Caleb nodded and left without a word, leaving through the hallway and presumably up some stairs somewhere.

Brandon and I locked eyes.

"Should I go too? Or, at least see how far I can get from Hanna without having to go back to my haunt? Which, by the way, how come she can't see me, but I'm still not zapped back to my haunt? This is weird."

I nodded, giving him a lost-looking shrug at the same time.

He followed off after the vampire, giving Hanna one last look before he left.

"Could you see the ghosts after you were resurrected?" Rose asked Hanna, bending down and getting uncomfortably close to her face as if the proximity would drag the answers out of her better.

It didn't matter how close she got, though, because not even Hanna knew what was happening.

"I—I'm not sure. Did something go wrong with the resurrection spell?" Hanna pulled away from Rose and deeper into the couch.

Huffing, Rose stood and looked at Theodore. "Well? Can you tell? How well did the spell work?"

Theodore shook his head with a perplexed shrug. "Everything seemed to go fine, as far as I can tell. She's not a zombie like my daughter. All seems perfectly normal."

In what was a super surreal experience, Brandon popped his head through the ceiling above the couch. "She's not wearing the glasses again, is she?"

We both looked at Rose who was studying Hanna with narrow eyes and not wearing the glasses. They sat on the table where she had put them earlier.

"Good. We've got company. Kieran is up here. She purposely made that sound to distract Caleb. At first, they were fighting, but then the queen managed to pin down Caleb, and is staring at him intently. I think something vampirey is going on. At first, I thought they were going to like make out, but then they didn't. Now I'm wondering if she's trying to use her queenly powers on him. Can she pull him away from Rose? You would think Rose would notice the battle for power going on inside her pet's head. Well, at least we know that Kieran could take Caleb in a fight. Hopefully, she's on our side."

I listened to Brandon prattle on with a pensive and concerned expression trained onto Hanna. I was worried about her, wanted to understand what had happened to her powers, and was worried if the same thing could happen to mine, but also didn't want to attract attention to Brandon in case Rose caught on.

I knew Kieran wanted to kill Rose, so as far as that went, she was on our side. Now, if she wanted to kill us as well, that was a whole different thing. If Kieran had come alone and still managed to get a hold of Caleb, we were at her mercy.

Honestly, though, I preferred to die at the hands of the vampire queen rather than the necromancer witch. I would be happy with how anything ended up as long as Rose didn't win...and Caleb or Hanna didn't die.

That would hurt.

"Have you ever resurrected a Seer before?" Rose asked Theodore, either unable to feel much for the wellbeing of her pet or too distracted to notice other things were going on.

Hanna watched their exchange with wide and focused eyes. I tried to snag her gaze without being obvious, but she was too enraptured by the discussion about her missing powers.

Can't say I blamed her.

Brandon kept popping his head up and down through the floor, keeping an eye on what was happening with Caleb and then coming back to tell me about it. "They're still having a mental battle. Rose still hasn't noticed? So weird."

Then the witch stopped mid-sentence about the effects magic might have on other magic and cinched her eyebrows.

As if answering her call, Caleb came strolling back down the hallway. He looked like her pet still, vague and determined, and Kieran was nowhere in sight.

I glanced up at Brandon with wide eyes to ask him what had happened, but he'd disappeared again.

"What's going on?" Theodore's gaze darted between Caleb and Rose in confusion.

"I'm not sure..." Rose began but stopped when Caleb side-stepped quickly and grabbed a hold of Theodore, his arm around the necromancer's neck.

Not even missing a beat, Rose grabbed Hanna, yanked her off the couch, and held a shiny dagger she'd seemingly pulled out of nowhere to my sister's throat.

I froze, having no idea what to do.

Hanna let out a strangled cry but didn't dare move much for fear of Rose slicing open her neck.

"Drop the girl." Caleb's voice was rigid.

"How did you escape?" Rose asked, her expression more curious than angry.

Theodore pulled against Caleb's arm, but it was no use. No necromancer could physically overcome a vampire.

"Don't even think about summoning any zombies to help you," Caleb snarled into Theodore's ear. "I'll snap your neck as soon as I smell anything putrid."

Brandon walked down the hallway and then paused as he saw the situation. "Holy—! Let her go!"

The ghost rushed over to tug on Rose's arm holding the weapon, but his hands simply went through her body.

My mind was racing with ideas as I tried to figure out what would be best. I knew I would only have one shot at doing something since any movement I made would be sure to end in Hanna's death.

Again.

"What do you want?" Rose's eyes locked with Theodore's.

It was unclear if she was asking Caleb or Theodore the question, but perhaps she wanted to know both answers.

"Me?" Caleb asked with a mockingly-innocent smile. "Oh, world peace, no child going hungry, stuff like that."

Hanna's eyes finally landed on me, and they were wide and panicked. My heart went out to her as I'm sure the last thing she wanted was to spend more time as a ghost. It was one of the last things I wanted, too.

Theodore grunted as he continued to struggle fruitlessly. His voice was gruff as he spoke while Caleb's arm was pressing onto his neck. "I can't take him over. Something is blocking his mind. Vampire, let me go. We don't care to kill this Seer. She's lost her powers. We've got no further need of her."

Caleb's eyes darted to Hanna's for a second as if to confirm the loss of her powers. I was reasonably sure he would still protect her even if she wasn't a valuable Seer, but I may have doubted for a tiny second.

Brandon came and kneeled next to me, his clothes having returned to the band t-shirt and those terrible 90s pants. "Well, this is stupid. I really need a body that can faze into real life when I need to so I can punch a witch in the face without any risk to myself or others, while also being able to go back to my ghostly form so I can move through walls and hide from people in plain sight. Plus, it's always hilarious to make fun of people while still being in the same room as them."

I was frowning when he started talking, but it slowly grew into a small smile. He had given me an idea.

Chapter 32 - Hanna

Rose's fingers were cold against my neck, but not nearly as cold as the dagger's sharp edge pressing into my skin. I was certain that it would slice me open with the barest movement from either me or Rose, and I'd be dead again.

It was perhaps easier to contemplate death now that I knew what it was like. There wasn't that great unknown stretching before me as I figured I'd go back to being a ghost again. Hopefully, my haunt would be somewhere more entertaining than the skatepark this time. I wouldn't mind hanging out with Frank at the movie theater for the rest of forever if I couldn't have my own bedroom where Brandon's haunt was.

I was glad to see that Caleb had somehow broken free of Rose's hold without us having to kill him. I wasn't sure if vampires got the whole soul situation and were able to become ghosts after death. Did vampires even have souls?

That didn't seem very fair for vampires like Caleb who weren't so bad during their undead life. Even if he got me killed...again... I was still convinced he was a good guy, trying his best to make up for letting my grandmother down.

It wasn't his fault he'd snapped my neck or done other evil things while Rose controlled him.

Yes, I was focusing on Caleb and thinking about the great mysteries of the universe to avoid trying to face my future as a normal person, unable to see ghosts anymore. A few months ago, that was all I wanted—to live a normal life with popular cheerleader friends and a football star boyfriend and only having to worry about getting good grades and fighting a reasonable amount with my parents.

But now...

I knew the world was so much more than that. I knew the potential of souls and how helping others was surely the best way to spend our short lives. Sure, there were many ways to help others even if I couldn't talk to ghosts, but there were far more wandering souls without help than there were alive ones. And even less Seers to help them.

"It's okay, Caleb," I said, trying to move my throat and chin as little as possible. "Take him out. It's better if he's dead and unable to hurt any more people than if I am alive."

Rose growled. "Do it, vampire, and she'll be dead. Or maybe you don't care now that she's not a Seer anymore. You were simply using her as a friend, after all, weren't you?"

Caleb narrowed his eyes. "I know you treat people like that, but all humans are valuable, whether they have special powers or not."

"You mean because you can always use them for a quick lunch?" Rose said tauntingly.

Her words gave me the nudge and idea I needed.

"This is for my grandma!' I yelled. Heedless of what would happen to me, I smacked my head backward and elbowed her in the gut at the same time.

Rose cried out in pain as a sickening sound came from her face where I hoped my skull had broken her nose. I fell to my knees as Rose released me and staggered away grabbing her face and her stomach.

Purple lightning zapped out around us but was cut off abruptly when Caleb twisted his arms and snapped Theodore's neck.

Not a second later, Trina tackled Rose, using her momentum to finally push the witch onto the carpet. Something gold flashed in her hand as she stabbed it into Rose's leg.

The witch screamed and collapsed into a wounded, bloody ball.

"What—" I tried to say, but my throat wasn't working, and warm redness was rushing down my front and dropping onto my fingers.

Strong arms wrapped around my shoulders and pulled me back to rest in his embrace. Caleb's dark eyes sparked with anger as he clamped his hand around my neck to stop the bleeding. "Did you really like being a ghost so much?"

I managed a grunt and a smile as I pointed to his mouth before passing out.

Chapter 33 - Trina

As soon as I put the gold letter opener I'd stolen from my mom's desk earlier into Rose's thigh, her body curled up in pain as her spirit floated out in confusion.

I sat back on my heels in triumph until I heard Hanna's gurgling breaths. Turning around, I saw Caleb cradling my sister as blood seeped through his fingers and dribbled onto her already-stained nightgown. As our eyes met, he seemed to ask me a question.

I nodded frantically as Rose's ghost finally figured out what had happened and started screaming.

Brandon was hovering over Hanna, heedless of anything else but the precious liquid that was coming out of her. "Oh no. Oh no! This can't be happening. Somebody do something *right now*!"

Caleb couldn't hear the ghost but after our exchange, he used a sharp canine to rip open the skin at his wrist and instantly put it into Hanna's mouth.

Brandon put his hands into his hair and grabbed it tightly. "I didn't mean *that*! You better not turn her into a vampire, you creepy—"

I tuned out the rest of his angry cursing, knowing Caleb would save Hanna's life, and turned to the blue form of Rose's spirit trying to get back into her body.

"What did you do?" she screamed at me for at least the third time. "Why can't I get back into my body? What did that item do to me?"

I tried to be graceful and not smirk, but I'm afraid I failed. "Only what you deserved. You killed so many people in your way-too-long life that I figured you could spend some time as a ghost, but not like as a real dead person, but as someone who has to watch your body be a zombie without you. Wouldn't that be fun?"

Indeed, her body was still breathing, curled up as it had been when she'd left, but other than that, appeared to be mostly resting. Her eyes were open, but the gaze was unfocused, vague, and her expression was completely relaxed, ready for any necromancer to make a simple command.

Rose screamed and stomped her blue foot onto the carpet. "You can't get away with this! I'll figure out how to break free from your curse!"

I shrugged. "I guess you might, but I still get to enjoy this moment of victory."

A presence appeared next to Rose that startled me into uncurling my legs and backing up a pace. "I can take it from here. Good work, sister."

I frowned at the vampire queen I had already known was in the house but had somehow forgotten about. "I'm not your sister. Nice of you to show up when the hard work is over."

"No, you're *the* sister." Kieran rolled her eyes. "Who do you think was helping Caleb withstand the necromancer's powers to overtake his mind again? I'm not sure if you've ever tried that before, but it's consuming business. Honestly, it wouldn't have even worked at all though without the help of a witch's potion. It's nice to have a magic user on retainer when you need one."

"Right." I glanced back at my friend and Hanna. He'd removed his hand away from her neck. While blood still coated everything in a sticky, already-crusting mess, at least the wound had been healed.

Hanna was still drinking slowly from Caleb's wrist, as if too weak to pull in much help, but even the small amount of blood was enough to heal her neck and provide her body with what she needed to keep on living for the moment.

"Thank you for helping set him free." I turned back to the queen.

Rose's ghost kept stomping and pacing around with snarls of frustration and cursing, but she must have been wise enough not to use up her ghostly energy to turn a part of her physical. Yet.

If I was a betting person, I would have put odds on the fact that she was simply biding her time.

Brandon was hovering over Hanna and Caleb, still snarling threats at the vampire but having calmed down a touch after he saw Caleb's actions were helping, even if they were creepy.

"You're welcome, but I didn't do it for you," Kieran said while distractedly looking at Rose's body. "Can she come back from this?"

"Probably. If anyone decided to pull out the letter opener. I'm sure she's going to enjoy watching her body rot." I sent her ghost a haughty nod.

Rose screamed some more. "Pull it out! So help me, I'm going to haunt you forever!"

"Good luck following me around. My powers don't allow ghosts to leave their haunt," I said, finding that I was braver when she was an incorporeal blue form.

"I can't take the risk," Kieran said.

"Wait! We've got to do something first." My chest fluttered with panic at what I had almost done as I turned back to Rose's ghost. "You need to set all those ghosts free. There are several still under your control. If you don't set them free right now, we're going to trap you inside a crystal, and then you'll be Phoenix's slave for the rest of existence."

She laughed, making me frown. "Is that supposed to scare me? First, you don't know how to do that spell. Second, neither does Phoenix. Third, even if I wanted to set them free, I can't do it here and now, like this."

I frowned even deeper.

Kieran watched me with a wary eye. "You know she's not going to cooperate with you after you stabbed her like that. I wouldn't either, to be fair."

"We can't kill her until those ghosts are free, or else we'd be just as bad as she is, damning those souls to some kind of weird, trapped existence." I wracked my brain as I spoke, trying to figure out what to do.

"She's right. I won't help." Rose glared and folded her arms across her chest.

"What if you tell us how to free them, and we agree to let you back into your body? That's what you want, right? To get back in there?"

Kieran narrowed her eyes at me but was at least wise enough not to speak and ruin whatever trick I was trying to pull.

Rose shook her head. "I can't trust you. No, put me back first, then I'll help you."

"And have you teleport never to be seen again? I don't think so."

She shrugged one ghostly shoulder. "Guess we're at an impasse then."

I turned back to Kieran. "We've got to save those souls. That's more important than anything else right now."

The vampire queen studied me for a moment as she thought. "I can possess her mind some as I drink her blood. There becomes this type of bond between vampire and host. Not every vampire can search a mind as thoroughly as I can, but you're in luck. I happen to be quite the expert. Not even Caleb can do what I can. I suppose it comes from age and experience."

I resisted the urge to make a comment on her age, pressed my lips together, and nodded. "Try it, but you've got to stop before you kill her so we can set those ghosts free. Can you do that?"

"What do you take me for, girl? An amateur?" Without any preamble or warning, she bit Rose's neck and started sucking.

"Uh, gross." I backed up until I bumped into Caleb, unsure of how I should be reacting.

Rose finally decided she was not going to tolerate being drained dry by the vampire and pulled energy from her soul to make her hand physical enough to grab onto the letter opener.

"Oh no you don't!" I scooted back over to keep her from pulling it out of her thigh.

Caleb must have put Hanna's body down to rest because he was suddenly beside me and steading my hand. There was no way Rose would be able to overpower both of us.

"Stop it! Don't let her drain me! It's not fair!" Rose wailed and screamed as we pushed her hand off the opener, and Kieran drank deeply.

I nudged Kieran's arm, feeling like I was poking a bear. "Remember not to kill her until we've freed those ghosts. We know some of them, and we can't let them be trapped."

Kieran grunted somewhere in her throat but didn't detach from Rose's neck.

A groaning sound came from behind us that was faint compared to Rose's screeches but creepy enough that it grabbed my attention.

"What is that?" I asked, keeping my hand on the handle of the letter opener, underneath Caleb's cool hand that was big enough to wrap around mine and my wrist. It had been nice to feel his touch even if it was a super weird situation.

Caleb frowned and followed my gaze to the heap that had been Theodore only minutes before.

Brandon, sitting next to Hanna's sleeping form in the carpet, had heard the sound too and was staring at the corpse, or what should have been a corpse.

Rose started using her fingers to pinch me in hopes that I'd let go, but it was easy to ignore. After another grunting groan came from Theodore, she looked over at her mentor's body and started to cackle.

"You're in for it now. Haven't you ever wondered why Theodore has been able to live so long? Maybe you're too dumb to even know much about him, but let's just say he's been around far longer than I have, and it isn't for lack of people killing him," she said, probably hoping I'd get so distracted she would be able to save herself. Or at least try to.

I doubted that even if she were able to get back into her body, she wouldn't be able to fight off Kieran's deathly embrace.

Caleb cursed, let go of my hand, and looked at me. "You got this?"

I nodded, gripping the letter opener so hard my knuckles turned white.

Kieran slowed in her drinking, and with a sickening slurping sound, she let go. Her mouth didn't have a drop of blood around it, which I was thankful for. "I know how to set them free, and we don't need her at all."

Rose screamed in anger and frustration.

I would have protested and demanded more answers from the vampire queen, but there was something else that demanded my attention.

Caleb approached the now-twitching body of Theodore. Crackles of purple lightning began popping up all over and around the necromancer as he slowly sat up.

"Be careful!" I yelled to Caleb, scared more from Rose's confidence of Theodore's rise than I would have been without it.

As his shoulders pulled upright, Theodore's neck popped and twisted until it was in the correct and functioning position. His expression was strained as he concentrated on pulling his body back together. It smelled like ozone as the purple lightning kept snapping and popping all over. Somehow, it helped him stand, but it took a few more seconds for his eyes to focus on us as an evil smile spread across his lips.

"Nice try, vampire. I appreciate a queen helping to fortify the mind of one of her seethe members. No one has figured out how to do that before, and it appears I need to find a way around that for next time. There won't be a next time for you, of course, but there is always a next time for me. It's funny, though, because you killed me, thus putting my body into resurrection mode where all this helpful lightning restores me for a time. It should be long enough to take you out."

I wasn't sure what would happen to Caleb if he touched the necromancer while the lightning zapped around his body like some kind of erratic forcefield, but Caleb must have been concerned about it as well because he didn't take any steps closer to Theodore. As far as I knew, vampires were fairly combustible.

Of course, lightning could take out pretty much any type of creature.

My whole body was trembling, but Kieran finally pulled away from the pale form of Rose's body. I felt confident enough in her demise that I let go of the letter opener and moved a few inches further away from the witch's corpse.

Rose's ghost was spiraling with different emotions, probably already going into instability. All bets were off when it came to the normal behavior of ghosts with Rose. Her spirit was old, like three hundred years old, and she had probably changed the very nature of it by consuming other souls. Then she'd tapped into whatever energy she had left to make her hand physical, and it seemed to take a quick toll. Not to mention, she had to watch a vampire drain her body dry, and then her mentor rise from the dead like Frankenstein's monster.

She kept screaming, but the words were incoherent. The screeches must have been able to reach into the physical world some, because they snagged Theodore's attention.

"What is that terrible wailing? Sounds like we have a poltergeist on our hands." Theodore looked around the room, still covered in that purple static light. It was possible that he could glimpse the ghost quickly going insane.

"Yeah, we killed your witch, and she doesn't seem too happy about it." I pulled myself into a standing position despite my knees that seemed to be weak with fear.

Kieran moved to stand next to Caleb. I wondered if he was tied to her again through seethe bonds. It would make sense since she'd had to help keep the necromancers out of his head, but I didn't know if he would be happy about it later.

Guess that was a future-us problem.

"Oh, then she can serve me well one more time," Theodore said and took a deep breath.

Panicking, I looked over at Brandon's spirit, but nothing seemed to be happening to him. He was sitting quietly next to Hanna, perhaps not even paying attention to anything else that was going on. He might have even been whispering encouraging words close to her ear that I wasn't sure she could hear anymore.

Theodore must have been able to target the only ghost he was aware of, because Rose, on the other hand, was being inexorably pulled toward the necromancer's wide mouth. There was no way to tell if she knew what was happening because she had been acting so crazed and panicked already.

She was gone with one more inhale, and he took a big swallow as if pushing her spirit into his chest.

My knees couldn't hold me up anymore, and I sunk back into the carpet. I was conflicted in feeling justice had happened to the witch while also wondering if those feelings were evil. She was a soul, after all. She should have paid for her crimes in the afterlife with whatever happened to bad spirits, if Hell even existed. Perhaps her being consumed was better than she deserved.

Even if it was some kind of poetic justice.

Theodore's grey-streaked hair grew into a rich brown. The wrinkles around his eyes and forehead smoothed out, and the skin around his jaw tightened to that of a young man. More lightning snapped around his body from the burst of new energy.

He laughed, making me wince. "I think I'll try to find more magic user souls. Those are delicious."

"You won't have a chance to eat anymore souls. We won't let you," Caleb said, his voice deep and determined.

I was behind the vampires so I couldn't see their faces, but I could imagine them standing before the lightning-covered man with fiery eyes and determined eyebrows.

"Oh? And what are you going to do?" Theodore asked as he brought his hand up, playing with the lightning as it jumped from one finger to the other. "It doesn't take much to fry a person, and even less to burn a vampire."

"We don't necessarily have to stop you ourselves, just distract you for a minute." Kieran bent over and tossed the nearest armchair at Theodore.

He used the lightning to force the chair away before it hit him. The smell of burning fabric mixed in with the ozone, and I watched in concern as flames started to lick the chair after it landed onto its side.

Caleb didn't hesitate as he followed the armchair with a wooden chair from the dining room table. Instead of throwing it, though, he lunged forward, using it as a bat with a swinging motion toward Theodore.

With mocking laughter, the necromancer ducked, spun around, and struck the chair with the force of several bolts. The wood lit up, adding more burning smells to the air and finally, the scent and sizzle of flesh as it came into contact with Caleb's hands.

Caleb dropped the chair with a hiss and more fire spread onto the carpet.

Deciding it was time to get out of there and leave the vampires to their fight, I crawled over to Hanna's body, trying to keep my nose and mouth covered so I didn't inhale too much smoke. My eyes were already burning, and I couldn't spare the time to see how the vampires were trying to take down the lightning monster.

"We've got to get her out of here," Brandon said as I neared him, finally seeming to realize things were happening.

I nodded, not wanting to spare oxygen on talking. I pulled my shirt over my nose, praying it would stay there as I put my hands under Hanna's armpits and pulled.

Trying not to panic or address the fear that we'd get burned alive, I drug my sister toward the wall, hoping I could slip around the outside of the battle without getting me or Hanna zapped by lightning or hit with another chair or burned by the flames eating up the carpet.

The smoke must have been getting to Theodore as well, because at that point, he shoved a big spiral of lightning toward the vampires and used the momentum to carry himself up, smash the ceiling, and out of the room. Smoke and fire gobbled up the influx of oxygen, and everything flew upward with a whoosh, including the vampires, I guessed.

It was really hard to see.

"C'mon! You can do it!" Brandon said, from somewhere to my right.

"Maybe just this once you can help out," I said through gasping coughs. "Take energy from me and help!"

"Oh. Right." Brandon grunted and suddenly Hanna's body felt easier to carry.

It was still a struggle to stumble through the smoke and down the hallway. I didn't even know we'd made it to the stairs until my foot bumped into something, and I nearly toppled over. Smoke was funneling out through the area, but the opening in the ceiling had helped draw the flames upward, giving us more of a chance for escape.

It took both of us, several gasping coughs and tears streaming down my face, but we finally made it up the stairs and out through a nearby window that had been smashed. It was one of those floor-to-ceiling windows rich people had in their kitchens sometimes, and the glass had been broken from something coming into the house. I didn't take the time to ponder that as I focused on carrying Hanna the rest of the way out, thankful that Brandon had been able to lift her feet enough that I didn't have to drag her through the sharp glass.

Chapter 34 - Hanna

I woke up in a hospital room. Gloomy light came in through the window and spilled onto the scratchy blanket that had seen too many decontamination washings. A beeping sound chirped out next to my head and must have been what had awoken me.

A nurse bustled into the room and went straight to the little box machine. She pushed a few buttons, one which stopped the incessant chirping, and then lightly squeezed one of the clear bags that was tethered both to the machine and an IV that stuck up out of my hand.

It wasn't until then that her eyes moved to me. A bright smile lit up her face as she saw I was awake.

"Hello, dear! How are you feeling?"

I blinked a few times, trying to figure out the answer to her question. "Actually, I feel pretty good."

She nodded. "That's great to hear. I know several people will be happy that you've woken up. Your mom hasn't left your side hardly at all. I finally managed to convince her to go home and take a shower and rest for a moment, but that's of course when you decide to wake up. Your dad is down getting coffee, I think."

I frowned. "How long have I been out?"

"Oh, it's nearly been twelve hours. I'm certain you're starving. I'll make sure to get a meal sent up straight away. Do you think you can eat?"

My stomach felt so hollow, I wasn't even sure it was there anymore. "Maybe."

"Well, try your best, dear. You look like you're wasting away into a corpse."

A bubble of laughter erupted from my throat. "You have no idea."

Thankfully, she didn't try to figure out what I meant from that, patted my hand, and left the room.

"Oh, I guess I should have said 'thank you'," I said to the empty chair sitting next to the bed.

Or was it really not empty, filled by a ghost I could no longer see?

Before I melted into fear and panic, I ripped my eyes away from the chair and looked around the room. There were several vases of flowers with small happy balloons in them wishing me a speedy recovery. The TV was on, but the volume was turned down low. It looked like it was playing that one pawn store show my dad liked.

I watched the dust dance in the sunlight for a few minutes as I tried to remember what had happened and how I had gotten there. It was difficult to think past the worry of not being able to see ghosts anymore, but I tried.

It wasn't too long before my dad came rushing into the room holding a cup of coffee. "Oh, thank goodness! The nurse just told me you'd woken up. How are you?"

He sat down into the chair, put his coffee on the side table, and grabbed my hand.

"I'm...okay."

I was sure Mom and Trina hadn't told him the truth, but I had no idea what story they had made up. Best to play the groggy and slightly confused patient.

Dad looked about the same since I'd seen him last at Thanksgiving a few weeks ago. He might have had some darker circles under his eyes, but other than that, he looked well. It probably felt like no time at all since he'd seen me to him, but, to me, it felt like years had gone by.

I'd battled zombies, fought alongside witches, been a ghost, and somehow escaped a magic user's slicing dagger during all that time.

Tears pooled in my eyes as I felt a surge of affection for my dad. Sure, he'd moved out, leaving my mom to figure out how to be a single parent, but there were circumstances and details about their marriage I was sure not to know about. He was still my dad. He was there for me, even if he lived in an apartment on the other side of town.

"Oh, sweetie." He squeezed my hand. "It's okay. I'm here. The doctors said your body was as fit as they'd seen. You only needed rest and food. In fact, between me and you, they seemed kind of puzzled with the numbers they got back from your blood work. They didn't give me details, but it seems like your injuries may be more of the mental or spiritual kind, maybe?"

I wiped at my eyes, feeling dumb for crying because I loved him so much. "The nurse said she was sending food up. What did Mom say about what happened?"

He furrowed his eyebrows. "Do you not remember? The CT scan and MRI came back normal. Does your head hurt?"

"No, everything just feels fuzzy."

"I suppose that's to be expected after what you've been through. They said you were on a ski trip with your friends and that you just had so much fun, you wore yourself out. Are you sure you didn't take any drugs or anything like that?"

I suppressed a small smile. "No, of course not. They're probably right. We had so much fun I kind of forgot I needed to rest and eat. I promise never to let myself go like that again. The aftermath does not feel good."

He kept a hold of my hand but sat back slightly in the chair with a furrowed forehead. "I can imagine. I'm having trouble believing that that's all that happened. I won't press it for now, but if you decide you ever want to talk more about it, I'll always be here."

I nodded and was saved from further trying to explain my carelessness by Mom and Trina rushing into the room.

"Hanna!"

"Oh, thank goodness! You're okay." Mom gave me a hug and sat on the edge of my bed, the opposite side of Dad's chair.

Trina stood behind Mom, and I had to admit, looked a bit worse than I felt.

"What happened to your hair?" I said, noticing Trina had gotten quite a short haircut and then saw the bandages on her hands. "And your hands? Are *you* okay?"

Trina smiled as she and Mom exchanged glances. "Oh, just a little cooking accident. I'll fill you in later."

Dad shook his head, put my hand down, and grabbed his coffee. "I sure have some clumsy girls, I guess."

As he took a sip, I gave Mom and Trina a wide-eyed look trying to convey that I really wanted to know what happened. It was nice to have Dad there for support, but it made things difficult to talk about since he still didn't know the kinds of things his kids kept getting into.

"So how do you feel, sweetie?" Mom wore a knowing smile as she patted my hand.

Trina was smiling down at me, but every once in a while, her eyes would drift to a place behind Dad's chair near the window. I pretended she was watching the dust motes float in through the sunshine and not looking at a ghost. I was going to have a breakdown later if I didn't get my powers back. Seriously. I'd gotten too used to having them around. I'd gotten so attached to a certain 90s kid that my heart hurt just thinking about not being able to see him anymore.

Even with Trina as an interpreter for us, it wouldn't have been the same.

So instead of worrying about it, I pushed it away, forcing myself to dwell on other things until either I got the powers back, or the loss was impossible to ignore.

"I feel...okay. For some reason, I don't think my vision is fully back." I gave Trina a meaningful look, so she knew I meant something other than regular sight. "But other than that, and heavy weakness, my body feels fine."

Mom gave me a soft smile. "I'm sure you'll recover fully soon. Say, Josh, do you think you could run to the house and pick up some belongings for Hanna? I totally forgot when I was just there. I'll text you a list while you drive. And you know, if you feel like you need to stop at your place for a while to rest, that would be okay. I'm sure they aren't going to let her out in the next few hours anyway, and you were so kind to stay while I took a break."

He drained his coffee cup before standing and nodding. "Is that okay with you, Hanna? I'll be back in a few hours, okay?"

I nodded, perhaps more enthusiastically than was needed. "Oh yes, I'm fine with that. Thank you so much."

He smiled, brushed my hair back from my forehead, and leaned in to give me a kiss. "I'm glad you're doing well, pumpkin. I don't know what I'd do if I lost either of my girls."

We shared silent giggles after he left the room. He had no idea that he'd lost me for a moment, and we were hoping we could keep it that way.

"So what *really* happened?" I asked after it'd been long enough for Dad to be out of earshot.

Mom turned to Trina with upraised eyebrows. "Care to fill her in? Then you can let her know how long both of you are grounded for."

Trina winced. "Yeah, I'm sorry. We didn't mean for all of that to happen. It all got out of hand."

I waved away Mom's comment. "Hey, after this, I have a feeling I'll enjoy being grounded for a few quiet weeks."

Trina filled me in with odd pauses and glances toward the window that I tried really hard to ignore. She explained what had happened after I'd headbutted Rose and jabbed her in the stomach—how she had stabbed Rose with a gold letter opener she'd stolen from Mom's desk and would happily repay Mom back for with chores, and what the ghostly effect she'd given it had done. Then she told me all about the fight between Caleb, Kieran, Theodore, and Rose, how everything had erupted in flames, and how she and Brandon had carried me up the stairs and out the back door.

Outside they had met up with some of the necromancers that had disagreed with David. They had formed a new branch of their order with Noah and Alberto as the leaders. They'd guessed Rose would retreat to Theodore's giant mansion, and their bet paid off as they'd found the house in time for Theodore to burst out the front door with Caleb and Kieran hot on his trail.

While the vampires had been able to keep the ancient necromancer busy, they'd been unable to work through his defenses enough to stop him. Lucky for all of us, the other necroes showed up and knew how to take him down.

"So he's dead? Like dead dead? Please tell me he's not coming back," I said, trembling from Trina's tale and how dangerous it had been while I'd essentially been a sack of potatoes.

Trina nodded. "Yes. Noah and the others threw enough zombies at him that he was too busy fighting, and Kieran was able to get in behind him and rip off his head. So unless he can grow a new head, which even a zombie can't do with a necro's help, I'm pretty sure he's gone for good."

I blew out a sigh of relief. "And I guess Rose's body burned up after Kieran drained her into a hollow husk. That's gross."

"Yeah, but even if her body was completely whole and fine, she's still not coming back. Theodore sucked her in like he was using a giant straw."

I shivered.

"Sounds like she got what she deserved if you ask me." Mom shook her head.

"True...although I'm not sure anyone really deserves that. So your hair and hands got burned in the fire?" My eyes danced across Trina's injuries.

She held her arms up to study the bandages. "Yeah, a little. These wraps make it look worse than it is."

"Thank you, Trina. Seriously. Thank you for coming to find me. Thank you for saving my life. Thank you even for letting that gross boyfriend of yours feed me his blood. No wonder the doctors were confused by my bloodwork."

Trina blushed as we all shared an amused chuckle when imagining the doctors' reactions.

"It's nothing you wouldn't have done for me," Trina said with soft eyes and a loving smile.

"Alright, so Noah and Alberto have taken care of the necromancers, hopefully getting the order back on track. What about David?" I asked, trying to get caught up with everything.

"They're going to have a trial by peers for him," Trina said. "I think this whole thing shook Noah up pretty good because I'm guessing David was a bit of a father figure for him, but he'll be okay."

"Yeah, I'm sure he'll work that out. What about the magic users? Have you heard from them?" I asked, remembering that Phoenix had been about to teleport me to safety when something had pushed them away.

"Phoenix dropped by a few times to check in on you. They told me a zombie had tackled them, but there weren't any injuries a little magic couldn't heal. Once the chaos died down, they even managed to find the evil book Rose and Theodore were using. They said they were going to keep it hidden and protected so nothing like this happens again.

"Oh, funny fact, though. Without Cordelia, we wouldn't have had Kieran's help. Once things got hairy, she teleported out to where Kieran was hiding, and brought her back in time for her to rescue Caleb from Bertram's snapping jaws."

My eyes widened. "Wow. I had forgotten about that. And then she must have been helping Caleb withstand Rose and Theodore's necromancer powers to control his mind. I never would have thought that crazy vampire queen would come to save the day."

Mom shook her head. "I still wouldn't trust her."

"For real. How did Cordelia know about her?" I asked.

"Oh, remember that witch Kieran mentioned having contact with? Or maybe you don't. I can't remember if you were conscious for that bit or not, but apparently, they've been working with each other for several years."

"I suppose that makes sense since they were both leaders of local groups of monsters. What about the wolves?" I felt a twinge of guilt for Gryphin. He'd helped me out so much, helped out our family even more, and I really hoped it wasn't because he was hoping we'd get together romantically at some point. Knowing him, though, it was probably simply out of the goodness of his heart.

"Oh, they had the yucky task of working through the hordes of zombies in and around the warehouse. I called Gryphin once you were safe and situated inside the hospital, and he filled me in with their side of the story. He said he wasn't sure he'd ever get the taste of zombies out of his mouth no matter how many times he brushed his teeth. Several of the pack were wounded in the fight, but they're quick healers. Honestly? I think they enjoyed having free reign to rip and tear stuff up. The tone in his voice was kind of excited as he talked about it. Oh, and he wanted to let me know they were all glad we made it out mostly safely."

I smiled as I thought about the cute curl that always dangled over Gryphin's forehead and the calming presence he had that helped me relax. "He's a good boy, that one. I have a feeling the wolves don't feel indebted to me anymore."

Trina grinned. "Probably not." She glanced again to the spot where no one was standing, nodded, and looked back to me. "We've also set the remaining trapped spirits free. I'm sure you've been worried about that."

"Oh." I put my hand to my mouth and took a breath. "Of course. Although, I feel bad they weren't what my first question was about. It's hard to remember everything."

"No need to worry. Kieran was able to infiltrate Rose's brain and pull out the secrets we needed. It was quite handy, actually."

"I have a feeling if we run into Kieran again, she's going to demand that we owe her. What did you need to do to get the spirits free?"

"Phoenix managed to help clean up the warehouse enough to at least grab the crystals. They were scattered after the werewolf attack, but they were able to collect them. Then all they had to do, after Kieran wrote it down for us later, was speak an incantation and burn the hair."

I crinkled my eyebrows together. "Well that seems super easy after all the trouble we had before. So now the ghosts are back...wherever their new haunts are?"

Trina nodded. "Yup, all we have to do is find their haunts, and we can begin to work on their unfinished business."

She looked again at the empty air and then back at me. "Which I'm sure I don't need to remind you, that there are a few certain siblings we can start with."

Neither of us pointed out that I couldn't currently interact with the ghosts. I wasn't ready to face it, and she must have sensed that. Plus, even though the glasses had most likely been destroyed in the fire, she could always make me another pair. Perhaps that's what the future of my ghost-helping was going to look like.

A nurse came in with a tray, interrupting our conversation, and set it on a nearby rolling table that she situated in front of me. The smells woke up my stomach, and it growled so long that even Mom and Trina were laughing after it stopped.

"Thank you," I said to the nurse who nodded and left the room.

Mom leaned over and removed the covering off the plate while I reached for my juice and struggled for a few seconds before getting it opened.

Hospital food wasn't typically my fare of choice, but at that moment, the cheeseburger and tater tots looked like the best thing I would ever eat.

Mom and Trina chatted politely as I scarfed down the food. Trina moved over to sit in the chair Dad had occupied after doing a weird waving motion and waiting for a second before sitting down.

I studiously ignored her odd behavior and continued to chew carefully so I wouldn't choke.

Then something weirder than her behavior happened. As I finished the burger and felt the effects of food filling my too-small stomach, a blue hue began to take shape near the window. At first, I thought I was seeing things, probably so hopeful that I didn't lose my powers that I was beginning to imagine.

Then he started talking, and I knew I wasn't making it up.

"This being ignored thing is getting old. And did you have to take my chair?" Brandon said, his arms folded across his chest as he half-sat on the window ledge. He was back in his clothes despite having changed while wearing the bracelet. It was a comfort to see those giant pants and those worn skater shoes. More comfort, at least, than I'd have imagined a pair of 90s pants would have ever given me.

My heart fluttered in my chest with relief and excitement. I couldn't even help the small smile that pulled up my lips as I chewed on a ketchup-covered tater tot.

"Maybe if you were less annoying, you wouldn't be getting ignored so much." I smirked, allowing my eyes to dart in his direction.

Immediately, he hopped off the ledge. "You can see me?"

Trina's eyes widened for a second and then a smile burst across her face while Mom pulled her eyebrows in confusion.

"Yes, and I have to ask you if you were in here the whole time like some creepy creep?" I put my juice down and gave him a look.

At least he had the decency to look a little ashamed, even if his grin told me he was as happy to see me see him again. "I was afraid if I left and went back to the haunt, I wouldn't be able to get back to you."

I frowned for a second and fiddled with my napkin. "Wait. So you've been able to be with me this whole time even though my powers were broken?"

He shrugged, came closer to my bed, and sat down next to my toes. "I guess?"

"Maybe the ability to allow ghosts to travel outside of their haunt is more of an unconscious latent kind of skill?" Trina said with hopeful eyebrows.

"Must be. Weird."

"But good weird, right? If I hadn't been here, I don't think Trina could have pulled you out of that fire by herself." He raised his eyebrows and looked at her.

"Yeah, yeah. You're the hero of the day." I waved my arm around but smiled teasingly.

Mom must have figured out what was happening because she sat back in her chair with a smile, content to let us talk to an invisible person for a bit.

It didn't take much food before my stomach felt like it was going to explode, but I was happy that I'd at least been able to eat most of the burger.

I laid back into the pillows and pushed the tray away a little. "You guys, I think I need to make some changes with myself."

"Are you going to start doing better with schoolwork?" Mom asked, giving me a raised eyebrow packed with meaning.

"Well, it'd be a heck of a lot easier to do more homework if I didn't have vampires and werewolves bugging me all the time... Not to mention all the ghosts I run into." I shared a small smile with Brandon, because at this point, I was pretty sure he knew I enjoyed his company.

"I suppose that's fair. Hopefully things can calm down some now that Rose is gone." Trina stole a fry off my plate.

"They had better. No, I think... This is harder to say than I imagined, but I've had some time to think here in this bed, and after losing my powers because I was clearly malnourished, I think I need to...maybe...get some therapy."

That grabbed Mom's attention, and she sat up toward the edge of her chair. "For what?"

Trina gave me a soft smile and patted my hand. "That's a brave thing to admit, you know. I'm proud of you."

Brandon was content to let this be a moment amongst our family members, but he did watch me with an understanding expression.

I returned the smile and looked at Mom. "You've probably noticed, but I've been trying not to eat so many calories. At first, I just wanted to lose some weight and fit in with the other girls at school more. But then it grew into an obsession, and after what I've just put my body through...before I died, of course, I'm pretty sure I need some outside help. Would that be okay? Maybe some of Dad's insurance can cover it."

Mom pressed her lips together tightly and grabbed my hand. Water pooled at the bottom of her eyes. "Oh, Hanna. I had begun to suspect something like that, especially after you didn't even touch your favorite pie at Thanksgiving. I'm so sorry you felt like you needed to lose weight. You're perfect as you are, no matter what you look like. I get it, though. There's lots of pressure to look like those computer-enhanced or definitely-sick models. We'll get you any help you need, and we'll be right here through the whole thing."

My hands trembled slightly as I worried what it would be like to go to therapy and confess my darkest secrets to essentially a stranger, but I knew it was the next best step. This struggle wasn't going to go away on its own.

"Thank you. It will be good to feel healthy again."

"I'm sure it will be. You'll get there." Mom squeezed my hand.

At the same time, Brandon said, "Plus, it's nice to be seen again. It was the weirdest thing to have Trina talk to me, but you couldn't."

"I bet." I grinned and looked back to Mom, squeezing her hand back. "I'm so glad to have such wonderful support. It's nice to be loved even with my flaws."

A few hours later, Mom and Trina decided to go out for dinner and let me have some alone time with Brandon or time to rest some more, whatever I needed.

I felt kind of nervous to be alone with him again after all that had happened. I also felt dumb for being nervous, but it was there all the same.

"After I get out of here, we should go looking for your siblings. Their haunt is probably somewhere they liked to hang out or visited often. It's quite possible that they are in three different places, but I promise we'll go looking for them." I gave him an encouraging smile in hopes that he wouldn't worry. "It won't take long at all before they're up where they belong. Oh, and we can figure out how much contact you want with your mom. Maybe we can even help her cross over. Won't that be good? I also need to check back in with her and let her know how much she helped us and how well the revenge went over. Maybe her UB will be learning about the revenge."

Brandon frowned, a reaction I hadn't expected.

"What? Why are you frowning?"

"What if that's my unfinished business? If we help them, I could cross over, too. I'm not ready to go...but I can't hold them back on the chance that it will set me free. I know we've talked about this before, but I still don't have an answer for it."

I took a slow breath. "Yeah. I can see how that's confusing. Maybe we'll take our time with them, help them carefully, and perhaps by the time the last one crosses over, you'll be ready to go, too? If that's what your UB is?"

We stared at each other for several seconds, both of our expressions were full of emotions and thoughts that we weren't sure we could say out loud.

"Hanna, I don't want to leave you. I'm not sure I'll ever be ready to go, no matter how much time passes."

My heart ached for him, and it broke a little more as I took in his pained eyes and furrowed eyebrows. "It's okay. We'll figure something out. We don't have to worry about it right now."

He nodded, and then his eyes trailed down to my lips. "I know you're not feeling one hundred percent right now, but do you think I could steal enough energy from you for a small kiss? Just a tiny one?"

I grinned, feeling a thrill of excitement rush through my chest. "How about enough for a long, deep one?"

He leaned in closer to me, and I hoped I didn't have ketchup breath. "I don't want to hurt you."

"You won't, but even if you did, it'll be worth it."

Color seeped into the soft curve of his mouth as he moved in closer to me, so close that his lips brushed across mine as he spoke. "I love you, Hanna."

The kiss stopped me from replying for a moment as our lips met, softly at first, and then he drew in a hitched breath, and we were pushing into each other with a passion I hadn't ever felt before.

It was overwhelming and swept away any other thought inside my head.

When we finally pulled away, we were both breathing heavily.

And then I said something that I regretted for the rest of my life.

"I'm not ready for you to go yet, either. Brandon, I know we shared how we feel about each other last time, but I feel like I need to say it again and add more to it. I love you. I love your stupid jokes, and the way you make fun of people who can't see you, and have no chance of defending themselves. I love how you tease me and make me feel like a normal girl despite the fact that I'm in love with a ghost.

"I love having you around. I love the light and purpose you've brought into my life. I didn't like it at first, but you've helped me learn to accept who I am and then showed me I can still be loved despite my powers. There will never be another person who means as much to me as you do. You mean everything to me, and I know I'm still young, but I'm still absolutely certain that I will *never* love anyone as much as I love you."

At first, he smiled, his eyes full of more life than I'd ever seen them, even when he'd been wearing the bracelet. Then his eyebrows pulled together, and his eyes widened.

"Oh damn," he breathed softly.

Goosebumps rushed across my arms as I brought a trembling hand to my mouth. "No...no! No! I take it back! I didn't mean any of it!"

His blue body began to fade and waver, but he kept his eyes locked with mine as he slowly disappeared. "I love you, too. I'll see you again. I promise."

When Mom and Trina came back a few hours later, I was still crying too hard to tell them what had happened. How could I have been so dumb?

Chapter 35 - Hanna

The next few days passed in a blur, mostly because I couldn't see much through the tears.

A parade of people came to visit me while I was in the hospital. Later, I felt bad that I didn't engage with them at all and probably hadn't even heard most of the things they'd said.

Addy and Emma brought me flowers and doughnuts. I don't know if I smelled the flowers or ate the sweets. I'm pretty sure I gave them at least a half-smile and agreed to hang out with them soon.

Noah stopped by at one point, toting a lost-looking Andrea with him. He explained how her father had been found dead in his own home, and Andrea hadn't been the same since. When she went to the bathroom, I mostly nodded while he talked about the future of the order. He lamented some more about Andrea's condition and not knowing what would be best to do next, but I had no advice to give him.

Gryphin and Mr. Tyler came by, but my teacher talked more with my mom than me while Gryphin simply held my hand. I know I cried then, the tears dampening my shirt. I wasn't even able to find the energy to care about the snot dripping down my face.

I had no idea if Gryphin knew why I was so upset, but he silently handed me a tissue and kept holding my hand, sensing that words would do nothing to help.

Trina and Caleb stopped by a few times, but again, I didn't pay much attention to them. I think I managed to offer a 'thank you' to the poor vampire but not much after that.

Three months later, I drove myself from a therapy session to the movie theater. Dad had given me a car and helped me pass the driver's exams. That picture was the first time I'd smiled in a long time.

It had been easy to find Justin, Brandon's little brother, because he happened to have the same haunt as Frank. We had no way of telling if the theater would have been his original haunt since Rose had snatched up his spirit right as he and his sisters had died.

It made sense as to why she killed them, though. Must have been a lot easier for her to snatch the dying spirits rather than force ghosts to get into the crystals.

Until she found me, that is.

I couldn't bring myself to even look at a ghost for a long time, but I knew I couldn't ignore them forever. Frank seemed like an easy spirit to start with, and I owed him for all the help he'd given me, so I forced myself to go visit his haunt.

"Oh, you're alive again. I was beginning to worry you were long gone." Frank sat down next to me on a pleather bench along the carpeted wall in the theater lobby.

"Sorry about your luck." I didn't even look over at him as I talked. Instead, I kept staring at my shoes, a pair I hadn't remembered putting on that morning.

At least they matched each other, if not my outfit.

"Well, it's nice of you to visit, anyway. I see you don't have a bodyguard. Things safer again?"

"Safe as things can get, I suppose. Have you figured out what your unfinished business is yet?"

"While I would usually appreciate the direct way you're wanting to get down to business, pun intended, in this instance, it feels kind of odd. Are you okay? Care to update me with everything that has happened? I hate to admit this, but I've been a bit worried and curious about how things panned out. Did Trina ever find the right warehouse?"

I sighed and leaned back against the scratchy wall and watched the few patrons walk around the lobby, visiting various arcade games or stopping to get some popcorn.

"I can see you're in a chatty mood." Frank studied me for a moment and then rested his head against the wall like I had, watching the lobby. "Well, since you don't want to talk, I'll tell you the news around these parts. We have a new ghost here, and you might be interested in finding out who it is."

I pulled my eyebrows together and finally looked at him. "Say what?"

"Yup, it's Brandon's little brother, Justin. He's a bit annoying, but I can appreciate his zest for the unlife. We've had fun pulling some pranks on alivers here and there. And before you ask, yes, we're careful not to spend too much of our own energy. We initially bonded over both being trapped inside Rose's crystals, although we never met each other. Then we swapped stories about you and theorized where his sisters' haunts might be. Are you interested in working the case?"

I blinked a few times as my brain processed all the words. "Yeah, actually. He's on my list of ghosts to help first. Where is he?"

And that was the restart of my career as a Seer. Frank understood I wasn't quite ready to talk about Rose or what had happened to Brandon. And while it was super painful looking at Justin and seeing the resemblance of his big brother, it was also nice to imagine them reuniting in Heaven. Brandon might have crossed over, but that didn't mean I couldn't help him anymore.

My name is Hanna, and I help dead people.

The End

Epilogue - Sixty Years Later

"You know, I hate to say this because it sounds crass, but it's impressive that we've lasted this long, and you are going out this way instead of being beheaded or stabbed or eaten by a zombie." Trina grabbed my hand and squeezed.

I had requested to die at home instead of the hospital. Hospice had been set up for home visits, and it was comforting to be able to look around my bedroom and lay underneath the quilt my gran had passed down through our family. Trina had insisted she would stay with me as long as I needed, and her presence was more comfort than I let on.

I squeezed Trina's hand in return and took a second to ponder our skin. We were both pale, wrinkled, and covered in age spots. When we were younger, it seemed like our age gap was huge, but now in our 70s, two years seemed like nothing but a breath.

"If I had to pick, I might choose something a bit faster than getting so old my organs don't want to work anymore. At least I didn't fall and die naked in the bathtub. That would have been terrible." My voice sounded hoarse and weak when it reached my ears, which still surprised me after all this time.

In my head, I sounded as I had most of my life.

"That's true, but I'd say you were doing pretty well considering you've been dead before."

"Yeah, please don't get the necroes to put me back though. I've worked hard not to owe them any more favors over the years."

We both laughed, hers a stronger sound than my breathless wheezes.

"Not all the necroes are bad. I'd say Noah turned out pretty okay. He's done well leading the order, and while it was difficult for him to come clean with Andrea and set her free all those years ago, it showed great strength of character." Trina gave me a soft smile as we revisited a conversation we'd had many times.

I grunted, finding it difficult to talk about too much. Half of me already felt like I had as a ghost—lost, memories falling out in pieces here and there, and unable to focus for long periods of time.

"You know, it's not too late to get turned into a vampire. I know of one or two who would be glad to help."

I scoffed. "And live for eternity in this body? No thank you."

"You could have said yes to Gryphin's marriage proposal fifty years ago. Then you could have been turned into a werewolf and lived a little bit of a longer life with extra healing powers and a whole pack of wolves to back you up."

"And been a doctor's wife while he worked long hours and was around all those attractive nurses? No," I paused for a few moments of intense coughing, "he was better off without me."

Trina handed me a glass of water, her own hand trembling some but not nearly as bad as mine was. I was shaking so hard, she had to help steady the glass against my lips.

She was frowning as she put the glass down on the side table. "I just worried about you a lot. I know I never told you, but it felt so selfish to go on living my own life, getting married, having kids, then eventually grandkids, while you...didn't."

"Oh, Frank and the ghosts kept me plenty company and busier than I'd have preferred. How many ghosts do you think we helped between the two of us?"

Trina turned to study the winter scene painting I'd placed on the opposite wall of my bedroom, presumably thinking about all the ghost work we'd done over the years. There had been several cases we'd worked together, but others she did on her own, with the use of her item-making skills, and even more that Frank and I had worked together. I'd been able to pay my bills by hosting an online group where I acted as a medium of sorts and helped people who had ghostly issues. It had been hard at first to take money for my services, but I had to eat somehow.

"It's hard to say," Trina started talking, pulling me out of my reminiscing. "It's got to be in the hundreds somewhere. You might have even hit a thousand at some point. You've basically made it your life's work."

"Mmm, that's when I knew I was dying. I couldn't see the ghosts anymore. Is Frank here?" I tried to raise my head and look around, but the muscles in my neck didn't respond.

Trina squeezed my hand and gave me one of her sympathetic smiles I'd seen too much of recently. "No, sweetie. He passed on about ten years ago, remember?"

I frowned. "No. What a relief. He was so grumpy."

"Almost as grumpy as you." Her smile morphed into a teasing one.

I'm not sure if she said anything more after that, but time seemed to pass. The only way I could tell was that the sun had moved the light in the room, making it gloomier, and the desk lamp was on.

Trina was gone, but I could hear shuffling sounds from somewhere in the house, so I figured I wasn't alone.

A small head peeked around the corner of my bedroom door. "Auntie?"

I spared a smile for Trina's youngest granddaughter, even if I couldn't remember her name. "Come in, dear."

She cautiously walked into the room, her hands holding a small paper. "I just wanted to give you this."

I waved with gnarled fingers for her to come closer. "What is it?"

"It's just a card I drew for you." She handed me the paper, and I had to squint and focus to make it out.

"Oh, is that me in bed?"

She nodded and pointed to what looked like a mound of blue scribbles next to me. "And this is the ghost that's come to visit a few times while Mamaw isn't looking. He's here right now, actually, and says it's time to take you home. Can you see him, Auntie? He's nicer than the others have been, but his pants are *huge*. Did everyone wear pants like that in the olden times?"

I paused and felt my heart flutter quicker than it'd worked in a long time. "Oh, I can see you. Where have you been?"

Acknowledgements

This is the first time I've written one of these, despite having published seven books. Even as a self-published author, my journey has not been a solitary one.

Mostly, I need to thank my poor friends and family for having to put up with the obsessive talk about my books and current projects. I have terrible news for you all in that while this is the last book in this series, I've already started working on another one, and the obsessive talk isn't going to end anytime soon.

My beta readers have been amazing. They're so kind to spend their free time helping me, finding typos, pointing out plot holes, and asking important questions, so I can head off any hating an online troll might drop on my books. They've also given me such amazingly kind words that have helped me continue on through the slog of writing.

Of course, I can't forget my proofreader, Jacelyn Schley, who has spent many hours forging through my ineligible, at times, writing. I've learned a lot from her, and I'm so grateful for her comments and added help through this process.

I want to thank anyone who has ever offered me support and encouragement anywhere along the process. Writing is such an inside battle between hope and imposter syndrome, and anyone who has offered me any kind of positive comment has helped me conquer most of the doubts (I'm afraid some will always be there).

There is one friend who has been so influential, I'm not sure I'd be here at all without her. Tara Wine-Queen and I made a pact in college that we'd both grow up to be famous authors and buy each other expensive gifts once we made it. Neither of us can buy the other a Maserati yet, but it's been a gift of its own to be able to struggle on this path together. She published her works first and showed me what was possible. I will be grateful forever for her friendship, even if I never get the fancy car (but I'm sure I will because she's freaking amazing).

Ashley, Melanie, and Michelle, we've lost touch over the years. I don't even know your last names now, but if you're out there, know that our silly games during sixth grade recess in a field forever changed my life. You guys taught me it was okay to be myself, and that there were others like me who preferred to play with their imaginations than stand around acting cool.

I need to thank my mom. If you know me personally, you know how strained our relationship is, and has been over the years, but I can't ignore that she helped foster a love of reading and stories inside my young mind. She has a large vocabulary and was great at teaching her young girls to use big words.

I also need to thank my dad who has been such a powerful example to me. He's had a difficult life, as most of us have, I imagine, but he's been able to conquer the inner demons of addiction and emerge a tall and stalwart example for his four children. Even now, he supports me so well, he'll read silly books about teenage girls in high school talking to ghosts.

My suffering husband has been a great sounding board for the many times I get stuck in the plot. I was blessed enough to find a fellow writing nerd as a companion, and we've had so much fun talking about stories and what we could do with them. Well, I'm not exactly sure if *he's* had fun, but I have. He's a great resource of ideas, and, even if I don't always take his suggestions, I can often work my way out of a situation with his help. He's generous enough to listen to my ramblings even when he's worked sixteen hours that day and is basically falling asleep on the couch. Find yourself a person who cares enough to do that for you, folks. It means everything.

I also have to thank and apologize to my girls. They're six and three at the time of this writing and have been little troopers while mom stands in the kitchen typing away at the computer and they play (kinda) quietly nearby. I couldn't have asked for sweeter babies, and I'm so blessed to be their mommy.

Lastly, thank you, dear reader, for giving me your time and spending it with me inside a world that was born from my head. It is through you that my dreams can come true.

Peter Pan in Wonderland

I nterested in more books by Jeni Conrad? Check out the *Mirror Island* series starting with *Peter Pan in Wonderland*.

With only a month to high school graduation, Peter is excited to get started on his life's next adventure—college and learning who he is without his adoptive family constantly around.

Too bad fate has other plans for him.

At a local amusement park called Wonderland, Peter has a chance encounter with his fencing rival, Jillian Hook. They fall through a creepy funhouse mirror and embark on an unimaginable journey searching for Peter's sister, Alice, who is lost on the mirror islands where fairies grant wishes, cats appear grin-first, and pirates rule the skies.

With reimagined, beloved characters, this dual POV, fairytale retelling boasts a vivid mixture of several worlds and stories. This series is perfect for fans of enemies to lovers, villain origin tales, magical worlds, whimsy, and *Once Upon a Time*.

About the Author

Jeni Conrad is a wife, mother, teacher, writer, reader, and a human (honest, she can pass those robot tests almost every time!). She usually writes YA fantasy or paranormal stories . Since fifteen years old, she worked in the restaurant business while getting through high school, a BA in English, and then an MA in sociology. Now she works from home while wrangling two small girls, a dog, and two crazy cats.

www.jeniconrad.com

Also By Jeni Conrad

The Lost Guardian Series
Part 1- Game On
Part 2- IRL

The Hanna Sanchez Series
Don't Haunt Ghosts
Don't Bite Vampires
Don't Hunt Werewolves
Don't Summon Necromancers
Don't Hex Witches

The Mirror Islands Series
Peter in Wonderland
Alice in Neverland
Wendy and the Lost Girls